CONSEQUENCES

#1 in the Consequences Series

CONSEQUENCES

REVIEWS:

I loved *Consequences* and can't wait until Truth! -Teresa Mummert, *New York Times & USA Today* Bestselling Author

Looking for a psychological thriller? Then you have found it! It's a good one! *Consequences* is definitely a book you have to read. I hope it evokes the same crazy emotions in you that it did in me and I hope you love it as much as I did! Bookie Nookie - *Bookie Nookie Reviews* and *The Romance Reviews*

Consequences is a good book, a book that makes you think how strong the persuasive powers of control and dependency are to a person's well-being. There is a lot that goes on and I can probably write an essay about all the psychological implications they produce but I'll just say it's worth reading and hopefully there will be sequel. Didi Hassan - *Choice Book Reviews*

Consequences is more *than* a psychological thriller or straight up suspense. The book is about one relationship, Tony and Claire, but it does not follow the typical relationship pattern. Bravo to Ms. Romig for shocking the heck out of me. Jen - *Fiction Vixen Book Reviews*

Seriously, I would have never thought a psycho-thriller book would appeal to me as much as *Consequences* has - but I MUST know the next phase in the story. For me, the appeal was the author's ability to draw such intensive emotion out of me throughout the entire story. Amy - *Smexy Book Reviews*

Consequences made me question my own limits. How can a story as disturbing and appalling as this one keep me compelled to keep going? It pushed my boundaries. Made me angry. And it was almost too painful to read at times. But, to be quite honest, not knowing where the story was going is what kept me glued to the pages. I HAD to know what happens with Claire and Anthony. And with the unpredictable, jaw dropping ending, I'm thrilled to find out *Truth* comes out November 1, 2012. I want it now! Paula – *Romantic Book Affairs*

COPYRIGHT AND LICENSE INFORMATION

Published by Aleatha Romig

Author's 2nd Edition 2012

Copyright © 2011 Aleatha Romig

ISBN-13: 978-0-9884891-3-4

ISBN-10: 0988489139

Acknowledgements:

Thank you especially to my wonderful husband, children, and mother. I love you all! You have my undying love and gratitude for indulging me while I pursued my dream.

Also, sincere appreciation to the readers of CONSEQUENCES, I thank all of you for reading my first novel. Please know you hold a special place in my heart. I love to hear from each and every one of you. My contact information is at the end. Feel free to let me know your thoughts!

Please know CONSEQUENCES is only the beginning of our saga. Anthony Rawlings and Claire Nichols' story continues in TRUTH, due for release November 2012. The conclusion of their story, and so many other characters you will learn to love and hate, is CONVICTED!

CONVICTED will be released in early 2014. Thank you for riding this amazing ride! It will be worth it – I promise!

*It is not the strongest of the species that survives,
not the most intelligent that survives.
It is the one that is the most adaptable to change.*
—Charles Darwin

Chapter 1

The fade into consciousness happens slowly like the melting of ice. The water is still present. It just changes form. Claire's mind couldn't process the entirety of her circumstance. She knew she was awakening, felt the warmth of soft sheets and a thick comforter against her skin, but it felt wrong. Where was she?

Suddenly, the ice was liquid and her veins filled with the cold, condensing fluid. Her heartbeat intensified as the poor muscle attempted to pump the viscous solution. The sting of her swollen eyelids brought back memories of her arrival to this place. She strained to listen, to hear anything. The only sound that registered was the incessant ringing within her ears. More with curiosity than courage, she cautiously opened her eyes. Peering around the room, she discovered that she was indeed alone. Momentary relief caused her chest to contract and a sigh to escape her lips.

Under other circumstances, she might relish the amazing softness of the silk sheets or the grandeur of the king-sized bed. Today, however, despite the warm cocoon, her body shivered as the fog of her mind cleared. The memories of the last previous night began to surface from the depths of her unconsciousness. Perhaps it was a nightmare. She tried to convince herself it wasn't real.

But if it wasn't real, how did she get here? And where was here?

Enormous windows, currently covered by golden drapes, allowed just enough sunlight for her eyes to adjust. For the first time since her arrival, she really looked at her surroundings, seeing the four ornately carved corner posts of the bed. They were exquisite, and looking beyond, so was the room where it sat. The alluring bedroom looked larger and more lavish than any she had ever seen. The room looked like heaven, but she already knew it was hell.

Again, she listened—nothing. The only sounds were the memories in her head. She heard herself screaming until her throat felt raw and pounding on the bedroom door until her clenched fist ached. No one heard. Or if anyone heard, no one cared. This beautiful room was her prison.

Slowly, she attempted to sit. The act in itself caused discomfort more evidence that last night was real. Slowly shifting, she managed to see more of her cell: a sitting area with an overstuffed chair, complementary sofa, small fireplace in the wall surrounded by marble tiles, and a cozy table for two with a crystal vase of fresh flowers. The intimacy of the table caused Claire's stomach to churn. The bile that seeped into her throat tasted vile. She tried desperately to swallow.

Conspicuously missing were dressers or other furniture usually associated with a bedroom. Yet dimly she remembered being told that this was her new bedroom. Looking around the perimeter of the room, she saw beautiful white woodwork: built-in bookcases, shelves, and three doors. The one farthest from her bed appeared solid, firm, and unharmed after the pounding she'd delivered the night before. There was no reason to believe that it would now be unlocked. What Claire did know, with some certainty, was that it held her only avenue to freedom. She needed to find her way back through that door.

Closing her eyes, she remembered the events of last night. As the memories started to flow from the recesses of her unconsciousness, her new goal was to stop them. She failed instead seeing him behind her closed lids.

Anthony Rawlings was so different from the man she met less than a week ago—the handsome tall man, with brown hair and the darkest eyes she'd ever seen. He'd been polite, kind, and gentlemanly. Last night, none of those words could be used to describe him. To say he was cruel would not explain what she endured. One could say demanding, aggressive, abrasive, controlling—but above all, brutal.

Shifting slightly, she realized that the slightest movement caused her muscles to ache. Her thighs throbbed, her body was tender. And her mouth felt swollen and raw. She remembered his scent, his taste, and the sound of his voice. Those thoughts instigated a revolt deep in the recesses of her stomach. At that moment, the images of him made her heart race—not in anticipation, but fear. This was insane. Things like this happened on crime shows and movies, not in real life and not to people like her.

She tried to censor the memories to find the one of him finally leaving the room, then the images of her futile barrage on the door. Tears fell from her swollen eyes as the visions replayed in her mind. She laid her head back on the velvety pillow allowing herself the luxury of more sleep and an escape from this reality.

The next time she woke, Claire knew she couldn't put off looking in the other doors any longer. She needed to find the entry to the bathroom. The sumptuous carpet enveloped her feet as she stepped from the bed. Despite the plush carpeting, the weight of her body made her legs cry out in pain. Sadly, she remembered crying out more than once. Her internal monologue screamed with unanswered questions: *How did this happen? How did I get here? Why am I here? And most crucially, how can I get out?*

The three doors she'd counted earlier were arranged with two near the bed and one by the sitting area. Claire knew the lone door was her passage to freedom. She wrapped a sheet around her aching body and slowly approached the massive barrier of solid wood. The doorknob was the kind that was really a lever. Anxiety induced trembling, causing her hands to shake as she slowly reached for the cold metal. If it moved, would she flee wrapped only in a sheet? Hell, yes!

Excitement quickly turned to disappointment as the lever remained perfectly horizontal. It didn't even wiggle, as many locked doors do. The solid impenetrable barrier stood unyielding. Despite the expected outcome, disappointment caused the pain within Claire's body to intensify. Turning around, she viewed her cell. One of the other two doors had the best chance of holding her desired destination. She opened the first door and revealed a closet, one the size of most bedrooms. It could more accurately be considered a dressing room with built-in drawers, shoe racks, shelves, and hanging racks. Surprisingly, the racks and shelves were full. These clothes seemed to come straight from a Saks photo shoot, not the kind Claire would or could choose for herself. She was more the Target or Vintage type. These clothes belonged to someone who lived the life of the rich and famous. Who was that someone? Claire wondered why she was in that person's room and why she remembered being told it was hers.

Opening the next door, Claire found her destination. She stepped into a bathroom like one she'd seen on television, large and very white. The coolness of the tile hit the soles of her bare feet. White marble, white porcelain, silver accents, and glass surrounded her. If it weren't for the plush purple towels, the room would be totally devoid of color. There was a large garden tub and a full glass shower that sported large and small showerheads from every direction. The sink adjoined a dressing table with a large lighted mirror and stool.

She turned to see the person in the mirror. The image frightened Claire as she studied the reflection. Her tangled brown hair framed an unfamiliar face. There were bruises around her lips trying to match the color of the towels, and her left temple appeared red and swollen. Slowly dropping the sheet, the visual evidence of the soreness she experienced could be seen as red and purple bruises over her body and extremities. The vision restarted her tears. With steely determination, she gripped the lever of another door within the bathroom and found the toilet.

A plush white bathrobe hung near the shower. Twisting the knobs to adjust the water, Claire decided a shower would make her feel better. Hot steamy water hit her skin as she stepped into the spacious stall. The prickling sensation of a thousand needles pierced her shoulders as the hot water flowed over her battered muscles. It was a sensation of both pleasure and pain. She allowed the water to continue its assault, and as time passed and the temperature remained high, her muscles relaxed. The sweet floral aroma of the shampoo and body soap replaced the odors of last night. A renewed sense of strength filled her resolve. Somehow, she would survive this nightmare.

Claire developed a plan as she used the luxurious lavender towel to dry her battered body. She would talk to Anthony and explain that this was a mistake. They could split ways, no questions asked and no charges pressed. The soft robe warmed her, providing a bogus sense of security.

The woman in the mirror looked better. However, her dark hair now fell messily in wet tangles. Without thinking, Claire began to open drawers and cabinets. Just like the closet, the bath was fully stocked. In front of her she saw thousands of dollars' worth of name-brand cosmetics. She found everything from skin care to eyeliner. Of course, there was also an array of hair supplies. She was wearing someone else's robe, sleeping in her bed, and showering in her bathroom. Using her hairbrush only added to the list of intrusions. Claire didn't have many options.

In the medicine cabinet she found a toothbrush still encased in cellophane. Claire couldn't resist. The shower, soap, shampoo, and now toothpaste all helped her feel less soiled.

When Claire opened the door to the bedroom, she was startled to see a tray of food waiting on the dining table. Prior to that moment, she ignored the pangs of hunger. God knows the thoughts of the previous night made her stomach turn. Yet, the aroma from the covered plate intrigued her. She lifted the lid to discover steaming scrambled eggs, toast, and a side of fresh fruit. On the tray, she also noticed a glass of orange juice, one of water, and a carafe of coffee.

With her stomach full, body relaxed from the shower, and no immediate path to freedom, Claire decided she wanted more sleep. It was then that she realized the bed was made, not only made, but the sheets had been changed. The room appeared as though the horror of last night never occurred. Her body screamed otherwise. She pulled back the covers, climbed between the soft satin sheets, inhaled the fresh clean scent, and closed her eyes. It wasn't the escape she wanted, but it was a temporary diversion.

The knocking at the door near the sitting area woke Claire. She'd been somewhere in a dream, far away. The knock and the unfamiliar surroundings left her temporarily disoriented. How long had she been sleeping? Sunlight, though not as bright, continued to seep from the edge of the drapes. The repeated raps brought her emotions and thoughts dramatically to the present. Fear gripped her being as she considered who was on the other side of the door. Yes, she was a twenty-six-year-old adult. Yet, at that moment, Claire decided to behave as any five-year-old child would and imitate sleep. Lying still in bed, she heard the door open.

Tentatively opening her eyes, she watched as a woman quietly entered the room. Given Claire's perspective, it was difficult to tell, but the woman appeared taller than her by a few inches with salt-and-pepper hair. Claire assumed she was about the age of her mother, had her mother been alive. As the woman approached, Claire decided to speak, "I'm sorry if I'm in your room."

10

"No, Ms. Claire. It is your suite, not mine. I am here to help you get ready for dinner. My name is Catherine."

Claire slowly sat in amazement. What the hell did she mean get ready for dinner? She was being held prisoner in some luxurious suite, covered in bruises, and this person was supposed to help her get ready for dinner. "I'm not trying to sound ungrateful. But what do you mean 'ready for dinner'?"

"Mr. Rawlings will be here precisely at 7:00 p.m. for dinner. He expects you to be ready and dressed accordingly. I presumed you might need some assistance."

At first, Claire couldn't wrap her mind around the entire scenario. He wanted her *dressed* for dinner. Who the hell did he think he was? "Listen, if you want to assist me, let me out of here." Claire did her best to keep her voice from raising another octave, yet the fear of seeing Anthony and the possibility of escape made that all but impossible.

"Ms. Claire, that is not up to me. I am here to assist you as I can." It didn't make any sense. Yet in the desperation of the situation, for some reason, Claire believed this lady. Catherine continued, "We only have an hour. Perhaps we could begin with your hair?"

Undaunted by Claire's appearance or even the circumstance of her presence, Catherine's calmness eased Claire. She shook her head and sighed. Remembering the resolve from her shower, she spoke with a convincing authority, "Catherine, thank you for offering to help, but I don't plan on dressing for dinner. I actually believe there has been a mistake. I will be leaving here soon." While Claire explained the misunderstanding, Catherine came and went from the closet with a blue cocktail dress and matching shoes. "Oh, I don't know whom those clothes belong to."

"Why, miss, they belong to you. Now, we really should move along. And even if you do not plan to eat, do you not need to wear clothes?" Claire noticed her pattern of speech seemed formal. She couldn't place the origin. It definitely wasn't the Georgia accent she'd learned to appreciate and tried desperately not to duplicate.

Catherine gently took Claire's hand and walked her into the bathroom. Claire obediently sat at the dressing table as Catherine began to gently brush her hair. She decided to not protest this kind woman. Instead, she would save her energy to face Anthony.

"There are cosmetics in the drawers in front of you. Perhaps you could begin to apply some while I do your hair." Then she added, "You are very pretty without it, but after sleeping most of the day, I believe it will make you feel better."

Claire looked into the mirror. Seeing her eyes, temple, and lips, she began to cry. It wasn't the sobs of earlier, but a rush of tears quietly flowing down her cheeks.

"Now Miss, that will not help the situation. Mr. Rawlings appreciates punctuality. Crying will only make the cosmetics run."

She began to explain to Catherine her desperation, "I don't want to face him." But after the first sentence, she hesitated. Claire didn't know this woman. She obviously worked for Anthony. Why would she confide in her? Then Claire looked in the reflection, not at herself but at the woman behind her. Her eyes were the color of steel, gray and soft. Her expression wasn't one of duty or pity, but somehow Claire sensed compassion. It may have been wishful thinking, but for some reason, the words continued to flow. "After last night, I feel so . . . dirty. You don't know what he did, what he made me do. I am too embarrassed." Her words came accompanied by tears, and her nose began to run.

Catherine's voice held no judgment for either Claire or Anthony, instead a means for understanding, as if that could be possible from Claire. "I have known Mr. Rawlings for a long time. Did anything happen last night that he did not want to happen?"

Claire shook her head *no*. "Everything that happened *he* wanted to happen."

"Then there is no need for you to be embarrassed. It is when you do something that he doesn't want you to do. That is when you do not want to face Mr. Rawlings."

Catherine went to the cabinet, removed a washcloth, and wet it in the sink. She handed it to Claire, who compliantly wiped her face and began to apply makeup. It wasn't long until they were satisfied with the results. The bruises were concealed quite well under a covering of foundation and powder. The lipstick made the swelling less noticeable. When Catherine entered the bathroom with the dress, Claire realized she was naked under the robe.

"Umm, I don't have any lingerie."

"Yes, miss. Do you not remember Mr. Rawlings's rules?" Without waiting for a response, Catherine continued, "No underclothes, ever." Claire fought the fog of last night. She couldn't understand why the memories were so fuzzy. Yet somewhere she had some recollection of such a conversation or, more accurately, a demand. But once again, this entered the world of ridiculous. Who the hell was he, that he even thought he could make such demands, and they would be followed?

Catherine assisted Claire with the dress, so as not to mess her hair and makeup.

Claire vowed to herself that this fiasco will be over. *I am not sure how or when. But I will leave here, get away from him, and go to a place where women wear underwear.*

Catherine smiled approvingly at Claire as she stepped in front of the mirror. "Mr. Rawlings will be pleased. Now I must go. He will be here soon." The reminder of his impending arrival sucked some of the resolve from Claire's demeanor as well as the air from her lungs. Catherine knew him. Maybe if she stayed, he would . . . Claire didn't know how to finish that thought. He would *be nice*? *Let her leave*? It just seemed safer around this woman.

"Perhaps you could stay until after his arrival?" Catherine didn't respond, but the look of satisfaction briefly changed to sadness. Instantaneously, Claire knew that Catherine's departure was beyond both of their control. Claire would be face-to-face with her fear, the man that abused and dominated her the night before. She also knew that he was her only means of escape. For that reason and that reason only, she would face him. "Thank you again for your help. I really doubt I will be here tomorrow. He and I will discuss it over dinner."

Catherine nodded. It was an acknowledgment of Claire's statement, not an affirmation of its accuracy. Then she left the bathroom. Claire heard a faint beep as she left the suite. It reminded her of the noise made by a car fob.

While still in the bathroom, her heart rate increased as she heard the faint beep again. He didn't knock. He just opened the door and entered. Claire imagined him surveying the empty suite. If she stayed in the bathroom, would he eventually come for her? Or perhaps he would leave. He waited silently in the bedroom. It took a minute or two. But slowly, Claire opened the bathroom door and entered the suite.

Determined to meet him head-on at his mind game, she used all her strength to suppress the fears that screamed to get out. The first things she saw as she entered the suite were his eyes, his dark black eyes. They resembled voids or black holes. His lips were moving. He was talking, yet Claire could only hear the memories of the previous night. She walked to the bookcase at the far end of the suite, feigning strength.

The fake resolve melted as she turned to see the eyes staring directly at her. Then almost instantaneously, he was there, right in front of her. His proximity caused her stomach to wrench, tasting the nasty bile from earlier.

He grabbed her chin, pulling her eyes and face toward the dark voids. His strong voice was deep, slow, and authoritative. "Shall we try this once more." It wasn't a question but a statement. "It is customary for one person to respond to the greeting of another. I said good evening."

Claire's knees went weak at his touch. She wanted to yell, to run, but she couldn't let herself. If she couldn't be strong, she could at least avoid fainting. "I'm sorry. I don't believe I am feeling well." Still holding her chin, she knew he could feel her body tremble.

He repeated, "Good evening, Claire." This time, it was more drawn-out. His eyes were so cold. Claire couldn't distinguish what they said, only see the depth of their infinite darkness.

"Good evening, Anthony." She would tell herself she sounded strong, but she didn't. At that moment, the door opened again, and a young man pushing a cart brought them their meal. Claire started to walk toward the table, but Anthony's hand seized her arm, stopping her. She looked back up at him, into those eyes. He reached with his other hand to lift her dress and place a hand on her buttocks. The shock of his touch quickly turned to anger. Her green eyes flashed fire, and her neck stiffened. "What the hell . . . ?" Her impulse was to lash out, but the hand that held her arm tightened its grip, causing her to forget her words.

"I see you can manage to follow at least one rule. Shall we eat?" His grip loosened as his voice attempted a reasonable tone. Anthony pulled back Claire's chair at the intimate table. She eyed the display, and her thoughts summed up the scene: *It all looks so nice and is such a masquerade.*

The food smelled wonderful, but Claire's stomach wouldn't allow her to eat. She managed a few bites although swallowing was difficult. Her anxiety made her mouth dry as cotton. All of her pep talks about standing up to him proved worthless. Instead, she sat politely, playing with her food and nodding attentively.

There was an attempt at conversation. Looking at the dinner, Claire felt that something was missing, besides common sense. The young man poured water into the glasses, yet to make the masquerade complete, there should be wine or champagne. It was almost as if he read her mind when Anthony commented, "I do not like to drink alcohol. It inhibits the senses." She immediately thought how nice it would be to have a fifth of Jack Daniels.

Anthony relished her discomfort. "Don't you like your food?"

"I do. I guess I'm just not hungry."

"I heard that today you have only eaten breakfast. I suggest you eat. You will need your strength." He grinned as he took a bite. His eyes didn't grin. She used every ounce of energy to remain seated and not run, although the door was shut, and she heard the faint beep when the waiter left.

If she had run, she could have avoided the next horrific hours of her life. Apparently, the night before was only a prelude. Once Anthony finished eating, he stood and took Claire's hand. Her trembling increased as she stood. He smiled and held her at arm's length. "Did you choose this dress for the evening?"

"No, it was Catherine." She remained tall and defiant even though she knew her will would not be considered in his plans.

"Yes, she knows me well. Now take it off." No sweet talk, no kisses, nothing—just a demand to remove her dress. She didn't move. She glared first at him and then at the floor.

Taking a deep breath and returning her eyes to his stare, she said, "I think we need to talk about this . . ." He waited for her to obey his command. When it seemed she had other plans, he redirected the conversation. In a sudden movement, the dress fell from her shoulders as he tore the lavish fabric from her body. Claire stood in shock wearing only high heels.

"Apparently, you do not remember all the rules. Rule number one is to do as you are told."

The trembling intensified as tears teetered on her painted eyelids. No words came from her mouth. It was all right. Anthony had other plans for her mouth. He pushed her down, directed her to kneel, and unzipped his pants. She noted immediately that he followed his own rules, no underwear. He didn't speak but roughly engaged her movement. At first, she thought she would suffocate. She attempted to fight, to back away, but he entwined his fingers in her hair and directed her as he found fit. From there, the evening continued until about one in the morning.

When Anthony finally left the room, Claire threw back the blankets, grabbed the robe, and rushed to the door. Her hand gripped the smooth gray lever and pulled with all her might. It didn't budge. She formed a fist and pounded again. Her hand throbbed, yet no one responded. The only answer was an eerie stillness.

Claire reached for something, anything. Finding the vase of flowers, she threw it against the wall. The crystal shattered, showering the wall and carpet with crystal shards and water. The flowers unable to drink, scattered on the

14

floor, left to wilt and die. Claire sank to the ground, tears flowing. Succumbing to the exhaustion and desperation, she fell asleep.

The next morning Anthony entered the suite. The sound of the beep and the opening door startled Claire. She rose to meet his gaze and their eyes met. He surveyed the suite: a lamp overturned by the bed, a scarf tied to one of the bedposts, and the broken vase near their feet. He smiled, "Good morning, Claire."

"Good morning, Anthony," she said with more determination than she'd been able to muster last evening. "I want you to know I have decided to go home. I will be leaving here today."

"Do you not like your accommodations?" Anthony's black eyes shone as his smile widened. "I do not believe you will be leaving so soon. We have a legally binding agreement." He removed a bar napkin from his suit pocket. "Dated and signed by both of us."

Claire stared, astonished as her mind started to turn. This whole situation was so idiotic it couldn't possibly be real. Who in their right mind thought a bar napkin was a legal agreement? And even if it was, which was like a snowball's chance in hell, it never gave rights to abuse, demean, or condemn a person to slavery. Dumbfounded, she stared - speechless.

Anthony continued, "Perhaps you do not remember. You agreed to work for me, to do whatever I deemed fit or pleasing, in exchange for me paying off all of your debts."

Claire's head throbbed. She recalled something of a napkin, maybe a job offer, but it was fuzzy. Besides, she would stay in debt and work double or triple shifts at the bar before agreeing to this!

"Apparently, you have been busy in the last twenty-six years. With education, rent, credit cards, and car, you have managed to accumulate approximately $215,000 of debt. This agreement was dated March 15, and as with any legally binding agreement, you or I had three days for recession. Today is March 20. I currently *own* you until your debt is paid. You will not be leaving until our agreement is complete. End of discussion."

In desperation, her trembling resumed and she found her voice. "It is not the end of this discussion. This is ludicrous. An agreement doesn't give you the right to rape me! I am leaving."

She eyed the door to the hallway, only a few feet away and miraculously left open. Without warning, Anthony's hand contacted her left cheek and sent her the other direction across the floor. He slowly walked to where she lay. He didn't bother to bend down, merely looked at her from high above, and repeated, "Perhaps in time, your memory will improve. It seems to be an issue. Let me remind you again, rule number one is that you will do as you are told. If I say a discussion is over, it is over." Picking up the napkin and placing it in his suit coat pocket, he continued, "And this written agreement states *whatever is pleasing to me*, means consensual, not rape."

Still towering over her, he straightened his suit jacket and smoothed his tie. "I have decided that it would be better if you do not leave your suite for a while. Don't worry. We have plenty of time, $215,000 worth of time." With that, he turned to leave the suite, the sound of broken crystal echoing from under his Gucci loafers. His controlled, imposing tone terrified Claire more than his words. He spoke with such authority it left her powerless to move or speak.

"I will tell the staff that you may have your breakfast, after you clean up this crystal." He disappeared behind the large white door.

Claire heard the beep and the lock as she allowed herself to reach up and touch her stinging cheek. The total silence returned as she looked at the mess before her. While a small, insignificant protest, she heard herself say, "I would rather starve than clean this up."

With tears in her eyes, and the sound of sniffles, a while later she found herself crawling around the floor retrieving pieces of crystal. She had most of the large pieces picked up when she noticed the blood on her robe. After investigating, Claire determined that it came from a cut on her hand. She tried unsuccessfully to remove the sliver of crystal from her palm; the blurriness of her vision made the task difficult. Suddenly, the too-familiar beep made her turn toward the door, terrified of Anthony's return.

Catherine entered, looked around, and shook her head. "Ms. Claire, let me clean that. You will end up cutting yourself."

"I believe I already have." Claire held out her hand. Very tenderly, Catherine led Claire into the bathroom and removed the crystal. She then cleaned and bandaged her hand. When they returned to the suite, the evidence of the previous night was gone. The suite was clean, no overturned lamps, no scarves, and the vase was gone. Sitting on the table was a tray of food.

Claire walked to the table and obediently ate her breakfast, alone. She was filled with an overwhelming feeling of desperation. She was trapped, alone, and didn't know what to do.

Grandma always said a new perspective was helpful. Claire decided to take a shower, and then hopefully, she would think of something.

The trust of the innocent is the liar's most useful tool.
—Stephen King

Chapter 2

Five days earlier . . .

The day filled with meetings served its purpose. First he met with the station manager, then endless hours with the sales team listening to budget reports followed by proposals. Truthfully, these meetings didn't usually warrant the attendance of the parent corporation's CEO. Judging by the way WKPZ's executives fell over themselves to justify every expense and augment every proposal, they demonstrated that they at least recognized this visit as extraordinary. Truth be known, Anthony Rawlings didn't give a damn about the two-bit television station. It already served its purpose. If he closed it tomorrow, he would lose no sleep. However, the meetings revealed that the station was turning a profit. And given the current state of economy, profitable is good. When he returned to the main office, he would assign a team to investigate an impending sale. Wouldn't it be great if this acquired station could reap both personal and monetary benefits?

After the conclusion of the meetings, he agreed to a social outing with the new station personnel director and his assistant. If they knew anything about him, they would realize this was completely out of character. His acceptance of their invitation came with one stipulation; they must go to the Red Wing. He'd heard it had the best fried green tomatoes in Atlanta, Georgia.

Thankfully, the two associates had families that were waiting earnestly for their return. He listened attentively to their personnel plans and thanked them for their devotion to WKPZ. After sipping a Red Wing signature beer and consuming a portion of the fried green tomato appetizer, Mr. Rawlings insisted that they take leave and spend time with their loved ones. However, if he were questioned under oath, he wouldn't be able to recall one word they said. His attention was focused on the brown-haired, green-eyed bartender.

She was scheduled to start her shift at four o'clock, and he knew she would be here. As soon as his associates left, he texted his driver and informed him that he would be at the Red Wing until late. Then he casually walked to an empty stool at the end of the bar, near the wall. It reduced the probability of anyone striking up conversation by 50 percent. He would have preferred 100, but damn, you can't have everything. The only object of his conversation and attention would be the smiling young woman on the other side of the shiny smooth wooden slab.

"Hey, handsome, do you need another beer?"

Anthony lifted his gaze to look into her emerald eyes. He had a handsome face and knew after many years of practice exactly how to use it. However, at this moment, his smile was genuine. She was finally talking to him. It had been a long, lonely road, but the destination was in sight. "Thank you, I would."

Sizing up the remaining contents of his glass, she asked, "Is that one of our custom wheats?"

"Well, yes, it is the La bière Blanche." She smiled sweetly and hurried away to fill him another glass. Returning with the amber liquid, she efficiently removed his empty tumbler, replaced it with the full glass, and a fresh Red Wing napkin. "I would like to start a tab."

"That would be great. If I could have your credit card, I will begin one right away."

Anthony opened his Armani jacket and removed the wallet from the inside pocket. He had so many things he wanted to say, but he had all night. He had forever. Her shift wouldn't end until ten, and he planned to spend the evening sitting right there. Handing her his platinum Visa, he watched as she read the name.

"Thank you, Mr. Rawlings. I'll return this to you in a minute." Her smile or expression never wavered. She turned away toward the cash register. Anthony sat back against the chair with a brief moment of satisfaction. She didn't know who he was. This was perfect.

During the next few hours, Anthony observed as Claire chatted and flirted with customer after customer. Her attentions were friendly and attentive, but never overtly personal. Some of the customers were greeted by name as they found their way to an empty seat. Many knew her name before she could introduce herself. Anthony assumed they were regulars. Both men and women appeared pleased to have her wait on them. She moved nonstop, clearing away empty glasses and plates and replacing them with more of the same or checks in need of payment. She wiped the shiny wooden bar and smiled even when a comment deserved a strong retort. After so much time watching her from afar, being this close gave him a rush greater than securing a multimillion-dollar deal. Perhaps it was the knowledge of what was to come.

After tending bar on and off again for years, Claire Nichols knew how to read people. More importantly, she genuinely liked the little quirks that made them real. For instance, take Mr. La bière Blanche, he'd been watching her for the last few hours like a lion sizing up its prey. She judged that he was at least ten years her senior but hid his age well behind that perfect smile, dark wavy styled hair, and amazing brown, almost-black eyes. Claire smiled a secretive smile as she watched him too.

"What time do you get off?" His strong husky voice resonated above the clamor of the bar, patrons, and music.

"Now, Anthony, isn't that what you said your name is?" Claire's chatty work tone contained the slightest of a Southern drawl, the kind of accent you pick up from being around it so much. Her roots in Indiana with a mother who taught English wouldn't allow her to drag those syllables out too far, unless on purpose.

Smiling a devilish grin and flashing those sensual eyes, he met her gaze. "Yes, that's correct. And if I recall, your name is Claire."

"And even though I'm flattered, I don't usually see my customers outside this esteemed establishment."

"All right, what time do you get off? Perhaps we could sit in one of those booths, right here . . . in this esteemed establishment . . . and talk? I would like to know more about you."

Damn. He was smoother talking than any of the regular Joes that sat on these stools. And now that his silk tie was in the pocket of his Armani suit coat, and the top button of his silk shirt was undone, his casual business persona was incredibly sexy.

"Now tell me again what brings you to Atlanta. You aren't from here, are you?" Claire said, leaning against the bar.

"Business, and no, but I think I am the one who wanted to ask the questions." His tone demonstrated a playful quality and at the same time exhibited focus and control.

Claire's intuition told her that he was used to getting his way. Something made her wonder if that's what made him successful in business. His appearance definitely said success. She pondered if that transcended to his personal life.

Claire listened and watched as Anthony's eyes glistened. He was tall. Now that his coat had been removed, she could tell he was muscular, with a wide chest and firm waist. Most importantly, his left hand had an empty fourth finger. That would definitely be a red flag. Against her better judgment, she decided she wanted to answer those questions.

"Okay." Claire smiled charmingly. "But I will've been standing behind this bar for six hours straight. I can't promise I will be the best company."

"Then I take that as a yes? But did you tell me the time? Or am I still waiting for that answer?" She found herself absorbed in his eyes.

"Yo! Hey, sweetheart, how about you give us some service down here?" Claire's attention was suddenly pulled away from the hold of those amazing eyes. The asshole down the bar needed more Jack and Coke. She started to walk away. Anthony reached for her hand, which was resting on the bar only inches from his. His warm touch made her skin tingle. He didn't ask again, but his expression did...

"At ten, I get off at ten." She removed her hand from under his, shook her head, and walked down the bar, smiling to herself. She needed to find out what the asshole wanted.

The deep red vinyl seat of the semicircular booth situated on the edge of the dance floor tried unsuccessfully to imitate fine upholstery. Music filled the air, too loud and too fast. In Anthony's mind, it created the perfect climate, requiring them to sit close to hear each other. He also had a bottle of the Red Wing's finest cabernet sauvignon. Looking at his watch for the hundredth time, he read the hands as they said 10:30 p.m. It was then that he saw Claire walking across the empty dance floor toward his booth.

This night was definitely filled with out-of-character behaviors. Not only did Anthony Rawlings not fraternize with regional associates, he *never* waited for anyone. Under any other circumstance, he would have been up and gone by 10:05. His friends, associates, and employees all knew his obsession with punctuality. But tonight was different. As Claire eased herself into the booth, she smiled a fatigued grin and apologized for the delay. Apparently there was a problem with the cash register, but all was well now.

He gently touched her hand. Momentarily, he became transfixed by the contrast—large and small. "I was beginning to wonder if you were standing me up." His grin hinted toward levity. "But since I could see you across the room, I hoped I might still have a chance at friendly conversation." Claire's exhale and upturned lips told him she was relieved. Was it because he was still waiting or merely that her shift was complete? "Perhaps we could have a glass of wine, and you could enjoy sitting instead of standing."

"I believe that would be very nice." Anthony poured the wine and noticed Claire's expression relax. The transformation occurring before him was from bartender to the real Claire Nichols. He watched as she took the glass, placed her lips on the rim, closed her eyes, and relished the thick red liquid on her tongue. Anthony fought the urge to think too much about her actions.

"So what's a classy girl like you doing waiting on stooges like us?" Anthony's rich voice refocused Claire's attention. Her eyes twinkled with emerald lights as she turned to face him.

"Why, Anthony, I do believe that self-deprecating statement was a compliment to me in a way." Her intonation held the Southern accent far from her native Indiana cadence. He only arched his eyebrows in response, waiting patiently for an answer. Claire shook her head succumbing to his charm. "I'm an out-of-work meteorologist. My news station was bought about a year ago. In their infinite wisdom they decided I was no longer needed, so this," she said as she glided her free hand open above the table, "is my new glamorous life. Don't knock it. It pays my student loans as well as multiple other bills."

His deep laughter was nonjudgmental. "Wouldn't you rather be doing the weather thing than this?"

"Of course, but honestly, this isn't so bad. I have some great friends here. There is always something happening, and I meet nice people like you."

20

Claire took another sip of the wine and leaned a little closer. "So that's my story in a nutshell. Sir, it is your turn. You said you are here on business. What kind of business do you do?"

"I am actually involved in many businesses. I came to Atlanta for an acquisition, and some associates convinced me to come here to your revered establishment to try the world-famous fried green tomatoes."

"Oh, they did. Did you?"

Anthony nodded. "Yes, I did."

Claire looked into her glass in an attempt to hide the snicker that escaped her lips. "Did you like them?"

He likewise looked into his glass. "No, I don't believe I am destined for Georgian cuisine." Unable to keep it silenced any longer, Claire's laughter caused him to look up. "Why are you laughing?"

"Because I think they are awful! Every time someone orders them, I want to whisper, 'No, don't do it.' It is just that they are so . . ."

"Slimy?" They said in unison and chuckled. The conversation progressed effortlessly. She asked about his acquisition. Would his trip be successful? Anthony was honestly surprised at her depth and knowledge. It was a shame that her news station had not kept her on. She deserved so much better than tending bar. Of course, that was what he told her. They discussed her career opportunities. Due to Anthony's involvement in multiple endeavors, he offered the possibility of assistance with more profitable employment. Claire thanked him for his offer, but doubted his ability or desire to truly assist.

"You know, your destiny could be as simple as an offer and a signature away." He channeled every deal he ever made, which were more than he could count or recall. Placing a napkin on the table, he drew her attention to the center design. "Just imagine, instead of the swirly lettering saying 'Red Wing' it is blocked and read, 'Weather Channel.'"

The bottle of cabernet sauvignon was almost empty. Claire closed her eyes and did as Anthony said, she imagined. Exhaling audibly, she said, "That would be wonderful. It would be the offer of a meteorologist's dreams."

Closing in on the deal, he said, "Well, Claire, if this napkin were that contract"— he reached for a pen in his breast pocket and wrote at the top of the napkin *Job Contract*—"would you be willing to sign? Would you really give this all up for a job offer?"

She didn't blink. "In a heartbeat!" Removing the pen from Anthony's hand, she signed, *Claire Nichols* next to the bar's insignia.

About midnight, Claire thanked Anthony for the lovely company and explained that she was very tired from her long day and needed to get home.

"I will be in town for a few more days. Perhaps I could call you for dinner? It isn't proper to offer a lady alcohol without food."

"Thank you. I'm honored, but I believe I will chuck this up to my brush with an amazing gentleman and go on with my glamorous existence. I fear that the Weather Channel will not be contacting me anytime soon."

Although her refusal surprised him, he didn't let it show. In the long run, it wouldn't matter, but he would play into her chastity. "I truly understand; dangerous man from out of town tries to learn your secrets and offers to help you with your aspirations. You are wise to keep your distance."

Although his grin had *sinister* written all over it, he assumed she would detect the facade.

"A girl can't be too careful. Truly, I'm honored, and I don't think you seem that dangerous." She began to scoot out of the booth, but he caught her hand. Their eyes met, he bowed his head, and kissed the back of her hand.

"It was wonderful to meet you, Claire Nichols." With a smile, she retrieved her hand and slowly slid from the booth. The next minute, he was alone. He took the pen, signed his name, and wrote the date on the same napkin. He carefully folded it and placed it in the pocket of his suit jacket. Then he pulled out his phone and texted his driver: *PICK ME UP NOW*. He always used full words. Text language was a joke. Closing his eyes, he thought, *yes - my acquisition is going quite well. Thank you for asking.*

To look backward for a while is to refresh the eye,
to restore it, and to render it the more fit for its prime function
of looking—forward.
—Margaret Fairless Barber, *The Roadmender*

Chapter 3

Claire contemplated her situation as she ate. She hadn't taken the napkin discussion seriously. Anthony probably expected that. She didn't prepare to move from her Atlanta apartment or even consider the possibility. His recollection of a document that legally bound them was a complete shock. Claire's gut told her it wasn't legal, but what recourse did she have to fight from this room? She'd searched high and low for a telephone, computer, or some way to call for help—nothing.

She actually thought she would walk out of this twisted nightmare. However, it wasn't a nightmare, twisted or otherwise. It was reality. Her mind searched for a way to survive and escape.

Claire relished the warm oatmeal, fruit, bacon, perfectly brewed coffee, and juice. Yesterday she'd hardly eaten. Today she was ravenous, devouring every ounce, even checking twice for more coffee in the carafe. At least starvation wasn't part of Anthony's plan.

Standing for a shower, she moved carefully, experiencing the same aches and pains of the day before, perhaps intensified. Claire wasn't sure if she wanted to see herself in the mirrors as she cautiously stepped into the generous bathroom and slowly approached the dressing table. The image that reflected back looked scary, hair messed and tangled, face sporting various shades of red and blue. The worst image had to be her lips, swollen - looking as if she'd received Botox injections. This time, there were no tears. Instead, she stared and considered.

Grandma Nichols told her more than once she was an unusually strong young woman. In Claire's mind, Grandma was always strong. Grandpa's work in law enforcement took him away from home. Grandma never complained. Instead, she was the heart of the family—always there for everyone and often giving advice, such as, "It is not the circumstances that make a person a success. It is how that person responds to those circumstances." Grandma

23

believed every situation could be made better by the right attitude. Claire dropped the robe. Beholding the vision in the mirror, she believed Grandma never anticipated a situation like this.

After the shower, Claire decided to *not* dress appropriately in expectation of an Anthony visitation. If he were to walk in her suite, he would find her in jeans, a T-shirt, and fuzzy socks. Furthermore, there would be no makeup and no hair primping. It may be a small act of rebellion, but Claire didn't have many rebellious options. Every bone in her body wanted to fight. She tried to fight during the past two nights, but that didn't work well.

Entering the grand closet/dressing room, Claire realized that yesterday she hadn't truly appreciated all it had to offer. First, she began to look for underwear but remembered that it didn't exist in any of the drawers. So Claire searched for jeans. There were multiple pairs, different shades of blue with different leg styles. Wearing jeans must not break any rules; if it did, they wouldn't be there. The brands she read on the labels she'd only seen in stores like Saks, Hudson, J Brand, and MIH. She never in her life tried on jeans like these. They were soft, amazingly comfortable, and fit perfectly.

Feeling a chill as she removed the robe, Claire decided a sweater would be better than a T-shirt. The countless choices were equally as fashionable. She decided on a Donna Karan pink, fuzzy cashmere sweater. Before putting it on, she looked for a bra. Apparently, bras were against the rules too, because she couldn't find one. However, she did find a drawer full of various colored camisoles; she chose pink.

It was like a treasure hunt as she searched the drawers and cabinets of the closet. Still rummaging for fuzzy socks, she found multiple drawers of lingerie. The silky black and red negligees in multiple lengths reminded her of a Victoria's Secret fashion show. Finally, she discovered socks. Claire couldn't comprehend that all of these lavish and extravagant clothes were for her. Truthfully, she didn't want them.

Driven by curiosity, she read the labels on the evening dresses: Aidan Mattox, Armani, Donna Karan, and Emilio Pucci. These dresses alone could pay her rent in Atlanta for six months. Fleetingly, she wondered about last night's dress. Its tag would remain a mystery. It disappeared when the room was cleaned.

Next she inspected the shoes: pumps, sandals, boots, and slip-ons—all with four-inch heels or more. The brands were equally as high-priced as the dresses: Prada, Calvin Klein, Dior, Kate Spade, and Yves Saint Lauren. Never really a *shoe person*, Claire usually wore casual footwear, Crocs and sneakers—rarely heels and never that high. Of course, every pair was her size.

Her mind slipped back to high school. Ten years ago, she would have done anything for a closet supplied like the one in which she stood. Back then, her sister helped her *fit in* despite her parents' modest income. Emily took her to consignment shops, bargain-hunted, and shopped sale racks. It worked. She was part of the *in* crowd, wearing the right clothes, shoes, and carrying the right purse. As she turned slowly and took in all the clothes, she wished she didn't have this closet or any of the memories.

She heard the beep, and the suite door opened. Her heart raced. Who was here? How long had she been in the closet? Stepping into the suite, she saw lunch being delivered by the same young man that brought dinner the night before. Claire hadn't notice last night, but he appeared Latino. She asked him about the food. He smiled and said, "I bring Ms. Claire lunch." She asked about Catherine, if she would be visiting. He replied, "I bring Ms. Claire lunch." Claire smiled and thanked him for the lunch. Other questions seemed senseless.

Each response and smile the young man offered was unaccompanied by eye contact. Claire thought about his job, bringing her food. Obviously with the lack of makeup, he could see her bruises. Hell, he opened a locked door to bring her food. What did he think of her, of the situation? The idea of seeing her plight from someone else's perspective weighed heavily on her chest. Sadness intensified at the realization, she once again was completely alone.

Instead of going to the table, Claire sat on the sofa and wrapped her arms around her knees. Staring into the fireplace, she contemplated turning it on. Time passed without record. She didn't remember sleeping. Her position didn't change. The unbearable quiet and isolation combined to create a kind of time-and-space continuum. It was after three on the bedside clock before she moved from the sofa. It was then she realized that the food remained on the table, untouched.

The subtle glow from behind the curtains reminded Claire that she hadn't looked out the windows since she awoke yesterday morning. When she checked for a means of escape the first night, everything was locked tight. At that time the nocturnal darkness wouldn't permit her to see past her own reflection.

Of the multiple golden draperies, the largest covered a section of wall near the sitting area. Claire moved toward it, searching for a cord to pull, to make the draperies move and reveal the secrets on the other side. After minutes of seeking, Claire found a switch. Tentatively, she pushed it up. Instantaneously the draperies opened, revealing tall French doors with a balcony beyond.

In her hysteria the other night, she hadn't noticed the French doors, thinking instead that they were only windows. She definitely didn't see the balcony. Her mind raced with possibilities: maybe from the balcony, she could climb down. Alas no, the French doors were locked and bolted. Expectedly the key was nowhere to be found. Claire had a good idea who possessed it.

The view beyond the doors revealed a massive uninhabited countryside, for miles only trees—thousands and thousands of trees—on very flat land. Once she stopped seeing the magnitude of unpopulated land, she realized that the trees weren't green, and the earth wasn't red. When she and Anthony made their *contractual agreement*, they were at a bar, the Red Wing, in Atlanta. What she saw from her locked balcony doors didn't look like Georgia.

She yearned for her home in Atlanta. Even though she wasn't from there, her career path had taken her to WKPZ, a local affiliate out of Atlanta. That path started with a major in meteorology at Valparaiso University in

Indiana. Being born and raised in Fishers, outside of Indianapolis, college in Indiana was expected. Her dreams almost ended when both of her parents tragically died during her junior year. Miraculously, she received a scholarship. That, with her student loans and bartending, allowed her to continue her education. After graduation, her path took her to a one-year unpaid internship in Upstate New York. Being in the weather business, she should have realized how much she would hate the weather in Albany. However, it was the ability to live with her sister and brother-in-law that made the offer easy to accept. Recently married, Emily and John were very willing to help Claire any way they could. Emily taught school, and John recently started practicing law with an esteemed firm in Albany. Since the two were high school sweethearts, Claire knew John most of her life. Living with them was easy. In hindsight, maybe not for the newlyweds; but for Claire, they were her only family.

When the offer came toward the end of her internship for WKPZ, Claire willingly followed her path to Atlanta. She figured the Vandersols needed some time alone, the weather was better in Atlanta, and the job was everything she'd prayed for. As the years continued, she learned more and more about the business, earned respect, notoriety, and a growing income. The station manager told her more than once that her willingness to learn and work made her a rising star.

The path hit a roadblock in April of 2009 when WKPZ was purchased by a large corporate network. Claire wasn't the only person to lose her job. Actually, over half of the veterans and most of the interns and assistants were *let go*. By then, she had student loans, an apartment, car and credit card debt. Honestly, that credit card and bartending kept food on the table while she looked for new employment. She considered leaving Atlanta. But she liked the city, climate, and people.

In Atlanta, she could depend on indigo blue skies and rusted red dirt. The vision out *her* window was black and white, like an old photograph. The ground, trees, and grass were colorless. The cloud-covered sky hung low and endless. The word that came to mind was *cold*. She could be in Indiana, Michigan, or anywhere in the Midwest. They all looked alike. She hated winter, the darkness, and lack of color. Now she was staring at it through the windows of her prison.

Claire wondered if she should have opened the drapes. Her discovery made her situation direr. If she wasn't in Atlanta, where was she? And how did she get here? She looked at the stupid switch and considered shutting away the bleak outside world. It wasn't helping her attitude. Claire decided the switch didn't help her attitude or the non-English speaking servant, the expensive clothes, or the lavish surroundings. She was being held prisoner by a crazy man who somehow believed that he now owned her. Her location, luxurious surroundings, fancy clothes—none of it mattered. She could have been in a cinder block cell. She was still a prisoner, and the stupid extravagant stuff wouldn't change that.

As hours and days passed, Claire had nothing to do but think. She mostly thought about escaping, fantasizing about running through the massive wooded forest outside her window. In her fantasy, salvation was through the trees. But she couldn't get outside the room, much less to the trees. After a few days, in a moment of heated desperation, Claire took one of the chairs from the table and tried to break the panes of glass on the French doors. The damn chair bounced off the glass. She searched the suite for anything heavy. The closest thing was a thick book. Even with repeated strikes, the windows remained intact.

The hours and days spent alone made her yearn for the hustle and bustle of the Red Wing. She wondered about the regulars and her coworkers. Had anyone reported her missing? These thoughts usually resulted in tears and a headache. In an attempt at self-preservation and sanity, she began to think about the past. Was there something in the past that led to this?

Liking earth science and weather, meteorology seemed a natural choice. She loved the unknown. As a teenager she experienced her first tornado. The power and unpredictability of the storm fascinated her. It exhilarated her to watch warm and cold fronts collide. She loved to learn more about the whys and hows. The computers could help you predict the weather. But it is such a small part. Why do some fronts stall and create floods when days before the models predicted only an inch of rain? How can a warm sunny day suddenly turn stormy? She wanted to understand it better, to control the outcomes in some way, and perhaps minimize its destructive forces. But now a degree in meteorology seemed useless.

Near the end of March . . .

He'd been in the little apartment on multiple occasions. Thankfully, this would be his last visit. Looking at his TAG Heuer watch, he knew the movers should be there in thirty minutes. He slowly walked around the small rooms. Starting in her bedroom, he surveyed her remaining belongings. Everything else, clothes and household items, had been placed in boxes labeled for donation. The full-sized bed was now stripped with only the mattress, boxed springs, and frame remaining.

On top of the dresser were the items Anthony pondered. There were pictures in frames, indicating sentimental attachment. He knew most of the faces. Some he'd seen in person. Others he'd learned about through whatever means necessary. There was a picture of her grandparents in one of those cheap frames labeled "Grandparents." Then there was an old picture of Claire with her sister, Emily, and their parents, taken in front of the Golden Gate Bridge. If he had to guess, Claire was about twelve or thirteen. There was a close-up of Claire and Emily at Emily's wedding. He would have known the location even without the evidence of Emily's veil. He remembered the day. It was hot and humid, even for Indiana. The last was a more recent photo of Emily and John sitting on a sofa.

A few pieces of jewelry sat on top of her dresser. The inexpensive pieces had been included in the donation boxes. These items, however, were of finer quality. A pearl necklace on a white gold chain was the same one she wore in the wedding picture with Emily. There was also a pair of diamond earrings.

As Anthony fingered the diamond studs with his gloved hands, he decided to put them into the donation box. The damn things couldn't be half a carat total weight. He grinned. If *he* wanted Claire to have diamond earrings, they sure as hell would be bigger than that.

Walking toward the living room, he glanced into the bathroom, completely empty. Most of its contents were thrown away. No one wants a used shower curtain. The living room was unnaturally sterile, dramatically contrasting the way he'd found it. Months ago, when he first entered the apartment to place the surveillance cameras, the small living room surprised him. He had closets bigger than this, yet it was *homey*, if that was possible. It may have been the pictures, plants, or eclectic furnishings—he really didn't know. It felt warm, like her.

Now the room was down to the bare essentials. He looked at his watch: seventeen more minutes. He picked up the laptop and placed it in the case. Going back to the bedroom, he decided to keep all the framed pictures and the pearl necklace. He put everything in the case with the laptop.

Reminiscing, the computer had been invaluable. With it, he'd been able to access her calendar, e-mail, and various accounts. He found all scheduled commitments and via e-mail regretfully canceled. He also e-mailed her employer, Facebook friends, and sister. They all received a similar message describing an amazing opportunity she received, how she'd be unreachable for a while, but would get back to them as soon as *her* decision regarding *her* future was made. Through the laptop, her bank accounts, credit cards, auto loan, utility bills, cellular phone—everything—was assessed. The balances now all read zero. After paying each final statement *in full*, the accounts were closed. The monies that went into her bank accounts were difficult to trace, but if someone took the time to do it, they would learn it was a settlement from WKPZ. Anthony hoped no one would investigate that thoroughly, but if they did, that discovery should pacify them. Of course, WKPZ had no record of such a transaction, but the probability of anyone investigating that thoroughly was low. The fact the monies had been deposited into her various savings and checking accounts four days before her disappearance led to the allusion. Smiling, he recalled sitting with her at the Red Wing, knowing she had an extra $200,000 plus in her accounts and was clueless. Anthony knew from his surveillance that Claire only checked her accounts on the weekend. At that time, she would sit down and attempt to make ends meet. The day after she did her little balancing act, the monies electronically appeared.

The settlement money and *"see you later"* e-mails combined to make her disappearance appear planned. If he could reach his own back, Anthony would give himself a hardy pat. He deserved it!

The manager at the Red Wing had been the most difficult to quiet. After the e-mail, he immediately began calling and texting her phone. Thankfully, Anthony had her Blackberry with him back in Iowa. *Claire* responded apologetically to the manager via text. *She* was so sorry to leave in such a rush, but you have to answer when opportunity knocks. Anthony was pretty sure that if she were to return to Atlanta, which she wouldn't, the Red Wing would *not* be willing to reemploy.

28

Keeping Claire's laptop, Anthony could check her e-mail and account balances. He would also be able to periodically send e-mails or post a Facebook status update to keep the curious from overreacting. Even though the computer would be in Iowa, the web address and URL wouldn't change. No one would know the point of origin.

Claire's Blackberry met an unfortunate accident. Many cellphones contain GPS trackers. Anthony wasn't willing to take that chance. A mass text went out explaining that Claire would have a new number and would contact everyone as soon as possible. And then, after removing the SIM card, Anthony backed his rental car over the device. It didn't survive. His case also contained the final hardware of his surveillance equipment. He definitely didn't want some stupid painter running across one of his cameras.

Six months of footage taught him much about Claire Nichols. She kept late hours and enjoyed sleeping late in the mornings. She liked to cook and bake, but gave a lot away. There were no boyfriends or male visitors to the apartment, which pleased Anthony. She liked to talk on the phone and chat with people on the computer. She rarely watched television except for a show called *Grey's Anatomy* and another on the same station. She liked to exercise, sometimes walking with the lady next door. Rarely did she stay around the apartment, going out with friends frequently. Many times, she would return home in a less than sober state, but always alone. During Christmas season, she put up decorations and even a tree. The best part of the surveillance was access to her schedules and passwords. The computer hacking would have been more difficult without those passwords. Oh, he could have done it, but this was easier.

Anthony heard the knock on the door. He removed his gloves, put them in his pockets, and opened the door. A burly man with underarm stains and a perspiration-drenched face met his gaze. He inquired. "Hi, are you John Vandersol?"

"Yeah, that's me. You the movers? Come on in." Anthony decided that even though he looked nothing like Claire's brother-in-law, his presence in her apartment made more sense than any other male. People rarely remembered faces anyway.

Anthony signed the contract and paid the man in cash, with a $200 tip. He explained that his sister-in-law moved to another city for a job and wanted all of her things taken to the local refuge for donation. The mover wasn't interested in the backstory, and Anthony didn't push. He gave enough information to make the transition plausible and not too much to make it sound contrived. Too bad Claire wouldn't be filing taxes. She could receive a hell of a deduction for her donations. It didn't take the men long to empty the apartment.

Her car sold for an amazingly low price. Actually, it hadn't been enough to pay off the loan, but the point was to get rid of it. Forging her signature on the paperwork wasn't difficult. He used her signature on the napkin as a pattern. The fortunate buyer didn't ask questions.

Caressing the case that held the only remnants of Claire's previous life, Anthony wiped the doorknob with his gloves, locked the door to the empty apartment, and placed the keys into an envelope. The complex had been e-mailed about Claire's sudden move, as well as reimbursed for severing the lease. The envelope was deposited into an open slot in the office door. Getting into the rented vehicle, he called his driver, *PICK ME UP AT BUDGET RENTAL, TEN MINUTES.*

Anthony didn't like doing all these tasks himself. Under different circumstances, he would hire someone to box the items, or wait for the movers. This however, wasn't normal circumstances. He couldn't risk others knowing his plan. He couldn't even trust his best friend and head of his legal team. This was all *very* private.

Eric, Anthony's driver, had some clue about things transpiring in Atlanta. Truthfully, he had more than a clue. He helped transport Claire back to Iowa. But Eric's allegiance was steadfast, as with the rest of his household staff.

Sighing as he parked the inconspicuous gray Toyota Camry in the lot of Budget, he thanked God this was done. Now to change into *his* kind of clothes, get back to *his* real life, prepare for *his* scheduled meetings overseas, *and* decide Claire's future. He flashed a private smile—the acquisition was complete.

Through humor, you can soften
some of the worst blows that life delivers.
And once you find laughter, no matter how painful
your situation might be, you can survive it.
—Bill Crosby

Chapter 4

Multiple times a day, she would think of her chance meeting with Anthony Rawlings. She believed his name sounded familiar, but didn't and still doesn't know why. God, she would love to put his name in Google and see what popped up; maybe *Crazy Abusive Man* or *Nut Job with a Supremacy Complex?*

She recalled that one day, while tending bar, they started to talk, not about anything particular, just chat. He was attentive and charming. His eyes mesmerized her, not with fear as they did now, more of a pull, an attraction. Her policy was not to see patrons socially. Yet for some reason, when Anthony invited her to a small booth after her shift, she accepted. In hindsight, Claire believed she was safe, still being *in* the Red Wing. Once there, they continued talking and drank some wine. At some point, he had a napkin and talked about helping her obtain a job. It was something about the Weather Channel—definitely not this. She remembered signing the napkin but couldn't recall him signing it. The entire scenario seemed harmless. She couldn't remember what was written on the napkin. It was never discussed again as they shared a few more glasses of cabernet sauvignon.

After that, she went home alone.

The next day she slept in, shopped for groceries, which now sat rotting in her refrigerator, and worked the closing shift. Had she known it was her last full day of freedom, she would have spent it in a more productive manner: visiting with friends, enjoying a crowd at the mall, or calling her sister. Claire wondered if Anthony returned to the bar that day. She didn't think so, but she did remember his call that evening, about a week ago...March 16...

The call surprised Claire. After their talk the night before and her refusal to see him for food, she never expected to hear from him again. Yet, the call came as the seats around the bar were beginning to fill. Her boss didn't appreciate personal calls at slow times of the day, much less during busy times. "Hello, this is Claire. May I help you?"

"Good evening, Claire." Her heart skipped a beat, immediately recognizing the deep husky voice that accompanied the handsome dark-haired, dark-eyed man.

"Anthony?"

First a chuckle, then, "I am impressed. You have a wonderful memory for voices."

Well, yeah, when they accompany people like you. "Thank you, I talk with people for a living. I am surprised you called. Did you forget or leave something?"

"Well, yes and no." The manager walked toward her. She covered the phone and whispered, "Customer from yesterday looking for something." He turned away and walked to the kitchen.

"Okay, if you let me know what it is, I can look around and call you back. First let me get your number."

"Oh, you definitely have my number. First I think you should know what I left." Claire waited impatiently. He sounded mysterious, but there were people waiting.

Finally, he said, "You, Claire . . ."

Her cheeks flushed. "Excuse me?"

"I have been thinking about you and would be honored if you would agree to accompany me to dinner."

Claire's mind scrambled. She tried to think, but the bar was filling with patrons all looking to her for service. Anthony was waiting for her to respond. Last night, he was so handsome and charming. The prospect of someone like him, older and successful, taking the time to call her after a few hours of chatting was flattering. She worked to sound resilient, "I'm sorry, I work until close. That's too late for dinner."

"Someone named Crystal, who answered the telephone earlier, said you work the early shift tomorrow. Or will you turn me down again and send me home heartbroken?"

Claire sighed. This was outside of her comfort zone. But then again, she didn't want to be responsible for sending some poor, successful, gorgeous businessman home heartbroken. "I am supposed to get off tomorrow at six, but if you recall from last night, it isn't always prompt. I could be ready by seven, if that isn't too late?"

His tone sounded lighter and quicker, "Wonderful. Should I pick you up at the Red Wing or your place?"

Oh god, she wasn't ready for him to know where she lived. "I can meet you—"

He cut her off. "I'm sure you can, but let me pick you up in style. I will see you at seven at the Red Wing. We are going to Chez Czar, until tomorrow, Claire." The telephone disconnected.

For the next sixty to seventy minutes, the barrage of orders and customers needing pacification kept her mind from fully registering her actions. She'd accepted an invitation to one of the most exclusive dining spots in Atlanta, with someone she barely knew. She broke her *no dating a customer* rule and her *no going in the same car on a first date* rule. But maybe the first date was in the booth at the Red Wing. Then this would officially be the second date, which was totally acceptable. Oh my, what would she wear?

The next morning she didn't have much time. However, after shaving her legs, Claire decided to swing by Greenbriar Mall and see if Macy's had anything appropriate for an evening with a man like Anthony Rawlings, in her price range. It turned out there was nothing for free, but she did find a simple black dress on its second markdown. It was shorter than she normally wore, but it fit, and she didn't have time to be picky. After a quick run through Burlington's, she purchased a pair of simple black heeled sandals. These items, accompanied by a black cotton half sweater that she had at home, would be perfect for a cool spring evening.

March 17th is a bigger holiday in the bar business than Christmas. Thankfully, Claire's shift ended at six o'clock. She wanted to be gone before the holiday crowd hit the Red Wing. St. Patrick's Day bestowed a claim of Irish roots on each patron. They all waited anxiously for green beer. By six-fifteen, she was officially clocked out, her register balanced. In the back of the bar, there was a small locker room where the female employees kept their purses, coats, and extra clothes. Opening her locker, she pulled out the black dress.

After changing her clothes and stuffing her Red Wing T-shirt and jeans back into the locker, Claire looked at herself in the mirror. Twisting and turning, her cheeks reddened, revealing uneasiness. This wasn't her. She was jeans, T-shirts, and tennis shoes. Pushing forward, she added eyeliner, mascara, and lip-gloss. That, accompanied by a quick brush through her hair, was as good as it would get.

Judging by the hoots from both sides of the bar when she entered the front of the Red Wing, she did all right. "Check you out, hot stuff. Where ya going all dolled up?" This flirting tone was one of the many voices Claire's manager had in his repertoire.

Feeling playful, she decided to throw it back to him and respond all *Southern belle*, "Why, sir"—the syllables drawn-out—"I don't know what you mean." He raised his eyebrows and stared. "Well, goodness gracious, I do have a little 'ole date with a tall, dark, handsome stranger."

A few minutes later, Claire saw a shiny black Porsche pull up to the front of the bar. "See y'all later. Don't wait up." The coworkers behind the bar did some more hoot'n and holler'n. Claire smiled as the voices faded into the sounds of the night on the other side of the door.

Anthony got out of the driver's side. His perfectly tailored light-colored Armani suit validated the purchase of her new black dress. Chivalrously, he kissed her hand and escorted her around to the passenger's door. At the time, Claire believed that the simple act seemed elegant.

33

Being a four-star authentic Italian restaurant in the heart of Atlanta, Chez Czar had a reputation for being a difficult place to get reservations. However, upon their arrival, the hostess greeted them warmly and guided them to a premium table.

When the waiter arrived with menus, Anthony immediately asked for their best bottle of Batasiolo Barolo. After the waiter departed, Claire began to look at the menu. She couldn't help notice there were no prices. What did that mean? When she looked up from behind the large leather-bound folder, Anthony was looking at her, not his menu. Once again, Claire felt her cheeks flush. "Do you already know what you want?" she asked.

"I believe I do." He reached for her menu. Claire released it, although she hadn't had a chance to really see her choices. The whole *no price* thing had her a little be fuddled. "And I can't see you behind that big menu." Claire smiled. She'd never met a man like Anthony. She felt like she had his full attention. It was nice but unsettling. When the waiter returned with the wine, he poured a small amount into a glass. Anthony tasted the liquid and replied, "Ahh, yes." The waiter poured two glasses.

Claire wondered if services like this was what people talked about on cruise ships. Goodness knows this wasn't how people were treated at the Red Wing or Applebee's for that matter. Before she realized what had happened, Anthony ordered dinner. Tentatively, she replied "Well, thank you."

"Do you not like Caesar salad and shrimp linguine?" he asked, dismayed.

"Oh, I do. I just have never had anyone order for me without asking me my preference." Claire thought to herself, *But then again, I have never met anyone like you.*

The tips of his lips moved upward and his eyes shone. "If you do not like your food, we can certainly send it back for something else."

She did like the food. As soon as the linguine arrived at the table and the aroma of garlic and butter penetrated her senses, she knew the taste would be even better. When the shrimp touched her tongue, she relished the seasoned flavor. Anthony was incredibly charming and polite. After dinner, as they waited for the valet, he gently placed his arm around her waist. He was much taller than she realized at the Red Wing. Leaning down to her ear, he whispered, "May I kiss you?"

Feeling the unstoppable sensation of his stare, Claire only nodded. As his lips touched hers, they were soft and full. Momentarily, she felt the rest of the world disappear. It ended too soon. When he pulled away from the contact, Anthony smiled, and Claire felt her cheeks flush. Once they were back in the car, he asked, "Are you ready to go back to the Red Wing, or should I take you to your home?" Claire contemplated her options. He offered her a third alternative. "Or would you like to join me in my suite, perhaps for some more wine, or we could call room service for dessert?"

Smiling, she responded, "I like dessert."

The hotel's foyer was exquisite—marble floors, large glowing chandeliers, and huge floral arrangements. Claire tried to not look around. She'd never entered such an exclusive establishment. His suite at the Ritz Carlton was as large as an apartment. Once inside, he remained suave and sensual with deep dark brown eyes. His glance transfixed her, giving her the sensation of chocolate, dark and melted. Although she didn't know him that well, she agreed to romance and sexual pleasures. Something about him made her break all her own rules. He was prepared, romantic, and attentive.

After midnight Claire lifted her head to meet Anthony's soft gaze. "I really need to go home." Claire enjoyed the soft 700-count sheets a little too much. "I don't want to disturb you, so I can get a taxi downstairs." She started to shift away as he gently reached for her.

"If I promise you a ride in the morning, would you consider some more dessert?" Anthony's expression, as well as another of his features, informed Claire that he wanted her to choose the dessert.

She knew she wasn't scheduled to be at work the next day. "I don't want to disrupt your schedule. I am sure you are busy."

"I promise this is not a disruption. And maybe after more dessert, we could have another glass of wine. There is still some in the bottle from room service." The last time she looked at a clock, it was 1:15 a.m. Even at that moment, Claire didn't realize the consequence of their *napkin agreement*.

As Claire lay on the sofa recalling the events that led her to this place and this situation, she couldn't recall traveling. She remembered a car but couldn't recall any other part of this house. She couldn't remember any other memories of Atlanta. That time, 1:15 a.m. was her last conscious memory of her life.

From the other windows near the bed, she could see only trees. She must be at the end of the dwelling because she couldn't see more of the house. Her windows were far from the ground. Even if they opened, she would break something from this height. Day after day, the skies lightened to shades of gray and then darkened too soon. Keeping track of the days became difficult.

Wondering where she was, Claire told herself that when Catherine returned she would ask about their location. Catherine didn't come, the young non-English speaking man did. Day after day, no one came to talk to her. The food came and the room was cleaned. Clothes were miraculously washed and returned to her closet or drawers, but no person was ever seen. She was alone. The isolation was hell. It may not have left physical markings, but there was no question in Claire's mind, it was a neater form of Anthony's abuse.

Claire wasn't a TV watcher, and the TV in her suite didn't receive many stations. However, she did check the news each day to learn what day it was. They'd begun to blend. On April 2, she finally heard a repeated knock at the door.

The thirteen days hadn't been a total loss. After two or three, Claire realized the weather channel would do *local* weather. The first time she sat to watch, she sat stunned. The midnight announcer, Shelby, graduated from Valparaiso the year before her. Claire watched in disbelief. Why was Shelby on the Weather Channel and she was being held prisoner in a house in Iowa? The local weather came from Iowa City, Iowa.

Claire discovered her windows faced southeast. During a few of the thirteen days of her seclusion, the sun shone. The hours of sunshine grew in length by minutes each day, but it still looked cold. With the insulated windows and warm fireplace, Claire's only knowledge of outdoor temperature remained Shelby and her co-anchors.

As a means of escape, Claire turned to reading. The built-in bookcases were filled with current bestsellers. There were series and individual books. She loved to read when she was a child, but life had become too busy. That no longer seemed to be a problem.

She also discovered a small refrigerator which stayed stocked with water and fruit. No one asked what she wanted to eat. Truly she wasn't hungry, considering she didn't do anything to build an appetite. She showered, dressed, and primped a little. The rebellion became meaningless with no one to rebel against. One sign of progress, the bruises faded from red, to blue, to purple, to green, and now a very indistinct yellow.

The knock came again. Food usually entered after the first knock this person was waiting for an invitation. Claire didn't think it was Anthony, he didn't knock. Could it be Catherine? Slowly, she approached the door.

"Yes? Who's there?" The anticipation of actually hearing a voice stimulated her as she waited for a response.

*Disappointment to a noble soul
is what cold water is to burning metal.
It strengthens, tempers, intensifies, but never destroys it*
—Unknown

Chapter 5

"**M**s. Claire, may I come in?"

Claire's heart leaped. The woman she barely knew was the one person Claire prayed would come to her each of the last thirteen days. Excited to use her voice again, she said, "Yes, Catherine, please come in." It wasn't as though Claire could open the door from her side. Claire heard the beep.

Catherine opened the door and smiled sadly at Claire. Claire wanted to hug her, but something in Catherine's eyes said, "No, not now. I was not able to come up here before." It was as if she spoke, yet her lips never moved.

"Ms. Claire, you seem . . . well rested. I have a message for you." Claire nodded, anticipating the message from Anthony. "Mr. Rawlings will be coming to see you tonight. He will be late in the city. He said to expect him between nine and ten."

Claire looked at the clock near the bed. It was only 4:35 p.m. "Okay." She didn't know what to do. She couldn't exactly refuse his entering. He didn't ask, only proclaimed. "Will we be dining?"

"You will dine alone. He will be here too late for dinner." Catherine looked as though she wanted to say more, but knew better. Maybe someday Claire would be like that, know better. Then again, hopefully, she would be out of here before then.

"Catherine, could you please help me prepare?"

"No, miss. I am sorry, but your attire and presentation are to be of your own doing." Catherine turned to leave the suite.

"Please wait. Catherine, can't you please stay and talk to me, even for a little while? After all, we have five hours before Mr. Rawlings will arrive."

"I must go, but may I say, you look beautiful. I like your face . . . well, ah . . . clear." Catherine smiled a real and tender smile and exited the suite.

Somehow Claire knew it was a mind game. He was testing her to see how she would dress, look, and act. He was also testing her to determine if the mere promise of his presence caused uneasiness. She decided this examination was an opportunity to respond to her circumstances, instead of react. He would take her body. That reality had been made painfully clear. However, she would *not* let him have her mind. He wanted her to spend the next five hours alone, dreading his arrival, filled with fear and trembling. She wouldn't give him the satisfaction.

Claire had five hours to prove she was in control of her life—if not to him, then at least to herself. She walked into her closet and, like a general selecting soldiers, perused the racks and shelves selecting an outfit that would bolster her self-confidence. She found it—a black dress with a long flowing skirt. The idea of being near him in a dress made her queasy, but she liked the boldness.

With each flash of the mascara, or zip of the flowing black satin dress, she reviewed her decision. Escape from this room was not possible. The only way to get out of here was to concede to whatever he demanded and find another path. Looking at herself in the mirror, Claire straightened her neck, righted her shoulders, and confirmed her mission. Physically fighting had been counterproductive, it only seemed to intensify Anthony's resolve. She needed to yield, temporarily, to his demands in order to access a means of exodus. Completing her hairstyle, she dissected her plan. It seemed like surrender, but her gut told her that resigning to him with a straight face and experiencing the effects of her verbalization took more control than the pleas, accusations, and fighting of two weeks earlier.

It was eight forty-five when Claire buckled the Jimmy Choo sandals. She felt confident she looked the part. She just needed to perform it. At nine thirty, her nerves wreaked havoc with her stomach. Damn him! That was his plan. She wouldn't give him the gratification. She reached for her current novel, by the bed, went to the overstuffed chair, and sat down. She started to read, but the words made no sense. Her chest thumped as her heart beat too rapidly, and her mouth tasted like cotton. Getting up, she retrieved a bottle of water. Her sweaty palms made opening the cap difficult. The water helped her dry mouth until it hit her stomach. Fearing she would need to run for the bathroom, she remembered to breathe - deep cleansing breaths. Her nerves began to calm. The flames of the fire warmed her as she attempted to concentrate on the words of her book.

At nine fifty-eight, preceded by the beep, her suite door opened. Anthony walked in like he'd been there earlier that day, not two weeks ago. Dressed in a dark gray double-breasted silk suit, he appeared heavier than she remembered; maybe not heavy, massive, broad-chested. She wasn't sure of his height, but would guess about six four, an entire twelve inches taller than her. His age showed in fine lines around his dark eyes. Estimating, Claire guessed, late thirties.

"Good evening, Claire."

The heat from the fireplace helped to ward off trembling. Claire stood and nodded. "Good evening, Anthony." Taking command, she suggested, "Shall we sit?"

Anthony sat on the sofa, leaned back, and unbuttoned his jacket. Claire sat on the edge of the chair and looked directly into his eyes. She wouldn't show fear, although his dark eyes were the scariest things she'd ever seen.

"Do you think you are ready to continue with our agreement? Or do you need some more time alone to consider the situation?"

"After consulting my attorney, I feel I have no choice but to continue with our agreement."

Anthony's eyes darkened at the mention of a consultation. "Claire, I know you are joking. But do you really think that is a good idea? Considering your circumstances?"

Keeping her smile intact, she said, "I have had a lot of time to think, joviality has sustained me."

"I must say your demeanor impresses me. I will need to deliberate on this new personality."

The two sat in silence while the fireplace blower hummed in the background. Claire used every ounce of control to appear calm while Anthony pondered. He remained seated against the back of the sofa, yet his jaw seemed to clench as his eyes devoured her, scanning and taking her in. She wished she could read his eyes. Then suddenly they caught hers. "Tell me what you have learned during your reflection time."

"I have learned I have many clothes, very nice clothes, may I add. I have a balcony that I cannot access because the door is locked. I have a refrigerator and small microwave. But honestly, the microwave seems unnecessary as I also have food brought to me three times a day."

"That is all very nice," Anthony said with a hint of sarcasm. "But what have you discovered about your situation? Do you even know where you are?" His mocking tone suggested his confidence that only he held the answer.

Claire contemplated her response. Should she be honest and tell him she learned Iowa City from the Weather Channel? What if that resulted in loss of TV stations; she might not know what day it is. Then again, if she lied and said she didn't know and he caught her in a lie, what would happen? Maintaining an air of confidence, she said, "I am in Iowa, or at least somewhere near Iowa City."

Gripping the arm of the sofa with his right hand, Claire watched his muscles tense. "And you learned this from whom?" Each word became more exaggerated as he spoke.

"I learned it from the Weather Channel, *Local on the Eights*. The local weather for this area comes from Iowa City, Iowa." Claire continued to sound as lighthearted as possible.

Anthony's body relaxed and he nodded his head in approval. "Very well, that will spare me telling you that information." Claire wanted to ask how she got there. "For the sake of clarity, since that seemed to be a problem in the past, you are aware that your indebtedness to me can only be determined paid by me?"

Claire swallowed. This is what she anticipated, smiling she nodded her head yes.

His voice strong and authoritative, "I prefer verbal confirmation."

"I am aware that you are the only one who can decide when my debt is paid in full." The calmness of her voice surprised even Claire. She said a silent prayer that he wouldn't notice her hands balled into fists with her nails biting into her own palms. If she concentrated, she could remember how to relax her hands. But at this moment, her concentration was needed elsewhere.

"You are also aware that your duties require you to be available to me whenever, wherever, and however I demand?" His eyes never faltered from her, yet his body language looked relaxed, arrogant. He was a man willing to push Claire to the brink. It was like watching a poker game, pushing the odds. Would there be a payoff? Or would someone blink?

"I am aware."

"You are aware that you must at all times obey my rules?" Anthony's eyes penetrated.

"I am aware that I must do as I am told." The words hurt her throat but sounded easily spoken. She was not going to let him fluster her. And damn, she didn't need that skin on her palms anyway. Her smile remained steady and undaunted.

Anthony remained silent for an extended period of time, watching Claire. Finally, he spoke, "Very well." He stood. Claire expected some kind of directive. Instead, he walked toward the door.

"Wait." She proclaimed. He turned to look at her. His expression displayed astonishment at her command. She immediately realized her words overstepped her bounds, but she couldn't go on locked alone in the suite. Her tone softened. "I'm sorry, but may I leave this suite?"

"As long as we are certain on the terms of our agreement *and* you follow the rules and orders given, I see no problem with you roaming the house." He reached for the door handle. "It is rather large. I will be working from home tomorrow. Your services will be utilized then, so be prepared for my call. When I have a chance, I will give you a tour of the house and define your limitations. I think it is best that you do not roam tonight. I do not want you getting lost." He started to leave. She heard the beep as he grabbed the lever.

"Anthony? I don't have any . . . duties tonight?" Her voice began to fail her. She sounded less like the strong, lighthearted woman she desperately tried to project and more like a child.

"I have recently arrived from a series of meetings in Europe and am quite tired. I am glad to know we have a mutual understanding. Good night, Claire."

"Good night, Anthony." He shut the door. She heard the beep and the lock. Her thoughts swirled. *He has been in Europe! I've been locked in here while he was on another continent! Okay, focus, the door will be open tomorrow. I engaged in a conversation, the first one in almost two weeks. He didn't say anything about my appearance, all that work and not a word. Perhaps compliments aren't his style, only criticism. That's all right, because tomorrow I'm leaving this suite And leaving the suite is one step closer to going home!*

Tossing and turning, Claire had too much energy to sleep. It wasn't just her body, her mind spun with the excitement of her impending release. During the past thirteen days her every need was met, except her need to be with people. She couldn't remember a time in her life that didn't include interaction. It was something she took for granted, until now. The isolation was unbearable. While it was happening, she wouldn't allow herself to think about it, but now that the end was near her anticipation mounted. She lay in bed and pondered Anthony Rawlings. What kind of man is he?

He obviously liked control, complete control. What did he mean when he said, "Be prepared for my call"? Did that mean she should be up early waiting for someone to come and get her? He didn't give her a time. She looked at the clock: 5:33. Should she get up now? What if she fell asleep and wasn't ready when he called? Could she end up locked in her suite another thirteen days? She couldn't take that. Claire needed companionship.

Her mind slipped back to college and recalled living in the sorority house surrounded by girls. She often longed for some *alone time*, away from the drama. There were always issues between sisters, with boyfriends, classes, or parents. She wished for a place of her own and time by herself. Another of Grandma's sayings came to mind, "Be careful what you wish for." She would love to have that camaraderie and even drama again.

At 6:00 a.m. she gave up, got out of bed, and went to the bathroom to get ready for whatever the day had in store. She spent almost two weeks doing the same thing. Now she prepared to venture into the unknown. It both scared and excited her. It was like the unpredictability of weather.

Her breakfast waited on the table when she left the bathroom. Her hair styled in a low ponytail, casual yet classy. Her makeup done, she decided to dress before eating and entered the closet. Stepping into the sea of material Claire wondered if every outfit would be so difficult to choose and if every action was a test? Decision made, she put on dark jeans and a sweater. Entering her suite, ready for coffee, she suddenly dropped her shoes and let out a startled, muffled scream.

Lost in her own thoughts, his presence caught her off guard. She hadn't heard him enter. Damn. Could he learn to knock? The look of surprise and shock on Claire's face accompanied by the dropping of her shoes made him smile. He'd startled her. She could tell that made him happy. "Good morning, Claire."

"Good morning, Anthony, I didn't hear you come in." She picked up her shoes and regained some composure.

"Are you ready for your tour?" He looked at her uneaten breakfast. "Did you plan to eat first? I have a web conference in forty-five minutes."

"What's a web conference?" Suddenly, she thought she shouldn't have asked, or should she? She just didn't know what to do or say. She knew it was just nice to have someone to talk to, even him.

"It is like a conference call between many different people, but instead of being on the phone it is over the Internet."

She couldn't believe how casual and friendly he spoke. He even looked more relaxed, wearing slacks and a shirt but no tie or jacket. It reminded her of the Anthony she met in Atlanta. "It's okay. I'm really not hungry. I'm more excited to get the tour." She put on her shoes and sipped a little coffee.

He began by explaining the shape of the house, a main section which housed the dining room, formal living room, sitting room, kitchen, and the grand foyer. The foyer contained the main stairway. Two large wings projected off from the main section. Stairways were also found at the end of each of those wings. The staff had access to an elevator for transporting carts and larger items to the second and lower level.

He continued to explain, Claire's suite was located on the second floor of the southeast wing, as they stepped out of the suite. Claire looked slowly down the great expanse of the hallway at many other doors. She hadn't heard anyone or anything her entire stay. Anthony moved five steps ahead before she remembered to walk. The sensation of stepping out of the suite was unnerving, like leaving the security of a nest.

She quickly caught him and did her best to walk at his fast pace. At times he wouldn't say a word, just walk. Other times he spoke at great length about this piece of art or that antique. Along the tour he showed her a library adorned with beautiful cherry woodwork and book-lined shelves. It occupied two stories and contained a back wall with a sliding ladder like you see in movies. She could get lost in there for days. She looked around for a computer. Didn't all libraries have computers? "Is there a computer in here, some way to find books?"

"I think it would be best for you to not have access to computers, the Internet, or telephones." Anthony's statement wasn't an answer to Claire's question, it was a proclamation.

The tour of his magnificent house held so many treasures that Claire momentarily forgot why she was there. His declaration brought the reason rushing back. She knew all forms of communication were absent from her suite, but assumed that outside the door there would be Wi-Fi. Even though she hadn't seen her Blackberry for over two weeks, she hoped she would once again be connected to the real world. He looked at her with his dark eyes as he spoke. She did her best to maintain his gaze, swallowed, and nodded in response.

Next he took her to an exercise room in the lower level, complete with all kinds of weight equipment, as well as a treadmill, elliptical, and stepper. Attached to the workout room was an indoor pool. Though not full sized, it was big enough to swim laps. When she saw the pool, the stunning mosaic tiles that covered the walls and floor, the windows that allowed sunlight to penetrate, and smelled the familiar chlorine, she let out a gasp.

"Do you like to swim?" he asked.

"Oh yes. This is amazing." Claire's eyes glowed.

"You shall have bathing suits tomorrow." His words surprised her. She hadn't asked. However, he was offering, and she did like to swim.

"Thank you."

The formal dining room was exquisite. The table currently held chairs for ten, but the room seemed as though it could seat at least three times as many. The intricate woodwork accented light yellow walls and included hand-carved trim, molding, and built-in cabinetry. The ceiling was divided into sections separated by wood trim, each section embellished with different designs and some sort of gold flaking that created a shimmer in the light of the sun. The cabinetry held what Claire believed to be very lavish crystal and china. The height of the ceiling allowed the windows and French doors to be taller than most, at least ten feet, and adorned by exquisite flowing draperies. "We will eat in here when I decide. If I am not home, you will eat in your suite."

Down the west corridor just off the main section was a set of grand double doors. "This is my office. Your services will be required in here on days I work from home, like today. My office is strictly forbidden without my permission. Is that clear?" Claire nodded. Anthony turned to look at her, standing very close. "Claire, I want verbal responses to my questions. Do not make me tell you that again."

"I understand. Your office is off-limits unless you tell me to be there." Her eyes fluttered from his eyes to the wall, straining to maintain eye contact. They hadn't made it down the rest of the west corridor when Anthony looked at his watch.

"I have business I must do. It is seven twenty-five. I want you back at my office at ten thirty. You have some debt to pay off." He obviously enjoyed the uncomfortable feeling his remarks produced. "Do you think you can find your way back to your suite?"

"Yes, I can. But do I have to?" She told him how she would like to go back to the library and look around. She promised she would be back by ten thirty.

He hesitated, but reluctantly agreed. "We have not discussed all of the rules pertaining to the house. At this point, do not go outside. Permission for entering the grounds will be contingent upon your ability to follow rules within the house."

"I understand, and I will be back by ten thirty." Filled with exhilaration, Claire walked down the marble corridor toward the library. The sensation of her shoes on the marble floor, the sound of her steps, and the coolness of the empty hall thrilled her senses. To be so deprived of anything except the same four walls, no matter how beautiful, and to be free to roam was ecstasy. She had three hours to spend in the library.

Anthony's collection of books was amazing. He had classics, "Tale of Two Cities," "Pride and Prejudice," "Great Expectations," "Moby Dick," and literally hundreds more. There were resource books, encyclopedias, dictionaries, and language translation books. She found biographies and memoirs, science fiction, romance, thrillers, and fantasy. Just as she entered another section Anthony met her face to face. Once again, she jumped. This time he wasn't smiling.

Claire's mind spun, *I can't be late, I've been watching the clock over there.* The clock read 10:37. Where had the time gone? "Oh, Anthony, I am so sorry. I was just engrossed in all you have—"

His hand struck her cheek. She didn't fall but wobbled off balance. He then pulled her toward him. His warm hand on the back of her neck, entwined in her hair, and caused her face to tilt upward until all she could see were his penetrating eyes.

"Simple instructions, which were what I gave you, perhaps you are not ready to leave your suite quite yet." He loosened the grip on her hair.

"No, please don't say that. I can follow instructions, I can." Claire didn't want to beg, but she couldn't stand the thought of being locked in her suite another day.

"Follow me to my office, now."

Each of his strides equaled three of Claire's; she practically ran to keep up. When they reached the double doors of his office, he opened one and shoved her inside. She had only seen his office doors, but now she looked around the interior. Like everything else in the mansion, it was lavish and substantial. The walls were surfaced with more of the impressive cherry paneling, decorative trim, and ornate bookcases. There was a very impressive mahogany desk, a leather sofa, chairs, and a conference table. His desk contained many computer screens as well as a large screen on the wall that could be one or divided into multiple screens. Currently, it was subdivided, and each screen contained stock market information. The lights on the telephone indicated that it held multiple lines.

He turned and locked the door. Claire's heart pounded in her chest, her face felt flush, and she could feel herself begin to tremble. Standing alone in the vastness of his office, she watched Anthony as he contemplated his next move. His angry expression included the completely black eyes she witnessed in her suite two weeks before. After a protracted silence, he spoke with an even flat tone.

"So you say you *can* follow instructions, we will see." The debate was over. It was the outcome that frightened Claire. A few hours ago he had been another person. Now the man standing before her was the same one who abused her so violently the first two nights of her stay. His grin wasn't playful, it was ruthless. "Let's start with you taking off your clothes."

Doing her best to be obedient, Claire did as she was told and removed her clothes, starting with her shoes and ending with her sweater. Next he told her to lie down on the carpet, face first and keep her eyes down. She did and felt the plush carpet rough against her skin. The vulnerability of the position alarmed her, intensifying her trembling. She couldn't see or hear his movements. Straining to listen she eventually heard his belt as it passed each loop. The first lash hit so unexpectedly that it made her scream out in agony and shock. She moved her hand to her mouth, bit down, and refused to scream anymore.

When she didn't respond he turned her over, stood above her, and removed his tie and slacks. He didn't say a word but watched for her reaction. Perhaps she was in shock. Whatever it was, Claire was unable to respond. She

44

waited, knowing that whatever he chose to do would be bad. His hands forcibly moved her legs while she observed, disengaged as if in another dimension. The scene she saw was brutal and domineering. By the grace of God, she felt everything in a removed yet present fashion.

She watched his actions and heard his demands. She was present, saw his expression, felt his body, smelled his skin, and tasted her shame. Yet she was somehow detached, not there. By the time he finished, her body exhibited various rug burns, and her hair was tangled and matted from the same lush carpet.

Anthony Rawlings callously stood and dressed. He paused for a moment, standing six feet above her, and then silently walked to the attached bathroom. There he combed his hair and replaced the tie he'd removed. Meanwhile, Claire sat in the middle of the room involuntarily shivering, holding her clothes, and silently weeping, unsure what to do.

Returning to the office he looked at her with disdain, his tone flat and cold. "You may go to your suite, clean yourself up, and get ready to demonstrate to me again your ability to follow instructions."

Claire began to gather her clothes and dress when he added "Do not leave your suite until I decide. Your pass to roam is revoked." Her mind was beyond comprehension; thinking outside of the box was more than she could handle. She remembered an agreement with herself for self-preservation, conceding to demands. Yet at this moment in time, Claire didn't know or understand what she was doing, agreeing to, or being forced to do. She was lost and most likely suffering from shock. She only remembered his directives to go back to her suite and clean up.

Leaving his office she turned toward the grand staircase. Beyond the stairs through the magnificent foyer with the high ceiling Claire saw the double doors leading to outside. They were tall and ornate. Without thinking she walked toward them, perhaps she should have run, but no one was around. The house was empty, like a museum or perhaps a tomb.

She could hear her heart pound in her ears as she approached the handle wondering if it would open. She wouldn't learn. Suddenly, she heard the sound of shoes on the marble floor of the corridor. The footsteps didn't sound rushed, but determined, and were getting closer. Claire quickly turned and began the ascent to the second floor. She didn't look back down. She didn't want to see the person that produced the footsteps, especially if that person would meet her gaze with a black-eyed stare. Instead, she walked toward her suite.

By the time she closed the door her internal monologue was in full gear. *He actually hit me with his belt! My god! The man is mad. I have to find a way out of here!*

At that moment, she didn't search for an escape. Instead, she showered, redid her hair, her makeup, and put on another outfit. While she *cleaned herself up* she contemplated fleeing. Questions arose. Where would she go? How would she get there? How far to civilization? And what were her chances of success? And most importantly, if she failed, what would he do?

Her lunch arrived. Even though she missed breakfast, she barely ate. She sat quietly on the sofa, read a book, stared into space, and waited for instructions. A feeling of helplessness settled into her chest like nothing she'd ever known.

About four thirty, the beep sounded, the door opened, and she dutifully obeyed. His demeanor, less malicious than before, seemed merely callous. The forbearance of the early morning and the tour were gone. Anthony had a goal for his actions. Claire needed to understand who was in control. She had done this to herself, he told her. She needed to do what she was told. But did she? No. He made her say, "No, I didn't do what I was told." And behaviors have consequences. Could she remember that? "Yes, I understand behaviors have consequences."

That evening they didn't dress appropriately for dinner in Claire's suite. Anthony decided he wanted her to model some of the lingerie. Dinner was eaten while wearing a flowing black silk negligee.

Every time she thought he was done and would leave, he regrouped. Maybe a drink of water or check the messages on his iPhone, then he resumed. The violence ended, but the domination continued. Claire wanted to scream. But she didn't. The more she obeyed, the less ruthless his instructions. After midnight, Anthony left her suite. He didn't say whether her door would be unlocked in the morning, and she couldn't remember if she heard the familiar beep. She wanted to check, but her body barely moved. Instead, she closed her eyes and went to sleep.

Human beings, by changing the inner attitudes of their minds,
can change the outer aspects of their live.
—William James

Chapter 6

Her eyes didn't open until she heard the door and her breakfast arrive. It usually came after she awoke. Looking at the clock, she saw that it was 10:30, the latest she'd slept since her initial arrival. The young lady with the food apologized. "I'm sorry, Ms. Claire. I know you were still asleep, but Mr. Rawlings would like you dressed and in his office by noon. Catherine said you need to eat." She handed Claire her robe as she got out of the bed.

"Is Mr. Rawlings working from home again today?" Claire's head pounded and body ached. This was way too late for coffee, and perhaps the activities of yesterday were affecting her.

"Miss, today is Sunday. Mr. Rawlings is usually home on Sundays." The young lady left the suite. Claire made a mental note: *Watch out for Sundays.*

Timidly, Claire approached the mirrors in the bathroom. Lowering the soft robe, she saw long red stripes on her back and new bruises. She didn't cry. She steamed with anger. Of course, it was directed toward *him* but also at herself. She wanted this nightmare to end, but she couldn't figure out the solution. Helplessness was not an emotion Claire was accustomed to feeling, and she didn't like it. Her only solution was to remain resolute until an opportunity arose.

At eleven fifty-seven, Claire knocked on Anthony's office door. The door opened, and he looked up from his desk. "Good afternoon, Claire."

Smiling respectfully, she said, "Good *morning*, Anthony. I believe it is still morning." She looked at his eyes and wondered who he would be today. Claire walked into his office and stood before his desk, the same place that twenty-four hours earlier had been the terrifying scene of his rage and domination.

She stood with her back straight, chin high, and smile plastered on her lips. The blouse she chose and her makeup covered the visible signs of the prior day's happenings. Anthony sat quietly and studied her. The silence made her uncomfortable. She prayed he couldn't hear her heart beating too fast or notice her wet palms. Long ago, she learned that awkward silences were an interview technique. She wouldn't be the one to break the silence.

Finally, "I believe you are correct, for another two minutes." Anthony's eyes seemed lighter. Claire breathed easier and smiled. She was on time. "Lunch will arrive here in a few minutes. I thought we would discuss some of the glitches that our business deal has encountered." He stood and moved toward Claire.

She kept her ground, neck straight, and watched as he circled the grand desk. He stopped only inches away. She could smell his fragrant cologne and needed to tilt her neck upward to see his face. He didn't speak but indicated with a gesture that they move to the conference table where he pulled out a chair for her to sit; she did. He sat at the head of the table with Claire to his right. The room was silent as Claire thought to herself how his *gentlemanly* behaviors were such a farce.

"Glitches? I'm not sure what you are referring to."

Before responding, he sat back and contemplated Claire Nichols. Her eyes contained an intense fire, and she possessed more daring than half of the presidents of his many companies. After what he put her through, he couldn't help but be astounded.

"I wasn't sure you would come here today."

"I wasn't aware I had a choice. I believe my job duties include doing as I am told."

"That is correct." He chose his words carefully. "Perhaps you can be trained."

Claire's mouth twitched, but she stayed steady. Getting upset would only accomplish losing control and giving it to him. He may take it, but by god, she wasn't giving it. "I am trying my best. Now glitches?"

A knock came as the door opened and their lunch arrived. They sat in silence as the young lady placed their food in front of them and asked Mr. Rawlings if they needed anything else. He informed her they were currently fine. She retreated from the office and closed the door behind her.

"Glitches, yes. I spent $215,000 for a business deal. I make deals that will be lucrative to me. I expected a better return for my money than I have experienced in the last three weeks."

If this was supposed to shock Claire, it didn't. She casually picked up her fork, ate a piece of broccoli, and responded, "I would believe that yesterday you successfully increased your return." And stabbing another piece of broccoli, she added, "Besides, wasn't it you that decided your business holding would be locked away for almost two weeks?" She ate more broccoli. Part of her feared retaliation, but the other part believed he appreciated the bravado.

"That is true. I'm considering the possibility that it was worth it, after what I'm currently witnessing." He watched her expression as he spoke. "And we have no deadline for completion of our contractual agreement."

Claire didn't know if she should be happy that he seemed impressed, and she did think an estimated timeline would be nice, but she didn't mention that either. Instead, she said, "Then apparently, the glitches have been resolved."

Claire felt she appeared respectful enough to avoid confrontation but impertinent enough to demonstrate resilience. She saw the light brown gleam around his irises, somehow knowing he wouldn't explode. She would learn to read him. They continued to eat.

Claire let Anthony do most of the talking. He discussed more of the *house rules*. She could roam the house. However, in anticipation of more glitches, she was not permitted to go outside or consider leaving the property. His office and the corridor of his suite were off-limits. Her schedule would be hers for most of the day, unless told otherwise by him or Catherine. He didn't work from home that often, but when he did she would be required to be nearby and available at all times. On days he went to the office his only requirement would be that Claire be back in her suite by 5:00 p.m. to receive evening instructions. He was a very busy man and wouldn't be home every evening to dine with her. However, on the nights he intended to be home she would receive instructions for time of dinner, apparel, and other plans he may have. If he were in town, she would receive instructions as to his intentions regarding visiting her suite and the estimated time of his arrival. She verbally responded to all of his rules.

The young lady with the food came back to clear the dishes and brought a carafe of coffee with two cups. Claire's headache was improving with food but more coffee would be helpful. Anthony told her that he and Ms. Claire would be having coffee on the sunporch. She thanked him and left with the coffee. Claire didn't remember a sunporch from the tour.

She walked beside Anthony as they left the office. Located in the rear of the main section, through the archways behind the grand stairs, and past the sitting room, they stepped down into a room made completely of glass. Claire felt faint as her eyes adjusted to the sunshine and she inhaled the fresh spring air. The room was decorated with brightly cushioned rattan furniture as well as tropical plants. Anthony sat on a loveseat and Claire on a chair. The sides of the room opened to allow a cool fresh breeze. Her bogus composure disappeared as the sensation of the fresh spring air blew her hair and she listened to the faint sounds of nature.

When she was a child, her dad, a policeman in Indianapolis, knew how much Claire loved the outdoors. Each spring he would take her to one of the many state parks. They would spend the weekend together hiking, fishing, talking, and wandering. Her grandfather, his father, had been FBI. It was ingrained in them to be cautious. On those weekends he let Claire believe she had control over their plans and the direction of their adventures. Remembering their activities she smiled, knowing he did most of the steering and all of the protecting. The aroma of the fresh spring air brought the memories of those adventures soaring back to Claire's consciousness.

49

Just off to the side of the sunporch she saw a large pool. The water was covered with a large tarp, furniture was absent from the deck, and fountains were nonoperational. Though not in season, it definitely had potential for a wonderful place to spend her *Claire time* once the weather warmed.

As they sat and sipped warm coffee with a cool breeze, Anthony informed Claire that he would be leaving for three days on a business trip. His businesses were all over and traveling was an important part of his work. He would leave later in the afternoon as his meetings were scheduled to begin very early in the morning. He planned to be home Wednesday evening. She would be informed if his plans changed. "Anthony, what do you do?"

"Do you truly not know who I am?"

It frightened her to bruise his ego but erring on honesty was always best. "I'm sorry if I should, but I don't. I thought at first that your name sounded familiar, Anthony Rawlings, but I have tried for over two weeks, and I admit I don't know."

He leaned back on the loveseat and offered a brief autobiographical synopsis. He called himself a businessman who had built his fortune from nothing. The beginning of and bulk of his success came with the Internet; he and a friend created one of the first Internet search engines. He later bought out his friend's part of the company, diversified his holdings, and has done pretty well.

Claire chuckled. "You made your fortune, because *this*," looking around the expanse of his mansion, "is more than doing pretty well, with the Internet? And the only technology in your home is in your office?"

"Perhaps I want my home to be an oasis from my business life."

Claire pondered that for a moment. "I understand. My grandfather and my father were both in law enforcement. They saw things that people should never see. Sometimes my grandfather would be gone for months at a time doing undercover work. Actually, I remember a story from when I was young where he was gone for around two years. My father was home each night. But anyways, my dad didn't want home to be anything like work. I couldn't even watch *COPS* on TV. I think it was like you were saying, an oasis."

Anthony went on to ask about Claire's family. She said her grandparents passed away before she graduated high school. Her parents were tragically killed in a car accident during her junior year of college. She did have a sister and brother-in-law in New York State. Fleetingly she wondered when she would talk to Emily again. With the breeze and the sound of birds, Claire casually went on talking. She asked Anthony about his family. As soon as her question left her lips she saw his eyes darken. She calmly added, "But if you don't want to say anything, I don't need to know."

Perhaps it was her quick observation or the realization that she could read him, but his eyes lightened. "My parents are also gone. It was an accident when I was twenty-four. I have no siblings, and my grandparents are also gone." The serenity returned as they both offered each other sincere condolences at their loss. Claire's coffee was gone and she didn't know what else to say or discuss. She could see Anthony watching her as she stared out to the pool area. Beyond the pool was the backyard. The corner of it could be seen from her room but not the pool or porch. Past the yard were trees. From the second story she knew they went on forever, but from this vantage they created a gray veil around the yard. Soon little starts of green would transform the bleak veil into a colorful curtain. Claire really enjoyed spring.

Anthony excused himself saying he needed to prepare for his trip. She was welcome to stay on the porch or go elsewhere in the house. He would look for her before he left. He smiled what appeared to be a real smile. "I'm pleased that the glitches have been resolved. I have plans for our agreement."

The smile seemed right, the unspoken portion of his statement made Claire shiver. After he left, she looked down at her arm and saw the goose bumps that rubbed her sleeves. She told herself they were caused by the breeze.

Claire returned to her suite recognizing that with the ability to roam she didn't feel the need. Besides, she was tired. Sleeping late can do that to a person. However, her gut told her yesterday's glitches were more likely the cause of her fatigue. Her body ached. She contemplated a nice long bath in her beautiful garden tub as she entered her room.

On the bed, laid out so she could see each one, were multiple bathing suits: one-piece suits like she wore in high school swim class and bikinis that would be perfect for the sun. She liked the styles but wondered if they would fit. Of course, they would, hadn't everything else? She had to wonder how a promise made Saturday morning could be so quickly fulfilled on a Sunday, seemingly far away from anywhere.

He told her that she would have bathing suits *tomorrow*. Apparently, he was a man of his word. That earned him *one* on the positive column. The negative column had more tallies than Claire could count.

Peeking out from under the white cover up was a wrapped gift. It was a small box wrapped in white paper with a gold foil ribbon. Claire usually liked gifts but she didn't feel good about this one. What did it mean? Was it because of how he had been or because of how he would be? She picked it up and decided she didn't want to know. She sat the gift on the corner of the bed and wearily entered the bathroom to soak in the tub.

After the bath she chose the same soft robe she wore before. It felt warm. With some slippers, she would be comfortable until she retired. She combed out her wet hair and didn't put on makeup. It was only five thirty but she was exhausted.

He said he would look for her before he left. She expected to find him in her suite. If she opened the door and he wasn't there, would she be disappointed? Only because she wanted him to leave, so seeing him one more time would be a means to that end. Upon opening the door, she wasn't disappointed, and his presence didn't startle her. He was seated at the table with the gift in his hand. "You haven't opened your present."

"I knew it was from you and thought you might want to see me open it," she lied.

He set the gift on the table and walked toward her. Although his height dominated her small frame, she held her ground and looked up at him as their bodies touched. He pulled her close and held her there with his strong solid arms. Her emerald eyes appeared weary as he examined her face. His soft brown eyes gleamed while his musky fragrance overwhelmed her senses. She wasn't afraid, only tired. She silently prayed, *Dear God, if he wants me to do something, I hope it is over soon.*

In one swift yet gentle motion he lifted her and carried her to the bed. Although he had a trip to take, he didn't seem rushed. Instead, he laid her on the bed and leisurely untied her robe. Claire remained still as he stood and looked at her body, completely nude, pink from the warm bath, and smelling of bath beads. Neither one spoke. There were no instructions, no insults, and no rules. He began to lightly touch her, tracing his fingers over her breasts, down her stomach, and over her hip bones. She could sense his burning carnal desire.

The heat intensified as he gently caressed her soft skin with the tips of his fingers and tenderly explored her body with his lips. Beginning at her neck, he nuzzled her collar bone, and then the flesh of her breasts. When he tenderly enticed her nipples with his tongue, she forgot the abrasive bristle of his five o'clock shadow. She didn't want to respond. She wanted to be unfazed by his touch. She kept telling herself, *This is the man that hurt me.* Her mind heard but her body stirred down deep, and uncontrollably her nipples hardened as her back arched, pushing her breasts toward his lips.

The open drapes allowed the room to fill with natural light. As his mouth tantalized her skin she sat forward allowing him to gently remove her robe. Anthony gasped.

Claire froze, unsure why he made such a sound, and turned to see his face. His features were softer and more concerned than she'd witnessed. He didn't say a word but tenderly caressed her neck and back with his mouth. His actions were sensual, careful, and tender.

Slowly, he joined her on the bed, and only after ensuring that she was moist and ready did he enter her body. He'd been there before, but this was different. The only sounds from his mouth were incomprehensible noises that made their meaning clear. Soon she responded with the same language. This time it wasn't just him that experienced fulfillment, Claire did too.

After they were both satisfied, she rested on the satin sheets and watched as he walked to the table completely nude and moist with perspiration. His muscles defined from exertion, he picked up the gift. She lifted her head from the pillow, her long damp brown hair cascaded in waves around her face. Her lips smiled weakly as he handed it to her. He watched as she removed the wrapping from the black velvet box that held a Swarovski wristwatch. She smiled.

"It is meant as a way to avoid *glitches* in the future," he said softly.

"Thank you. I would really like to avoid those."

She handed him the box and lowered her head to the pillow. Completely drained of energy, she closed her eyes and felt the soft warmth as Anthony lifted the covers over her body. She could still smell his musky scent as she drifted into unconsciousness. She didn't wake until Monday morning.

In that time between sleep and wakefulness, Claire wondered if yesterday evening had been real. How could it be real if Saturday was too?

Could Anthony Rawlings really be two such different men? As the fog began to clear she realized that whoever he was he was gone for the next two and a half days. This comprehension gave her a renewed vitality. She didn't know what she would do with her sixty-five hours of *freedom* but she knew she would find something.

Her breakfast sat on the table when she exited the bathroom and the drapes were opened. The sky radiated a very light shade of blue and there seemed to be clouds forming in the distance. It was spring in Iowa. The weather could be unpredictable. After breakfast she decided to try the indoor pool. She swam laps for forty minutes and rested in the hot tub. It felt wonderful to push her muscles beyond their limit. Other than her duties, she'd done nothing to exercise in almost three weeks. Surprisingly the lack of physical activity didn't seem to cause weight gain. She didn't have a scale, but she could tell in the mirror and with her new clothes. If anything she lost weight. She lay back and closed her eyes amid the hum and bubbling of the tub and realized it was her diet. In three weeks she hadn't had any alcohol, not even a glass of wine. She also hadn't consumed one ounce of dessert, not a cookie, brownie, or even a piece of dark chocolate. Now that the realization hit her, she craved chocolate.

The sixty-five hours passed without event. She thoroughly investigated the house. It was luxurious, vast, and held many amenities. However, the more she explored the more she realized it was still a prison. She couldn't leave. She couldn't go outside. It may be bigger and grander than her suite, but it still had walls.

She made an effort to get to know the names of the staff. The young lady who brings food is Cindy. The young man who speaks little English is Carlos. Anthony's driver is Eric. There were others that clean, cook, do laundry, and tend the grounds but Claire rarely saw them, so she didn't have the chance to learn their names. Yet, whenever she passed one or encountered them in a hallway, they would nod and acknowledge her, "Ms. Claire."

On Wednesday, before Anthony was scheduled to return, Claire watched from the sunporch as nimbostratus clouds formed in the west. This would have thrilled her a month earlier. Watching storms form, either in person or on the radar screen, had filled her with excitement. As the dark clouds approached, she began to hear the distant rumbling of thunder. She could feel the distinct drop in pressure. Claire knew that Iowa, like Indiana, had its share of tornadoes. Despite the drop in pressure, her instincts told her this was going to be just a good old-fashioned spring thunderstorm, the kind that is loud and boisterous but usually blows over with little damage. It mesmerized her, she watched and listened. Didn't it seem that she'd been too busy to just wait and listen to the weather? Now she had the time and she just stood.

Catherine finally broke the spell, "Ms. Claire, please come in. We need to shut the windows. You will get wet."

Claire came in and went to her suite. The howling of the wind electrified her emotions. She knew he would return today. She hated him with every bit of her being. She detested his patronizing demeanor, his callous attitude, and above all his abusive mentality. And she hated being alone. She liked

Catherine very much, but she treated Claire like a guest or a superior. Claire longed for someone to talk to, to laugh with, and to just be near. With all her heart and soul, she didn't want that person to be Anthony Rawlings. So when five o'clock arrived and Claire waited for word of his arrival, she should have been pleased with Catherine's report, "Mr. Rawlings is delayed due to the storm fronts. The pilot will not fly west of Chicago due to high cloud banks. He will be home tomorrow evening and plans to dine with you at that time. You will know more tomorrow."

Claire thanked Catherine for the information, ate her dinner, read a little, and went to bed.

After Anthony returned, the schedule he discussed went into full gear. She was in her suite at five each evening to learn his plans. Things were very busy with his work and many nights he didn't visit at all. Sometimes they ate in her suite and sometimes in the dining room. Sometimes he called upon her for her duties, other times he said he had work to do. The days turned to weeks and the weeks to another month.

The positive aspect had to be that there'd been no more *glitches*. That didn't mean that Claire experienced anything like the afternoon in her suite. On the contrary, each task to fulfill her contractual agreement was about him. Nonetheless, she felt content to avoid the explosive unpredictable glitches.

At some point during the beginning of May after Anthony was finished with Claire, he chose to stay in her bed. She realized this after she fell asleep and woke in the middle of the night to the sound of his breathing, steady and rhythmic. The consciousness of his presence frightened her. Did he have additional plans? Should she be doing something? She was too afraid to wake him and ask. Instead, she quietly slowly moved to the edge of *her side* of the bed and fell back to sleep. When she awoke in the morning, he was gone.

On May 12, a Sunday, Catherine informed Claire that she and Mr. Rawlings would be eating on the back patio. The temperature had steadily increased and the backyard was vibrant with color, intense shades of greens, ruby reds from the red bud trees, and pure white from the dogwood trees. Anthony employed groundskeepers that had been busily planting thousands of annual flowers in the gardens, beautiful clay pots, and flowing hanging baskets. The pool was recently opened with ever-flowing fountains. At night they produced a colorful light show that changed the water from clear to pink to blue to green to red and back to clear.

Claire remembered the day, because as they sat to eat Anthony asked, "Have you been swimming in the outdoor pool yet? It's heated."

After so much time following his rules and being incarcerated inside, her bravado failed; she started to cry. Her reaction obviously surprised him. Through muffled tears Claire replied, "This is the first time I have been outside in two months. I didn't think I was allowed to go outside."

If he had been moved initially at her emotional response, he quickly recovered. "Yes, that is correct. I do know exactly how long it has been since you have been outside." His voice resumed the authoritative tone she despised. "And I am happy to see you still remember who is in control of your access to additional privileges."

Claire nodded her head ever so slightly to indicate yes, she understood. Anthony cleared his throat. She looked into his eyes trying to blink the tears from hers. "Yes, I understand. But, I truly love being outside."

"Surely you are smart enough to figure this out," Anthony teased.

Confused and upset by the loss of her falsely perceived equality, she said, "I'm not sure what you mean."

"Claire, I am an important man. I have hundreds of thousands of people in hundreds of companies who depend upon me for their livelihood. I balance a lot on my plate. Being observant to your wants and whims is not on my list of priorities. If you want to go outside, ask."

The simplicity startled her and the reality nauseated her. She was an adult and she was asking permission to go outside. Her memory seemed foggy, but she couldn't recall doing that since she was maybe ten or eleven. It was one of his tests. Would she surrender to his authority or would she refuse and spend the summer inside? If she surrendered was it really submission or was it her way of controlling the situation? The internal debate continued for a short time.

"Anthony, may I please leave the house and go outside?"

"You may be outside. Do not leave the property without me or my permission." His tone continued, but Claire's only concern was his meaning, "Remember to be available to me whenever I am here. Therefore, no wandering the grounds if I'm present, and you must be in your suite by five each evening for instructions. Can you follow these rules?"

"Oh yes, I can." It may still be a prison, but it had just multiplied in size.

Greed, for lack of a better word is good
Greed in all its forms for life,
for money, for love, for knowledge has marked
the upward surge of mankind.
—Gordon Gekko, *Wallstreet*

Chapter 7

The cloud of smoke levitating near the suspended ceiling created a haze, making the florescent lights appear dim within the small office. Nathaniel clenched his teeth while analyzing the figures. Since taking the company public, the numbers showed profits. The stock continued to grow, and industry reports were favorable. Rawls Corporation was in the black. And considering the current economic climate of the seventies, that was good. The problem was Nathaniel Rawls didn't want good. He wasn't content with black. He wanted more, a lot more. The sound of the furnace blowing warm air created a hypnotizing hum. He leaned back, took a long draw on his cigarette, and rubbed his temples. How could he make the figures in the profit column multiply? Hell, others were doing it. He wanted to too.

Punching the black button on the small box, he bellowed, "Connie, get Samuel in here now."

The crackling voice responded immediately, "Yes, sir, Mr. Rawls."

Samuel entered the small paneled office inhaling the suspended cloud. The sight of his father hunched over the books and spreadsheets meant only one thing: he was in for the "*We can do better*" speech. "Yes, Father, did you want to see me?"

"Have you seen the latest figures?"

"Yes. Sales to major distributors are up 18 percent."

"That is chicken feed. Textiles can't make shit in the United States. We have to revisit the idea of moving operations out of country. In Mexico we can produce the same merchandise for less than a quarter of what it costs here. Hell, the unions here in Jersey are costing us a fortune."

Samuel learned long ago to pacify his father, let him blow off some steam and things would settle. "We have looked into that. The problem is that we would lay off hundreds of workers who have been loyal through the years. Besides, as I said, we are in the black."

Nathaniel blew a cloud of smoke toward his son. "I've decided to hire Jared Clawson as CFO, chief financial officer. The man has some innovative ideas."

"Didn't he just leave New England Energy amid allegations of illegal activities?"

"Nothing was proven. Besides, I have seen the figures. When Clawson was assisting with finance at NE Energy, their profits were through the roof. Since his departure, they're doing well to keep the grids going." Samuel remained silent. "The man is a damn genius. We've met a few times. He believes Rawls has potential and he has some great ideas."

Samuel knew his opinion didn't matter. If Nathaniel's mind was made up, Jared Clawson was coming on board. The only thing he could do was watch and do his best to stop anything illegal before it began. "The contracts with Huntington House are in their final stages. They have plans for a new clothing line. The potential for revenue is huge. They have distributors all up and down the East Coast."

"Damn chicken feed."

*A strong positive mental attitude will create
more miracles than any wonder drug.*
—Patricia Neal

Chapter 8

Survival for the last two months was facilitated by a technique Claire called *compartmentalization*. She couldn't bear the entirety of her situation, but she could handle a part at a time. The colossal lapse in judgment that brought her to this circumstance; the treatment, punishment, or consequence that *he* felt he had the right or ability to carry out -- the duties he could tell her to do, and the fact that she obeyed—were all too much. She had to separate them and deal with them in small manageable bits. Some days that was possible. Other days it was more difficult.

Her morning workouts now included swimming and weight training. Exercise supposedly produced endorphins and endorphins helped elevate mood. That seemed like a good idea.

Before she was allowed outside, Claire spent many afternoons with a blanket and a good movie. The lower level of the house contained a movie theater. With Anthony's busy schedule, she wondered if he ever used it. It held hundreds, if not thousands, of digital movies. Claire loved the classics, especially musicals. She could lose an entire afternoon curled up in a large soft recliner watching happy people sing and dance. It was a magnificent escape from reality.

It was near the end of May, and Claire had taken advantage of her outdoor liberty every chance she could by lounging at the pool, walking in the gardens, and reading books in the yard. Now she wanted to explore. The woods held the possibility of both plant and animal life. It had been a few years since she studied Earth science, but she believed it would come back. Anthony said his house had been on this land for fourteen or fifteen years. Claire believed no one had been back in the woods for years. The potential for real undisturbed wildlife excited her. Not that there would be bears or lions, but deer, rabbits, birds, and rodents. In her current situation, self-preservation encouraged her to find happiness wherever possible.

Three days earlier she asked Anthony for hiking boots. Now she was tying them and preparing for her new adventure. Inhaling the sweet smells of nature, Claire contemplated her path as Catherine came rushing toward her. "Ms. Claire, I am so glad I didn't miss you."

Claire's tranquility evaporated into the afternoon haze. "No, it looks like you caught me. And I promise to be back before five."

"Ms. Claire, I just received a call from Mr. Rawlings. He has an engagement tonight in Davenport. It is a fund-raiser at the Adler Theater for the Quad City Symphony."

"So he won't be back tonight?" she said, thinking that perhaps she could stay out in the woods later than five.

"No, miss, he will be back."

"What?"

"He will be here at six to pick you up. You are to accompany him to the symphony."

Claire stared at Catherine in disbelief. She'd just been permitted outdoors, and now she was going to Davenport to the symphony. Saying "*No, thank you*" didn't seem to be an option. Her mind swirled. "Catherine, I've never been to a symphony before. Can you please help me?" Claire prayed that this wasn't another test about appropriate dress.

"Of course -- I will, miss. Now let's go up to your room, and we will get started."

They did. Catherine went directly into the closet and came out with a long black evening gown. It was simple, yet amazingly beautiful. Claire showered again. Catherine helped with her makeup and hair. They straightened, pinned, and curled her long chestnut locks until they were piled on her head with cascading curls dangling down her neck. There were even exquisite sparkling earrings for Claire to wear. Securing them in her pierced ears, she thought how long it had been since she'd worn jewelry and how nice they looked with her hair up.

Another accessory that surprised Claire was the handbag. She hadn't gone anywhere or needed a handbag, but tonight Catherine had one for her. Anthony would be home and ready at six. Apparently, the symphony began at eight, with cocktails at seven. Catherine explained that it took one hour to drive to Davenport, and Eric would chauffeur them in the limousine.

Before she dressed, still wearing her robe with her hair done and makeup perfect, Claire sat on the edge of the large marble tub and asked Catherine for advice. What did Mr. Rawlings expect of her this evening? How should she act? If he had rules for being out, he hadn't told her; and if Catherine knew, Claire would truly appreciate being informed.

Catherine's eyes shone with care and concern. She wanted to help Claire. She would do anything to make this evening a success for both Claire and Mr. Rawlings. Catherine sat next to Claire and gently took her hands in her own. "Ms. Claire, you are to look beautiful, and you do." Her smile reassured Claire who nodded as Catherine spoke. "Mr. Rawlings is a very influential businessman. He is a fervent believer in appearance. If things look right on the surface the underside is rarely questioned. However, things may be great in reality, but if one perceives them to be amiss, it is difficult to change that

59

perception. Therefore, Ms. Claire, you are expected to be the perfect companion: beautiful, polite, contented, and appreciative."

Claire thought to herself, *Well, perfect . . . okay, no pressure.*

Catherine continued, "A man of Mr. Rawlings's standing is constantly observed by others. Some watch to imitate, others to mar. That is why he requires his home to be a place of quietude. He has to do so much for so many that he needs a place to repose and refuel. That is where you have been so good for him." Claire looked into Catherine's eyes; she was sincere. Claire believed Catherine had Mr. Rawlings's best interests at heart. However, she was sure Catherine didn't understand the ways he expected to be *helped.* "But, above all, Mr. Rawlings requires confidentiality on the part of anyone who works for him or is near to him." Claire pondered that thought. "Ms. Claire, you have had the rare opportunity to get to know Mr. Rawlings in a way most do not. The information you hold must not be shared with anyone. He has allowed you to see a more intimate side of himself. The Mr. Rawlings the world knows is much more guarded. He has placed a trust in you. You should know he does not fully trust many people. Do not ever discuss Mr. Rawlings or your relationship with anyone." Catherine smiled and squeezed Claire's hands. "I know you will be wonderful, Ms. Claire. Mr. Rawlings will be proud to have you on his arm."

For a moment, Claire sat silently contemplating Catherine's words. *Rare opportunity? A trust? Intimate side of himself?* She hadn't asked for any of this. With all honesty, she considered the possibility of bolting from the symphony. Did Catherine expect her to feel honored? She mostly felt . . . well, conflicted.

Catherine insisted that Claire eat a light dinner before dressing. The beaded silk gown with the halter bodice fit like it was custom made for Claire. With the Ralph Lauren black high-heeled shoes the dress' length was perfect. The beading made the material heavier than Claire had anticipated. Watching herself in the mirror, Claire turned ever so slightly and the skirt pitched that direction. It was the most stunning dress Claire had ever seen, much less worn. Next Catherine assisted Claire with a lightweight black silk wrap and matching handbag. Inside the handbag she placed lipstick and powder. Catherine reminded her, there will be people everywhere, remember *appearances* are everything.

"Ms. Claire, you are striking!" Catherine's eyes shone in approval. Claire looked at herself again in the mirror. She felt like she was viewing someone else. Tentatively smiling at that person in the mirror, Claire agreed she looked beautiful.

At five fifty they left the suite for the foyer. Instead of the usual route, Catherine took Claire the longer way, forcing them to descend the grand stairs. When they reached the top of the stairs Catherine coughed ever so slightly. She looked up at Claire, taller than her in her heels, and gave her one more reassuring smile. Catherine gestured for Claire to descend the staircase first.

Waiting by the front door, iPhone in hand texting, stood Anthony. He emitted confidence and animal magnetism. His tuxedo, obviously tailored specifically for him, looked exquisite as it accented his broad shoulders. There wasn't a piece of his dark hair out of place as it was gelled and combed to perfection. His face smooth like he'd recently shaven. Claire couldn't help but think that he looked incredibly handsome. Following the sound of Catherine's cough he glanced to the top of the stairs. Suddenly, the business that was demanding his attention appeared to be forgotten. He watched as Claire gracefully descended the flight of steps. As his eyes beheld her every move she wondered if she should smile. She wasn't sure how he would react. His expression emanated favor. Claire wanted his approval. She told herself she didn't need it. She was happy with the way she looked, but she knew she wanted it.

Once at the bottom of the stairs she proceeded to Anthony's side. He didn't speak at first, then not to Claire but to Catherine, "My dear Catherine, you have outdone yourself. You are an artist." He bowed to her at the waist.

"Mr. Rawlings, an artist is only as good as her canvas. You are accompanying a beautiful canvas."

"Or should we say, she is accompanying me." Now to Claire, "We must go, Eric is waiting."

If Claire were concerned about conversation topics on the drive to Davenport, she needn't have been. After assisting Claire into the back of the limousine Anthony once again became engrossed in his iPhone and multitasked with his iPad. On days he worked from home, Claire was often expected to stay in his office in case her services were required. She overheard many business calls, web conferences, and webinars. Therefore, listening to him discuss some dealings on the phone on the way to the symphony seemed strangely comfortable.

Claire wanted to thank him, tell him how excited she was to leave the house and see something, anything. However, his work preoccupied him throughout the ride. She was busy too, watching out the tinted window, seeing different views and different things. Even the sensation of being in a car exhilarated her. She had never ridden in a limousine. The interior was exquisite and she could smell the soft leather seats that formed a horseshoe.

They approached Davenport as the sky filled with a mixture of pink and purple; it reminded her of vibrant paints swirled together. Soon the sky began to darken and the lights of the city illuminated the horizon. It was the most splendid combination of sky and skyline she'd ever seen.

Minutes before their arrival, Anthony ceased his business and turned to Claire. "Has Catherine prepared your behavior for the evening as well as she has your appearance?"

Claire thought to herself, *Somewhere in that statement is a compliment. I'm going to take it.* "She has given me her advice, but I would feel better if I heard yours."

"Very well, when we arrive there will probably be photographers. Do not act surprised or shocked by the attention. Just flash a beautiful smile and radiate confidence. Stay next to me at all times. There will be reporters who will try to learn your identity. I have a publicist who will know the time to release any necessary information. That is not you. I will do most of the talking. However, common sense will need to be with you. If spoken to, you will respond, but do not share information that is privileged. Do you understand?"

"I do."

"I have been asked to attend this event because of a donation I made to the Quad City Symphony and the Support the Arts Foundation. Have you ever been to a symphony before?" Claire said that she had not. Anthony continued as the limousine snaked and crawled along narrow streets. Traffic was stop and go. Claire thought this meant they were getting closer. "The symphony is a delightful evening. I believe you will enjoy the music. This conductor is incredibly talented."

"Thank you, Anthony, for allowing me to join you this evening."

"I admit you have learned your lessons well. Now it is time to see if you can continue to follow the rules outside the boundaries of my estate."

"I will do my best."

Anthony gently took Claire's chin and turned it toward him, "You will succeed. Failure in a public setting is not an option." Their eyes locked on each other.

"Yes, Anthony. I will continue to follow your rules." The car slowed and stopped.

Anthony whispered, "Wait for Eric, he will open the door and assist you in getting out. I will be right behind you and we will enter the theater together."

Catherine said there would be people looking at them and Anthony warned about photographers, but Claire hadn't expected the *Emmy red carpet* treatment. There were cameras everywhere and people shouting questions. At WKPZ there was a meteorologist, Jennifer, about ten years Claire's senior. She took Claire under her wing and taught her all about working for a news station. Jennifer was preparing Claire for the cameras, prior to the buyout. The stage advice Jennifer gave her about appearance and demeanor proved helpful. She told Claire, "When those cameras turn on and your image transcends people's living rooms, they don't care if your dog just died, your boyfriend cheated, or you won the lottery. They care about the weather. So find a mask, keep it polished, and when that red light turns on, wear it proudly." It worked for Jennifer. She retained her position after the buyout.

Eric opened the door. Claire gently swung her legs outside the car and put on her mask. It was the mask of the beautiful face she'd seen smiling back at her in the bathroom mirror earlier that evening. Her movements flowed gracefully and her smile never waned. She diligently followed everyone's advice.

Anthony exited the car, nodded with a handsome smile to the crowd, and gently placed his hand in the small of Claire's back. Her nervousness changed to exhilaration as they advanced through the crowd and into the theater. Waiting inside the doors was a man who enthusiastically greeted Mr. Rawlings and escorted them upstairs to a private room. Once there, the reporters were gone, but the people remaining were equally anxious to speak with Anthony Rawlings.

As they mingled, Anthony took two crystal flutes of champagne and handed one to Claire. His voice sounded different, chatty, as he greeted and was greeted by people. He graciously introduced his companion, Claire Nichols, to the individuals and couples they encountered. Claire smiled politely, shook hands, and made small talk. Claire watched the man she'd come to know; he seemed so different. Many people wanted to talk to him and he knew all their names. His social skills captivated her.

After the lights flashed, he gently touched her elbow and led her to their seats. They stepped through the black curtain, and Claire could see the entire theater. Anthony had directed her to a private box above and to the right of the stage. They sat and she beheld the magnificent view, ornate walls, crowds of nicely dressed people, and beautiful velvet curtain. Too quickly, the auditorium darkened and the spotlight hit the stage.

A woman with a German accent began to speak. "Before we begin tonight's performance, I would like to thank everyone for their attendance. I would like to ask you, the audience, to join us at the Quad City Symphony in thanking the one man who made this evening's performance, as well as future performances, possible, Mr. Anthony Rawlings."

Suddenly, the spotlight shone directly into their box. The crowd erupted in applause and a standing ovation. Claire watched as Anthony stood and acknowledged the gratitude with a dashing smile and a wave. He sat back down, and with the light still on them, leaned over and took Claire's hand. She smiled at him; his eyes were so light. The spotlight turned off and the symphony began.

They hardly spoke during the entire performance other than to comment on a musical piece. When not occupied with applauding, Anthony's hand continued to gently hold Claire's. The entire concert ended too soon. The lights came up and they stood to go. Whispering in his ear Claire thanked him again. It was more than she could have imagined. He smiled, gently placed his hand in the small of her back, and led her through the crowd to the foyer. Once outside, Eric opened the door of the waiting car and Anthony assisted Claire as she entered the limousine.

The stark contrast in volume left Claire's ears ringing as the limousine pulled away from the curb. Her mind swirled with thoughts, the evening was wonderful—music, champagne, people, theater, everything. They were riding for a few minutes when she realized Anthony hadn't spoken since they entered the limousine. Her heart rate increased as she contemplated the possibility he was upset. She told herself he couldn't be. She did everything everyone told her to do. She kept up appearances and let him do most of the talking. She felt his eyes upon her, but was afraid to turn and face them. The ringing in her ears turned to silence - completely devoid of sound - silence. She adjusted her new mask and turned. "That was a magnificent evening, thank you again."

"Do you really think so?" She wondered if he was asking about the symphony or her.

"I do. The music was performed beautifully and you were right about the conductor." Her pulse quickened, unable to take the suspense any longer, she asked, "Did I do all right?"

"What do you think?"

She contemplated her answer and all he told her. "I think I did well. I listened to Catherine and to you and did well." She hoped her voice didn't expose her insecurity.

Anthony didn't respond but reached into his briefcase. Claire assumed the conversation was now over, and he planned to resume work. She decided if the conversation was over and he didn't say she failed, she must have succeeded. She exhaled. Suddenly, he turned to her and extended a square black velvet box. "I believe you did well." She liked the tone of his voice, it sounded like the man at the theater.

"I told you every action has a consequence. That can be negative, as we've seen, or positive. I believe you earned a positive consequence."

"Anthony, I don't need a gift. I wanted to make you proud. If I did that, then I am happy and that's enough."

"It is a gift, or at least I believe it was. However, it is not new." Anthony still held the box before Claire. With the running lights illuminating the cabin she could see his smile: genuine, not cruel or sadistic. "Is it always going to be this difficult to get you to open gifts?"

She took the box. "You have my curiosity peaked. What are you giving me that is old?"

She opened the velvet hinged box. The lump in her throat made her choke, unable to speak. The dainty white gold chain with a pearl on a white gold cross hung on the satin. The surprise overwhelmed her. She only saw the necklace for a millisecond before her eyes filled with tears. She looked at Anthony again, tears trickling down her cheeks. "How did you? Where did you get this? It was my grandmother's."

"It was in your apartment in Atlanta when it was cleaned out. I thought you might want to have it. Do you?"

Claire listened to his words. Her apartment had been cleaned out. Where were the rest of her things? She needed to compartmentalize. Right now, she concentrated on her grandmother's necklace. "Oh yes, I do!"

He asked if he could help her put it on. She nodded yes, a verbal answer wasn't required. Next, he took the box out of her hand and started to remove the satin board. Claire observed his tenderness as he held the fine chain and delicate clasp. She turned away and he draped the necklace around her neck. Taking the compact out of her purse, she watched as the pearl moved up and down to the beat of her heart.

"Anthony, there isn't a necklace you could have bought that would mean more to me than this." Her tears dried, yet her emerald-green eyes sparkled.

"People who know me well, and they are numbered, call me Tony. You may call me Tony."

"Thank you, Tony. This is the best night of my life. How can I ever thank you?"

Tony turned off the riding lights in the cabin. Home was still over a half hour away and the window between them and Eric was closed. His smile morphed into a devilish grin, "I have a few ideas."

*My formula for living is quite simple. I get up in the morning
and I go to bed at night. In between, I occupy myself as best I can.*
—Cary Grant

Chapter 9

The weather continued to warm. Claire could now sunbathe in her new bikinis. Each time she stepped through the door onto the deck of the pool, she felt like she was entering a resort. She could eat at one of the umbrella tables or read in a lounge chair or swim in the tepid water. The Iowa sunshine resulted in a beautiful, golden tan. Her hair, which was always brown, now shimmered with golden highlights contrasting the normal chestnut shade.

It seemed impossible, but Claire actually felt busy. She would wake, work out, shower, and eat breakfast. Then if Tony were out of the house, the possibilities were numerous. The pool remained a good option. However, Claire preferred that in the afternoon. What she enjoyed beyond anything was exploring the woods. The land around Anthony Rawlings's estate extended for miles in most directions. One evening, she asked if walking in the woods was permitted. Tony explained that she could probably walk hours and not reach the property line. He never ventured into the woods but had flown over in a helicopter to survey the land, determining the best location for the house. This made her feel better about exploring. He didn't want her leaving his property without him or his permission, but she could wander and roam and still follow the rules. The fact that even Tony hadn't been out there made it more appealing.

Claire wanted to learn all about the land. To do this she decided to go different directions each time she ventured through the trees. She discovered areas where the trees were so dense there was no ground vegetation and remained cool even as the temperatures of summer increased. She also found spontaneous clearings usually filled with flowers. The earlier in the morning Claire went into the forest, the more flowers she would see. There were morning glories blue as the sky above. After the sun's warmth caused those to close, the white daisies and yellow mustard flowers would fill the void and

65

create a multicolored canvas. With flowers came insects. Claire watched the bees busily pollinating and the multiple kinds of butterflies fluttering about. She decided to check Tony's library to see if he had a book that would help her classify the different species.

Catherine expected Claire back for lunch each day, so she tried not to venture farther than an hour and a half in any direction. During her past life, she walked for exercise, sometimes at a gym but more often around her neighborhood in Atlanta. Walking on sidewalks and through a nearby park she measured distance by time. One mile took fifteen minutes. Lately her adventures took her along the path less traveled. It wasn't unusual for her to climb over fallen trees or up steep embankments. Due to these obstacles Claire estimated that one mile took closer to twenty minutes. With those calculations she traveled approximately four miles away from the house on each adventure.

One morning, she happened upon a den of foxes. Initially frightened, she watched them from a distance. There were two large and three small foxes. The small ones ventured away from the den, but the larger ones would always be within sight. It reminded Claire of camping with her dad. It filled her with warmth and a reassuring glow of protection.

It seemed like more recently she thought about her childhood and not her pre-contractual adult life. Perhaps it was a compartmentalization thing. Childhood was the past. It couldn't be changed, only remembered.

Her life before March 15 was actually present, or should be present. She *should* be in Atlanta, tending bar at the Red Wing and trying desperately to find another job in meteorology. She *should* be going out with friends and drinking so much her head hurt the next morning. She *should* be talking to her sister on the phone or e-mailing her and learning about her and John.

Currently nearing the end of June, Emily would be out of school for the summer. John was a busy associate in a law firm. Before Claire *disappeared*, Emily mentioned visiting Claire. "You know I'm off work in the summer and John is busy. I could come spend some time with you in Atlanta."

"Gosh, that would be great, but it gets really hot here in the summer. And I have to work, so you would probably be bored." Claire now felt bad that she hadn't been more encouraging. Honestly, she worried that Emily would disapprove of her tending bar or something else. Claire hadn't wanted to listen to her advice. Now she would love to hear her advice or even her voice. Claire sighed and wondered about Emily, did she wonder where Claire had gone? Had she tried to contact her? Soon she realized the wooded scene in front of her was blurry. The tears were spilling over her lids onto her cheeks. Claire decided to avoid those thoughts. Put them away in that compartment labeled *later*. Childhood provided safer thoughts and memories.

Tony explained that his land was virtually pie-shaped. The front of the property was where the drive met the highway, then the house, and then the land fanned out from there. Claire felt as though she was getting a handle on the layout of the property but it was taking time. *Luckily*, she thought *that is the one thing I have plenty of, because there's a lot of land to explore.* Of course, that followed with thoughts of the mysterious timetable. When would her debt be considered paid?

One cool morning Claire sat on her jacket at the edge of a beautiful clearing and watched a magnificent wildlife performance. First she saw deer run across the open field. With each jump their white tails caught the sun like bright white powder puffs. The longer she sat the more deer she saw. They would slowly approach the clearing, run across, and slow again once in the safety of the trees. There was no threat to them at that time, but instinct told them that the trees held security. Claire wondered where her security was. Or perhaps this was a lesson in instinct?

Claire contemplated talking to Catherine about packing a lunch so that she could stay out in the woods longer. Then she decided that might be something to do when Tony was out of town. She didn't want to get lost and not be back to the suite by 5:00 p.m. She hated his rules, but following them made her life more pleasant.

On days Tony stayed home exploring wasn't an option. He required her to stay near in the event her services were needed. She was often told to stay in his office where she would read, sitting on the soft leather sofa until he summoned her. There were days when he never requested her services, yet she wasted the entire day in his office. Claire knew it was more of the continued power play. He controlled her time, her body, and her life.

To continue her busy days, after lunch Claire sunbathed by the pool or read on the sunporch. She also had the library that could captivate her for hours at a time. If it rained she might opt for a movie in the theater. There were so many things to do. The addition of an occasional evening out with Tony was the biggest change to Claire's busy schedule. It started with the symphony. Since that time she accompanied him to a few other events. None as formal as the symphony, and all charity related, different foundations having dinners or cocktail parties or benefits. Each time Tony would tell Catherine that Claire needed to be ready for a specific event. She liked getting out away from the estate but an invitation instead of a mandate would be nice. Apparently, companionship to events had now been added to her job description. Claire believed she did well at each turn and felt confident as long as Tony was near her. He would handle any situation that came her way.

At an event to honor donors of the University of Iowa's Children's Hospital, Claire stood dutifully at Anthony's side while he spoke with a gentleman to whom she'd been introduced. Another man began to speak to her. It started innocently enough, "Hello, Ms. Nichols, I'm not sure if you remember me? We met a few weeks ago at the Quad City Symphony." His volume was low -- to either lure her away from Tony or not be heard by him. Claire believed she remembered him. She tried to remember names as well as Tony, but she could only recall his face. He then introduced himself, "Charles Jackson," and made small talk about the symphony. He started asking her about her place of residence, did she live in the Quad City region? Chicago? What brought her to this area? The entire time Claire stayed steady to Tony. She didn't want to interrupt Tony's conversation, but her instincts told her this wasn't good. She successfully avoided direct answers, but he persisted beyond political correctness. She decided she needed to get Tony involved before this man dragged something out of her she wasn't allowed to divulge. She lightly placed her hand on Tony's arm. At first, he didn't respond, so she squeezed it a little. When he excused himself from his conversation, he turned to Claire. She hated that she interrupted him, but she wore her mask and politely motioned toward the gentleman.

"Anthony, this is Charles Jackson." Anthony turned to Charles and shook his hand. Charles appeared uncomfortable, but not Tony. "Mr. Jackson has been incredibly inquisitive. I thought you might be able to be of assistance to him."

Claire stood back a half a step, still holding Anthony's arm, and watched as he turned to Mr. Jackson, who looked increasingly pale.

Anthony's voice was one Claire recognized immediately. It was not his chatty social voice, "Mr. Jackson, I am very good with names and faces. I remember seeing you at the symphony. I do not believe we were introduced. It is not my practice to converse with members of the press. It is my policy to allow my publicist to discuss such matters. I recommend that you speak to her, not my companion."

Mr. Jackson didn't have difficulty distinguishing the tone or the meaning. He apologized profusely to Anthony and then to Claire and made his way out of the event. Claire felt ill. She honestly didn't know how she would have handled it without his help. Tony placed his hand on top of Claire's as Mr. Jackson walked away.

"Tony, I'm sorry I interrupted your conversation. I just felt uncomfortable."

Leaning down to her ear and squeezing her hand, he whispered, "It is fine. You made the right decision." She exhaled with relief.

Her current *job* passed its three-month anniversary. She still felt trapped and hated that she was there, but she didn't hate every day. She thought of each day as a new possibility, and like everyone else in the world, some days were better than others. She knew the difference with her life was that her barometer was not her. It summed up her dependence on Anthony Rawlings. The tone of her life depended totally and completely upon *his* frame of mind.

He traveled a few days a week every couple of weeks. While she was secluded to her suite, he'd been in Europe, which apparently happened with some regularity. These momentary *freedoms* upset her. Instead of relishing them, she felt lonely. There would be some evenings that he had business obligations and wouldn't dine with her or even come to her suite. Some of his ideas for her job requirements didn't settle well, but she came to prefer that to being alone.

June came and went. Since Claire chose to not watch television, she didn't know that the entire country was enduring a heat wave. She just knew that the outside air was heavy and within minutes could feel the perspiration dripping between her breasts and down her back. If a breeze blew it felt sticky and oppressive, not refreshing. Even being at the pool was uncomfortable unless early or late.

One evening, Catherine told Claire that Mr. Rawlings wouldn't be home until late. Claire didn't like vague terms like *late*. Normally she would wait in her suite to see if he came to her, but the day was scorching and she knew *late* could mean *not at all*. With the sunset, she decided to take a swim.

Walking to the pool, Claire realized she rarely ventured out of her suite at night. The house seemed eerily quiet, like a museum after closing. The staff were mostly retired to their rooms and the lights were low. Her flip-flops echoed as she stepped onto the marble floor at the base of the staircase. After four months, Claire didn't need lights, she knew her way through the arches and into the sitting room. She paused at the windows and looked out to the pool. The water changed from pink to green to yellow to purple to blue to clear and back to pink. The deck lights were off, creating the illusion of a colorful abyss engulfed in complete darkness. She considered turning on the deck lights and decided against it.

Stepping into the summer night, the air sat heavy and still. The contrast from the air conditioning reminded her why she stayed indoors all day. Looking toward heaven she knew she made the right decision about the lights. The velvety sky glistened with a million stars. The water enveloped her body as she walked down the steps, its temperature barely varied from the air and she quickly submerged herself. After swimming a few laps she floated on her back, watching the sky and thinking about constellations. Suddenly, Claire froze.

Deep in thought and enjoying the stars, she realized Tony was standing at the edge of the pool. He'd been speaking, but her ears were submerged and she couldn't hear him. Seeing his silhouette from the lights of the fountain startled her. She lifted her head out of the water to clear her ears and began to tread water.

"Tony, you startled me. Catherine said you wouldn't be home until late." She couldn't see his eyes. She waited for him to respond. He stood in silence for a moment; she thought about talking. While she debated, he walked to a chair hidden in darkness. When he returned she could only see his silhouette but knew he was now nude.

Still not speaking, Tony dove into the pool. He swam up to Claire and wrapped his arms around her. Within seconds, Claire's bathing suit disappeared. His actions were fast and rough. Their mouths united as their tongues wildly searched for one another. He moved from her lips to the nape of her neck and all places in between. The pool depth allowed Tony to touch but not Claire. She wrapped her legs around his torso, allowing him to support her. He continued to nuzzle her neck, lifting her body so her round supple breasts found his lips. His kisses became nips and he gently bit the tips of her hard nipples. Claire groaned with pleasure.

His hurried movements caused his bristled face to scratch her soft skin. However, the pain of his beard was quickly forgotten as the pleasure from his touch filled her consciousness. His mouth tantalized and his hands explored. Claire's back arched as she pressed her breasts toward his mouth and wrapped her fingers in his wet hair. In the silence of the country night her moans echoed as her body convulsed. Though the night was hot, Claire's arms and legs cloaked with goose bumps.

Tony eventually led Claire out of the pool, onto a chaise lounge. He resumed his exploration but not with his hands. They still hadn't spoken. Claire's mind teetered between the cognizant *he doesn't seem upset* and the unconscious *ecstasy*. His actions slowed, became more deliberate and sensual, causing sensations deep inside of her. She held on to his massive shoulders and accepted everything he had to offer.

The carnal heat intensified by the night's humidity instigated perspiration. Claire tasted it as her lips and tongue seduced his neck. The salty sweat mixed with chlorine creating an amazing potion. When he finished they were both moist, more from one another than the pool.

Panting, they lay still, listening to the cicadas and crickets. Finally, with a grin, Tony spoke, "Good evening, Claire." His eyes were soft suede brown. "I wasn't happy when you weren't in your suite." Claire started to speak but stopped as Tony's finger lightly touched her lips. "But your idea of a swim on this hot evening was much better than what I planned."

Claire smiled. They moved back into the water to cool off but found that even in the water they had problems staying cool.

Later that night in Claire's suite, Tony brought up the situation at the University of Iowa Children's Hospital Event. He told her it hadn't been a planned test. However, had it been she would have passed. He believed she could be trusted with more responsibilities and independence. Therefore, on her table was a wallet containing her ID—a driver's license and a new credit card. The card was on his account and was for her use when he wasn't around.

"What do you mean when you are not around?" Her voice didn't hide her fear. Tony smiled at her trepidation.

"You will only leave the grounds without me, with Eric, and my permission. But I will need to travel to Europe for at least a week next month. You have behaved well." He smiled and ran his hand over her bare thigh and buttocks. "Very well. And you have followed instructions much better than I would have given you credit for a few months ago." His hands roamed and Claire's eyes closed as her body responded. Tony's voice was both masterful and playful, "As a matter of fact, I believe right now you would do as I say."

Opening her eyes, she gazed into his, and answered, "I would." Her voice yearned as her body mindlessly obeyed, responding to his touch.

"I think we should continue to test that theory,"he said with a devilish grin. "But first I believe you have earned the ability to do some shopping for yourself."

Claire's first thought was she didn't want to be by herself. What if someone like Mr. Jackson approached? But then again, wasn't that what she'd wanted since she arrived, to be out, away, alone forever? She would need to file these thoughts, compartmentalize, and think about them tomorrow.

Tony was testing his theory. She needed to hear his every word. The directives for this test were proving playful and exciting. Claire knew she could pass.

Life is not what it's supposed to be. It's what it is.
The way you cope with it is what makes the difference.
—Virginia Satir

Chapter 10

Standing at the rail of her balcony, Claire stared at the scene in front of her. The rays of moonlight illuminated the yard and tops of the trees, changing the familiar objects to unfamiliar colors. Under its brilliance, the trees appeared black and the grass silver. The multitude of stars glistened as she listened to the sounds of coyotes in the distance. This noise worried her. She thought about the smaller animals in the woods and hoped for their safety.

Although she hadn't been outside long, the humid air caused her to perspire. She could feel her hair stick to her neck as droplets of sweat rolled down her back. Claire received word Mr. Rawlings wouldn't be home until after ten and she would dine alone. This was the third night in a row. Last night, he hadn't come to her suite at all. The night before, it'd only been for a few minutes to *touch base*. Apparently, things had been extremely busy.

The clock said 11:00 when she retreated to the balcony. She hadn't seen him, or received a message, and wanted to do something—anything. Patience wasn't a virtue she possessed in her old life. Now as she gazed at the countryside, she knew she was losing what little she'd recently been forced to acquire. She was thinking about how even the air smelled warm when the door behind her opened. "Oh, hi, Tony, you startled me."

"I thought perhaps I would need to search for you again. Then I noticed the drapes."

"I didn't know if you were coming tonight."

He indicated for her to come back inside. She complied. And he shut the door. "You didn't get my message?"

"I did. It's just later than normal." Seeing him in the light, she realized he looked tired and thought how he rarely appeared anything but ideal. Things must really be rough with work. She wanted to talk to him about it, but in the past, he didn't, or wouldn't, try to explain things.

"I came to let you know I am flying to New York tomorrow. I have a business deal which apparently will fall apart if I don't get personally involved."

"How long will you be gone?"

"Damn it, Claire, I don't know for sure." He told her to come to him, and she did. He held her so close that she needed to look up to see his eyes. He lowered his face to her hair. With her head against his chest, she heard him sigh. "This has been a pain-in-the-ass deal. It has been in the pipeline for years. The time alone has cost me millions, what with research and analysis. Now it seems like everything is falling through."

Claire didn't know anything about the deal. She did know this was more than he'd disclosed to her at one time. She wanted to help, to make him feel better. She didn't want to do anything because he *owned* her, but because she wanted to. As terrifying as Anthony Rawlings could be when he was strong and controlling, she didn't like seeing him meek and worn down either. "Tony, is there anything I can do?"

He moved her away, to see her face. "Are you asking me? I don't think that has happened before."

She leaned back into his chest. "I want to help you relax before this big meeting." She stood on her toes and kissed his cheek and neck as her hands unfastened his belt and slacks. She pulled his hand and led him to the bed, where he sat. Claire knelt in front of him, his hands held her face, and she moved toward him.

The entire night, Claire was in control. She did what she wanted, what she believed would help him. Her pace was slow and more thorough. Tony tended to move fast, rough, and hard. Claire moved steadily, softly, and completely. He'd told her exactly what he wanted and how he wanted it for over three months. She knew what he liked. The most surprising part to Claire was that he allowed it. He would sometimes grab her and push, deeper and harder. Then he would allow Claire to take over again.

Lying together in Claire's bed, Tony surprised her again. "Thank you." He rolled to face her. "Thank you for giving yourself. You keep me totally amazed."

They were both almost a sleep when Tony announced, "You are coming with me to New York tomorrow. You can use that new credit card again while I have my meetings. And after tonight, I may need more of this, depending on how the meetings go." Claire had a million questions, but stayed silent while Tony continued, "No, I *will* need more of this, no matter how the meetings go." They fell asleep.

By six in the morning, they boarded Tony's private jet. Catherine woke Claire about four-thirty. Since she and Tony fell asleep after midnight, wake-up came very early. Tony was no longer in her suite. She showered as Catherine packed her luggage. There would've been a time when Claire would've been horrified to have someone else pack her belongings for a trip, but today it reassured her. Catherine seemed to know exactly what Claire needed and when she needed it. Allowing Catherine to take care of her needs had become second nature.

Claire's light yellow slacks and a flowing white blouse were laid out. She obediently put them on. Her luggage was packed. She had a new Prada purse containing her wallet, ID, and credit card, as well as cosmetics, tissues, and other needed items. Carlos came to her suite to take her belongings down to the waiting car.

Before they left Claire's suite Catherine informed her she would be staying with Mr. Rawlings at his Manhattan apartment. And although she may be tired this morning, do not let it show, she must maintain appearances. Mr. Rawlings would be off to his work as soon as they arrived in the city, she would then be able to rest at the apartment. Claire nodded her understanding.

While Eric drove them to the local private airport, Tony spoke more directly and less compassionately than the night before. "You will be at my apartment while I'm working today. Eric will drive you there after he takes my associates and me to our meeting." Claire smiled and said that was fine. She didn't have a choice. She knew that, and so did he. "Upon reaching the airport, we will be met by Brent Simmons, the head of my legal team; Sharon Michaels, his associate; and David Field, one of my lead negotiators. They will join us on the flight to New York. I will introduce you. Brent is already aware of you. Once we board my jet, you will sit away from us while we begin our preparations."

Claire said she understood. "Tony, I don't want to get in the way. I'm here because you want me to be."

"Yes." He was looking at his iPhone, which had just buzzed. "That is true. It is my choice, and I do want you here. I believe your presence will benefit me." He became engrossed in his texting.

Benefit him? Why couldn't he just say "I want you here"? Her stomach tied in knots as she wondered what Brent Simmons knew about her. Did he know what she did? Did he think she was a companion or an employee or worse? As they rode in the backseat of the Mercedes Benz, Claire decided this was time for a *mask*. Finding it through all the apprehension that surged through her mind was difficult, but she did, and put it on.

Claire didn't know what to expect from a private jet. On the outside it seemed smaller than she anticipated. Once they climbed the steps, she was pleasantly surprised by the spacious interior. To her left was the door to the cockpit and to her right was an open space with a table and four chairs. Beyond was a sofa along one wall facing three reclining chairs along the other. Everything was secured and contained seat belts like you would expect on a plane. The chairs and some of the walls were luxuriously covered with white leather and accented with woodlike trim. There was additional space behind the far wall. Claire guessed that it contained a bathroom, maybe more.

Tony introduced Claire to his associates and motioned for her to take a seat on the sofa near the wall. Everyone was polite and friendly. She went to the sofa as she was told. Tony, Mr. Simmons, Ms. Michaels, and Mr. Fields sat around the oval table. Eric joined them on the plane after loading their luggage into a compartment below. Surprisingly, he sat in the copilot's seat.

His talents suddenly impressed Claire. He obviously was the world's most versatile chauffeur.

Claire watched and listened as Tony and the others discussed the impending deal. She honestly didn't care about the deal other than its impact on Tony. She liked to watch him work. She liked his expertise, his intelligence, and his control. He respected the knowledge and wisdom of his associates, asked questions, and listened intently to their responses and opinions. With that said, Claire knew when the time came for decisions, the only opinion that mattered would be his.

After they were in the air and the discussion at the table became mundane, Claire thought about napping and remembered Catherine's advice. To stay awake, she looked in her purse -- another treasure hunt. First, she opened her wallet. Staring back at her was her picture from her Georgia driver's license. She read the identification card and saw her Atlanta address. Compartmentalize. Her picture didn't look like her. The picture was taken two years earlier and her face had changed: slimmed, tanned, and just changed. Her height, five four, was the same; her weight, one hundred and twenty-five, was closer to actual. That hadn't been the case four months ago. The listed weight was accurate when she was sixteen and like with everyone else it had inched up through the years. However, now it seemed accurate if not erroneously high. Next, Claire spotted the American Express platinum card with *Claire Nichols* embossed on the front.

When Tony first *gave* Claire the card, she didn't want to use it. She thanked him for the confidence and faith and tried to explain there was nothing she needed. She had all the clothes she could possibly wear. She actually had many she'd never worn. Food came to her three times a day and she had a roof over her head. She had no interest in jewelry; having her grandmother's necklace was all she wanted. She loved to read, but so far the library contained more than she could hope to read.

Tony wouldn't accept any of her excuses. He told her to ask him when she wanted to go shopping. She didn't ask. After a week, he apparently gave up. One evening, over dinner, he proclaimed, "Eric is taking you into Davenport tomorrow to shop." Claire remembered suddenly feeling ill. She didn't speak at first and only stared, "Claire, did you hear me?" He knew she did; he wanted verbal confirmation.

"Yes, Tony, I heard you. I thought we discussed this and decided I had no pressing need for anything."

"I am pretty sure we discussed it, and I said you are going tomorrow."

"But, don't you need Eric tomorrow?"

His eyes darkened as his tone slowed, "Are you arguing? You were a confident woman when I met you. You have learned your lessons well. You need to get out in the world. And for the record, this conversation is now over. Unless you feel it would be beneficial to argue?"

Claire wanted to complain and explain that she worried about the Charles Jacksons of the world. But she'd made that mistake before. She swallowed. "What time does Eric need me to be ready?"

74

The trip to Davenport was unnerving. Eric picked Claire up in a black BMW. She sat in the backseat and felt awkward without Tony. Driving away from the house, she told herself he was right. She had been a confident woman, and besides, one day she would be leaving here. She also knew the truth. This was a test to determine if she could be trusted out by herself. And she learned from earlier *glitches* the best way to pass a test was to avoid it. Tony made it clear: avoiding this was not an option.

Eric took her to the River Walk Shoppes, higher-end boutiques in the Quad Cities. She entered each shop and took her time looking around. At first, her senses were on high alert, afraid of everyone that approached her. She soon realized no one paid that much attention to her. The clerks were attentive and she was shown everything and anything she wanted. People didn't browse these shops if they couldn't buy.

Claire saw no reporters. No one stared or asked questions. By the time she made it down the street to a small coffee shop she felt better about her outing, and even drank coffee sitting at an outside table. She sipped the aromatic rich brew and watched people as they rushed down the sidewalks. She missed being around people. However, the idea of speaking to anyone frightened her. What if she said something wrong?

By the time Eric returned to pick her up, she found a few books on butterflies and some casual clothes for her busy event-filled days. It wasn't a lot, but she did what she'd been told to do and honestly enjoyed it.

Tony seemed disappointed that she hadn't bought more, but also pleased she'd done as he instructed. He then expected her to give him a fashion show of her finds and suggested next time she buy some items he would like too. That meant fashions with much less material.

Once the jet landed the five of them entered a waiting limousine. The four continued to discuss their impending meeting. Claire sat silently listening, trying to go unnoticed. It was nine twenty and their meeting was to start at ten. Eric rode in the passenger seat next to the driver. In no time they were in the throes of New York City grid-lock traffic. The car traveled in short, accelerated movements.

Claire experienced this traffic from the back of a taxi when she lived with Emily and John and knew it could stifle travel and wreak havoc on schedules. Tony didn't seem concerned. Their car pulled up to their destination with minutes to spare. The four associates got out and proceeded through the big glass doors. Claire found herself alone in a large limousine. She didn't know where she was going or how long she would be there. Her life was no longer in her hands, and she was somehow coming to terms with that.

Peering around the marble floored foyer, Claire knew his apartment wasn't like any she'd seen before. Her anxiety eased with the housekeeper's warm greeting, "Ms. Claire, welcome. My name is Jan. Let me show you to Mr. Rawlings's room. We will put your belongings in there and show you around."

Claire thanked Jan and followed her up the ornate staircase which ascended to a railed landing on the second floor. The apartment included a massive sitting room complete with fireplace, a dining room, a kitchen, and an office on the first level. Claire called it the first level, but in actuality it was seventy-six stories from the ground. The sitting and dining rooms had floor to ceiling windows which looked out over the city and toward the water. She'd spent many days and nights in NYC but had never seen such a spectacular view.

Tony's bedroom was large and decorated in dark masculine colors. A large high bed with a leather headboard and complementary leather furniture filled the room. Jan carried Claire's hanging bag, and two other staff members assisted with the rest of their luggage. Once things were put away Jan asked Claire if she would like some lunch or if she would rather rest. Claire decided a little lunch before a nap would be good.

Tony arrived at the apartment at about seven o'clock. He wasn't alone. Brent Simmons was with him. They arrived conversing about something that happened during the day. Their conversation continued into the dining room, where they opened briefcases, laptops, and resumed their debate. Jan asked Mr. Rawlings if he would like dinner. He told her to just bring them something they could eat while working.

Claire hoped for a night out under the New York lights. Instead, she settled for dinner alone in his bedroom and a night with her book. Wearing a black silk nightgown she fell asleep before Tony ever made it to bed. He left before she awoke. If the covers on his side weren't rumpled, she wouldn't have known he'd been there. In the morning she found a note next to the bed:

> *Eric is available to you all day. Have*
> *a good day in the city. Be back by 6.*
> *Do not disappoint me.*

And there was cash, with a separate note:
> *For tipping, remember, appearances!*

Okay, she thought. *I'm stuck in New York. I might as well enjoy myself.*

After her shower, Jan served her a wonderful breakfast and promised she would be notified as soon as Eric returned from taking Mr. Rawlings to his office. By ten Claire sat in the back of the limousine with Eric driving her to some shopping therapy. She decided if Tony wanted her to shop so badly, this definitely was the place to do it. She always enjoyed shopping in NYC, but this would be a new experience. The vastness of the city, along with the quantity of people, gave Claire the feeling of anonymity – something she didn't have in Davenport. No one would even notice her here. She could do as she pleased.

"To Fifth Avenue and Fifty-first Street, please." Eric didn't hesitate. Claire decided she could keep herself busy with Versace, Prada, Bendel, and Louis Vuitton for at least four or five hours. Eric gave Claire a card with his cell phone number and explained that she needn't worry about carrying any purchases. Tell the clerk to call him, her driver. He would pick up everything she bought. He dropped her off near East Fifty-First and Madison and promised to pick her up near the Plaza Hotel at East Fifty-Eighth Street at two. At that time, he would be happy to take her to her next destination.

Claire stepped from the car, her high-heeled sandals hit the concrete and her chiffon sundress blew slightly in the breeze; she felt like a model doing a magazine shoot. It didn't seem real. She kept telling herself, *Play the part.* The summer heat radiating in waves off the pavement and the sounds of the city invigorated her as she fought the crowds of people along the sidewalk.

First, she entered Versace. The ornate limestone facade with the large glass doors, and an unlimited amount of money in her purse gave her a rush of adrenaline. It felt different from exercise. It was the strange sensation that she could buy anything and everything she wanted. She did her best to feign the image of someone accustomed to spending. It didn't take long before she believed it as much as the store's associates.

She tried very hard not to notice prices as she chose dress possibilities. She liked a cotton pique sheath dress and a gathered bodice sheath dress. They accentuated her trimmer figure. As she looked at herself in the mirror, she judged her image by *would Tony like this?* She decided he would. According to the associate she also needed shoes. When all was said and done, and she paid for her two outfits, she almost lost her composure. The associate smiled and said, "That will be $3,657. Would you like to place that on an existing account?"

Claire worked diligently to keep her mask intact, despite the dramatic increase in heart rate. "No, I'll pay for it now and my driver will pick it up. Let me give you his number and he will work out the details." She handed the associate her American Express.

"Thank you, madam, I will be glad to take care of that for you." She rang the transaction. This kind associate definitely needed a tip, appearances.

Claire preceded north, next stop Cartier. She was determined to make it back to the apartment with items to show Tony. She decided on a nice little pair of sunglasses for only $500. She thought about the $10 sunglasses she wore all four years of college. Her shopping adventure continued. The crowds of people talking, the cash registers ringing, the smells of exhaust, the sights of tall buildings as she looked up to the sky, all worked together to create the feeling of elation.

By one o'clock, Claire was exhausted. She purchased a few dresses, some shoes, a few new lingerie items, and sunglasses. She successfully spent over $5,000. It truly seemed ridiculous, but she was determined to *make Tony proud.* She didn't want to shop anymore. She stopped at the Trump Tower, less than two blocks from her pick-up destination, for lunch. She'd been there before and remembered the Trump Café. The people and beauty of the glass caught her attention as she entered the Atrium, but her mind focused on food.

In the past four months she hadn't made one decision about food. Now she salivated at the idea of ordering anything she wanted. There were even desserts. She took a few minutes wandering around the cases, so many choices. The aroma from the grill caused her to think of hamburgers in the summertime. She could almost taste the foods as she inhaled their delicious scents. She silently debated her options.

Claire found a table near the window and ate her spinach salad, iced tea, and yogurt. It was still her choice but eating healthy made more sense. She ate and watched. New York had always been fun, and even today, by herself, she found it fun. She glanced at her watch, one forty. She finished her lunch and walked toward the Plaza Hotel. Tony wouldn't be waiting. But she didn't want Eric to tell him she was late.

When Eric pulled the car to the curb, Claire was ready. However, she waited for Eric to park, get out, and open her door. She'd learned to perform her part well. Once back on the road he inquired as to the next destination. "I believe I'm tired and would like to go back to the apartment. Oh, did you pick up my purchases?" Yes, they were in the trunk. He would have someone take them to Mr. Rawlings's room immediately upon arriving at the apartment.

Claire sat back, closed her eyes, and let herself be taken back to Tony's apartment. It wasn't until she was almost back that it occurred to her, Emily and John were only three hours out of the city. She could get there by train. If she had Eric drop her off near a station, she could get to their house and be back in the span of a day. She used to ride the train all the time. No one would ever know. She couldn't do it today but excitement brewed as she began to work out the details in her head for tomorrow.

Napping soundly on his large bed, late in the afternoon, Tony's voice brought Claire back to reality. "We did it! The deal is complete."

She pushed the sleepy fog from her mind and tried to concentrate on his words. "That's great. I'm happy for you."

"I believe a celebration is in order!" Smiling at his enthusiasm, Claire began to get out of bed.

"Where are you going?" His intimidating tone caused her to focus on the man across the room. She watched as his expression of accomplishment quickly morphed into a new menacing gaze.

Claire felt a chill, despite the warmth of the blankets. "I thought you wanted to celebrate. I need to dress."

"Yes, you do, but first you need to undress." Tony removed his Brooks Brothers suit jacket and silk tie, letting them fall to the floor, and unbuttoned his shirt. "Our celebration will begin here."

Claire hadn't expected him to return this early and was napping in shorts and a camisole. Her instincts told her the vigor and energy acquired from his successful business dealings would be unleashed here and now. Thankful she'd napped, she obeyed and removed her shorts and top.

Apprehensively, Claire watched as Tony approached. His clothes created a trail from the doorway to near the foot of the bed. Adjusting her eyes to the dim light, she beheld his completely nude body. She'd been groggy when he first entered the room, but something about his demeanor alarmed her, like the warning rumble of thunder indicating an imminent storm. Now fully awake, her body quivered. Coming toward her, she beheld his wide chest, defined, and covered with dark hair, his trim abdomen, obviously the result of keeping fit, and his narrow hips and waist which held a light trail of hair, leading to where Claire could plainly see he was ready to celebrate. She didn't need to help him. Everything about his presence said *power*.

She steadied herself as Tony pushed his body against her petite form. Moving fast and rough, he pulled her into his embrace. Forcibly engaging her lips, she tasted coffee and attempted to slow his movements, trying to control his explosion of energy. But it was a matter of momentum. Claire was helpless to slow this force of nature. Her only defense was to move with it. Anticipating his actions she expected to be lifted onto the bed. Instead, he turned her and pushed her to the bed. Her cheek felt the softness of the satin covered, down comforter. His plans were unexpected, and he hadn't prepared her. She stifled the urge to cry out in pain, as her fingers gripped the cover, forming fists. Dominating, Anthony Rawlings showed no meekness, only total control.

His voracious need only momentarily satisfied, he instructed Claire to kneel, held her head and dictated her movements until he was ready again. Insatiable, the afternoon went on and on. There was no longer a rush. Tony took his time. His authoritative tone resumed, as did instructions and directions. Eventually he led her to the shower. They needed to get ready to go out. The soap, the multiple shower heads, he continued.

Finally, gratified, Tony took shampoo and began to wash Claire's hair. After ravaging her body, he reverently caressed her chestnut trusses. Suddenly, his movements were tender and gentle. Outwardly she responded appropriately, but inwardly she burned with loathing. One day she wanted to help him, to be with him, the next he treated her like a whore. It made her furious and her heart ache, but she stopped the tears. He'd already taken too much. She wasn't giving him those too.

That night, dressed in a sleek black strapless dress with black heels, Claire was escorted by Tony to Daniel, a four-star restaurant in Manhattan. Located on the Upper East Side, it was known for its elegant ambiance and delicious French cuisine. En route, Tony reminded Claire about his rules: do as she was told, keep up appearances, and the severity of punishment for public failure. Perhaps he could sense her unspoken revulsion and overwhelming desire to flee and felt the need to reiterate the consequences if she tried.

When they arrived to Daniel, they went to the lounge where Tony ordered cocktails. They sipped drinks while Tony chatted about his amazing rescue of this sensational deal. Claire felt like she was spending the evening with two different men. He could chastise her in one breath and be refined and charming in the next. While talking about his deal he said he didn't like to talk about money, but today he made more than most people do in an entire lifetime, quoting, "Hell, more than most families do in their lifetimes."

When the maître d' informed them their table was ready, they moved to the exquisite dining room. Again, Tony ordered their meal. Claire's attention was completely centered on him. He required that, maintaining appearances. She discovered Tony spoke French. Since she did not, she didn't know what was said to the waiter. When the bottle of wine arrived, after sipping on cocktails, Claire tried unsuccessfully to hide her surprise. Tony explained, "This is a special occasion."

The waiter poured a small amount of wine into a glass and offered it to him. He approved and two glasses were poured.

If the prelude hadn't been so tempestuous, the dinner would have been more pleasurable. Claire remembered Tony saying he didn't approve of alcohol because it diminished the senses. Currently, feeling her body, head, and heart ache, she welcomed the diminishing effects. Of course, she didn't show her uneasiness with the return of the Anthony Rawlings she'd known. She obeyed the rules and remained the perfect companion.

On the way back to the apartment, Eric drove them around Manhattan to enjoy the lights, sights, and sounds. New York City was truly spectacular. It had been so long since Claire had experienced so many people and so much energy. If Tony weren't running his hand up her thigh, it would have been more enjoyable.

Tony informed her they would return to Iowa in the morning. As they were about to fall asleep, he asked about shopping. Her body exhausted, her head spinning from the alcohol, she replied, "It was nice... may I please show you the purchases in the morning?" They both fell asleep.

We shall draw from the heart of suffering
itself the means of inspiration and survival.
—Sir Winston Churchill

Chapter 11

His alarm sounded, and Mr. Rawlings called for the car. It would be ready to take them to the airport at 6:00 a.m. Claire knew she would rather be back in her suite, waking at eight, working out, eating, and being on her own schedule. When she worked at WKPZ, she needed to wake before three every morning. But back then, she went to bed much earlier and, most importantly, alone.

A little before five, she sleepily entered the shower. Turning her face to the hot spray, she desperately tried to revive her senses and dull the aches in her body. The water began the process, but the real awakening came as she heard the glass door slide, and saw Tony enter the steamy stall. His only expectation was to get clean. However, the act, the sharing of this personal space non-sexually, was more intimate than Claire anticipated or desired.

Once on the jet, she asked about his associates. Tony explained Mr. Simmons and Mr. Field stayed behind to complete the contracts and Ms. Michaels had left on another company jet yesterday. During the two-and-a-half-hour flight, it was only the two of them in the cabin. Tony busily read his computer screen while Claire watched the clouds under the plane and contemplated the trip: disappointing and short. She thought pensively about her missed opportunity to contact Emily and John. She hadn't spoken to anyone from her past for almost four months. Did anyone wonder what happened to her? Were they concerned she'd dropped off the earth? But then she thought about Tony. He'd taken her out and introduced her to the world. She couldn't be a missing person or the police would have gotten involved. She wasn't sure how this publicity thing worked. Maybe Emily knew she was seen out with Mr. Anthony Rawlings. Claire berated herself. She'd worried more about *not disappointing* Tony than thinking to contact her sister.

Suddenly, Tony broke the silence. "Now, tell me about your shopping trip." The domineering man from the night before was gone. His tone was friendly and inquisitive.

Claire did her best to respond with the appropriate tone and inflection. "It was amazing. New York is such a bustling city. I wasn't worried about people, or should I say reporters, approaching me."

"That concerns you?"

"Yes. After that scene at the benefit, I'm terrified someone will approach me. I know how much appearance and privacy means to you."

Satisfied, Tony smiled smugly. "Very well, that is interesting. Go on, what did you buy?"

"Well, first I went to Versace and found a couple of dresses and some shoes. I think you will like them. I made my way along Fifth Avenue and bought some sunglasses. Oh, they're here in my purse." She pulled the glasses out and put them on.

Tony smiled and removed them from her green eyes. He liked her eyes and didn't want them covered.

Claire continued chattily, "I also found some lingerie," managing to smile coyly, "which I believe you will like."

His eyes were soft, fully focused, and his expression was amused. "It sounds like you did well. Do you mind telling me how much you spent?"

Claire's eyes dropped to the floor. She knew five thousand was nothing to Tony, but it would have been a month's salary for her parents. Two outfits, shoes, sunglasses, and some silk and lace seemed like such a small accumulation for so much money. Tony gently lifted her chin to resume eye contact. Her eyes shone as she flashed a smile and spoke. "About five thousand."

His reaction surprised her. He laughed. She waited to see if it was a laugh leading to something else, but no, it was just a laugh. Finally, he responded, "Good job, Claire. You may get the hang of this yet. I look forward to my private fashion show tonight when I return to the house."

It bothered Claire that he could treat her in such a demeaning manner in the bedroom or wherever he chose and then turn around and act like nothing happened. She needed to work on compartmentalizing the sex away from the rest of her life. That was harder than it sounded.

Once they arrived back to Iowa, they entered Tony's waiting car and Eric drove them back to the house. Tony needed to get a few things before heading into the office in Iowa City. He would be leaving tomorrow for ten days in Europe and had some loose ends which required his immediate attention.

After the car entered the gates to the estate, they took the long winding drive and approached the mansion. Claire usually saw the house from the back. She rarely left the property, but when she did it was usually at night. Now seeing it in daylight, the beautiful combination of river stone, limestone, and brick, combined with the Romanesque style architecture, gave her a new appreciation. Tony had said he'd built the house about fifteen years ago, but it looked older. It didn't look outdated or antiquated. It looked as if it had been designed for an earlier time. Claire couldn't help but ask, "Tony, you said you built your house about fifteen years ago?"

"Yes," he answered as Eric came around the front drive. "Why do you ask?"

"I'm not used to seeing it from the front. It's beautiful!" He thanked her. She continued, "But it looks older than fifteen years to me, the style I mean."

"I patterned it after my family's home from when I was a child."

Claire knew he lost his parents and didn't want to stir up bad memories, but her curiosity got the best of her. "I thought you built your fortune from nothing. How did your parents have a house like this?" They were now getting out of the car.

"It was my grandfather's, not my parents'. My father was weak. However, my grandfather's house and money were all lost over twenty-five years ago. My grandfather trusted the wrong people."

That seemed like a wealth of information. She wasn't sure what it meant. Catherine told her that Mr. Rawlings didn't allow many people to get close. She was sure this family history had something to do with that. As they walked to his office she tried for a little more information. "It truly is amazing. Did you pattern the inside after it, as well?"

"Mostly, I even found and purchased some of the original artwork and antiques. However, I wanted my home equipped with all the modern conveniences and security equipment. Every inch of this house is under constant surveillance. I will not make the same mistake my grandfather made." Claire considered what he was saying; he meant every inch of the perimeter. He was stopping someone from getting in who wasn't supposed to be there. "Haven't you ever wondered how the staff knows exactly when to enter your suite?" Tony now stood behind his desk, punching some buttons on his computer and rummaging through papers.

Claire's knees became weak and she thought she may need to sit down. "You mean my suite is under surveillance? Like there are cameras?"

Tony looked up from the papers and met Claire's eyes. He saw the repugnance and slowly smiled. His words slowed, adding malice, "Yes, of course. It is all video recorded and saved." Claire sat on the nearest chair. He was suddenly making the most of her newfound discomfort. "Perhaps we could have a premier viewing, critique, and work on revisions."

She detested his existence. "Tony, please tell me you are joking, some sort of sick joke."

His vile smirk gave spark to his darkening eyes. "But, my dear Claire, I am not. Now the staff does not have access to the view of your bed, only I have that. But they do have view of the sitting area and the doorways to and from your dressing room and bath. That is how they have been able to come and go without you seeing them."

"But why? Why would you do that? Why would you keep it?"

Tony picked up his needed papers and a flash drive and moved to leave his office, "Because I can. I can watch and decide what I like and what I believe can be improved. You will understand after you get a chance to view it. Maybe tonight, but now I must be going." He started to walk toward the hall doors. Claire didn't think her legs could support her weight; she stayed seated. The thought of him watching them, of her watching him with her, it all made her physically sick. She seriously believed if she stood she wouldn't be able to control the revolt currently occurring in her stomach. Tony reiterated, "It is time to exit my office." He watched as she sat motionless and heartlessly added, "And in case you were wondering, yes, this too is under surveillance, except for my desk. But I do have a great view of the sofa and this open area." He nastily grinned and gestured to the setting of one of her worse nightmares. Something she'd pushed away. Now she knew he had it on video and watched it! "Claire, I need to go. Get out of the chair, now."

She absently stood, only thinking about keeping her breakfast down. She tried desperately to keep all other thoughts out of her head as she left his office. Before she knew it, she was back in her suite. Her head spun. She wanted to flop on the sofa and stop the thoughts that bombarded her mind, but he could see her. Was there anywhere he couldn't see her?

That night they dined on the back patio. It was shaded and the night air felt warm. The yard looked picture perfect. Even with the recent heat wave which had been accompanied by a drought, his lawn was lush and green thanks to the marvels of a sprinkling system and ground's crew. Tony was doing what she despised, talking about his trip to Europe, the time in New York, anything except the cameras and videos.

Claire couldn't understand how he could behave one way, say something, and then act as if it never happened. She, however, was having difficulty thinking of anything else. Her appetite gone, she barely ate any of her dinner.

Once they were done dining, Tony led Claire to the movie theater. It was her retreat, a place to escape, watch singing and dancing. Tonight, Tony didn't intend to watch a musical. He programmed the video system and entered a passcode. Suddenly, the screen was full of dates and locations, such as "2010, May 05, S.E. suite." He had the ability to scroll to different dates and different locations. It wasn't just her room. There were locations like garages, kitchen, foyer, stairs, theater, pool, S.E. 2 floor hall, S.E. 1 floor hall, etc.

In some humiliating form of torture he chose, 2010 March 20, S.E Suite, and then programmed the time. He scrolled up and the time decreased, 9, 8, 7. He returned to approximately 8:00 a.m. He hit enter, and there on the movie screen, bigger than life, was Claire's suite. She wore a white robe and lay curled up on the floor near the hall door. Claire didn't need to watch, she knew too well what would happen. She also knew the Claire on the screen was covered in bruises, her hair was a mess, and she could see the demolition of the room. Now she heard a beep and the door opened. The screen Claire jumped up, also hearing the sound and seeing Tony enter. "Good morning, Claire." Screen Claire looked at Tony. "Good morning, Anthony. I want you to know, I have decided to go home. I will be leaving here today." Screen Tony then spoke, his black eyes shining. He was smiling, "Do you not like your accommodations?" His smile widened. "I do not believe you will be leaving so soon. We have a legally binding agreement." The real Claire watched as the

Tony on the screen took a bar napkin from his suit pocket and continued, "Dated and signed by both of us."

Claire didn't want to watch anymore. "Please, Tony. I don't want to see this." She covered her eyes.

Tony physically removed her hands from her eyes. "I promised a viewing. I said you will watch. And you will watch."

The video had progressed in real time. Claire looked up in time to hear her own voice obviously filled with alarm. "It is not the end of this discussion. This is ludicrous. An agreement doesn't give you the right to rape me! I am leaving." Knowing what was to come. Claire closed her eyes as she heard Tony's hand contact the screen Claire's left cheek.

Unknowingly, her own fingers drift toward her left cheek. Opening her eyes she saw herself fly across the floor and Tony walk over to that Claire. She closed her eyes again, hearing the voice on the screen with the cruel tone, "Perhaps in time your memory will improve. It seems to be an issue. Let me remind you again, rule number one is that you will do as you are told. If I say a discussion is over, it is over, and this written agreement which states *whatever is pleasing to me*, means consensual, not rape." The real Claire still had her eyes shut. She knew the Tony on the screen was straightening his jacket. She could hear him continue in a disturbing, authoritative voice, "I have decided that it would be better if you did not leave your suite for a while. Don't worry, we have plenty of time, $215,000 worth of time" She opened her eyes again to see the screen Tony step on broken crystal and speak again in a tone that made the real Claire shiver, "I will tell the staff that you may have your breakfast after you clean up this crystal." The Tony on the screen left Claire's room.

"Please stop the video," Claire cried. She couldn't help it. "Please, I can't watch anymore."

Relishing Claire's suffering, Tony said, "Oh, there are so many videos. We can watch for hours." He hit some buttons and went back to the menu. "For example," the screen read, March 19, 2010, "how do you suppose your suite got into that condition? I'm sure we could find out."

"Please!" she pleaded. Her head hurt and stomach twisted in knots. She couldn't stand this. She tried desperately to make it stop. "Please, you are leaving tomorrow. Wouldn't you rather spend tonight making movies instead of watching?"

Her eyes were red and puffy and her nose ran from crying.

Tony smirked at her desperation. His tone dripped with ruthlessness, "But maybe we should watch some more, find out where you need improvement."

"I will do anything you say, anything you want me to do differently, just tell me. Just please don't make me watch." Claire was now on the floor in front of Tony, kneeling, crying. She hated that she'd been reduced to begging, but this ruined her whole compartmentalization. How could she keep these awful memories hidden if he made her watch them?

His dark eyes pierced her soul and his voice was ice cold. "You will do whatever I say, even if it is to watch. But . . ." He hesitated to add emphasis. "I do not want to spend my last night for over a week here with you in this condition." He stood, causing her to fall back onto the floor. "I will be in your suite in a few minutes." Claire stood.

He continued, "Go up and get ready. Wash your face! You look like hell, and as far as attire . . . I am thinking some new lingerie."

She started to leave the theater as Tony gripped her arm. She stopped, met his gaze, and listened to his steely tone, "Claire, what do you say?"

She looked at him, fire in her moist eyes. They stood silent for a moment while Claire's confused mind spun. She couldn't fathom what he wanted. When it hit her she almost screamed. It took all her resolve to not lash out. Instead, she managed, "Thank you, Tony."

Loosening his grip he responded, "You may demonstrate your gratitude when I get upstairs."

Claire continued to stand, afraid to move. Her mind was a mess, not knowing what to do or say, all she could do was pray she would never see another of those videos. As if sensing her bewilderment, Tony remained in control of her motion, "You may go to your suite now."

It was after sunrise when Claire felt Tony get out of her bed. She listened as he picked up his clothes and knew he was dressing. Next, she heard him open a drawer and rifle through it. She opened her eyes and in the dim light saw him writing a note. When he turned to look at her, she closed her eyes and pretended to sleep. Doing her best to keep her breathing steady, she remembered he wouldn't be back for over a week.

At this moment in time, she detested everything about Anthony Rawlings.

Lust and greed are more gullible than innocence.
--Mason Cooley

Chapter 12

Nathaniel didn't mind the commute between New York and New Jersey, especially when he drove the winding drive toward his home. Each time the beautiful combination of river stone, limestone, and brick came into view, he momentarily remembered the two-room apartment he'd shared with his wife. For a young soldier recently home from fighting the Japs, it was ample. Being a soldier and a veteran were the only attributes Sharron's family saw in him. That was the only reason they allowed their daughter to marry Nathaniel Rawls.

Today as he stepped into the marble entry, he wished her high-and-mighty father could see his daughter now. Oh yes, Nathaniel Rawls did make something out of himself. And now, with Clawson's ideas, there is so much more to be made. If his father-in-law were still alive he would gladly shove this up his—

"Good evening, Nathaniel." Sharron's greeting came from the archway to the sitting room. She had his bourbon waiting. Dinner would be precisely at seven. Everyone knew that. Perhaps it was the military training, but punctuality was never questioned. "How was your day?"

"It's better now." He took the glass she handed to him and kissed his wife's cheek. The sparkle of his wife's eyes reflected the flames from the large fireplace. "How was your day, my love?"

Sharron chatted about the pressing concerns regarding the household staff while Nathaniel thought about Rawls Corp. Of course he responded and acknowledged her concerns, but his mind swirled with Clawson's ideas. Just before seven they heard Samuel and Amanda descending the grand stairs. They all congregated in the dining room.

He may think about work, but dinner was not the time to discuss it. Even though Nathaniel and Samuel had spent the day together debating ideas, Nathaniel and his son spent dinner talking with their wives, discussing weather, politics, sports, movies, etc...

A man's home was his castle and Nathaniel loved the castle his queen and family were able to enjoy.

Look deep into nature, and then you will
understand everything better.
—Albert Einstein

Chapter 13

Claire waited about ten minutes after hearing the door to her suite shut. During that time, she lay still, barely breathing, and pretended to sleep. She didn't want to face him, talk to him, or even see him. Though appearing peacefully asleep, her mind was a whirlwind of questions: *How long until I'm sure he won't come back? Can he see me? Is he watching? Oh god! What did he write?*

Finally, her curiosity won. She got out of bed and started to walk to the table to read his note. Suddenly, the thought hit her like a physical strike. She remembered the cameras and the staff. She reached for her robe on the floor and put it on. Sitting on the table where he left it, was his note.

I believe we have a blockbuster on our hands. It is
hard to say, until we thoroughly review the footage
I plan to return a week from Wednesday. Eric is
available if you want to visit the Quad Cities. I trust
last night's film reminded you of my rules. Don't
disappoint me.

Never in her life had she remembered being so overwhelmed with emotion. Her entire being emitted loathing, directed completely and totally toward one man, Anthony Rawlings. She hated him, his sadistic ploys, and nasty reminders. She picked up the note, crumbled it into a ball, and threw it against the wall. It created significantly less mess than the vase of flowers had months earlier.

Her mind tried desperately to compartmentalize the videos. She wanted to put them away, someplace she would never find them. *Think of something else*, she told herself, but it was too difficult. She climbed back into bed and smelled his aftershave. Turning over the pillow, the cool side smelled fresh. That, with the realization he wouldn't return until a week from Wednesday, gave her a sliver of peace. She tried to concentrate. *What day is it now? Sunday*. She felt her muscles relax. It was Sunday, his day to be home . . . but he was gone. Her eyes closed as tears began to slip onto her pillow. She drifted away to another place.

"Ms. Claire? Ms. Claire, you must wake."

Claire tried to focus. She'd been somewhere in a dream. Now hearing Catherine's voice, she rolled over and saw her standing at the edge of her bed.

"Catherine, what are you doing?"

"Ms. Claire, it is after one in the afternoon. You need to wake and eat. You have already missed breakfast and now lunch. I am worried about you."

Opening her eyes caused pain. They felt puffy. However, Claire could see Catherine's concerned expression and hear it in her tone. From the moment he left the room and she read the note, she'd been crying, even in her sleep. Her body ached, head ached, and heart ached. She felt more alone and isolated than she'd ever felt. "Thank you, Catherine, for your concern. But I believe I'll stay in bed today. I'm not feeling well." She tried to sound strong, but as the words came, so did more tears. They stung her swollen eyes. Claire wanted to concentrate on Catherine but her mind wouldn't stop thinking of him and what he'd done. She didn't want Catherine to see her in this condition. Claire rolled her face into her pillow, making her words muffled. "Please leave me alone."

Catherine didn't leave. Instead, she sat on the edge of Claire's bed and tenderly stroked Claire's hair as her head moved with the sobs. Catherine remained silent and comforted her until the sobs subsided and Claire caught her breath. "Ms. Claire, you will feel better if you shower and eat. Please let me help you." Catherine's concern and affection reminded Claire of her mother or grandmother. However, she knew if they were here, they would be telling her to run, not shower.

Claire didn't want to eat, shower, or even get out of bed. The only thing she wanted to do was to be out of *his* house. At that moment, she didn't care if it was by car or death, she just wanted out. The feeling of helplessness sat heavily on her chest. She had tried to survive this ordeal. She had even convinced herself she could handle whatever he sent her way. But this new situation was too much. He broke her. Since March she maintained her spirit despite the loss of her body. Yesterday he took that too. She turned to look Catherine in the eyes. "How have you been able to work for *him* all this time?"

Catherine stopped stroking Claire's hair and gently took her hand. "Mr. Rawlings is a good man, Ms. Claire. He truly is."

Claire shook her head. The tears and sobs resumed. "No! No, he isn't. I have never met a more sadistic, cruel, bad man." She closed her eyes, feeling the sting of the tears, the pounding in her head, and taste of her runny nose. Catherine handed Claire a tissue.

"Mr. Rawlings hides his feelings with certain behaviors. He is afraid to face his own emotions, and he uses this dark persona as a cover. It is not who he truly is. I have known him a long time."

Her words came between whimpers. "Catherine, I can't. I can't get up. I can't face the staff. They all know. They have all seen me, seen him . . . I just can't."

"No, Ms. Claire, only I have access to view the inside of your room." Claire pulled her hand away from Catherine and rolled from her gaze. Catherine reached out to lightly touch her shoulder. "I only use that access to know when to send the staff inside or to check on your safety." Claire continued to face away from Catherine. "And now I am concerned about you. Ms. Claire. Please let me help you. It is a beautiful day outside." Claire didn't move. "Would you like your lunch in here or downstairs?"

Claire shook her head no. "I don't want lunch. Thank you for your concern, but I am too . . . too . . ." She turned around to face Catherine. "I don't know what I am. I don't even know who I am anymore."

"Ms. Claire, you are a beautiful strong woman. That is what Mr. Rawlings finds so attractive. He is astounded by your strength and resilience."

"That isn't true. He hates strength in anyone but himself. He has to have total control." Claire replayed scenes from the past that caused her body to shiver.

"Miss, you are partially right, Mr. Rawlings does not want to let anyone else have any power over him. Therefore, *if* he admits he has feelings toward you, he gives up control. And if I may, that scares him."

Claire really didn't think that anything scared Anthony Rawlings. "I don't want his feelings. I want out. I want to go to Atlanta and forget I was ever here. I promise I won't tell any of his secrets. I just want to go home." Tears flowed with increased intensity and her next question was barely audible. "Do you think he will ever let me go?"

Catherine looked into her eyes. "Mr. Rawlings is a man of his word. If he said he will release you when your debt is paid, then he will." The obvious question was when would that be? "Now after you shower, would you like your lunch in here or downstairs?"

Claire began to get out of the bed as Catherine helped with her robe. "I will shower, but I'm really not hungry."

"It is sunny and beautiful outside, the sun will make you feel better. I will have your lunch brought to the pool." Catherine started for the door and stopped, "Unless you need my assistance?"

"No thank you, I will be all right. I'll be down to the pool in a little while."

Claire slowly walked into the bathroom. She turned the shower on as hot as possible, stood under the stream and let the flow hit her face and skin. It didn't stop her head from aching, but it washed away the scent of him. As the steam built and her skin turned red, she found herself sitting on the bench, liquid needles hitting her hair, and tears flowing.

She couldn't be sure how long she sat in that position but the temperature of the water began to cool when she snapped back to reality. Drying, she noticed new bruises, both hip bones and left forearm were red and tender to the touch, and when placing sunscreen she found some more on her legs. Momentarily, she considered the need to camouflage them while at the pool, then she realized, why? Maybe the staff didn't have access to the videos of her room, but what about the pool, his office, and any other place he chose to require her services?

She combed her wet hair, put on a bikini, a beach cover, flip-flops, and found her new sunglasses. Her eyes looked scary in the mirror. The sunglasses would definitely help. On her way to the pool she stopped in the library and grabbed an older magazine, *People*. Some light nonsense reading to help her mind stray.

As soon as she stepped outside of the house Claire realized Catherine was right about the weather; lower humidity with bright sunshine. When she reached the pool, Cindy brought a tray with her lunch: a turkey sandwich, mixed fresh fruit, and an iced tea. She asked if Claire needed anything else.

"No, Cindy, I'm fine. Thank you for lunch." The sound of defeat flowed thickly through her voice. The sight of the food made her ill. It reminded her of dining, and dining of Tony, and Tony of his rules, instructions, and video surveillance. She started to shove the tray off the table but stopped. Someone would need to clean it up and that seemed unnecessary. She picked up the glass of iced tea and walked toward a chaise lounge.

Remembering scenes on that lounge chair, she chose another.

The sun felt wonderful on her skin and the tea tasted refreshing. Her head still ached and eyes hurt. She suddenly wished she had asked Cindy for some headache medicine. Thumbing through the magazine she looked at pictures of celebrities. They all smiled, pretty and happy. She read an article about a little girl who was saved by her dog, sweet.

Then the latest gossip, who was with whom and who was splitting from whom. It was then she saw the picture. In a section called "Star Tracks," it was her! The photo showed her and Tony sitting in the private box at the symphony, her smiling at him and him holding her hand. It contained the title: **Mystery Beauty?** The caption read:

Anthony Rawlings, forty–five, confirmed bachelor,

mega millionaire and red–hot sexy has been seen at numerous

events in the last month with this beautiful woman. Sources say her

name is Claire Nichols, but who is she? Mr. Rawlings's publicist would

not comment regarding speculation that there could be someone

special in his life.

Claire looked at the photo in disbelief. Tony is forty-five, really? And who would care that she was at the symphony? Well other than her, since it was her first time *allowed* out of the house in two months. Has Emily seen this? What about her friends in Atlanta? The stupid magazine was supposed to take her mind off everything, not make it public. Claire flipped the magazine over. It was dated June 14. Today was Sunday, but what was the date? It was August, August 8, and Tony won't return until the eighteenth. When she thought of it that way, it seemed even longer. She smiled, threw the magazine on the ground, and closed her eyes. The clock by the pool house read 3:15 when Catherine woke her again.

"I brought you something special, Ms. Claire." Claire opened her eyes to see Catherine holding a tall glass containing something that looked like a smoothie. "It is my secret recipe: banana, strawberry, and yogurt."

Claire appreciated Catherine's persistence and took the drink. It tasted sweet and felt cool in her throat as she swallowed. The nutritional ingredients gave her body the sustenance it needed. While she drank Catherine pulled up a chair and chatted. Claire knew she was being watched. This wasn't a depraved voyeur. It was an act of compassion and concern. Catherine didn't talk about anything that happened, she just talked. Claire liked the sound of her voice. Once she finished, Catherine left with the glass.

Claire closed her eyes and recognized a new sense of emptiness and relief. Four months of despair had been washed out of her through gallons of tears. She remembered her grandmother saying sometimes we all need a good cry. To that end, Grandma would read a sad book or watch a sad movie. Claire decided she'd watched the sad movie.

The sun still shimmered on high but began to move toward the front of the house, casting shadows on the pool and deck. Claire decided to go back upstairs, but realized she had no privacy in her suite.

At that moment, she noticed the trees. Her mind worked slowly; it had been through quite an ordeal in the past twenty-four hours. As she stood staring at the green leaves and thick forest, she saw freedom. Not freedom to Atlanta or completely away from him, but freedom from cameras, instructions, rules, and freedom to relax. The realization energized Claire like nothing had all day. Tomorrow she was heading into the woods.

Monday morning Claire woke with a start. She'd been dreaming, but she couldn't remember about what. She just knew her heart pounded, she gasped for breath, and she felt like she was suffocating. As her mind cleared and she looked around her suite, she saw reality. She was alone, the night had been peaceful, and today was a new day. She quickly showered and dressed for her exploration. When she stepped from the closet/ dressing room, because she vowed to never be unclothed in her main room again, her door was closing.

"Wait please," she shouted toward the door.

"I'm sorry, miss, I should have been faster."

"Oh no, Cindy, you're fine. I just need a favor."

"Anything, miss, what can I do for you?" Claire explained to Cindy that she planned a day trip into the woods. She needed a packed lunch and some water bottles. Cindy listened intently and promised to help.

Claire sat down to her breakfast. It wouldn't take much for Claire's appetite to disappear, just a few thoughts of reality. So she chose not to do that . . . she would get them into that compartment no matter what it took.

Instead, she thought about her impending adventure. She thought about hiking boots and bug spray and ate.

There was a knock on her door. Claire called for the person to come in. "Ms. Claire, could you please explain to me what Cindy is asking?" She told Catherine about her plans to explore, how she didn't want to return for lunch, and she knew Catherine wouldn't want her to skip a meal. Therefore, she would need a packed lunch and some water bottles. Catherine seemed apprehensive. "I am sorry, miss, but if you didn't come back?"

Although that sounded wonderful, Claire was surprised by Catherine's concern. "Catherine, I have no plans for that. First, I wouldn't do that to you. I can only imagine Mr. Rawlings's reaction if I didn't return. And second, *his* reaction. I can truthfully say if I left, I would be looking over my shoulder for the rest of my life," which, she didn't say audibly, she believed deep in her soul might not be very long. "I just want to explore and be outside, away from everything. Mr. Rawlings gave me permission to go into the woods. I've done it before. I just want to be out longer, without concern for curfews. Besides, we both know that this conversation is being recorded. I promise to return. If I don't, he will see it was I who lied, you just believed me. But, I promise I will be back."

There was a spark in Claire's green eyes. The same eyes that only yesterday were red, swollen, and lifeless. Catherine told Claire she would have her lunch and water packed in a few minutes, but asked that she be back by six for dinner. Claire promised she would. As soon as Catherine left the room, Claire went to the dressing table and found her watch. She didn't want to disappoint her.

That morning Claire abandoned her strategy of dissecting the woods. She remembered the large clearing with the flowers and headed in that direction. In the past she only went as far as the clearing, today she planned to go beyond it. She found the clearing right where she thought it would be. The heat of the summer transformed the green grass into long brown straw, only the weeds were green. Claire didn't mind, the weeds had pretty, colorful flowers. Unlike Tony's flowers, which were sentenced to his yard, gardens, or clay pots, these flowers grew free wherever they wanted. Furthermore, weeds were survivors. When all else died, the weeds remained. Yes, Claire liked weeds.

She glanced at her watch. She'd reached the clearing by ten in the morning.

When she left the house there was a slight chill, so she brought a sweatshirt. With steadily increasing temperatures, now its only purpose was to sit upon. She laid it out in the middle of the clearing and sat. A faint breeze blew her hair and caused the leaves of the trees to rustle. Even though it was only the beginning of August, due to the recent dryness, the leaves were beginning to change.

That bothered her. She moved, or was brought, to Iowa in March. At that time, the leaves hadn't formed and now they were beginning to change. Time slipped away from her and she couldn't hold on. It made her think of a soap opera her mother used to watch. The opening said something like, "Sands through the hour glass . . ."

She laid her head on the hard ground and gazed at the open sky. There were a few white fluffy clouds. The expanse of the sky glowed blue and clear. The longer she lay immobile, the more she blended into the surroundings. Firs, she noticed the butterflies which fluttered just above the grass. Then, she saw the chipmunks. One would run around a tree, the next would run up the tree, chasing and being chased. Eventually, she sat up, opened one of her water bottles, and continued to sit and contemplate.

Once she stepped through the trees, leaving the confines of Tony's backyard, Claire believed she escaped the range of his top-notch security. It felt like being released from a prison. Even the air smelled sweeter as she inhaled and relaxed. She smiled at the irony, definitely feeling more secure without security.

She didn't look at her watch, enjoying her *freedom*. After much consideration she decided to head west, northwest. There was no reason for that direction, more of a yearning, but it was solely hers, so she did it. She walked and walked. Close to the earth, she experienced a coolness that comes only from the shade of very tall trees. When she looked up, the trees reminded her of a kaleidoscope. The blue sky radiated beyond the ever-changing design of leaves. Since she hadn't checked the time when she left the clearing, she didn't know how long she'd walked when she reached the shore.

The lake wasn't big, but then again it wasn't small. She could see the other end, a distance away. Nothing but nature surrounded the water in every direction. Looking down as she stood on the shore, her boots stood upon thousands of small smooth pebbles. Suddenly, she wondered if she could skip one. Remembering from childhood, she knew it needed to be smooth. It took her three tries, but she did it. It skipped four times, each hit going a little deeper, creating a slightly larger ring upon the water. The rings grew until they faded into the waves of the lake. For the first time in days, she felt hungry.

Catherine never disappointed when it came to food. Claire found a sandwich—turkey or chicken --she would soon find out—fruit in a small sealed cup, and some carrots. She sat at the water's edge, broke off some of her bread and threw it in the water. The crumbs floated, rising and falling with the water. Suddenly, each crumb became surrounded by four or five minnows. They jumped and nibbled. Once they ate all the bread, Claire broke off more and fed them again. This time more minnows came to the feast.

The sounds of the lake exemplified peace. Claire closed her eyes and lost herself in the rhythm. Small waves lapped the earth making a consistent beat, swoosh, swoosh, swoosh. The leaves rustled, creating a gentle on again, off again reverberation. The sun moved steadily toward the other end of the lake. Claire's new sunglasses were a smart accessory for her adventure. It wasn't just the sun, but its reflection off the water, that sparkled and shined as prisms of light and color danced off the waves. She could sit and watch for hours. Occasionally there would be a splash and Claire would see the telltale rings left behind from a fish that jumped out of the lake only to go back down.

Just before Claire decided to check her watch, she saw, about one hundred yards down the shore, a doe and a fawn. They cautiously approached the lake's edge. The doe kept a watchful eye on the surroundings while the fawn concentrated on drinking the cool clear water. She didn't want to move or disturb them but the sun continued to lean west.

With a heavy heart, she looked at her watch. It was four thirty. It took forty-five minutes to get from the clearing to the house, but she didn't know how long it took to get from the lake to the clearing. Tony wouldn't be home, but Catherine had been so kind and supportive. She didn't want to disappoint her either.

Slowly, she stood, having no idea how long she'd been sitting on the shore. Her muscles ached. She wondered if the cause could be sitting on the smooth pebbles or if it was the activities of Friday and Saturday night. When those memories entered her mind, she felt her stomach knot. Eight more days she knew without a doubt this would be where they were spent.

Survival is not so much about the body,
but rather it is about the triumph of the human spirit.
—Danita Vance

Chapter 14

Wednesday arrived sooner than Claire hoped. Since the discovery of her lake oasis, she spent every day there and returned to the house by six each evening, as promised. Truly, the first night had been close. She even needed to run part of the way, but she made it. Now she knew the way and knew it took an hour and forty-five minutes each direction.

As the week progressed, Claire took more supplies: a blanket, a book, and her lunch with water to drink. She even started wearing her bathing suit under her shorts so that she could sunbathe on the shore. This made her feel like a rebel. The bathing suit was a lot like underwear.

When she walked the path approaching the lake, she began to recognize the sights, sounds, and also the smells. It was a clean fresh aroma that penetrated deep into her lungs. As the days passed, she soaked in the serenity of this secret haven and her strength and resolve returned. When Tony left for Europe, she'd felt as low as she had felt since her arrival—actually, in her entire life. She wanted out and would have been willing to die to accomplish that goal, if only the means had been present.

Now she was thankful that they weren't. When he returned he would be the same, but she would be different. He hurt her—not just physically, but also emotionally—down to her core. He humiliated her, and seemed to enjoy humiliating her routinely, since she arrived. Forcing her to view herself in those situations was agony. Previously, she tried to put away the memories to create a separation between her daily life and her daily duties. To some extent, she'd been successful. This compartmentalization had facilitated her survival. His appalling videos documenting his brutal treatment and merciless instructions exposed her to herself. It broke her.

The lake, nature, sunshine, and freedom, rejuvenated her. She felt like the Six-Million Dollar Man: stronger, faster, and better. She would gain sustenance and strength from the memories of the crystal waves shining and flashing in the sunlight. He could say, do, or make her do anything, anywhere, and her mind would be hearing the leaves rustle, birds sing, and waves lap the shore. She knew it wouldn't be easy, but she also knew the routine. There would be breaks when he needed to travel and hopefully be gone, faraway for long periods of time. She would live for those breaks, until the time came when her debt was paid and she would be the one to leave.

Claire asked Catherine, but she hadn't heard the time of his arrival. It didn't surprise Claire. It was part of his game, a test. He wanted to know if she read his note, if she would be prepared for his return. She also knew that on the day of his arrival she shouldn't leave the immediate grounds. She planned to be ready when he arrived. She was.

Claire ate lunch in her suite and sat on the sofa reading a book, a crime novel - except it was funny, the fifth in a series. She didn't know for sure how many there were, but she enjoyed reading them. She painstakingly chose her attire: white capris, a black and white top which accentuated her figure, and black sandals with a shorter heel. Her hair had lightened and grown quite long since March. She had it half up and half down, with the ends curled. Her makeup was flawless. If he didn't show up until later, she had another outfit for then. She planned to meet him head-on. The miserable wretched woman he left was gone.

The door opened without warning. Claire's heart skipped a beat, but she controlled her breathing, and remained still and relaxed as she looked up from her book. He walked in and greeted her, "Good afternoon, Claire."

Slowly, she placed her bookmark in her book, laid the book on the end table, and stood. Her smile radiated as pleasant a welcome as she could muster. Her mask was not only on, but polished and intact. "Good afternoon, Anthony." Their eyes met. "It is nice to have you home. How was your trip?"

She didn't walk toward him, but she stood straight, tall, and defiant. He approached her, not touching, yet standing close, and watched for her reaction. She stood her ground, smiling, waiting for his reply. Asking for a verbal answer to her question was not a good idea, so she remained silent and refused to drop eye contact.

"My trip was long. I'm pleased with your greeting. Does this mean your temper tantrum from before my trip reached its conclusion?" His body only inches from hers. She could smell his cologne and feared if she inhaled too deeply, they would touch.

"Yes, I believe it has. I apologize for my behavior. It was childish and unnecessary."

He grinned, wondering if she was sincere or playing him. His tone and words tried to enlist her motivation. "As I recall, a good deal of your behavior was far from childish." He paused, no reaction. "But my memory could be failing me, it has been a long trip. I know how we could find out." Another pause, no reaction. "Or review?"

Claire didn't react. She didn't take his bait. Instead, she responded, "You are right, it was very adult. I would be glad to do whatever it is you tell me to

98

do again. I believe I have a debt to repay, my goal is to make that happen as soon as possible, and that is the means to that end."

He pulled her against him and looked down into her eyes. He saw a fire, one which ten days ago had been dowsed with tears. She smiled, said all the right things, but her eyes were fighting. He bent down and kissed her. It started slowly, but soon became hard and forceful. She hesitated for only a split second and responded with equal force. She didn't back away. He hadn't intended for their reunion to go this direction. He had expected someone different.

About six thirty he used his cell phone to call the kitchen and have dinner brought to her suite. The flight had been long. By nine thirty he was sound asleep in her bed. She sat up and watched him. She still loathed him, but Claire felt she had won this battle. She stood strong and quieted the fury in his approach. She gave in without incidence. That made him less aggressive. The final result would be similar no matter the mode, but this way it happened without violence and without video replay. To Claire that was a victory. She read her book for a few hours before joining him in sleep.

The next morning when she awoke, he was gone. She knew the tedious schedule of her daily duties had resumed. She didn't mope. Instead she headed to the exercise room and worked out, back to her suite and showered, then ate breakfast and learned of Tony's location. Today he was at the office, not home. She sighed with relief. That meant she had until five to do whatever she wanted. Already ten, traveling to and from the lake was a three-and-a-half-hour journey. She would need to get up earlier on days she wanted to go there. Perhaps that would be something she did on days he was out of town. She would miss her lake, but Claire was determined she wasn't going to risk losing her piece of paradise. She'd wait until a better time to go. Of course, that didn't mean she couldn't go into the woods for a walk. So she did. It still felt liberating to get away from the cameras.

That afternoon she spent at the pool. She returned to her suite and showered, ready for instructions by five. Catherine brought word; Mr. Rawlings would be home and they would dine in the dining room at seven. Claire didn't need Catherine's help with appropriate clothing, dining room meant formal. She knew how to follow the rules.

At six forty-five Claire went down to the sitting room and waited for dinner. A little after seven Tony joined her. "Good evening, Claire."

"Good evening, Anthony." They walked to the dining room.

"I went to your suite expecting to find you there."

"I apologize. I was told dinner would be in the dining room at seven, I didn't want to be late." She emphasized her obedience to his rules. Tony pulled out a chair, she sat. She couldn't help notice his eyes, black as night. She knew her impudence had an effect on him and she needed to be cautious. She was walking a slim hazardous line.

"Your punctuality is dutifully noted. It seems that my absence has helped you remember who is in charge and what guidelines you are to follow."

"Yes, your absence was advantageous on many counts." She placed the napkin on her lap. Tony's eyes were piercing. After a prolonged silence, Claire decided to lighten the mood. "I believe it helped me recognize I owe you much, not just the money to repay my debt, but the confidence you've shown in me." He was listening, "The confidence to trust me with your intimate beliefs." She paused and waited. He didn't comment. "I will not betray that confidence."

Cindy and Carlos entered the dining room, placed plates with food, and poured water and tea. Claire and Tony remained silent until the staff exited the dining room.

"Claire, if you are sincere, then you never cease to amaze me. If, however, you are playing me, you will regret it." His eyes were intense. He wanted to make her confess her scheme.

"Tony, what would I gain by playing you? I'm aware my present, future, and release are solely in your hands. I'm sorry for my behavior before you left." She was pretty sure she sounded earnest.

Tony seemed satisfied. He didn't tell her it was all right, instead he changed the subject, and they ate. After dinner they went out to the gardens for a stroll. It was there he asked about her walks in the woods. How far did she walk? Where did she go? How long was she gone? Claire didn't want to tell him about the lake, but she was afraid to lie. He could see on the video surveillance she left the yard at one time and didn't return until another.

She told him about the multiple clearings, insects, flowers, and animals. Then she told him about the lake. He seemed surprised. He'd seen the lake on his flyovers but it had to be six or seven miles from the house. Suddenly, she worried. "Is it still on your land?"

He appreciated her concern, but yes, she'd stayed on his land. As they conversed his eyes lightened. He reached into his breast pocket and brought out a black velvet box. "I found these for you in Italy. I thought they made a nice complement to your necklace."

Claire opened the box. Inside she discovered a pair of pearl earrings. The large cream colored pearls almost identical in size and color to the one on her grandmother's necklace were offset by white gold circles. They were pretty but not the same. Claire tried to understand his meaning.

Tony explained, "Your necklace is a cross, which is an X on its side. Now your earrings are O's - X's and O's." He smiled.

It wasn't as if she suddenly liked him, she didn't. However, she appreciated the thought he put into his gift. It was a sweet and unexpected gesture. "Thank you, Tony. That was very kind of you to think of me during your busy trip."

They made it through this storm. Leaving wasn't an option, but they seemed to reach an understanding. Tony knew he was in control. He didn't need to prove it. Claire knew she was in control of her actions, she could choose to fight or complain. Her plan was for self-preservation until she was free. This had been a good old-fashioned thunderstorm, loud and boisterous but no real damage.

Days passed and turned into weeks. It was the end of August and Claire's schedule remained constant. The only variable was Tony's work location. Before he left for Europe, he offered Eric for her use. Since his return he hadn't mentioned her leaving the property. She hadn't been off the estate since New York and that was a month ago. Truthfully, she didn't miss the cities, she missed the lake. She kept praying for him to be called away for a few days; it didn't happen.

Something else that hadn't happened since Tony's return was his threat of video screening. Other than the first night back, trying to bait her, he hadn't mentioned the videos. It was as if they no longer existed. Claire knew that wasn't true, but the illusion helped her compartmentalize.

Sundays usually involved staying at home, in his office, her suite, at the pool, anywhere that allowed for relaxation. Tony often needed to read or talk to Brent Simmons about something, but he slated Sundays for *his time* to *do as he pleased*. It was Sunday, the twenty-ninth of August, when Claire decided to ask Tony for a favor.

He told her once that if she wanted something she needed to ask. They lounged at the pool, enjoying the last few days of the season. "Tony, I have a favor to ask of you."

He lay on a lounge chair, his dark hair soft and wavy after drying in the sun, relaxing following a recent encounter in the pool. He wore swim trunks, which showed his firm, defined, tanned body. His eyes hidden behind sunglasses, he didn't move, but answered, "Go ahead."

"I would like to call my sister."

He sat up slowly, removed his sunglasses, and shot his piercing eyes her direction. "I believe this has been discussed and you know my decision. I have determined it is better that you don't have contact with your family." It sounded like a final statement. She persisted.

I remember you saying that. However, a lot of time has passed. I won't say anything to her you don't want me to." She could see Tony becoming irritated but decided to add more information, "Her birthday is on the thirty-first."

He took a breath, exhaled, and lay back down. Claire waited, he didn't answer. She put her head back on the chair and contemplated how to revisit the subject without being disrespectful of his answer, or lack thereof.

Tony closed his eyes against the sunlight. He thought about the framed pictures hidden in his suite, the ones from Claire's Atlanta apartment. He'd wondered how long it would take for her to ask to contact her family. It took five months. No doubt if the means had been available she would have contacted them sooner.

If her family consisted of poor farmers from Indiana, the call wouldn't be much of a risk. Actually, Tony wasn't concerned about her sister. It was her brother-in-law, John Vandersol, an accomplished attorney that was a potential threat. From humble beginnings, utilizing his intelligence and intuition, he had become an associate at a top-notch law firm in Albany, New York. This was a firm that rarely hired outside of Ivy League schools. The man was even under early consideration for partnership. Tony didn't feel comfortable with Claire having contact with him.

As far as Tony was concerned, the past five months had taken favorable, unexpected turns. Claire's behavior was a pleasant surprise, much better than he'd anticipated while planning her acquisition. Truthfully, while wanting to keep her and use her for himself, he hadn't been sure it would work. Plan B had always been and supposedly was still an option. But now that she'd been seen with him in public, it would be difficult to remain completely detached. He didn't want the addition of Emily, and especially John Vandersol, to upset his perfect equation.

Tony contemplated and a rush of fury swept his consciousness. He realized she was questioning—no, arguing his decision. Not only was she arguing, but he was considering her request. It was the damned pictures in the stupid frames. A small part of him cared that he'd taken all that away from her. That hadn't bothered him five months ago. It had actually been quite the coup, but now . . . Hell, it was just one call. Maybe *if* he could control the content. Reassuring himself—of course *he* could control the content, *he* controlled her. He could control a telephone call. Tony decided first he would see how badly she wanted to make this call. He would stand back and watch, see how far Claire would push, observing her resolve in the face of much adversity, as she attempted to manipulate him. Yeah, no lie, that courage turned him on. Finally, he said, "I will think about it."

He didn't bring up the subject again on Sunday. Monday came and went, they spent time together but he didn't bring up her request. Tuesday was Emily's birthday. He could sense Claire's impatience. Her self-control since Sunday was impressive. He wondered if she would just abandon the idea if he didn't bring it up.

Claire wasn't sure if Tony thought that by avoiding the subject she would forget her own sister's birthday, but she didn't. She'd been good and hadn't pushed. She rationalized -- he's busy, maybe he forgot. Deciding to wait through dinner, if he didn't mention it, she would bring it up.

They ate on the back patio with a slight breeze blowing her hair. The evenings were becoming increasingly cool and Claire regretted not bringing a sweater or light jacket to dinner. When they'd finished eating, Tony began to stand. Claire bit her lip and spoke, "Tony, today is Emily's birthday." She'd created an illusion of equality in her mind and didn't want to beg.

He resumed sitting and leaned into Claire, his voice slow and deliberate. "So you have decided that this is a subject worth risking reprimand? I believe that my last answer had been I would think about it."

Claire swallowed, held her head high, and looked directly into his dark eyes. "Yes, I feel talking to Emily on her birthday is worth the penalty you believe I deserve for pursuing the subject." Tony didn't speak but intently maintained their gaze. She waited for his response. Finally, she spoke again, "Tony, may I please call my sister for her birthday?"

"I have her telephone number in my office. You may call her from there." Claire's heart jumped and her eyes sparkled. She started to stand but he

102

indicated for her to remain seated. "You will speak to her on a speaker phone with me present. Before you call, we will discuss the limitations of your discussion." She hated his tone, the one he used when he felt the need to show his authority, but his words were saying she could talk to Emily. The rest didn't matter.

Claire nodded her head as Anthony spoke. "I understand. Thank you, Tony."

Walking down the marble corridor toward Tony's office Claire thought about her sister. They hadn't spoken in over five months. She fought the incredible urge to run the length of the corridor and grab his telephone. Once in his office, Tony instructed her to sit near his desk. She could see the phone; the anticipation was agony. First he proclaimed the guidelines she must follow: do not tell Emily or John that she had been or was living in Tony's house, only that she lived and worked in Iowa, near the Quad Cities. Claire should keep the conversation focused on Emily, avoid discussion of herself. If pressed, she could admit to accompanying him to various events. But this was *not* to be initiated by Claire. If the subject of *getting together* came up, Claire was to be evasive. The shorter the conversation the better the chance she wouldn't make a mistake. To emphasize her obedience, he added, "Disobeying these rules is *not* an option; the consequence will not be pleasant." He then asked if she had any questions, understood his rules, and was ready to call.

"I don't have any questions, Tony. I promise I understand the rules, and oh yes, I'm ready."

He removed a piece of paper from the top drawer of his desk and dialed the phone. Then, as if just occurring to him, he added, "There is a block on this line. My number will not appear on their caller ID." He hit the speaker button and Claire could hear Emily's line ring.

It rang and rang. Then she heard John's voice, but it wasn't really him, it was their voice mail. Her heart sank. She looked to Tony, "May I leave a message?" He nodded yes. John was still talking on the voice mail. "May I tell her I will try to reach her again?" The recording beeped. Finally, Tony nodded yes.

Keeping her tone as light as possible, considering the disappointment of reaching their voice mail, she said, "Hi Emily and John, it's Claire. I wanted to call and wish Emily a happy birthday. I'm sorry I missed you. I hope you're having a great day. Things are very busy, but I'll try to reach you again, happy birthday!" Tony hit the disconnect button. Claire didn't want to stop talking. She lowered her head and felt the tears. Resolved to accept the outcome, she looked up into Tony's gaze. "Thank you for allowing me to make that call. Do you need me right now or may I go to my room?"

"You may leave." Dejected, she rose. Tony continued, "I will be up to join you later. I have some work to complete first." Claire verbally acknowledged his plans and continued to walk toward the grand double doors. As she reached for the handle, he continued, his initial authoritative tone now more mellow. "Claire, New York is an hour later than Iowa. Perhaps they went out to dinner and a movie. You can try again later."

She didn't turn back around. She didn't want him to see the tears cascading down her cheeks. Though fighting sobs, she feigned resolve and articulated, "Thank you."

As she stepped into the cool corridor and closed the door to his office, Claire melted onto the marble floor. The staggering disappointment momentarily debilitated her. Eventually, her resolve grew. She regained composure and walked to her suite. Truthfully, she did appreciate his offer.

About nine in Iowa, they went back to his office to try again. To expedite the process, Claire looked to Tony and proclaimed she remembered the rules and wouldn't fail. The phone began to ring on the speaker. It only rang once when the voice of a woman on the other end answered, "Claire, is that you?"

Claire's heart soared, "Yes, Emily, it's me. Happy birthday, sis!"

Emily's voice hadn't changed. Claire heard the excitement of their reunion coming through the speaker. "Thank you. Hearing from you is the best birthday gift ever. Where are you? Are you all right? Why haven't you called us?"

Claire looked from the phone to Tony and then back to the phone. Tony's eyes spoke volumes. "Hey, slow down. I have a new job that keeps me very busy, but I couldn't miss talking to you on your special day. How are you doing? How is John? How is his law firm?" She'd done it. She succeeded in getting Emily to talk about them.

Emily said she was fine. School had recently started, and she thought this was going to be a good class. John was fine, just very busy. The law firm was good, he was an associate now and the more hours he billed the better chance he had of making partner. Claire could have spoken with her for hours. They had so much catching up to do. Instead, Claire apologized and told her she needed to run. She loved her and please give John her love. Emily said she would, but John was right there and would like to talk to her. Claire looked at Tony. His eyes darkened and he shook his head no.

Claire said she would like to, but another time, she really needed to run. "Have a great birthday. Bye." Tony pressed the disconnect button.

Claire stared at the telephone for the longest time. This was one of those junctures. She could be sad the conversation was short or she could choose to be happy there had been a conversation. She decided to pick *B*.

Standing to leave Tony's office, she looked up to see him leaning back in his chair. His eyes devoured her as he unbuckled his belt. With sickening comprehension Claire understood, in his mind he'd shown a kindness, now he expected gratitude - *quid pro quo*.

*If life were predictable it would cease to be life
and be without flavor.*
—Eleanor Roosevelt

Chapter 15

"**W**e have been invited to a Labor Day barbeque tomorrow." Sitting on the sunporch, reading her new novel, and enjoying the Sunday afternoon, Tony's casual announcement surprised Claire. The warm gentle breeze and faint smell of cut grass gave way to a rush of anxiety and disbelief. "We? Who would invite me?"

"Courtney, Brent Simmons' wife," Tony said while lounging on the loveseat with his laptop on his outstretched legs. His light brown eyes gazed at Claire as she questioned him.

"Why? What does she know about me?"

"Well, Brent met you when I brought you to New York, and Courtney knows I have been seen with the same woman on multiple occasions. Since they are probably my closest friends, she wants to meet you and invited both of us to tomorrow's barbeque."

Despite her sudden rush of anxiety at meeting his *closest friends*, Claire knew her fate wasn't in her hands. "Are we going?"

"Yes. It starts at noon and we will leave here by eleven thirty."

"I guess it sounds like fun." Her tone was tentative. She wondered what these friends would think of her, if they would know him well enough to know the truth about her. If they didn't, how should she act? Her stomach began to knot with unanswered concerns. "Please let me know if there are different instructions for an intimate barbeque versus a public event."

Tony set his laptop on the table and contemplated Claire's honest question. His words sounded instructive, but his tone wasn't authoritative, just matter-of-fact as they looked at one another. The late summer breeze caused strands of her long golden brown hair to float around her beautiful face. Her green eyes saw only him as her expression reflected her sincere interest in his advice. "You have done well at public events, this will be different. I believe there will be four or five couples present. You met Brent. His wife is Courtney. They have two children who are grown and live away. Brent's law partner Thomas Miller will be there. His wife is Beverly. She owns a renowned design firm in Bettendorf. Brent is a few years my senior. Thomas and Beverly are closer to my age, they have no children. Another guest will be Elijah Summer and his long-time companion MaryAnn. Elijah is another client of Brent and Tom's. He has made a fortune in the entertainment business. He enjoys telling stories about some of his more famous clients. Personally I believe he enjoys hearing himself talk," Tony paused and smiled, "much more than I like to hear him talk. And the last couple will be Timothy Bronson and his wife Sue. Tim is a junior vice president at my local office. He is young, but has proven himself. I asked Brent to invite him, make him feel involved."

That was all helpful information, Claire desperately tried to remember names: Brent and Courtney, Thomas and Beverly, Elijah and Sue . . . no, Elijah and Mary Ann, Timothy and Sue. But that really didn't answer her question. Claire thought to herself -- there were wives and long-time companions, what did that make her? "Tony, who am I?"

"You are a *rumor*." Perhaps it was the calm setting of the sunporch or their recent understanding, whatever the reason, Tony spoke thoughtfully. He explained he had spent his entire life working, accomplishing goals, and fulfilling self-made agendas. He'd been in relationships, most very short-lived. He believed strongly in appearances and had not been willing to risk the perception people have of him on a woman. Claire thought about his words and his honesty, and right or wrong believed him. "You told me that you would not betray my confidence."

"I did, and I still mean that."

"I believe you know what could happen if you did." Feeling the prickling sensation which accompanies chills along your arms and legs, Claire believed she did know, but she didn't confirm that verbally. She allowed Tony to continue talking. "And therefore I have allowed you to become part of my life." She thought he honestly meant that as a compliment, and she should be flattered; however, it felt more ominous.

She wondered and worried about her release. This quiet peaceful setting wasn't the time or place to voice her concerns. Instead, she decided to put it away and deal with it later. "Since you have been seen with me at various events, and I'm rarely seen with the same woman over time, you are a rumor. There have been countless speculations about you. Everyone, like the man at the benefit, wants to know who you are and what you are to me."

Claire admitted to herself she too would like the answer to those questions. "I saw our picture in a *People Magazine* from your library."

He said their picture had appeared in many publications. His publicist had kept information limited to the basics: her name and that she lived in Atlanta. The people at this barbeque were part of his inner circle and wouldn't betray his trust. Other than Elijah Summer, their jobs and livelihood depended on Tony. Elijah was a more public person, but he respected Tony and wouldn't compromise their mutual friendship.

106

She tried one more time, "And I am . . ."

"Persistent." His eyes were soft and light with a contented expression. He spoke as he moved from the loveseat to the floor of the sunporch. "Well, I would say more than an acquaintance." Kneeling in front of her, gently spreading her knees, he moved his hand under the hem of her skirt. Their eyes met as the sides of his mouth turned upward into a devilish grin. "Shall we say... *companion?*"

If that was a question, she didn't answer. Her attentions were turned to his actions. His touch eventually directed her from the chair to the rug. The windows and doors were open and they were exposed to the world. It was *his* house, he didn't care. Although the straw rug was rough, his movements were calm like his tone. The staff didn't return until they were done.

Late Sunday night, Shelby on the Weather Channel, said a cold front would pass over Iowa. Claire awoke and opened the drapes to find condensation on the windows with crystal clear skies beyond. She stepped onto her balcony, looked at the trees, and smelled the fresh autumn air. The cool concrete beneath her bare feet and the goose bumps on her arms and legs confirmed the decrease in temperature. Wrapping her arms and her thick cashmere robe around her body, she entertained fleeting memories of autumns past. She always loved summers but autumns were special too, with cookouts and football games. Today the change of season brought sadness, another reminder of time slipping away.

While in the shower, she contemplated the impending barbeque. It was a new situation, a new test, and it made her anxious. She hadn't received a direct answer to her question, so Claire decided to approach the people like she was told to approach Emily. She would try to turn conversation away from herself and divulge as little information as possible. Evasive answers would be best. There was a time she loved parties, getting together with people, laughing, talking, and sharing. Now she was petrified of saying or doing something wrong.

Stepping from the shower, Claire discovered her clothes on her bed. Sometimes that upset her, other times, like today, it was reassuring—one less decision to mess up. She did her hair, makeup, and dressed. At ten thirty she was ready, an hour before they were to leave.

The balcony held two chairs. She sat plaintively and watched the trees through sunglassed eyes. The bright sunshine caused a rapid increase in temperature as the trees rustled in the gentle breeze. Vibrant hues of yellow and orange were beginning to emerge from the green canvas. Her mind wandered through the woods to her lake. She hadn't been back since Tony's return. That is to say, physically. Mentally she would be sitting on the shore, watching the minnows or listening to the water rhythmically lap the shore. As a matter of fact she was sitting on the shore in her mind when Tony materialized behind her. "Oh, good morning, Tony, I didn't hear you enter."

He eased himself into the other chair. "Good morning, where were you?"

"I've been here. I have nowhere else to go."

"You seemed faraway."

"I was thinking about the trees," being partially honest. "Their leaves are changing already."

It was as if he never really looked at them, so he did. "I guess they are. That happens." He didn't concern himself with matters he couldn't influence. "Are you ready for our outing?" She said she was and they proceeded down the grand stairs. "I have a car out front, we can go."

When Tony opened the door she saw a small Lexus SC 10 convertible, but no Eric. Tony opened the passenger door and she got in. He went around to the driver's seat. She couldn't help but smile at him. He wore jeans that accentuated his trim waist, a button-down shirt, white, which showed his tan, his powerful chest, and shoulders. His hair was perfect, and as she beheld his profile she saw the "red-hot sexy" *People Magazine* mentioned. He glanced at her as he started the car, her smile seemed different. "What?" he asked.

"I guess I forgot you drive, without Eric I mean."

Tony smiled. "I love to drive. However, it's more advantageous to be driven and accomplish work during my commutes." The convertible felt liberating with the wind and air invigorating their senses. Thankfully, Claire had decided to wear her hair in a side braid. She laid her head on the headrest and watched the road twist and turn, the vibrant sapphire blue of the sky and the autumn colors made for picture-perfect views as Tony drove the narrow country roads. The aroma of autumn was in the air. Claire inhaled as memories of pumpkins and leaves filled her subconscious.

The car slowed to a stop along a quiet side road. Tony gently touched Claire's braid. "Good choice of style." He smiled "I am needed in Chicago for a couple of days next week." He continued to play with the end of her braid. Claire thought about her lake. "I have made you an appointment at a very exclusive spa in my apartment building." Her attention refocused on him and his words. "Your hair needs trimming and you can have a manicure, pedicure, full body message, sauna, whatever you desire."

She started to respond, "Thanks, but no thanks." He stopped her and went on, "I just trust that it will not need to be canceled."

Confused, Claire asked, "Why would it need to be canceled?" As the words escaped her lips she wondered why she cared, she actually didn't want to go to a spa. She wanted time alone to go to the lake.

His hand moved from her braid, gently removed her sunglasses, and lifted her chin, holding her eyes to his. She watched as the dark deepened. "If today doesn't go as I believe it should, a massage may not be possible. We wouldn't want appearances to be questioned." There was no ambiguity to his statement. Claire received his meaning loud and clear. She suddenly felt chilled.

Maintaining his forced eye contact, Claire responded, "Tony, I fully comprehend the importance of appearances. I will not let you down."

He handed her the sunglasses, moved his hands back to the steering wheel, and put the car in gear. "As long as we are clear, public failure is not an option." Claire reassured him, they were clear.

The Simmonses' home was grand, probably about a quarter of the size of Tony's but large by normal standards, with a good deal of land. The Lexus moved slowly through the gates and up their drive as Tony turned to view Claire. She felt his gaze and maintained her mask. By all outward appearance she looked beautiful and content, the ingredients to the perfect companion. She saw his grip on the wheel relax and knew his brown eyes were muted.

They parked on a brick circle directly in front of the home beside many equally nice automobiles. The front door opened as Tony opened Claire's door. He gently put his arm around her and led her toward the entry. Claire remembered Brent, but Courtney wasn't what she had pictured. She looked younger than a woman with two grown children. Courtney was slender, with short brown hair, soft blue eyes, and a refreshingly engaging smile. Instantly, Claire liked her. Brent may owe his livelihood to Tony, but Courtney obviously felt very comfortable around both of them.

Courtney immediately hugged Claire. "You must be Claire. I am so excited to finally meet you. My dear, you are more beautiful than your pictures!" Claire felt overwhelmed. She introduced herself and called Courtney *Mrs. Simmons*. When she looked to Tony, he was already in conversation with Brent.

"Oh goodness, call me Courtney. We will let those two get their business out of the way so we can have some fun, and I'll take you around and introduce you to our other guests." Tony didn't seem to object, so Claire allowed herself to be ushered off.

The house was stunning yet homey, not like Tony's. Children played on these floors, a family laughed, loved, and each room contained priceless memories. Courtney walked Claire through her home toward the kitchen. Designed very modern, brushed stainless steel appliances, granite countertops, and tall cabinets were accentuated with intricate tile. Golden lighting fixtures hung at appropriate intervals, not for light but ambiance. The kitchen wasn't only functional, but was also intended as the centerpiece of the home. The stove was located on a large island that contained a wraparound bar with six tall stools. Out from the kitchen Claire could see a large family room leading to a sunporch and their backyard.

Claire couldn't see beyond the porch, but she did notice the suddenly silent room of guests. She couldn't help but feel their eyes on her, assessing and evaluating. Keeping her mask in place she moved forward. She hadn't expected to face these people without Tony.

Courtney didn't leave Claire's side as she introduced her to the others. First, she met Tom and Bev. Claire did her best to be polite and social. "It is so nice to meet you. I believe Tony told me that you," looking at Tom, "and Brent are partners?" They continued with some polite conversation. Claire asked Bev about her design business. Years of bartending taught Claire the art of small talk.

Next were Sue and Tim. "Tim, I have heard wonderful things about you." Claire watched as Sue's smile widened and Tim's expression softened. She could tell he seemed stressed. Working for Tony could do that to a person. Perhaps some positive reinforcement would help.

Then it was on to Eli and MaryAnn. It didn't take Claire long to understand what Tony meant by Elijah enjoying his own stories. Lastly, Courtney introduced Claire to the couple with Eli and MaryAnn, Chance and

Bonnie. Claire wasn't prepared for this couple. She wondered if Tony knew they were there. Courtney explained that Chance was an associate of Eli's in town for a visit, so of course they were welcome to join them. Chance seemed nice enough, but Bonnie made no secret of her evaluation of Claire.

Courtney offered Claire a drink. Requesting water, Courtney obliged but suggested Claire consider something a little more fun. "We have some fantastic sangria."

Just then Tony and Brent joined them in the kitchen. Tony looked so relaxed wearing jeans and holding a beer, it almost made Claire laugh. Appearances were everything.

Brent did his own barbequing, and the men joined him out on the patio. The women gathered around the island as Courtney busied with side dishes. They all offered to help but she wouldn't hear of it, confessing she hadn't prepared a thing. Her cook did it all yesterday and now she was only putting them into the appropriate dishes. The conversation quickly went to cooking. Some enjoyed it, others did not. Did Claire enjoy cooking? She told them she did. Did Tony like her cooking? She laughed and said she hadn't prepared many meals for him. She left out the part about her not cooking in over five months because she'd been held hostage.

It seemed like Bonnie tried to ask more *Claire specific* questions, but Courtney did a fantastic job of moving the conversation. Claire had apparently made a quick friend of Sue by complimenting her husband. Sue ran flank for Courtney helping Claire avoid the invasive inquiries.

Sue looked about Claire's age, mid to late twenties, very pretty, blonde and tan. It was nice to talk to a female who was her contemporary. While the men cooked, Claire learned that Sue had a degree in art appreciation and worked part-time at the art museum in Davenport. Tim didn't feel Sue needed to work. Financially she didn't. However, Tim worked long hours and she needed something to do with her time. After she mentioned the long hours, Sue immediately added, "But he is glad to do it." It took a minute, but Claire realized the additional information was because she was the boss' *companion*.

The dinner tasted fabulous. Claire hadn't eaten *normal* food in five months, everything was always healthy. She wanted to devour the entire platter of hamburgers. She, however, chose the barbecued chicken or Tony did for her. She managed some of Courtney's homemade side dishes and savored every bite.

The conversation remained benign and chatty. Bonnie didn't only question Claire any chance she could, she also approached Tony. When they were introduced, Chance had the good sense to address Tony as Mr. Rawlings. Bonnie wasn't as astute. Of course, Tony told Chance that at gatherings of friends he could call him Anthony.

Tony had been right about his inner circle. Even Eli was annoyed at Bonnie's abrasive curiosity. Claire didn't need to lie or deceive. Bonnie continually found herself cut off before Claire had a chance to respond.

After they ate, the men retired to a lower level. Claire would later learn that it contained a beautiful handcrafted bar, pool table, and large television.

The women took a bottle of wine and sat on the sunporch. The sunshine with the cool air felt wonderful. To be sitting with five other women chatting felt like a performance, unreal. Their conversation ran from books, to movies, to sexy movie stars. MaryAnn shared some inside scoop on some of Eli's clients. Sexy stars led to sex. Claire politely excused herself and asked Courtney about the ladies' room.

It was on her way back to the porch when she overheard MaryAnn and Bonnie in a room off the main hall. "Bonnie, what is your problem? You are embarrassing yourself with your persistence about Claire and Tony."

"I'm an inquisitive person. I want to find out what the rest of the world wants to know. Why is he, Anthony Rawlings, interested in her? She's a nobody."

"Frankly, Bonnie, it's none of your damn business. It is none of any of our business. Tony is a private man. And as far as a *nobody*, I guess that depends on who you ask. Tony must think she is somebody. If he wants Claire in his life, good for him."

"Hell no! Good for her," Bonnie exclaimed. "The guy is drop-dead gorgeous and has money to burn. He hardly takes his eyes off her. Do you think she paid for those clothes she is wearing? The blouse alone is over $500. She's getting herself a sugar daddy. Look how young and skinny she is, why she—"

"Stop it. Stop it now or we will tell Courtney we need to leave. I will tell Eli what you have done and you and Chance will go back to California. Perhaps you can get started on Chance's job search." MaryAnn's control of the situation made Claire smile. Bonnie told MaryAnn she would stop. Claire let them proceed to the porch and waited a few minutes before joining the group. Once there, she smiled at MaryAnn but didn't glance toward Bonnie.

The men and women came together outside for some conversation, dessert, and drinks. Claire passed on the dessert and sat with Tony's arm around her shoulders. Brent had a fire pit built into his patio. The cool autumn evening, crackling fire, warmth, and distinct aroma created a pleasurable atmosphere. At about six thirty Tony whispered to Claire that they should leave. Everyone seemed genuinely saddened, Claire included.

It had been a nice day, better than anticipated.

As they said goodbyes, Sue handed Claire a piece of paper. Surprised, Claire opened it. It was a telephone number. "Call me, we can do lunch." Claire smiled and said she would try.

They went to the car and drove away. Perhaps they drove a mile, maybe two when Tony stopped the car on the side of the road and put out his hand. He didn't speak but she knew what he wanted. She placed Sue's telephone number in his palm. "Tony—"

With the same hand that held the little white piece of paper he roughly covered her mouth. "Not now. We will discuss it when we get home." He let go of her face and resumed driving.

No words were uttered during their drive home. Claire's internal monologue, however, raged: *this is ridiculous. Sue was being friendly. I had no idea she would do such a thing. What is the big deal? Why does he have to react so fast and so violent like a freak'n tornado?*

Tony pulled the car to the front door. He didn't open Claire's door. Instead, he told her to go to her suite, he would be up later. He had things to do, like cancel a spa appointment. His tone was curt and his eyes dark. She wanted to run. Instead she got out of the car and walked boldly into the house, through the large doors, up the grand staircase, and down the southeast corridor to her suite. Once she closed her door, she felt her heart race and her internal monologue continue: *this was such a nice day. I met Tony's friends and they were nice. I wanted to tell him about what I heard. I wanted to tell him what a great time I had.*

Claire knew what Anthony was doing. Starting in the car, he was contemplating, overthinking, and overanalyzing the entire situation. She knew if he would just let her, she could explain. Oh god! She wanted to lie down, scream, and cry. But she also knew he could be watching right now. She refused to give him the satisfaction, refused to let him know how worried she was about his decision. Truthfully, she was worried - actually, terrified. Claire feared the possible return of his other persona.

There are two things a person should never be angry at,
what they can help, and what they cannot.
—Plato

Chapter 16

Claire sat at her table, writing. Tony couldn't see what she was writing. The cameras didn't have enough zooming capability. Her body language didn't look nervous. It showed a proud and defiant pose. He watched as she wrote, sitting straight, her neck tall and proud. The only hint of uneasiness would be the way her feet fidgeted under her chair.

From his office screens, he could access different views of the room. From another view, she sat farther away, and he could see her bed in the background. Of course, there was the view that kept the bed centered, but the table wasn't visible from that one.

Trying to contemplate his options and the consequences of her actions, Tony closed his eyes and reviewed the day. When he entered her suite, he anticipated anxiety, but found calm. And that smile when they got in the car. God! Her smile when it was real melted him. Her emerald eyes could glisten and shine. Of course, he didn't see her real smile much. He did today, and seeing her with his friends, she was perfect.

He told himself the reason he had trouble keeping his eyes off her was strictly because he needed to monitor her behavior. It had nothing to do with how beautiful she looked. Now, as he watched the screens, he wondered what she was thinking. Was she thinking about him, about her future? It was all up to him. She knew that. He knew that. The power didn't give him the satisfaction it once had.

Damn, why in the hell did Sue give her that phone number? What did they talk about when he wasn't there? His head filled with unanswered questions and plausible scenarios. She wanted to leave him. Why wouldn't she? Did she initiate a plan? Why wouldn't she follow his rules?

His internal monologue momentarily caused him to lose focus of the screens. Now as he scanned, she was gone. He scanned the other views until he noticed the open door to the balcony. He could only see the back of her head. He needed another camera installed.

Over an hour had passed since they came home. Making Claire wait for him was part of his plan. But watching her, it seemed she controlled her nerves better than he. Maybe he needed fresh air too. No, he needed to make a decision. It was his mantra. She knew the rules. It didn't matter if you do something 99 percent right, perfection was required. The fact remained she must have broken his rules. He needed to make a decision. Behaviors have consequences, consequences can be unpleasant. Tony told himself he had warned her, *she* chose not to listen.

She inhaled and exhaled. The country air filled her lungs with cool, refreshing strength. Claire thought about the people she'd met and about talking and laughing. It was fantastic. Courtney's reassurance and Tony's unusually kind smiles relieved her initial anxiety. She knew it was a charade. But it was fun, getting out around people. Then the telephone number came. It boggled her mind that something so incredibly simple could cause such ridiculous repercussions.

She thought about Tony. He would enter her suite soon, of course without knocking. And he would have some verdict regarding her insubordination. The fact that she wasn't insubordinate wouldn't alter his decision. She wondered if he handled business issues this way too, without input. With her mind scrambling, she asked herself, *Do I have any options?*

Her wild emotions caused a rush of adrenaline concealing the cool night air from her consciousness. His impending decision terrified her. His smiles today gratified her and his physique in jeans aroused her. How could her body defy her mind so severely? Claire believed her body was the true offender of insubordination!

Thinking about Bonnie made Claire laugh at the irony. She thought Claire was securing a *sugar daddy*. The reality couldn't be farther from the truth. However, at that moment, instead of wanting to explain, she was honored to be associated with Anthony Rawlings. *Irrational* best described her thoughts. Maybe if she could get her body and mind to work together she could devise some kind of plan. The sound of the suite door closing brought her thoughts to the present.

Tony didn't speak, but his eyes did, acknowledging Claire on the balcony and bidding her to enter. She did. Determined to continue the bogus act of strength, she walked within inches of him and stood her ground. He didn't greet her, instead he lifted her chin. His eyes looked as cold as his icy hand felt. Claire knew without a doubt, this will *not* be good. "What did we discuss just before we arrived at the Simmons?"

Her eyes flashed fire but her words sounded respectful. "I told you I wouldn't let you down and I didn't."

"Actions have consequences, I have told you that. Why is that difficult for you to understand?"

"Tony, it isn't. If—" He stopped her, not with a gentle finger to the lips but with a slap to her left cheek. Claire stopped speaking, her eyes moist; she refused to look away or back down.

"Actions have consequences. I have been thinking quite a bit about an appropriate punishment."

Claire decided she had nothing to lose. There was punishment coming, so she might as well push her luck. "Tony, if you would please let me speak. I know your decision is set, but allow me to talk." Impressed by her strength, he nodded and told her to make it quick. "I was nervous about going to this barbeque today, but I had a wonderful time. Courtney was the perfect hostess and very charming. Everyone was nice to me. I really didn't know what to expect." She tried to hurry. "Well, everyone except Bonnie. By the way, I overheard Bonnie and MaryAnn talking and everyone there had your back. That includes me. And Sue, well Sue is lonely. She told me Tim works long hours, which she mentioned he enjoys, but she is lonely. At some point, she asked me for my number. I don't have one -- as you know. But I thought that sounded dumb, everyone has a cell phone, so I just said I didn't have it with me and I didn't know my number. I never call myself. So I am guessing that's why she gave me her number. I really didn't know she was going to do it. If I did, would I have her do it right in front of you?"

Tony hadn't stopped her, so she decided to keep rambling, pacing a little. "When Courtney introduced me to Tim and Sue, I told Tim I'd heard good things about him from you. I can only guess that made Sue and I instant friends. Women love to hear good things about their husbands. I would have told you if I'd gotten the number without you knowing. I have no way of calling. And if I just didn't call, it would appear rude. I know how you feel about appearances." She didn't know what else to say, but at least she had said her piece. "I really did well today, this is just a misunderstanding, and your friends are very nice."

She stood and maintained eye contact. Tony continued speaking as if no words had been uttered. "I have decided you may choose. Perhaps you would like to know your choices?"

Claire's heart sank. She lowered herself into a chair at the table and looked away. Nothing she said mattered. He hadn't listened to a word. "Tony, your decision is made, I don't care." Defeat filled her voice. She looked at the table, where on a piece of paper was a list of *positives* from her day.

"The first option is a two-week timeout in your suite."

What? That never crossed her mind. There was no way, she couldn't take that. She glared at him.

Tony watched. She stood and met him face to face. God, her strength captivated him. "Then I choose number two." Claire's voice sounded resilient. He didn't respond.

The silence grew. He wanted her. He wanted to tell her he was sorry, he overreacted, but that wasn't him. He couldn't.

"Very well, undress."

She didn't hesitate, she obeyed his command. She started by unbuttoning her blouse, one button at a time. Then she shimmied out of her slacks, she didn't argue or complain, and maintained eye contact the entire time. Tony's arousal was becoming difficult to conceal. Her body trembled slightly before him and his demeanor dissolved.

"Claire, come here." She did. He held her shoulders and looked into her green eyes. "Damn you, Claire." He pulled her close. "I make snap decisions based on the visible evidence. Appearances are important. I assumed you had something planned with Sue, something I hadn't approved. I was wrong. Your speech," he lifted her chin, gently this time, as his tone softened, "was very brave." He watched her expression. "It helped me see I'd jumped to the wrong conclusion."

He put his head down on her hair. Claire exhaled at the unexpected revelation: Anthony Rawlings was apologizing. She stood still while he encircled her with his arms, her trembling ceased and she let her face fall against his chest, inhaling the scent of smoke on his shirt. She felt his erection against her hips and the tension began to build within her depths. Tony's tone, now mellow, "Up until the moment Sue handed you that note, I was extremely proud of you. You were amazing. Courtney told me that about ten times." Claire lifted her eyes to see his expression. It was smiling like his tone. Claire smiled and felt her body relax against his. "There is something I would like us to do."

The relief of his apology overwhelmed her. Her body continued its disregard for reason. She wanted him to take her and didn't hesitate. "Whatever it is, yes."

"Your hair, smells like smoke. I would like us to shower." Claire took Tony's hand and led him to her shower. He followed. Once there she helped him undress, and he started undoing her braid. Under the warm spray of the shower he wet her hair, added shampoo, and gently massaged. "Your hair is beautiful, but it really needs trimming. And the weather is getting colder, so maybe some highlights. I believe you will enjoy the spa. It has a great reputation."

She turned to face him. "You didn't cancel my appointment?"

Smiling tenderly he said, "No, I guess I hoped something would change my mind." After working the cream rinse into her hair, he took the shower gel and began to lather Claire's back. Wrapping his arms around her, he lathered her breasts and stomach. Finally, he couldn't control himself any longer. Claire didn't want him to.

His tender touch caused an ache deep inside of her. He turned her around and lifted her body. She wrapped her legs around him and his mouth excitedly nibbled her breasts. His tongue created intense sensations as it tantalized her hard round nipples. She gripped his wide shoulders and let her fingers run through his wet hair. His strong arms and torso kept her body pinned against the wall of the shower. She yearned for him.

He tempted her with his fingers until self-control was beyond his reach. He filled her completely. Thunderous convulsions overtook her body. She expected his actions, but the fulfillment made her back arch and sounds escape her lips. Their bodies moved as one, not because of instructions or

116

demands. Instead, the cause was erotic carnal physical instinct. In time the ardent passion moved from the shower to the bed. He received his desires, but he made sure Claire did too.

At some point during the night, Tony asked Claire what she overheard. She told him. At first, she didn't want to say anything about her looking for a sugar daddy, but why hide anything now? Tony laughed.

He was happy to learn about MaryAnn, and that Courtney and Sue were so helpful throughout the day. She told Tony how much she liked seeing him in jeans. Definitely sexy, Claire told him. He told her he preferred her without jeans or anything else. That started them again.

Claire's spa appointment would be the following Wednesday. Initially she didn't want to go, but now she thought about Chicago and Tony's apartment. "How many apartments do you have?"

"As many as I need. I don't like hotels much." They both drifted off to sleep.

Tony woke before his alarm. Hearing Claire's soft and delicate breathing, he saw her curled into a ball on the far side of the bed, covered only by a sheet. With the pale light of the lingering moon he noticed her chestnut hair fanned around her head, damp and wavy, her body petite, soft, and supple. He carefully lifted the blankets and covered her. As he watched, the warmth of the blankets allowed her to unconsciously relax and settle into a deeper slumber.

This was not his plan. Things had been in the works for so long and now emotions were wreaking havoc. It was supposed to be easy. Her only purpose was for physical enjoyment, release of energy, and personal pleasure. He had watched her for so long. He told himself he deserved that. Yet somehow, now while at work, in a meeting, on a plane, anywhere, without warning he would recall something she said or did and a smile would come to his lips. Tony even noticed strange looks from Brent, a visible sign his thoughts were revealing themselves.

This was wrong. Tony didn't want to have feelings. The sex was great. It was okay to want her, dominate her, and control her. It was *not* okay to *want* to be with her, *please* her, and *love* her. Yet every one of his senses desired Claire. Watching her sleep, he wanted to see her emerald-green eyes that flared when she was upset, her neck that straightened with defiance even when her words accommodated his demands, and her body that filled his every waking thought. He wanted to touch her skin, warm, soft yet firm, and her long silky hair. He wanted to taste her. He wanted to smell her scent when he first came home, clean and fresh with her chosen perfume; and the aroma of her after sex, warm, moist, and exhausted. And he wanted to hear her. At this moment, he heard her faint breathing but he also liked to hear her endless talk. He knew she longed for companionship and camaraderie. He also knew he was currently her only choice. He tried desperately to appear uninterested, but her voice filled him with an intense desire he'd never experienced. That desire had a sexual component, but it also contained a desire to fulfill her yearnings. Anthony Rawlings never previously considered fulfilling someone else's desires. His entire adult life had been about *his* wants, goals, ambitions, and needs.

As his mind pondered these dilemmas, he thought about her just a few feet away. He wanted her again. He knew he could wake her and she would accommodate his demands. Laying his head back on the pillow he remembered the sex they experienced and wondered *when did this happen?* He no longer wanted to dominate but to satisfy.

This situation was completely unplanned. His entire life, business, everything was calculated, *how could this happen?*

He hadn't realized until he heard himself apologize. When he entered her suite he knew what he was going to say. It wasn't what he said. Anthony Rawlings could count on one hand the people to whom he'd apologized. Now this woman, a piece of his plan, was on that shortlist.

At the Simmonses she performed beyond his expectation. Then his overreaction almost ruined everything. Claire's strength, standing up to him, explaining the situation, and then not complaining yet complying with his punishment touched him. But when she was relieved by his realization, instead of upset by his overreaction, she melted him.

In reflection he berated himself. He should have stayed indifferent, dominant, and in charge. The words from his past echoed in his memory, "Only the weak apologize." He reconsidered waking her, fulfilling the indifferent domineering qualities that would prove he wasn't weak. Then he saw her peaceful expression and thought of her giving and surrendering herself over and over. Quietly, he got out of bed, put on his jeans, and left her suite. Stepping into the corridor, he decided to workout.

There is something perverse about more than enough.
When we have more, it is never enough. It is always somewhere
out there, just out of reach. The more we acquire,
the more elusive enough becomes.
—Unknown

Chapter 17

Clawson tried one more time. "It is very easy. Textiles have made you a fortune, a fortune you can now plant and invest to grow a lot more. This is 1977. The real money isn't in creating. It is in owning and selling. See these figures?" He handed Nathaniel the reports. "You have capital not only in profit margins but also in secured retirement plans. That money is just sitting there, waiting for those employees to get old. Hell, many of them won't be eligible for retirement for another twenty years. Use that money, invest it. Grow it. Right now it's just rotting away in these accounts."

Samuel stayed quiet as long as he could. His father's dark eyes were starting to flash dollar signs. "Clawson, the problem with your plan is that our employees own that money, not us. They've entrusted us to keep that money for them so it will be available when they retire. And it is growing interest."

"With all due respect, Mr. Rawls, have you seen the interest rates? Your employees will have their money because you aren't going to lose it. You're growing it. Then when the day is done, they'll have their retirement and Rawls Corp. will have additional profits." Clawson spoke to Samuel but hoped Nathaniel was the one listening.

He was. Nathaniel said, "Jesus, Samuel, have you looked at these reports? Where are the figures on Hong Kong Industrials? Since the exchange-trade options change of seventy-three, it's a cake-walk to manipulate these options." Clawson handed Nathaniel the reports. "We set our strike price. If the stock price starts to move out of the option near expiration, we set the cap."

Clawson smiled. The old man was finally getting it. "You have the capital to do that."

Samuel threw a report on the table. "It *isn't* our capital."

Looking first to the suddenly disorganized stacks of papers, then to his son, Nathaniel's brown eyes darkened. "Like hell it isn't. It is my goddamn company. I built it from nothing. Do you think those employees you're so damned concerned about would have a job if I didn't work my ass off thirty years ago?"

*Who will tell whether one happy moment of love or the joy of
breathing or walking on a bright morning and smelling the fresh
air is not worth all the suffering and effort which life implies.*
—Erich Fromm

Chapter 18

A week later they flew to Chicago. Tony absorbed himself in his work and laptop as Claire sat quietly and thought about the city. It had been a frequent haunt during her college days. Valparaiso was only an hour and twenty minutes from the Loop. She and her sorority sisters would spend entire afternoons or evenings enjoying the sights. They would shop, dine, or go to the theater. They knew their way to all the best deals.

Claire remembered the fun as they rode the L or the train around the city. Sometimes they would go with guys to a baseball game, usually the Cubs. She enjoyed watching people at Wrigley Field. Not really a baseball fan, she liked warm evenings with a group of friends, enjoying hot dogs and beer. They would all pile into someone's vehicle and road-trip. It really didn't get better than that. They were even known to blow off classes for a day at Wrigley. Claire rationalized it as academic research, her major being meteorology and baseball held outdoors, it all made sense.

Friends made baseball fun. To Claire, the guys, all from the same fraternity, were more like brothers. After a brief romance her freshman year she decided to concentrate on school instead of love. Suddenly, Claire realized her reminiscing made her sad. She wondered where those friends were today. She became so busy concentrating on her career that she lost touch with most of them. Maybe if they'd stayed connected they would have noticed her missing last March.

As the jet approached the private airport, Claire saw the skyline against the blue of the lake. She told herself to put the sadness away. Compartmentalize. She should concentrate on great times in Chicago. But she wondered, when driving there in an old minivan, she knew fun times were ahead; now leaving the private jet and entering the backseat of the leased limousine, what was in store?

Eric chauffeured the limousine as they drove toward the lake at seven thirty in the morning. Claire could see the buildings, smell the exhaust, and feel the vibration of the road as the car turned north on Lake Shore Drive. She felt more at home than she had in months. Filled with excitement, she wanted to talk about everything they passed: McCormick Place, Soldier Field, and Grant Park. As they approached Millennium Park, she thought about the concerts which took place all summer long.

However, she didn't speak. Tony was occupied on his cell phone. He'd been in a conversation with someone since they landed. His voice sounded amicable, but she could see his body language. It told another story. Listening to Claire give a tour of Chicago wouldn't help his disposition. She also worried he may not approve of her comfort level with Chicago. Originally she didn't want to join him on this trip, now she couldn't wait to enjoy the city.

The limousine pulled up to the Reliance Building and Tony gathered his briefcase, laptop, and cell phone. Eric came around and opened the door. Still talking on his phone, Tony nodded to Claire and got out. She found herself in the familiar situation, being chauffeured to a completely unknown destination.

Before they arrived, Tony informed her she could rest at his apartment. He hadn't mentioned the location or when he would return. She took a deep breath and waited while Eric moved the car through the crowded streets. In a short time the limousine idled in a line approaching the front entrance to the Trump Tower.

Eric lowered the window that separated the two compartments and gave Claire the first information on her destination. "Ms. Claire, Mr. Rawlings' apartment is the eighty-ninth floor of Trump Tower. Security has your name and will allow you access. As you enter the main doors, walk to the left. You will see a security desk. They will help you reach the apartment. I will park the car and bring your and Mr. Rawlings' bags up as soon as I can. The staff of the apartment will be available to assist you once you reach the eighty-ninth floor. Do you have any questions, miss?"

"No, thank you, Eric, I will be fine." Then she waited while he stopped the car and came around to open her door. Only having five hours sleep, Claire felt like a mouse placed in a maze. Would she be able to find the cheese?

The cool lake breeze hit her legs as she stepped from the car and proceeded into the Trump Tower. She thought about her appearance, the blouse, skirt, sophisticated heels, and hair pulled up and back. She didn't resemble the college girl who used to roam these streets with her friends. Doors opened and the bellman nodded as she passed.

She looked like she belonged in a limousine. The guard at the security desk didn't question her as she spoke with confidence, "Hello, I am Claire Nichols. Please show me to Mr. Rawlings' apartment."

"Yes, Ms. Nichols, we have been expecting you. We hope your flight was enjoyable. Please follow me this way." The guard tried his best to make small talk, but Claire's mind lingered six years behind.

Once the elevator reached the eighty-ninth floor, Claire tipped the guard, thanked him, and entered the open door to the apartment. Immediately, a charming gentleman greeted her, "Hello, Ms. Claire, my name is Charles. I am very pleased to meet you." He showed her to Mr. Rawlings's room. "Miss, would you be interested in some breakfast, coffee, or anything else?"

Tony's room reminded her of his apartment in New York, more of the masculine natural colors. The shades were drawn and Claire asked Charles to open them. The room felt dark and dreary and she knew on the other side of the shades the sun shone brightly. The view, as he opened the drapes, took her breath away. The windows faced north toward the lake. Far above most of the city, she could stand close to the window and look down at the buildings. Just a little to the left she could see Navy Pier and out on the lake boats. The beautiful vista hypnotized her. She loved Chicago, and there it was -- eighty-nine stories below.

"Ms. Nichols, will you be staying or going out?"

Pulled from her trance, she knew her desire and reality differed. She and Tony hadn't discussed her activities. "I believe I will be staying here for now, and I would like some coffee please."

Charles returned with coffee and their luggage. If she were back in Iowa she could be on her way to her lake. Instead, she was sequestered in Tony's apartment. She lay down on his big luxurious cold bed, covered herself with blankets, and fell asleep. When she awoke the clock said 12:30. Tony might not be back for at least five hours. If only she could contact him, find out his plans. Instead she investigated his apartment.

Not surprisingly, it was magnificent and apparently took the entire eighty-ninth floor. Like his New York apartment, there were floor-to-ceiling windows throughout the dwelling. She found an office that contained computers and telephones, no doubt Tony's *home* office in Chicago. She opened the office door, looked around, and closed it. Under no circumstance was she permitted in his home office without him. There was no reason to believe the rules would be different here.

It occurred to Claire that perhaps Eric would be able to contact Tony and find out his expectations. Charles informed her that Eric was with Mr. Rawlings. He didn't know when they planned to return.

Next Charles served lunch. It bore a striking resemblance to her everyday lunches in Iowa. Claire knew there were restaurants with various delicious foods, just an elevator ride away. Her appetite disappeared, and she settled onto the sofa in the living room with a book. Between the stunning view and the undeniable yearning to be in the city, she had difficulty concentrating. Finally, at four thirty, Charles informed her Mr. Rawlings called. They had dinner reservations for six and tickets to the theater, the eight thirty showing of "Wicked."

As she prepared for the evening, Claire opened her garment bag to a Nicole Miller taupe strapless dress with sequins. She'd never seen the dress before, but of course it would fit perfectly. The matching Gucci shoes and handbag completed the ensemble. It even had a small jacket with matching sequins, just right for an autumn evening. She piled her hair on top of her head with large spiral curls dangling down her neck.

As she completed the finishing touches to her makeup, Tony entered the bedroom, greeted Claire, and went to the adjoining bath for a quick shower. She smiled. His tone sounded chatty, like other people were near, and his eyes were milk chocolate. He emerged from the bath clean-shaven, hair wet, with a towel around his waist. The aroma of aftershave filled the bedroom.

Watching him, she momentarily thought about an ongoing conversation she'd been having lately with herself. It usually started with thoughts of him, pleasant thoughts. Then she would think about the way he made her feel or how much she liked to see him happy. It would then turn to questioning, something like, *Are you completely crazy or only unstable.* She didn't know how she could be feeling this way about *him*. After all, he kidnapped her. He hurt her, but when he was good . . . Claire tried to remember, there was a song or something that said: when he is good, he is *so* good—and that summed it up.

She pondered the many puzzling sides of this enigma as she watched him in the mirror. First, looking at him as he removed the towel, her pulse quickened and she forgot about her primping. No one could deny his incredibly handsome physique. Hell, he was gorgeous. Despite the almost twenty-year age difference, she observed his defined muscles, broad shoulders, and firm abdomen. Momentarily, she fantasized about the feel of his skin against hers. Second, he was undoubtedly an extremely successful businessman who desired to keep his life private. Third, he utterly and completely believed in appearances. Fourth, he had an insatiable sex drive. In that arena Claire had come to terms with his varying approaches, anywhere from tenderness to domination. However, the side of Tony that bothered Claire the most was his unpredictability. His temperament could shift without warning making an Indiana tornado seem docile.

Due to his position, his desire for privacy and appearances were understandable. It was the swiftness with which he could go from serene to furious that concerned her. Nevertheless, as Claire watched him dress, smelled his cologne, and heard him chat, her body tingled in anticipation. She looked forward to being on his arm, enjoying Chicago's nightlife.

Their dinner reservations were for Sixteen, a fine restaurant on the sixteenth floor of the Trump Tower. They were escorted to a premium table with an amazing view of the Wrigley Clock Tower. Tony ordered their wine, appetizers, and meals. The reputation for outstanding cuisine proved true; everything tasted delectable. They chatted throughout the meal, mostly about Chicago and its many possibilities. Claire didn't complain about spending the day in the apartment, but she mentioned that after the spa she would like to do some shopping. After all, wasn't it Tony who kept encouraging her to shop?

124

After dinner, Tony suggested they walk the short distance from Trump Tower to Cadillac Palace Theater. Having wanted outside all day, Claire thought his idea was fantastic. Feeling the warm city breeze, walking arm in arm down South Street through the crowds of people, gave her a rush of anonymity. They talked and laughed as the evening faded into night. Claire's deprived senses filled with sounds of traffic, the feel of a crowd, and visions of buildings transforming into monuments of architecture as darkness descended and lights illuminated.

Claire could have walked forever. Even the sensation of her shoes hitting the hard concrete delighted her, but their journey ended too soon. Upon entering the theater, she saw the show bill high above their heads. She'd long been a fan of the "Wizard of Oz" and immediately became excited about watching the performance of "Wicked."

Of course, they were seated in prime seats. Claire remembered shows she saw in the same theater years earlier, sitting somewhere near the top of the balcony. Currently, they had an excellent view of the stage and orchestra. For the next few hours, Claire became lost in the performance: the acting, dancing, and singing. When Elphaba sang "Defying Gravity," Claire was absolutely mesmerized. Her life disappeared into the performance. Every now and again she would notice Tony watching her, not the show. She chose to ignore his gazes and enjoy the show. She believed her behavior was appropriate and knew without a doubt if it weren't, he would let her know.

After the show they walked back to Trump Tower. Tony talked about Claire's appointment scheduled for nine in the morning. She had a massage, facial, and hair services scheduled, but if she wanted more she only needed to let them know. Everything would be billed to Tony's apartment. Her only concern would be generous tipping, and he would give her all the cash she needed. The spa was actually in the tower and Charles would be available to help her find it. They would provide lunch if her services took that long and they probably would.

That night Tony's bed wasn't cold like it had been earlier in the day. Claire believed his business in Chicago must be going well. That night he was generous, demonstrative, sensual, and erotic. Perhaps he felt apologetic for his quick judgment the week earlier. Whatever the motive, Claire loved the results!

In the past, during the nights Tony stayed in Claire's bed, it seemed like they slept on polar-opposite sides. Tonight's finale concluded differently. They fell asleep with Claire's cheek on his chest, his arm around her bare shoulder, and her arm over his tight abdomen. She felt his warmth as his chest hair tickled her nose. Her head rose and fell with each of his breaths, and the sound of his heartbeat in her ear. She inhaled his intoxicating scent and drifted into a deep, peaceful sleep.

The next morning, she awoke alone. Due to the heavy draperies, the room was dark, making it difficult for Claire to judge time. The clock read 7:10. She hadn't heard Tony get out of bed, shower or dress, and had no idea how long he'd been gone.

Putting on a robe, she decided to find coffee. At home it would have been brought to her immediately upon waking. Then she thought—no, hoped—perhaps this room didn't have the quality surveillance of her room in Iowa. In the dining room Charles poured coffee and informed her that Mr. Rawlings left thirty minutes earlier for his Chicago office.

Sipping the rich bold liquid, Claire's mind recalled the pleasures of last night. Not just the sex, which was great, it was memories of his voice and expressions. Blissfully walking back to the bedroom, Claire told Charles she would wait until after she dressed for breakfast.

Back in Tony's room she found his note:

> *I am sure you remember that your appointment*
> *is at 9:00, don't be late.*
> *I plan to be back to the apartment by 6:00 p.m.*
> *You mentioned shopping last night at dinner.*
> *I have left you your credit card and ID. There is*
> *also ample cash for tipping and incidentals.*
> *After your spa day, Charles will help you with*
> *transportation to shopping.*
> *Do not forget my rules. I trust you know better than that.*

He never began his notes with a salutation or signed them. Claire looked in the envelope under the note. It contained her ID and credit card, as well as over $1,000 in different denominations.

Claire thought it was unnecessary that Tony *kept* her ID and credit card. It wasn't as if she had the opportunity to use it whenever she wanted. And the amount of cash seemed excessive until she saw the small Post-It note on one of the bills:

> *$100 per stylist that assists you*

Claire decided that was helpful, she wouldn't have considered tipping that much. Maybe some instruction was helpful.

She arrived at the Day Spa ten minutes early. They greeted her and ushered her to one of the treatment rooms. Instead of music, the air permeated with sounds of nature and the aroma of scented candles. Indirect lighting helped to complete the relaxing atmosphere. To begin her day of pampering they directed her to a large whirlpool tub. Once submerged, the assistant added a special mixture of oils and powders based on Claire's answers to some preference questions. After the tub, Claire was led to the massage table, where they asked her to lie with her face submerged in a hole.

Suddenly, besieged by a rush of unpleasant memories, she did her best to control her emotions and lie down. The masseuse began with Claire's shoulders and commented on the tightness of her muscles. It didn't take long for the combination of the bath oils, ambiance, and magic of the masseuse's hands to ease the tension. At the conclusion of the massage, every muscle in Claire's body felt loose and relaxed.

126

Next, they proceeded to the hair salon. Apparently, when making Claire's reservations a highlight procedure was requested. Never in all of her life had she colored her hair. The apprehension brought back some tension to her shoulders. However, she knew Tony was the one to plan her treatment, so the idea of changing it was more unsettling. While the color sat on her hair, they treated her to a facial which claimed skin rejuvenation. After they washed and conditioned her hair, the stylist began trimming and styling.

When Claire's chair spun around, she gazed at her auburn tresses which now contained generous caramel and light blonde highlights. It all blended beautifully, and the length hadn't really changed. The result looked healthy, shaped, stunning, and different.

Next, they offered Claire a menu. She enthusiastically ordered her own lunch, deciding on a sushi variety plate with a side salad. Claire decided Tony must not like sushi. She hadn't eaten any in months. It tasted wonderful. Following lunch she chose to receive a manicure and pedicure while the cosmetic specialist completed her makeup. Claire yearned to walk around outside, yet she was truly enjoying the pampering. Smiling, she recalled Tony's enthusiasm about her spa experience.

It was nearing two o'clock when the receptionist brought Claire the telephone. "Ms. Nichols, you have a call." At first, she just stared. Other than Emily over a week ago, Claire hadn't spoken on a phone for almost six months. She immediately believed this was a test.

Looking at her nails under the dryer, she said, "Thank you, could you please ask who it is?"

The receptionist inquired and continued, "Mr. Rawlings would like to speak with you."

Claire carefully took the phone. "Hello, Tony?"

"Very good, Claire." She smiled. "I'm on my way to the airport. I need to make an emergency trip to New York." Tony's voice sounded informative but preoccupied.

"All right. Will I be going too?"

"No, Eric will be back in Chicago this evening and accompany you home. Just continue your plans and be back at the apartment by six. Charles will see that you get to the airport for your flight."

Claire wanted to ask about the shopping. She felt pretty and didn't want to spend the afternoon in the apartment. He said to continue her plans. She chose to believe that included shopping. If she didn't ask, she could plead ignorance when questioned.

"Okay, I will." She didn't want to say anything inappropriate with people listening. "Do you know when you will be back?"

"Not for sure. I believe Saturday. I need to go, we are at the airport."

"I will see you then. Have a safe trip."

"Claire," he paused, "do not disappoint me."

"I won't, Tony. I will see you Saturday." The telephone disconnected from his end. Claire handed the telephone back to one of the clinicians and inspected her nails, holding the phone hadn't caused any damage. Her fingers and toes glistened shiny red, and her makeup had been expertly applied.

127

Claire stepped in front of the mirror. She wished with all her might that Tony could see her now, she felt stunning.

There were a total of six assistants that worked directly with Claire. She went to the front desk, signed the charge slip, and gave the tip money to the receptionist, with an additional fifty for her. Claire smiled and thanked her for bringing her the telephone.

Back at the apartment Claire changed clothes, wanting to get outside and enjoy the shops before she needed to return at six. Looking out of the windows, she could tell the day was warm. The waves on the lake also told her that the breeze was strong. But of course, that was why they call it the windy city!

She had a little over three hours to shop and she wanted to make every minute count! All of a sudden, time slipped back six years. She needed to shop fast in order to get back to class. The biggest difference between then and now was her goal—instead of bargains, she looked for the buys that would please Tony.

Charles offered Claire a driver, but she wanted to walk. The busy city and warm weather created an exhilarating atmosphere. She longed to be outside and on her own short schedule. Cartier was her first stop. She found another pair of sunglasses. They were like the ones from New York, except black, which would be better for winter.

Although that was her thought, she wondered if she would really be with Tony all winter. Compartmentalize. Right now, her plan was to enjoy this afternoon and some shopping, the rest would work itself out.

Her familiarity with the magnificent mile proved advantageous to her goal. She didn't have Eric to pick up packages, so she didn't buy anything too bulky. However, she managed some smaller bags from Saks, Anne Fontaine, Armani, and Louis Vuitton.

Claire approached the Trump Tower and her watch said she had thirty minutes to spare. She stopped in the coffee shop for a quick café mocha. In Iowa she mostly drank plain coffee with cream, very high quality and amazingly delicious. This afternoon she was *living* and decided a little chocolate would hit the spot.

Sitting at the table surrounded by her packages, sipping her café mocha, Claire's mind wandered. Her life seemed to have taken a turn. The last few weeks were much better than months earlier, so much better than she could have predicted. She talked with Emily, if only for a few minutes. She thought about the rules: speaker phone, limitations, and the briefness of the call. It took a magnitude of compartmentalization to concentrate on the affirmative aspect of the conversation. Nonetheless, she spoke with her sister and that made her happy. Then there was the barbeque, minus the unfortunate misunderstanding, which was a success. Tony introduced her to his friends, and they were nice to her. The date with Tony the night before was romantic: dinner, walking, the play, and the activities until they fell asleep. Now, she was sitting in Chicago, a destination she loved.

Smiling, she sipped her café mocha and thought about him. She hated him one day and then allowed her hair to change colors because he requested

128

it. The more she thought about it, maybe *allow* wasn't the appropriate word. Really, did she have an option? How could he hurt her one day and then make her feel so fulfilled the next? Her internal debate continued.

As she thought of him, feelings of lust pushed away the old feelings of fear. Remembering the sensation of his touch, sound of his voice, and taste of his skin, she wanted to believe this was a significant improvement. She wondered how she could be having these feelings, how she could enjoy his presence, and even look forward to being with him. She had read about *Stockholm syndrome*, maybe that was it. She knew it didn't make sense, but she couldn't deny the way she was beginning to feel.

Preoccupied in her thoughts, she didn't notice the woman approaching until she stood directly above her. "Claire? Claire Nichols is that really you?"

Claire looked up in disbelief, realizing that someone actually addressed her. She recognized Meredith Banks immediately. She was a sorority sister from Valparaiso. It made sense, Valparaiso was nearby.

"Hello, Meredith, how are you?" Her voice reflected her genuine excitement and surprise at seeing someone from her past. They had roamed these streets together in another life.

"Gosh, I'm great. How are you? You look amazing. I haven't heard from you in ages!" Meredith looked at the other chair. "Do you mind if I join you for a few minutes?"

Apprehensively, Claire looked at her watch. She needed to be upstairs by six -- it was five forty. She considered appearances. It would be rude to not allow her to sit.

Claire motioned with her hand. "Yes, please do."

The two ladies talked about what brought them to Chicago. Meredith noted, looking at the booty surrounding Claire's chair, she was obviously doing some shopping. She even noted it was higher-end shopping than they did in college. Claire laughed it off, saying even these stores had great deals. She couldn't help think about Bonnie who had gauged the value of her clothing, wondering if Meredith was doing the same.

Meredith asked if she saw any shows while in town. Claire told her she saw "Wicked" and enjoyed it very much. Did Claire remember the fun shows they used to watch and the concerts? Meredith mentioned she was in town for work. Where was Claire working? She seemed to know Claire had been in Atlanta. Claire wondered if they had spoken while she was there, they must have. Meredith lived out west these days, in California. Did Claire ever make it out that way? Where was she living?

Claire did her best to be evasive yet friendly. This was her sorority sister being friendly, not some paparazzi. Finally, Meredith started talking about her husband. She married Jerry from the fraternity and their group. Did Claire know that? No, she didn't. How long had they been married? And Anne and Shaun were engaged! If Claire would give Meredith her address, she was sure that Anne would want to invite her. Meredith wondered if Claire was married. Was she seeing anyone? Hadn't she heard rumors?

That word sounded an alarm. *Rumor*. Wasn't that the word Tony used to describe her, a rumor? Claire laughed again. "Oh, Meredith, didn't we learn years ago you should never trust rumors."

Checking her watch again, it was five till six. "It was great seeing you, but I really do need to go. We should catch up sometime." Claire tried to not be rude, but she didn't want to talk any longer. She went directly to the security counter, where the guard recognized her and helped her with her bags as they went to the residential elevators.

By eight o'clock, Claire sat in Tony's jet by herself, flying back to Iowa. Eric copiloted; she had the entire cabin to herself. She tried not to think about her conversation with Meredith. She decided compartmentalization was best, she would think about it another time. She decided to think about Thursday and Friday with Tony out of town. Smiling, she told herself, *I'm going to my lake!*

Experience: is the most brutal of teachers.
But you learn, my god, do you learn.
-C. S. Lewis

Chapter 19

Claire woke Thursday morning to the unfamiliar sound of rain. With the dryness of the summer, at first she questioned the pitter-patter. But as her mind cleared, the noise made sense. Going directly to the window, she saw droplets on the window, gray clouds, and puddles on the ground below. She was so excited about the lake but didn't want to walk five miles each direction in the rain and mud. The disappointment overwhelmed her. How could it rain on the one day she wanted sun? With Tony gone, the day drug on endlessly.

Friday morning, she lay in bed and listened for the sound of rain. Straining her ears, she only heard silence. Tentatively looking out the window, Claire beheld the crystal clear blue sky. It was as though the rain washed the dust and dryness of the summer away. Everything looked fresh and clean. The bright early morning sunshine glistened on the moist leaves.

Wearing her robe, she went out onto the balcony and immediately realized the drop in temperature. Shivering, she wrapped her arms around herself and gazed out over the polychromatic woods. The crisp autumn fragrance penetrated deep into her lungs. It would be muddy, but she didn't care. She would wear an older pair of shoes and make her way to her lake.

Getting ready that morning, her reflection caught her by surprise. The new lighter hair made her skin tone lighter and her eyes deeper green. It wasn't as if she suddenly looked like Marilyn Monroe, but her reflection looked more blonde than ever before. Claire wasn't sure what she thought of her new look, but she did know Tony wouldn't be back until tomorrow. So she pulled it back in a ponytail.

While dressing, Claire realized she didn't own anything *old* as in old shoes. Everything was new or at least looked new. The clothes which had been in her closet almost six months ago were gone, now too large. Whether she shopped or not, her wardrobe never waned. Currently, sweaters and jackets multiplied while she slept.

Luckily, her feet weren't changing size, so the hiking boots she requested months ago were waiting and ready. She decided she would just clean them when she got home. Catherine didn't approve of Claire's plan. The ground would be muddy and slippery. What if she fell and twisted something? Claire promised she would be safe. She told Catherine it had been so long since she hiked in the woods. She wanted to stay out as long as possible. She would return -- she simply didn't know when.

Catherine promised dinner upon her arrival, no matter how late. She also provided Claire with a packed lunch complete with water bottles and a thermos of warm coffee. It was after ten when she left the backyard.

It had been almost a month, but Claire knew each turn to find her lake. At almost noon she reached her destination. The shore looked exactly like she remembered, except now the trees surrounding the lake were multicolored with rich vibrant reds, yellows, and oranges. Green was definitely the minority. Certain varieties of deciduous trees were completely bare. She suddenly wondered what made some trees lose their leaves earlier than others. She had some research to do.

The scent of autumn filled the air, thick, poignant, fresh, and spicy. After yesterday's wind and rain the air was still, the remaining leaves didn't rustle, and the lake was calm. The water resembled a giant mirror. The colorful trees on the shoreline reflected on the water. Claire wished she had a camera. The simplistic beauty made a picture-perfect postcard.

The sounds of nature were everywhere: bees or yellow jackets buzzed in the autumn sunshine, birds sang, and forest rodents scurried through the fallen leaves. She watched as ducks swam on the beautiful smooth lake, leaving wakes as their trail. Some floated near the shore, occasionally dipping their heads under the water, filling their stomachs for their flight south. September was almost half done; she would head south too if she could. Hopefully she would be going to Atlanta before long. When Claire dressed, she put on jeans, a workout T-shirt, and a jacket. Now that the sun glowed high and strong, the warmth allowed her to remove the jacket. By late afternoon she even took off her boots, rolled up her jeans, and waded into the water.

Part of her recognized the possibility she may not make it back to the lake before winter. She wanted to experience as much of it as she could. Of course, she hoped her debt would soon be considered paid. More realistically she realized her duties now included travel. If she were expected to accompany Tony out of town, she wouldn't be home to explore.

The cold water made her feet tingle. She watched her brightly polished toes as she stepped on pebbles and her feet squished the underwater terra. When she stood still, the minnows swarmed, investigating the bright red toenails. Some even nibbled at her toes; it tickled.

Claire had eaten her lunch midafternoon, but her stomach told her she needed dinner soon. Finding some coffee in the thermos, no longer warm, she pretended it was a Frappuccino without the crushed ice. It helped to fill

132

the void until she reached the promise of Catherine's dinner. The daylight hours were decreasing and before she knew it the sky began to redden.

Glancing at her watch, it was after seven. She wondered where the day had gone as the most beautiful scene unfolded before her eyes. Sitting on the shore she watched the sky as the sun settled over the lake. She couldn't make herself get up and go back to the house as the lovely postcard picture transformed into a stunning explosion of crimson.

The setting sun caused the few cumuliform clouds to change from white to gray to pink, and then to a vibrant red. The radiance beamed onto the leaves, altering their color. The scene continued to improve in brilliance and the beauty continued to grow. Claire sat patiently and watched with a new sense of contentment.

Once the sun reached the line of trees at the far end of the lake, the darkness quickly extended over the land. Claire remembered Catherine; she would be worried. The idea of walking back in the dark woods should have frightened her, but it didn't. She knew her way. In the daylight it took her an hour and forty-five minutes to reach the house or an hour to reach the clearing.

When she stepped into the clearing the illumination from the moon allowed her to see her watch, eight thirty. She wasn't making bad time but it would be almost nine-thirty before she reached home. The air had cooled but still tasted fresh and clean, she inhaled and set off as fast as she could. Direction wasn't the issue, it was safety. The ground not only had limbs and roots as obstacles, but the rain left muddy areas which made her slip. One time her left foot slid, making her right knee muddy. When she stepped into the backyard, her eyes focused on her watch, it was nine thirty-five. The last leg of her trip took longer than normal. Her stomach growled for dinner, but her first priority was removing the muddy boots, jeans, and taking a shower or a nice bath. She left the boots on the back stoop.

The carpeted floor of the southeast corridor felt soft under her feet compared to the hiking boots. It also quieted her steps. As she opened the door to her suite, her thoughts ran between removing her muddy jeans and a warm shower. Although the room was dark, navigation was easy. She even considered leaving the light off. Then she remembered Catherine. Turning on the light would let her know she'd returned. As she reached for the light switch, she sensed his presence. Before she could speak an arm came down over her neck and her head turned sharply upward as her ponytail was pulled back. It all happened so fast, she gasped.

His fierce voice in the darkness was unmistakable, "Where the fuck have you been?"

She tried to respond, but the arm around her neck restricted her air intake. She couldn't breathe, much less speak. He let go of her momentarily while he spun her around. Now she faced him. His hands gripped her shoulders with a force she'd never experienced. His warm breath hit her face with each word. "I asked you a question. Where the fuck have you been?"

She coughed at the sudden intake of oxygen and tried to respond, "Tony, I didn't think you were coming home until tomorrow."

That wasn't an answer to his question. Although the lights were still off, her eyes adjusted quickly as the bright moonlight streamed through the unblocked windows. With diminished light, distinguishing color was difficult, but Claire didn't need to see color to know his eyes contained none. He released the grip on her shoulder with his right hand and struck her. His left hand stopped her from falling. He supported her only to confront her again. "I have asked you a question twice. I will not ask again." And his hand contacted her cheek again, harder this time.

"Tony, please stop." She gasped for breath as her temple and cheek stung. "I was hiking in the woods."

He let go of her shoulders, shoving her onto the sofa. He followed her and loomed over her body as she lay against the cushions. "Do you expect me to believe you were in the woods until this time of night?"

She tried to explain, "I was in the woods. The sun was setting. It was so beautiful." Her words came in gasps.

Finally, he yelled, "Shut the fuck up! You were out there because you knew I was coming home and you didn't want to face me after what you did."

Claire's mind spun. She didn't know what she had done. "I don't know what you mean. You told me you were coming home on Saturday, this is still Friday. I haven't done anything."

Tony slapped her again and called her a liar. Then he walked over to the light switch and turned it on. Claire watched him. His suit coat was gone and his shirt and slacks looked wrinkled. His chest visibly expanded and contracted with labored breaths and his eyes were not only black but violent. In the past he'd been upset, but in control. Tonight his self-control was replaced with rage. She knew he'd passed some invisible threshold. Claire just didn't know why, but the reason scared the hell out of her. He walked to her dining table and picked up some papers.

"Then tell me, tell me how this is a misunderstanding." He shook the pages in his hand while his words came too close together. "I jumped to conclusions last time. Tell me how I'm doing that now."

Claire feared talking, but she did. "Tony, I'm sorry. I really don't know what you are talking about." He threw the pages at her; they scattered on the floor near her feet. When he didn't move, she bent down to pick them up. Her vision now blurry from tears, she tried desperately to blink and focus on the pages. They were typed, from the Internet. The last two pages contained pictures: pictures of the two of them at the symphony, at some event she couldn't distinguish, in New York, and walking down the street in Chicago, arm in arm. Then there were pictures of Claire, in college, with friends and one of her and Meredith sitting at a table talking. The breath in her chest suddenly dissipated. Her eyes focused on the words:

"Questions Answered—the Mystery Woman in Anthony

Rawlings's Life Agrees to a One on One Interview."

Claire's eyes grew wide and immediately overflowed with a flood of tears. She couldn't believe what she read. Oh my god! She didn't agree to an interview. She wouldn't do that! "Tony, oh my god, I did *not* agree to an interview."

"So you are telling me that the picture of you talking to this woman is a print shop fabrication and this is a colossal misunderstanding?" He pointed to the picture as he stood over Claire. His closeness filled her with dread. It was her talking to Meredith, but it wasn't an interview.

"It is me, but—" His hands picked her off the sofa and pinned her against a wall.

"I wasn't giving an interview." She hit the wall with enough force for a picture to fall. His grip hurt her arms, she could taste the salt of her tears, and her ears reverberated with his booming voice and rang from his repeated slaps.

His face descended upon hers. "Then what in the hell are you doing?" He shook her again. "Claire, I trusted you! You told me I could trust you and I believed you. I sent you to a spa day. This is how you thank me? By breaking all my rules, by public failure?" he dropped her to the floor like a rag doll.

Claire scurried to pick up the papers. She wanted to know what the article said. "What is this?"

"It is an exclusive Internet release of an upcoming story. It will run simultaneously in *People* and *Rolling Stone*." He hovered over her and then turned abruptly away. He went to the bookshelf, picked up a book, and threw it into the fireplace. He tried to gain control of his anger and of himself. "Shelly, my publicist, found it today and immediately forwarded a copy to me. I flew home as soon as I could." She wondered how long he'd been waiting and brewing in her suite.

She desperately tried to read:

Well, you believe you know Anthony Rawlings, forty-five, self-made billionaire?

Or maybe you would like to know him? You may be too late. Since May of 2010 Anthony has been seen out on the town with the same mystery woman. Up until now we have not known much about Anthony's special woman. That is until she agreed to sit down with old friend and freelance writer Meredith Banks. The woman in Anthony Rawlings's life is Claire Nichols, twenty-six. She is originally from Fishers, Indiana, just outside of Indianapolis.

Claire graduated from Valparaiso University, Valparaiso, Indiana in 2006 with a bachelor's degree in meteorology. Ms. Nichols and Meredith were in the same sorority from 2003 through 2006. It is believed that this long-time friendship is why Claire finally agreed to sit down and discuss her relationship with one of the world's top bachelors.

Claire looked up from the page in her hand. Tony sat on the sofa and watched her reaction as she sat on the floor and read. Her whole body trembled as nausea erupted in her empty stomach.

"Tony, I did go to school with Meredith, she did come up to me the other day and started talking. I didn't know she was a reporter. I wasn't giving an interview. I didn't say anything about you. Your name was never mentioned!"

He didn't speak. Instead, he nodded toward the pages and she continued to read.

Anthony Rawlings has long been seen as a wonderful catch for that one deserving woman. He dated such women as supermodel Cynthia Simmons and recording artist Julia Owens. However, none of his previous relationships lasted long. That is until now, now that Rawlings and Nichols have been together. These two were first seen together in late May (see picture) at the Quad City Symphony not far from the large wooded estate of Anthony Rawlings. And since that time, they have been spotted by curious onlookers at various charity events, as well as taking on two of the nation's biggest cities, New York (see picture) and Chicago (see picture).

The question all eligible bachelorettes are asking, why Claire? What makes her the woman for a man like Anthony Rawlings? Perhaps it is her youth, her beauty, or her style. Obviously, from her college days to present, she has found her flair!

While Claire would neither confirm nor deny that she and Anthony Rawlings were involved. She didn't deny living in the Iowa City area. Could that address perhaps be the same as Mr. Rawlings'?

Social Security records indicate that Ms. Nichols' only employment has been as a bartender since losing her job in 2009 at WKPZ in Atlanta, Georgia. WKPZ was purchased by TTT–TV, resulting in the layoff of many employees. Yet, despite this loss of employment, Ms. Nichols was seen shopping in Chicago at such stores as Saks Fifth Avenue, Anne Fontaine, Cartier, Giorgio Armani, and Louis Vuitton. It is also rumored that Ms. Nichols spent the better part of the day enjoying all the comforts money could buy at one of the most exclusive day spas in Chicago.

Claire used to spend her days in Chicago (see picture) with many different men from Valparaiso University. Now it seems she is enjoying the better life with only one man. (see picture). The two of them walking arm in arm on their way to the theater. The performers will be happy to know that Claire and Anthony enjoyed the performance of "Wicked."

The final bit of evidence confirming their involvement came when Ms. Claire Nichols was ushered to the eighty–ninth floor of Trump Tower, the private city dwelling belonging to none other than Mr. Anthony Rawlings. Emily Vandersol, twenty–nine, sister and only living relative of Ms. Nichols was asked about her knowledge of Claire and Anthony's relationship. Mrs. Vandersol informed Ms. Banks she recently spoke to Claire and she sounded well. There was no mention of Anthony Rawlings during their conversation. Mrs. Vandersol had no further comment.

Sorry, ladies, it seems that Ms. Claire Nichols is holding on to Anthony Rawlings. What will she tell us about this private man? We are anxiously waiting to learn.

Byline: Meredith Banks

Claire held the papers even though she finished the article. She desperately searched for something to say, some explanation. Finally, she set the pages on the floor but didn't look up. She knew there was nothing to say. The article hadn't revealed any information, although the sensational title alluded it would. Tony knew that, he flew all the way home. He obviously read the article multiple times. It was her in the picture. She was talking to Meredith. It wasn't what it seemed, but in her head she could hear him, she could hear his voice. Now she could hear him getting up and walking toward her. "Appearances, Claire, how many times have I told you? Appearances mean everything. There is a picture right here of you sitting with her, the author. It doesn't matter if what she writes is accurate, it is believable because she is seen talking to you."

He wasn't yelling, he'd regained some control, yet the aura of rage remained. Claire didn't want to look into his black eyes even though she could feel their penetrating stare.

"Get up." She knew she should, but she didn't move. She couldn't, her body was paralyzed with fear. She had no defense and had disobeyed his rules. His volume increased, "Claire, get up!"

The tears dripped off her nose. "Please, Tony," she sobbed, "I'm so sorry." He lifted her by her arm. She felt helpless. His voice exuded wrath. "The entire way home I was praying that somehow this was another misunderstanding. You wouldn't do this after I put my trust in you. But I knew if it wasn't a misunderstanding there had to be consequences. There had to be a punishment for this blatant disregard for the most fundamental of rules."

She saw his hand move and instinctively veered to avoid another blow. The miss of her cheek infuriated him, his control gone, he swung again. His hand caught her pearl necklace. The fine chain proved no contest for Tony's anger and power. The pearl charm flew as the broken chain slid from around Claire's neck. The next impact put her back on the floor. This time she tasted blood. She didn't know if it was her nose or her lip, she started to reach to find the source. His voice continued, "And I believe some time away from people, some time alone will help you remember who and who not to talk to."

She tried to turn and to twist herself. She pleaded for him to stop. He continued to hurt her and she was sorry, tried to yell, but couldn't get away. She tried to protect her face, her body. Time wasn't moving. She wondered how long this was happening. It could have been only seconds, maybe hours, Claire didn't know.

Suddenly thrown backward by a forceful blow, his voice seemed to drift far away. Her body cried out in agony from the abuse, yet there was a sudden onset of intense pain. She tried to get up, to speak, but she couldn't. Then the stillness grew and everything—Tony, the room, tears, fear, and pain—all faded to darkness.

*Enjoy the little things in life, for one day you may look back
and realize they were the big things.*
—Author anonymous

Chapter 20

She couldn't remember why she was afraid, only that she was terribly afraid and alone. Then with time, the dark and cold that enveloped her being began to dissipate. She heard music and felt warmth. Keeping her eyes shut, the dark continued, but the familiar music grew louder and more comforting. Bette Midler sang "Wind Beneath My Wings." Her mom loved that song. She would turn up the radio and sing every word. Mom used to say, "It isn't about the sound of your voice, but the happiness that makes you sing."

"Shirley, do you know where my wallet is?" Jordan called from down the hall. "Mom, Claire, took my Pop-Tart." Emily's voice sounded different, so young. Claire opened her eyes. She saw a scene, like a movie, except she was there and not there. She also saw her mom, dad, and sister. Claire watched herself, but the Claire she saw was young, maybe five or six years old. Their small house was chaotic and full of affection.

She watched as her mom made Emily another Pop-Tart, scolded Claire, and gave her a loving kiss on top of her head. Dad walked into the kitchen wearing his police uniform. Claire couldn't believe how young everyone looked, how warm and full of love she felt watching this scene from her childhood. Dad walked behind Mom and put his arms tenderly around her. She noticed Emily and Claire playing with one another and their breakfast. They weren't seeing the devotion and adoration Claire now saw between her parents. Mom giggled as Dad kissed her neck, and she handed him his wallet from the kitchen counter. He whispered in her ear, Claire strained to hear, "What would I ever do without you?"

"Well, you aren't going to get the chance to find out. I plan on sticking around forever."

As they looked at one another, the two little girls at the table started to distract them with their giggling, bickering, and suddenly the spilling of a glass of orange juice all over the table. Little Emily and little Claire both became silent, neither one would tell on the other. Claire heard her dad's voice, "Girls, see what happens when you mess around." His voice wasn't angry. He cleaned the juice with a paper towel and Mom helped with a wet cloth. "Try to be careful, you sillies." He kissed their foreheads as he turned to leave, taking the time to hug their mom.

The scene began to fade. Claire didn't want to leave the warm feeling. She took one last look at the sisters eating their cereal and laughing. The spilled juice is forgotten. The darkness returned . . . coolness . . .

"Ms. Claire, Ms. Claire, can you hear me?" The familiar voice teemed with concern. The warmth she felt from her childhood was gone. She didn't want to go to the voice. She wanted to go back. Claire wanted more sleep, more tranquility . . .

"Come on, Claire, the movie starts in half an hour," Grandma's voice came from the bottom of the stairs. Claire opened her eyes. She wondered where she was, her grandparent's house. She must be staying over. Now she wondered if Emily was there too. She could see herself no longer a child but an awkward teenager. Grandma called up the stairs again, "Claire, your sister said she'd pick you and your friend up, hurry down." Grandma's expression reflected concern for Claire's movie. The real Claire wondered if the teenage Claire would see Grandma's distress.

Young Claire stomped down the stairs. "Fine, I'm ready. I called Amy, she can't go now. And I don't want to see 'A Bug's Life' with Emily. John will be there. He'll think it's stupid."

"Let's call Emily, and tell her Grandpa, you, and I are going to the movies." As Claire watched she prayed her counterpart would accept Grandma's offer. She also wondered her age, probably fourteen or fifteen. Then she remembered Grandpa died when she was fourteen, so if he was going to the movies she had to be thirteen or fourteen. Teenage Claire made a face at her grandmother's suggestion.

"Where are we going?" Grandpa's green eyes shone and his voice boomed jovially as he joined them from the other room. Claire's heart ached to see her grandparents, yet at the same time it swelled with affection.

"To the movies," Grandma said, smiling at Grandpa. Her grandparents were having an entire conversation through their sparkling eyes and facial expressions. Young Claire didn't notice, too self-absorbed. Grandpa put his arm around Claire.

"Great, I have been trying to get Grandma to go to the new 'Lethal Weapon.' You know I love me some police drama."

Grandma smiled at him. "Oh no, that's rated R. Claire would rather see 'Ever After.'" They were doing it, pulling Claire out of her funk. She wasn't budging willingly, but they were doing it.

"Oh no, Grandma, I don't want to see 'Ever After,' it's a Cinderella story . . . stupid." Grudgingly, smiling at Grandpa, she said, "I want to see Mel Gibson's butt!"

140

Her grandparents smiled at one another and continued the amorous charade. "I don't think Shirley and Jordan will approve," Grandma said as she grabbed the newspaper. "Let me look at the movie times for 'Ever After.'"

Teenage Claire looked over her grandma's shoulder. "Grandpa, 'Lethal Weapon' starts in twenty minutes. If we hurry we can make it." Her sulking forgotten, she believed she'd just gotten her way. Claire filled with warmth as she watched herself be lovingly manipulated.

Grandma surprised Claire. "Hey, I'm going too. I don't want to miss Mel's butt." Grandma winked at Grandpa. The scene began to fade away. The last thing she saw was the three of them going out the door to the movie.

Claire wondered why she hadn't remembered this before. Then she realized it wasn't unusual. She was raised by an amazing family with unconditional love and consideration. Somewhere along the way, she'd forgotten how that felt, a warmth which made everyone within its aura feel happy. The darkness returned with the quietness of a feeling of serenity and warmth.

Gradually, the darkness intensified; the warmth melted away. In the cool darkness she heard voices again. She waited.

"Claire, talk to us. Open your eyes." It wasn't a command. Tony's desperate voice was requesting.

She didn't want to open her eyes. She wanted to feel the warmth, to sleep.

"Ms. Nichols, Ms. Nichols." The deep unfamiliar voice no longer spoke to her, but to someone else. "We will need to begin intravenous feeding if she doesn't regain consciousness soon. The medicine to keep her unconscious should be out of her system. She is responding to some commands, but we can't be sure of her condition until she fully wakes. Sometimes the body will do this on its own, shut itself down to heal and to avoid the pain." There were voices and then she heard the unfamiliar one speaking again. "Her pain seems to have subsided with the medication. It should help her wake."

Claire didn't want to listen to them anymore or know who they are talking about. She just wanted to sleep, to feel warm, and go back to her memories.

"Get up, sleepyhead. You have a room of your own." Claire heard her own voice. It sounded happy and playful. However, she couldn't see herself or to whom she spoke.

"But I like this room better. I like this bed better," the other voice teased and laughed.

"Really, a twin bunk bed? That's what you like?" They both giggled.

"As long as you're here." Claire saw the two of them, a big mound under the covers, laughing and playing. As the covers moved she recognized herself and Simon, Simon Johnson. She hadn't thought of him in years. She'd made herself compartmentalize him away. Their hair disheveled, they looked too young for such activities. This was her freshman dorm room.

"Claire, I want to marry you."

"Yeah, right." She didn't believe him. Her plans didn't include marriage. Young Simon, however, meant every word he said. Now as Claire watched she wondered: *what if?*

"No, really. We can wait until we are through school or we can run away today. I'm not busy, how about you?" He pretended to be playful, but his tone held more than a hint of sincerity.

"Give me a rain check, okay?" Claire nibbled his ear. "I think my dad might be upset if I decide to throw away a year of school to get married during spring semester."

"I want to marry you, not stop your dreams . . . we can still finish school and you can be a famous meteorologist," Simon didn't get upset. He smiled tenderly and continued, "A famous meteorologist named Johnson." He playfully nibbled her ear and let her take a turn on his. They lay in that little twin bunk bed and talked for hours.

Claire watched them and memories flooded her consciousness. The two of them shared so much of themselves, their dreams, ambitions, troubles, failures, hopes, and accomplishments. Nothing could stop the mutual admiration and affection of their first love. She watched as they finally got out of bed and dressed wearing sweatpants and Valparaiso University sweatshirts. Claire put her hair in a ponytail. Looking at her now, Claire chastised herself. She needed a shower, some makeup, and definitely a brush. Simon didn't notice. Compliments came between hugs and kisses. He thought she looked beautiful and doted on each word. They were both completely in love. They discussed the finer dining establishments near campus, Taco Bell, McDonald's, Pizza Hut, or Wendy's.

With a warm loving kiss they mutually decided it would be Taco Bell. No pretense, no rules, only warmth and an undying need to be together. As they left the dorm room, Claire looked at the mess: clothes on the floor, bed unmade, a pizza box next to the trash can, and she saw the comforts of home. The scene vanished, fading to black, the feeling of love remained.

After watching, all she could think was: *please don't fade. I want to keep this going.* But it did. It faded.

Slowly, it evaporated, slipped away into cool darkness. Claire felt so cold. She wanted a blanket, something, anything with heat . . . please. She would beg if necessary. The cold was so . . . cold!

"Claire, the doctor said you may be able to hear us when we talk. Catherine and I have been talking to you for days -- for over a week. He said you will wake up when your pain decreases and you are ready. Please be ready soon. This liquid crap they're putting in your arm may have nutrients, but you're wasting away. Catherine has had the cook prepare all the foods you like every day, just in case you wake and want something." Tony's voice sounded close. She could sense his distress and concern.

She had to wonder, if I open my eyes will he be right there. Did he say over a week? I have been asleep for over a week? How did that happen? Why was a doctor here? Claire couldn't remember the whys or how, all she could remember were her parents, her grandparents, her sister, and Simon. Those memories filled her with hope and promise, and yet Tony sounded like he needed her. She knew she needed to go to Tony.

She didn't want to make him wait. But, she felt so tired and weak. Maybe a little more rest before she opened her eyes. Someone must have put blankets on her because she felt warmer. Along with the warmth Claire felt the stiffness of her dress, it was sea foam green. She was seeing herself in a full length mirror as Emily watched. They were in a big dressing room.

"I love it!" Emily observed Claire from all sides. "It is perfect for my wedding."

"Seriously, Em, you want me to wear green?" Claire's tone sounded joking, but she meant it. She remembered not liking the dress, but of course she would wear it if that was what Emily wanted.

"Yes. With your eyes, it's stunning." Claire watched the two sisters and again became self-critical, the self she saw looked too heavy and her hair was too thick and bushy. Emily was seeing someone different as she played with Claire's hair, twisting it and talking, "With your hair up and some dangly earrings. I know you can wear Grandma's necklace. It has a pearl. And I'll wear Mom's strand of pearls. They'll look great, and that will be my something *old*. You will almost be as pretty as me."

The mention of Grandma's necklace triggered something sad. Yet, Claire couldn't remember why the sadness came. She couldn't seem to remember . .
.

Emily, being three years older than Claire, was the bride. But, she also had the responsibilities of the mother of the bride. Their mother should be there, but she wasn't. The girls only had each other. It was Emily's wedding, yet *she* encouraged Claire.

Claire smiled at her sister and her green eyes sparkled, "Yeah, you wish. I just want you to know John secretly loves me! We wanted to tell you, but you know?"

"Honey, he isn't secretive about that. He loves you, you are his little sister."

"Yeah, I know. I have to beat the men off with sticks. Okay, I'll wear green. But for my wedding, I am finding you the gaudiest bubblegum pink dress you've ever seen." The two sisters laughed. Emily helped Claire out of the dress and they continued their shopping. They had so many things to do before the wedding. Together they would do it all.

Just like the little girls with the juice, they were there for one another. After their parents died it was the two of them against the world. John understood. He never tried to come between them. Even when Claire moved in with them as newlyweds, they welcomed her.

Briefly Claire saw their home in Troy, New York. Not large, it could be described as crowded. Seeing it again from afar filled Claire with affection and warmth. John worked long hours, and Emily had her teaching responsibilities. But they still managed to make Claire feel welcome. She suddenly wondered if she'd ever thanked them. She couldn't remember . . .

The scenes faded faster now. The warmth and strength evaporated. The blackness returned and pulled her in. Claire instinctively wanted to get away from the blackness.

The serenity transformed into coldness. She opened her eyes and saw it, the cold blackness staring back at her. She gasped and closed her eyes, but then she could hear the voices again coming from different directions. "Claire, are you awake?"

"Ms. Claire, please come back to us."

Tony spoke fast, "She opened her eyes. I saw it, just a second ago." She could feel his hand on hers. "Can you hear me?" He continued speaking to Catherine, "Go get the doctor. He's getting food in the kitchen. Let him know she is finally waking." And with a different tone, one of desperation and affection, he said, "Claire, please open your eyes."

Do you know what happens to scar tissue?
It's the strongest part of the skin
—Michael R. Mantell

Chapter 21

Claire inhaled, her chest felt tight, and there was a deep ache on her right side. She tried to remember. How did she get this way? She felt so weak. She tried to move her hand to touch Tony's, even the attempt exhausted her. There was an odd feeling on her left arm. She turned her head to see what was making her arm feel strange. Everything blurred out of focus. The light in the room was so intense -- she couldn't see. Tony noticed her eyes squint, immediately got up from the side of her bed, and closed the drapes. He returned and picked up her hand.

"It was too bright in here. I closed the drapes for you. Is that better?"

Claire tried to respond; she couldn't speak. Her mouth was too dry. She moved her head ever so slightly, indicating *"Yes, it is better."* The movement of her head made her dizzy. The inability to speak frightened her. Her eyes moistened. She closed them, and a tear escaped down her cheek.

"It's okay, you don't need to talk." Tony's tone was kind and loving. "Please open your eyes again. It was so good to see your beautiful emerald eyes." He continued gently holding her hand. Claire opened her eyes and looked at the needle taped to the bend of her left arm. As if reading her mind, he explained, "That is how you have been eating for almost two weeks. And it has some pain medicine too, trying to make you more comfortable."

Claire started to remember: she was in the woods; she came home and Tony . . . The memory made her eyes open wider. She looked at Tony. Her eyes filled with panic.

She remembered.

Tony's voice continued, gentle and comforting, "Can you remember what happened? You had an accident." Claire tried to say, "No, you did this," but she couldn't. It may have been the dryness of her tongue or the horror of the images, but she just stared at him as he continued. "You had an accident in the woods. When we found you, your jeans and boots were all muddy, and you had multiple injuries. Did you fall? Did you slip? Did someone or something hurt you out there? We've had the woods searched. Nothing was found. Claire, we've been so worried about you."

The stiffness in her neck made turning painful, and the dizziness made focusing difficult. She heard Catherine. Someone was with her. Was it the doctor? Whoever he was, he was right in front of her; an older man with a very pleasant, encouraging, deep voice.

"Ms. Nichols, I am Dr. Leonard. I've been taking care of you since Mr. Rawlings found you in the woods. Can you talk to me?"

Claire lifted her right hand to her throat. It tired her to make the slightest movement.

"Catherine, could you please get Ms. Nichols some water?" Catherine hurried for the liquid. Claire watched as Catherine came back with a glass and a straw. She handed it to the doctor, who put the straw to Claire's lips. "Drink slow, your stomach has been empty for a while." Claire began to sip. The water felt cool and refreshing. She kept drinking. The doctor talked to Tony. Claire continued to drink. She felt the invigorating liquid lubricate her throat. As she sipped she only heard a buzz inside her head. The doctor's lips moved as did Tony's, but the only sound was the buzz. He removed the straw from her lips. The buzzing ceased.

"Please, that was so good," Claire spoke. The room went silent. Everyone turned to her.

"Claire, thank god. How do you feel?" Tony leaned over her. She realized she wasn't in her bed, it was a hospital bed. That made sense. She wondered how she'd sat up. But, she wasn't in a hospital room, it was her suite.

"I feel . . . I feel . . . tired . . . and kind of dizzy" Her voice quivered weakly with uncertainty and pain.

Dr. Leonard asked Tony and Catherine to allow him to examine Claire alone. Catherine agreed and began to leave but Tony stayed, saying Claire wouldn't mind him being there. Claire started to say it was all right, Tony could stay when Dr. Leonard continued, "Mr. Rawlings, I realize you hired me. However, as a medical doctor, I need to see and talk to Ms. Nichols alone. You will be welcomed back as soon as we are done." Tony just stared at Dr. Leonard. The doctor continued, "Mr. Rawlings, she is not related to you. We must allow her some privacy."

Claire watched and thought, *Tony can handle this. It's his battle.* But he didn't battle. "I'm sorry. You are right. It is just that it has been so long since she has been awake. I don't want to leave her." Standing, he continued, "But I will. I will be right outside the door. Please call me when you are finished." Then he leaned over, kissed Claire on her forehead, and left the room.

The doctor spoke soothingly as he helped Claire remove her nightgown and removed tubes. Claire mindlessly thought about the doctor's breath; it smelled like coffee, she liked coffee. He pushed on her side and asked if it hurt. He touched her face, her cheek, her temple, did any of it hurt? He examined her head, touching her skull, front and back, and near the neck. Then he focused on her arms and legs. Lastly, he touched her back, pushing harder in some spots. Claire could see the remnants of the bruises on her

146

arms, legs, and midsection. She felt them elsewhere. Her back and midsection hurt the most from the doctor's pressure, and her face felt tender. Looking at her legs covered in brown and yellow marks, she wondered if her face looked as bad as her legs. After he finished with his examination, and yes, no questions, he helped her put her nightgown back on.

"Ms. Nichols, I need you to be completely honest with me, do you understand?" Claire said she did, but she was getting very tired. "Please tell me what you remember from the night of your accident."

"Dr. Leonard, I'm very tired and my memories are fuzzy." As she spoke her head continued to buzz. Her throat felt raw. The combination made talking difficult.

"It's all right. Let me put your bed back." He pushed the button to recline the bed and continued to inquire, "Now please, what do you remember?"

The fatigue overwhelmed Claire. Abruptly her stomach revolted against the water. Initially queasy, she instantly knew she would be sick. "Doctor, I'm going to get sick." She sat up. He grabbed a basin, and the water she drank came back up. Dr. Leonard explained it was normal, her stomach had been empty for too long. The vomiting made her shake, and suddenly her head and ribs throbbed. The fierce pain caused her to cry.

"Ms. Nichols, your pain medicine has started to wear off. I will get you some more, but I want you to be thinking straight. Please tell me what happened." He was persistent.

Claire felt faint and her body felt limp. She wanted food, but her stomach wouldn't even hold water. The doctor wanted to know what happened and she knew. When she closed her eyes and felt the pain she saw Tony. She saw his rage, his fury, his unwillingness to let her explain. She remembered every terrifying minute until she blacked out. It happened two weeks ago but she still felt the agony.

The weakness, combined with the unsettled stomach, told her it wasn't going to end anytime soon. She wanted to go back to her visions. Nevertheless, the doctor waited for the answer to his question. He gave her some more water but instructed her to only rinse and spit into the basin. It helped the terrible taste go away. Her mouth felt moist again. She could speak.

"I went for a walk in the woods, I like the woods. It rained the day before and the ground was slippery in some spots. I made it into the woods fine, but I let it get dark. I watched the sun set. I remember it being crimson and beautiful." She laid her head back on the pillow and closed her eyes. Softly tears trickled down her cheeks. Dr. Leonard was determined, he asked her to continue. She did, but with closed eyes. "So it was dark by the time I headed back to the house. I remember getting to the clearing, which is about forty-five minutes from here. The sun . . . I mean, moon, was bright. I tried to get back. Catherine had dinner waiting for me." Her eyelids were heavy and her words slowed and slurred. She never remembered feeling so incredibly tired, all she wanted to do was sleep. Please God, she prayed, let me sleep.

"Ms. Nichols, did you make it back to the house?" Dr. Leonard spoke softly.

"I don't remember." Her decision was made. Telling the truth wouldn't do any good. Actually, it would be a direct violation of Tony's rules. She wasn't allowed to discuss private matters. She learned her lesson well. As her ribs, head, and stomach ached, the lesson was reinforced. "I remember slipping in the mud. There were roots and limbs. It was very dark under the trees. After that, I just don't know."

"Please know, Ms. Nichols, anything you disclose to me is said in confidence. I am bound by complete patient-doctor confidentiality," he spoke quietly. Despite her physical exhaustion, Claire's mind was astute. She knew every word they uttered was recorded and possibly overheard as they spoke.

"Doctor, I'm not sure what you are asking me or what you are implying, but I can't remember what happened that night. Perhaps I hit my head." Her eyes were open and brimming with tears. She felt so tired. "Please, may I rest?" Her eyes closed and she slipped away.

Hours later, Claire opened her eyes to see Catherine holding a glass of her famous banana strawberry yogurt smoothie. She told the caring woman she was afraid it would make her sick, like the water. Catherine explained the doctor had put some medicine in her IV. It would help with the pain and nausea. Claire reached for the button to sit herself up, but before she could get to it, Tony did. His presence made her involuntarily tremble. His eyes weren't dark; instead, they were soft suede brown. He gently touched her face. "You need to listen to Catherine. Please try to drink the smoothie. You need to get better, and to do that you need to eat." She looked at him and wondered if he knew about her recent confidential conversation. He continued to plead, "Please, Claire."

She drank some of the smoothie, closed her eyes, and fell asleep.

The next time she woke her suite burst with flowers. They looked beautiful and their aroma permeated her dreams. Over the next few weeks they were constantly replaced. It seemed as if they never wilted. They were meant to make her feel better, but they reminded her of the funeral home after her parents' death.

She even received *get well* cards and flowers from the Simmons', Millers, and Bronsons. Apparently, Tony's secretary, Patricia, called Sue to apologize. Claire had been so busy recently, and with her *accident* she hadn't been able to call. But, she would when she felt better and got the chance. It made Claire feel so much better knowing that even though she'd almost died, appearances were maintained. Claire recovered slowly and gradually. Dr. Leonard continued to treat her, coming to the estate every day during the first week after she woke. After that, the length between visits steadily increased. He never questioned her memory again. He did push her to recover. He pushed her to eat, walk, and go outside. He wasn't the only one pushing. Catherine pushed. She pushed Claire to eat, shower, and do her hair and makeup.

The provoking seemed necessary. Claire would have lain in bed all day if they would let her. The only motivation she possessed was to return to the visions she'd experienced during her unconsciousness. Unfortunately, they didn't reappear in any of her dreams.

It wasn't that she felt sad, she didn't. She didn't feel scared, and with enough medication she didn't feel pain. Accurately, she felt nothing. Consciously or unconsciously she'd compartmentalized everything away. Nothing remained. With each prompt she obeyed. She ate. She walked -- with difficulty at first. Her muscles lost tone in just two weeks. And her weight dropped below anything she ever remembered. She showered, at first with assistance and then on her own. She conceded to Catherine's pleas for hair and makeup. However, every activity tired her. Therefore, sleep became a natural and accepted escape.

The one person who didn't pressure Claire was Tony. He was, however, omnipresent every day. Catherine told Claire he hadn't left her side while she was unconscious. Now, he went to work but returned every evening. He spent most of his time in Claire's suite, sometimes with his laptop, reading a book, talking, always willing to listen, and every night sleeping. While Claire stayed in the hospital bed, he slept in a recliner that was brought to her room. Once she made the transition to her big bed, he *asked* if he could sleep with her.

Claire said yes, but . . . Tony said he just wanted to sleep near her. Dr. Leonard hadn't given her the go-ahead on all normal activities. She'd suffered a concussion which attributed to her unconsciousness and headaches. However, it was her broken ribs that caused the problem. Claire couldn't lay certain ways. Her own weight caused intense pain. She knew Tony's weight would be agony. She didn't assume she had a choice in his sleeping site and truly didn't care as long as she could sleep. He didn't complain.

Each milestone—getting out of bed alone, walking to the bathroom alone, walking to the dining room, or going into the backyard received a gift. Some were simple tokens: a book, a journal, or a scarf—apparently very *in style* this season. But others, like for her first dinner in the dining room, were extravagant. The dining room warranted a new *journey* necklace, with three diamonds in increasing sizes to represent past, present, and future. The entire carat weight was easily over three. It was remarkable, but Claire missed her grandmother's necklace. She remembered it too was a casualty of the *accident*.

It appeared the giving of gifts gave Tony pleasure, so she accepted them. The journey necklace representing past, present, and future didn't sit well. She knew even in her fragile state, she didn't want *any* of the represented time periods. The jewelry was so excessive Claire began to think of it as costume. It made accepting it easier. She tried to act happy about the gifts and the attention. However, she felt like his eyes had been—devoid of emotion. There was nothing inside of her.

Catherine knew Claire liked being outside and encouraged Tony to take her out into the yard. The scene didn't help her state of mind. The blue skies rarely shone and the green of spring and summer had dispelled like brown withered leaves in the wind. The foliage gone, the trees were bare, and the outside was gray. Now all that remained was the black and white photo of landscape Claire saw when she first arrived.

One day, while walking the perimeter of the backyard wearing warm coats and soft gloves, she asked Tony, "Do you have any idea when my debt will be paid?" The question caught him off guard. She witnessed the fluctuation of his eyes. The intensity changed, finally settling on light brown.

"My dear Claire, the last time you were on your own, which was for only a day, look what happened. I think you need me. I don't want you to have more accidents." And then he added, "Do you?" Claire knew without a doubt she didn't want any more accidents.

They didn't discuss her accident. They discussed travel. The idea of leaving the estate frightened Claire. She felt confident she could avoid accidents if she stayed put. Tony said when she was better he would like to have her join him while he traveled. He talked about Chicago, New York, Phoenix, San Francisco, and overseas destinations. Claire asked if she needed a passport if they flew on a private jet. Tony said he would have Brent work on getting her one.

On a Saturday in mid-November, two months after her accident, Claire was technically pronounced physically well. She'd become stronger with time. Her bruises had disappeared, ribs totally healed, headaches less frequent, and she could eat, although she had no appetite. Dr. Leonard visited the estate the day before and released her from his care.

Tony decided they should go on a drive. Claire hadn't left the property or even the immediate house since early September. Faced with the reality of getting into the car caused an explosive and unexpected trauma.

That morning she obediently dressed in the clothes she found laid out for her which happened every day since she was well enough to dress. The sun shone and the temperature felt unseasonably warm. She anticipated going outside, but when Tony announced he had the Lexus out front, Claire panicked. Her reaction was quick and unpredicted. She started to cry and shake. She didn't want to go.

For the first time since the *accident* Tony pushed. He didn't ask, he declared; they were going for a drive. It was the best thing he could do. She needed to get out, but Claire couldn't think straight. She sat down on the front steps and refused to get up. Finally, Tony reached for her arm. She reacted in a way she hadn't since the first days of her arrival. Her entire body filled with anguish. Violently trembling, she started to scream, "I remember everything! I know the truth! *Please* do not touch me!" Her torment erupted as her volume increased, "I hate you! Leave me alone!" He looked at her with disbelief. She stared at him with vengeance.

Her screaming caused Catherine and Cindy to come running. By the time they arrived, Claire's words were unintelligible, overlapped by sobs and whimpers. She sat on the steps, shaking, holding her knees, and rocking back and forth. Eventually her sobs subsided into freely flowing tears. She didn't speak as Catherine gently helped her to her feet and calmly walked her to the car.

They began the drive in silence. Tony didn't do or say anything. He drove and let Claire cry. It had been two months since her *accident*. She hadn't cried or said a word, and suddenly it all exploded.

150

Dr. Leonard had given his clearance. Tony had been patient. Claire knew what he wanted and she was petrified to be with him again. He drove them to a meadow. She'd never been there before or even seen it. It was very secluded. Claire's crying subsided. Tony tenderly helped her out of the car, and while holding her hand he offered his overdue apology. "Claire, I'm sorry."

She looked up at his eyes, they glistened light brown. "You are sorry? Why are you sorry?"

His tone was remorseful and sincere. "I am sorry for your *accident*." She didn't respond and looked away from his eyes. He continued, "Yes, I admit what happened that night was me. I admit I lost control, something which doesn't usually happen. I admit I feel terrible, and Catherine has made me feel worse. I admit I was beyond furious with you and the article by Meredith Banks. I wasn't thinking straight." His eyes were getting darker. "I trusted you. I believed you wouldn't betray my confidence and then . . ." His shoulders stiffened then relaxed, "Claire, I would do anything to have that night to do over."

They stood by the car, no longer touching. The breeze gently rustled the tall grass, blew wisps of hair around her face, and filled her lungs with the smell of impending winter. Claire watched his expression as he spoke. It had been so long since she'd felt anything. Suddenly, she fought the rapid mixture of emotions stirring inside of her.

Tony watched as her eyes, which had been dull and dead, contained a small spark.

"Tony, I remember. I remember what you were doing and saying. I remember you saying I would need to be alone for a while, to think about who to talk to and who not to talk to." Tony nodded his head. He'd said that. Claire's eyes brimmed with tears and her chest swelled with fear, but she needed to know. "Is that still coming?"

He reached for her shoulders. He intended to be gentle, but Claire remembered fury and backed away, tripped, and fell onto the ground. His eyes said gentle but she remembered anger. She didn't know what to think or feel. Not feeling was so much easier. Confusion, apprehension, anger, and dread all showed in her eyes. He followed her to the ground.

"Claire, please stop." He knelt beside her. "No, that isn't coming. I don't think you need any more reminders on how to behave, do you?" She said no, she didn't. "Claire, may I please touch you?"

Her trembling resumed. Sobs again resonated from her chest. His voice still gentle but firm, "You know I don't need your permission to touch you. I don't need your permission to do anything."

Claire's eyes closed as she tried to swallow her sobs. She nodded her head yes. She knew too well her permission was not necessary.

"But I would like to have it. Please, may I have your consent?"

She braced herself and opened her eyes. She looked at him, his expression, and his eyes. She closed her eyes again and meekly replied, "Okay."

He scooted next to her, sitting on the cold hard ground, and softly placed his arm around her back. He felt her tension and gently bent down and tenderly kissed her lips, very lightly brushing his lips against hers. She didn't back away. The aroma of her shampoo filled the air as her hair blew in the breeze. It reminded him of flowers. "Have I told you how much I like the highlights in your hair?" She shook her head no. He lightly stroked her hair. "I think you are amazing. You are so strong and resilient. I don't deserve your forgiveness for what I did, but you deserve to hear me ask for it."

She didn't want to look at him. Her emotions were too raw. She wanted to forgive him.

He didn't touch her, instead he moved himself in front of her so they were eye to eye. "Claire, I am sorry I hurt you." She felt the tears as she tried to maintain eye contact. He gently took her hands. "I ask that one day you will consider forgiving me."

He kissed her hands.

When she looked into his eyes she saw sadness and remorse. The swirl of emotions that had so violently erupted at the estate now settled into her chest. She wanted the sadness to go away. He'd been so patient. He was being so tender. She didn't forgive him, but she began to respond to his advances. It started with kissing, he kissed her and she began to kiss him. Then she felt her hands as they caressed his arms and shoulders.

Tony bulged with excitement, yet he didn't rush or push. He stayed compassionate and tender.

"Tony, I'm scared."

"I promise I'll be gentle." Although she had every reason to not believe him, she did.

"Can we please go home to a nice soft bed?" He quietly stood and helped Claire to her feet. She took his offered hand. They walked back to the car. This time, she got in willingly.

When they pulled up to the house, Claire leaned over. "I really want this. But please be gentle."

He parked, walked around to her door, and helped her out of the car. They walked up the front steps hand in hand. Only a few hours ago this had been the scene of her hysterics. When he opened the door he scooped Claire into his arms and instead of going up to her suite, carried her to *his* room. While he held her, she closed her eyes and nuzzled his neck. The aroma of his skin and cologne intoxicated her.

She had never, in all the time she'd been there, been in his bedroom. It was grand, almost royal. The walls were covered with cherry paneling and ornate carpentry. One wall was covered with a large screen framed like a picture, like the one in his office. His bed was massive, tall and larger than a normal king-sized. There were steps to reach the height of the mattress.

He gently placed her on his bed. She watched as he slowly removed her shoes. Then, he unbuttoned and tenderly removed her jacket, her blouse, and her jeans. He removed his own clothes while she observed his every move. He was gorgeous, and his moves were slow and sensual. He softly kissed her, causing her to lie back. She looked up at the beautiful ornate ceiling. She felt his lips move down her body. They lingered at her neck, at her breast, stopping to lick and suckle her nipples. Claire's back arched, and she pressed her breasts toward Tony.

He continued to touch her warm body, taste her skin, and inhale her scent.

She hadn't realized it before that moment, but after experiencing satisfaction routinely, the void of the past two months left her wanting. Her body was now alive, on full alert, with every nerve electrified. He fondled her breasts and gently twisted her nipples. She moaned in ecstasy. He stopped. "Did I hurt you? I'm sorry. Do you want me to stop?"

She pleaded, "No, god no. Please don't stop."

He allowed his lips to move from her breasts to her flat stomach and over her protruding hipbones. He tenderly spread her legs and kissed her inner thighs. She feared she would explode before he ever reached his destination. Next, his mouth affectionately awakened her desires. He satisfied every need she'd ever had and ones she'd forgotten. He moved slowly and deliberately, sensual and romantic, compassionate and loving.

He was patient and remorseful. Now it was his turn to experience a favorable consequence. His pleasure came by pleasing her. His actions took everything away. And now his actions brought everything back and more.

Nothing is more common on earth
than to deceive and be deceived.
—Johann G. Seume

Chapter 22

The ashtray overflowed with cigarette butts. Samuel Rawls and Jared Clawson sat while Nathaniel Rawls paced. The large polished conference table was barely visible beneath the magnitude of papers. The players no longer worked from the New Jersey office above the textile factory as they had five years ago. Instead, the view from the conference table or large mahogany desk is now that of Cedar Street in the heart of Manhattan's financial district.

"Rawls stock is up another five-eighths after heavy trading. The rumors that circulated today about the quarterly report helped with that increase," Clawson said as he leaned back in the comfortable leather chair, adjusting his suit jacket. Nathaniel's track around the large office included peering out toward the NYSE and circling the desk to see the large computer screens which relayed up-to-the-minute stock information. Exhaling a large gray cloud, he asked the question that sat heavily on his and Samuel's minds, "But what happens when it is discovered the rumors and reality are different?"

"Shit hits the fan." Clawson smiled. "So -- we don't tell anyone."

Samuel rubbed his throbbing head. "What do you mean we don't tell anyone? The quarterly earnings report will be released tomorrow. The investors will find out that our capital is down. That last string of investments wiped out millions."

"Numbers are funny things. I have a copy here of an alternative report. The numbers are all legitimate, but the information is written with a positive slant." Clawson distributed the report. The room filled with uncomfortable silence as the two Rawls men read the new report.

"Where is the original report?" Nathaniel bellowed. Immediately, Clawson pulled the requested pages from the cluttered table. The elder Rawls took the two reports and sat heavily at his desk. Page by page he compared

154

the figures. Samuel and Clawson watched as the tips of Nathaniel's lips moved from south to north. The telephone rang, breaking the silence. Instead of answering, Nathaniel hit the button on the intercom. "Connie, I said *no* calls!"

The voice from the box spoke apologetically, "I'm sorry, Mr. Rawls. It's your personal line. I'll take care of it." Immediately, the ringing stopped.

The sight of Nathaniel's smile had differing effects. Clawson resumed his leaned back position and lit another cigarette. Samuel leaned forward and held his head in his hands. Confronting his father in front of Clawson wasn't a good idea, but it had to be done. This whole damn thing was getting out of hand.

It is difficult to know at what moment love begins;
it is less difficult to know it has begun
—Henry Wadsworth Longfellow

Chapter 23

His head rested on his arm as he listened to her breathing and watched her sleep. The discussion in his head had raged for hours. Sensing her warmth, inhaling her scent, and wanting to taste her lips . . . the voice of love prevailed.

Claire floated in that place before consciousness. She had difficulty distinguishing reality from fantasy, unsure of what she was feeling. The epiphany came with the realization she was --feeling. It had been so long since she felt anything. She felt warm, safe, and secure. Her mind tried to convince her it was a dream, but she remembered feeling that way before she fell asleep. She questioned herself, *is this real?* Her soft skin rolled on the silky sheets and felt radiating warmth. Hesitantly, she opened her eyes. Right in front of her, close enough to touch, was Tony's firm broad chest. Again, the questions, *is he really here?* He usually left her bed before she woke. *Why is he still here?* Now as Claire rolled onto her back and saw the beautiful ornate ceiling she wondered, *Where is here? This isn't my room.*

With a rich raspy tone, he greeted her, "Good morning, Claire." His smile revealed the winner of his internal monologue; adoration and love showed through. He leaned down to kiss her head.

"Good morning, what are you doing still in bed?" The room was quite dark. "Or is it morning? It's so dark." The eyes watching her weren't.

"I've been watching you sleep." He slid his arm under her back, placing her head upon his shoulder. His aroma was exhilarating. His hard strong shoulder made the perfect pillow as his arm gently surrounded her warm body.

"Why would you do that? I need a shower and probably look awful." She buried her face into his chest, allowing his hairs to tickle her cheeks. She inhaled deeply.

He took her chin and turned her face toward his, gently kissing her lips. "I have been watching you because you are so beautiful. Your face is flawless." Claire tried to look away from his eyes. They were light, honest, and real. The candidness made her uneasy. "Please don't look away. I see you now and think about what your face looked like, what I did to you. I'm not going to keep bringing this up, but I want you to know how much I regret it. And how amazing I think you are. You went through so much. I don't want anything like that to ever happen again."

She couldn't stop the tears from trickling down her cheeks. She wanted to hide her face, but he held her chin firmly. "Tony, I'm glad to know you're sorry. I'm sorry too." He let go of her chin, but she continued watching as she spoke. "I'm sorry about Meredith. I really didn't say anything to her. She walked up and recognized me. Like the article said, we were sorority sisters. I never suspected she was a reporter. She asked if she could join me. I didn't want her to, I thought about your rules, but then I thought about appearances, and I decided telling her no would be rude. I'm sorry I made the wrong decision."

He rolled her over onto her back. The skin of his chest pressed against her bare breasts. Looking up into his face she saw his eyes darken only slightly. His features looked like those of a model, prominent cheek bones and strong jaw line. His gaze went on for an eternity before he finally spoke. "I can't promise I will never get upset. I can probably promise I will. However, I promise I will do my best to never hurt you like that again. But, I need something from you."

She assumed it involved gratification, and she didn't mind. "What do you want me to do?"

"I want you to make me a promise." Claire raised her eyebrows. "A promise, that you will do your best to follow my rules. That you will do your best -- to never give me cause to hurt you again."

"Tony, I promise I will do my best to make you proud. And I accept your apology. You don't need to keep apologizing." Looking at his expression she read a mixture of emotions: gratitude, adoration, and relief.

"Have I told you how amazing you were? I've watched you with Dr. Leonard fifty times. You were in such pain. God, even water made you sick. Yet, you were perfect and made me so proud. I listened to your answers over and over. I understand his concern. Our story didn't hold water. I was just so worried about you, lying on the floor, and I couldn't get you to wake. I had to get you some medical help. I was upset about what I thought you'd done. The longer I waited for you to get home that night, the more betrayed I felt. I lost control." Claire saw such honesty in his eyes. It was like a window exposing his soul, one she didn't think he allowed many people to see. "When you quit moving I realized what happened and I became more upset about what I'd done. Suddenly, getting you help was more important than appearances." He gently smoothed her hair. "You had the chance to tell someone about me, and what I did. I deserved that and more. But no, even in your condition you were perfect."

He lowered his face to her collar bone. His rough beard growth prickled her skin. "I don't deserve your forgiveness, but . . ." looking again into her emerald eyes, "thank you for giving it to me."

He started to kiss her. Her body responded, but her mind thought about the cameras and surveillance. She knew they were there. Compartmentalize. She had a lot to put away. She needed bigger compartments.

Claire felt his hardness on her leg as his lips moved down her neck to her collar bone. Her breasts pressed upward in anticipation of his mouth and her nipples hardened as his lips lightly brushed their tips. Trying to suppress her heated desires, Claire asked for a favor, "Tony, while we're asking for things, may I have something from you?"

"I have something for you right now," he said between kisses, inching his way down her body, gently spreading her legs.

"And, I want that." Claire smiled as she lifted her head to catch his eyes. "But first, can I have a promise?" Tony moved up, kissed her lips, and asked what she wanted him to promise. "You were right, there was pain. But what haunted me for two months was the threat of you locking me in my suite. Please don't use my honesty against me. I don't want to be locked up alone again. It was unbearable. I know you don't have to, but I'm asking you . . . please promise you will never threaten me with that or do that to me again."

"Claire, I promise I will not lock you in your suite again. And if we each keep our promises, maintaining them all will be easier."

"Thank you," she sighed, his promise removed a tremendous weight. Her body yearned. "Now what did you say about having something for me?"

He looked at her smile. It was real, extending to her gleaming green eyes, and it was for him. Tony grinned back, a little more mischievous this time.

Breakfast was served in Tony's suite. They ate with wet hair while wrapped in thick soft white robes. Claire's appetite returned with a vengeance. She ate eggs, turkey bacon, toast, and fruit. She even thought about hash browns. She decided maybe she should tell Catherine she liked hash browns. Tony's voice took Claire's attention away from her food. "I have a confession. I think I'm an example of my own rule." Claire told him she didn't know what he meant. He explained that although he's thrilled with the outcome of yesterday's drive, it wasn't his goal.

Claire smiled and responded, "Well appearances," looking at their wet hair and robes, "would say differently." She used her toe to rub up and down his leg. "I'm happy with the outcome too. But, what was your goal?" He told her it was simply to get her to leave the estate to go somewhere. He wanted to get her away before they *needed* to go somewhere. Claire reflected on the past twenty-four hours. Okay, he did that too. "Why? When do we need to go somewhere? And where do we need to go?" Her toe still wandered.

"If you keep that up, we'll be late." Tony's voice didn't sound concerned. He glanced at the clock by his bed, eleven seventeen. "Well, we are supposed to be at Brent and Courtney's for dinner at three thirty this afternoon."

158

Claire did some math in her head, they had four hours. "I really would rather stay here, but I suspect I don't have a choice. How many people will be there?"

Tony confirmed she was correct. They were going and it would just be the four of them. Courtney had been asking Tony to bring Claire over since the beginning of October. They sent her flowers and cards, they must have known about her *accident*. Claire liked Courtney, Tony obviously trusted them. She could do it.

While she thought about the Simmons' and refocused on her breakfast, her toe was stopped in its exploration and lifted. She followed the sensation and found Tony on the ground, holding her foot.

He slowly put her toe in his mouth and began to suck. He watched her reaction as her brain forgot the breakfast and impending dinner. The slight gasp that escaped her lips made him smile.

She immediately felt the sensation on her toe ignite pulsations elsewhere. His lips moved from her toe, to her foot, ankle, and leg. He opened her robe and pulled her toward him. Claire's body tingled in anticipation. Too soon he gave her unimaginable thrills.

Finding their way back to his bed, Tony supported himself above her lean, blossoming body. With a raspy voice he inquired, "Claire, what do you want?" She looked in his eyes again, still so light and real. He had never asked her what *she* wanted. He kissed her neck, her back arched and pressed against him. He continued, "I want to hear you, no forcing, and no directions. What do you want?" His desires were clear and rubbing across her thighs.

"I want you."

That wasn't enough, Tony wanted to hear more. "Tell me what you want. I need to know you want it as much as I do."

"Oh god, Tony, I want you. I want you inside of me." Her body was on the brink of explosion. "Please. Please take me." She closed her eyes as he did what she asked.

Grabbing his shoulders, she wanted every bit of him, every inch, and now that he was there, she lost control. Her body responded to his every movement; no consciousness, only carnal desire. More than once he elicited earthshaking convulsions. There was no question this was consensual. Claire was getting what she asked for and wanted more.

Tony drove to and from the Simmons'. This time they took the Mercedes. It was a great ride from the back when Eric drove, but it was even better from the passenger's seat, smooth and quiet. Tony tuned the satellite radio to a classical station. The warm car, soft music, and smooth ride almost had Claire napping. Her energy wasn't at its pre-accident level, and her eyes began to close. Catherine told her one time not to act tired, but she wasn't acting. Tony noticed. "It's all right. Why don't you lay the seat back and I'll wake you when we arrive." She did.

They had a good time with Brent and Courtney. Courtney told Claire a thousand times she needed to gain some weight. The unfortunate accident in the woods left her too thin, but she quickly added, "But you're still beautiful." After the delicious dinner they retired to the lower level; the Vikings and the

Packers were playing. Apparently, Brent and Tony were Vikings fans. Claire wondered how she didn't know that.

While they watched the game and argued with the television, Claire and Courtney chatted. It was nice to talk to someone else. Courtney made Claire feel warm and secure. She didn't pry but wanted to know about Claire's accident and recovery. Apparently, Brent told her how upset Tony was. He couldn't believe something like that could happen on his land. Did they ever find out if someone had been out in the woods?

The football game didn't turn out like the men wanted. Undaunted they all sipped red wine and played cards. Claire hadn't *played* a game in so long. It was truly enjoyable. They left the Simmons' home after eleven. Courtney hugged Claire, "Now you promise to eat." Claire nodded. "We're so happy you're feeling better."

On the way home Tony praised Claire for all she did and said. He also informed her he needed to be in New York the following week. It was up to her if she joined him. However, she may not realize Thursday of next week would be Thanksgiving. He couldn't promise he would be back. He may have to stay until Friday. He would like her to join him if she was up to it. Claire knew the intense therapy of the last two days had helped revitalize her. "I may need naps, but I want to go."

During the week between the Simmons and New York, Claire made strides in her recovery. It was like a black veil had been lifted. For weeks, even months, the entire world had been gray. The release of suppressed emotions and Tony's promise removed the veil. The trees were still leafless and the grass still lacked color, but the world was once again alive.

Instead of sleeping to get energy, Claire began moving. First, she walked around the house, then swam in the indoor pool, and enjoyed the hot tub. She even ventured to the theater room and made herself watch a movie. It was a musical, "Hairspray" with John Travolta. She smiled. It was her first trip to the theater room since Tony had taken her there.

Monday evening they flew to New York watching the sky grow dark as they headed east. Eric drove them directly to Tony's apartment, and Jan waited for their arrival with dinner. From the spectacular view of the seventy-sixth floor, the city vibrantly glistened with lights and activity. They ate in the dining room and watched little cars drive on busy little streets far below.

That night, exhausted from traveling, they settled into Tony's bed and he handed Claire a black velvet box. Her shoulders slumped. "Tony, please stop. No more black velvet boxes. I have plenty of jewelry. I love it all, but I don't need it. I feel bad about you spending all this money on me."

"Well, first, if you haven't noticed, money isn't an issue. And what good is money if it doesn't buy the things I want? Besides, this is a special gift." Claire raised her eyebrows.

He continued, "Somehow, with all that happened in the past two months, I made an awful mistake." Claire feared he was talking about the accident again. "I realized it when I was getting you your ID and credit card."

Now she knew what he meant. He'd missed her birthday. "It's all right. I've received plenty of gifts lately." She tried to give him back the box.

160

"No," he declared adamantly. "It is not all right. You had a birthday, your twenty-seventh, on October 17." He firmly yet tenderly held her hands with the box in them, while his tone softened. "The other gifts were because of your accomplishments." *And your guilt*, Claire mentally added. "This one is for your birthday." She looked helplessly at the box. He continued, "Okay, I'm a cheapskate." With a frisky grin he added, "I'm regifting, again."

Looking at the box Claire pondered the possibilities of his regifting. Her eyes opened wide. She lifted the velvet lid to reveal her grandmother's necklace. It looked perfect, absolutely no evidence of the *accident* it had endured. She beamed at Tony, closed the box, and put it on the bedside stand. Scooting close to him, resting her head on his chest, her green eyes gleamed with moisture. "I think you're doing a great job of enticing me to feeling better. I wonder sometimes how I got here." The fatigue made her head pound. She closed her eyes, the moisture escaped as tears onto Tony's chest. Her shields were down and mask gone. "I know I'm here because you *own* me and my debt. Sometimes I feel that way, but other times you make me feel special." She nuzzled into his warm embrace. Her words slowed, fatigue prevailed, "I don't know any more if you're using me or if you care about me. I know what I hope."

He listened to her. Her words ran together but she continued, "I want you to know it didn't start this way, but, Tony, I'm willing to do what you ask, not because of my debt but because I want you to be happy." She couldn't give him gifts in black velvet boxes. She could only give herself.

He kissed her hair, tasting her scent mixed with hairspray and perfume. He held her soft body against his. "Thank you for making me happy." Caressing her silky shoulder, he wanted her, all of her.

"Thank you for helping my necklace too." Her breathing became rhythmic and even. She fell asleep with her head on his chest.

"God help me, I do care about you." Gently hugging her against his body, he tenderly moved her hair away from her angelic face. Seeing her sleep, peaceful and trusting, his thoughts of waking her for his desires were quickly replaced. He held her close, closed his eyes, and joined her in sleep.

Love comforteth like sunshine after rain.
—William Shakespeare

Chapter 24

Tuesday morning bustled with activity. Tony left early for meetings. Eric chauffeured Claire to a spa appointment for a highlight treatment. During the two months since her last appointment, she'd barely ventured outside. She needed sun and blonde to maintain her hair. The sun wasn't going to happen, but the blonde could. Claire agreed to a hair appointment and a manicure but declined other services. The idea of having a massage, someone touching her, made her very uncomfortable.

Afterward she had Eric bring her back to the apartment where she rested until Tony returned in the evening. He informed her they had plans for the following evening. He also asked if she went shopping. She explained, "I waited for you here. My head ached and I think traveling wore me out. I was just too tired." The answers didn't please him, but he didn't complain or argue.

Wednesday late afternoon Claire prepared for their plans. She didn't know what they were or where they were going, only to be ready by five. The night before Tony looked through the closet and inspected the clothes Catherine packed. After only brief scrutiny, Tony announced that nothing she brought would do for their plans. He wanted her to wear something special, something she chose, and everything brand-new.

It took her the better part of the day. She left the apartment early in the morning and visited Manhattan, Soho, and the Upper East Side. All of her work paid off, she'd done it. Actually, she'd gotten her new outfit and a few more items. Due to her post *accident* leaner body, she decided some new slacks, jeans, and sweaters were in order. She refused to even calculate the total of her expenditures. Tony would know with a click of his computer, but she wasn't concerned. He liked her to spend money. With Eric available to get her packages, the shopping was getting easier. Her new outfit consisted of a black one-shouldered silk crepe dress with a long-sleeved overlay from a quaint little boutique in Soho. The Valentino bow pumps were a perfect match from Nordstrom's. The Kate Spade shoulder bag and stretch wool long coat came from Saks. Due to the cool November temperature the associate recommended hosiery. When they showed her the thigh-high sheer hose, she knew she'd successfully followed Tony's rules and covered her legs at the same time. Of the extra items she found, her favorite was a cashmere hoodie, dusty rose, and amazingly soft. It would be perfect for snuggling up at home with a book on a cold winter day.

Something about the thought of *home* meaning Tony's house perplexed Claire. She decided it was what it was. As he had put it, her actions in Chicago resulted in the consequence of *needing* him to *keep her from having more accidents*. It wasn't up for debate. She also knew things could be considerably worse than snuggling with a book, by the fire, in her suite, in her cashmere hoodie, and some comfortable jeans. She did her best to compartmentalize. It made the fire, book, and hoodie all very pleasant.

Tony entered the bedroom as she wore a black silk robe and worked on her hair. She knew during her recovery he only visited his district offices via Internet. He'd sent Timothy to do some of his bidding, but his presence had more influence. Some things needed to be dealt with in person. If his mood was any indication, the business dealings were going well.

He came up behind her and kissed her neck, igniting an immediate fire within her soul. Her busy day allowed only a short nap, but his kiss sparked her to full alert. Her hair was pinned up and she was curling the ends.

"Good evening, Claire. I trust you were successful with your shopping endeavors today?" She happily informed him that she'd done very well, even finding some extra items. His grin showed his approval. "I can't wait to see tonight's ensemble."

He went to the dressing room to prepare for his shower. Completely nude and ready to enter the steamy water, he paused to caress Claire's skin. Reaching his arms around her, he maneuvered his hands under her flimsy robe. "Do you think joining me in the shower would be detrimental to your hair and makeup?" He nuzzled her neck.

She could smell his intoxicating scent. His chin's stubble triggered goose bumps on her arms and legs. "I think it would." Her voice resonated unconvincingly.

"Then perhaps we should plan it for another time?" His hands didn't obey his words and continued to fondle.

"Or . . . we could postpone your plans?" Claire's eyes closed, head tilted against his chest, and hands massaged his strong arms. She turned to face him. He was visibly glad to be near her.

His voice gravely and low, he said, "Oh god, I want to, but we have plenty of time for that. Tonight I have special plans for you." He gently pulled away from her. "And so far you look amazing. I believe I like your outfit now better than the one you bought."

Claire flashed a modest smile accompanied by blushed cheeks. He'd removed the robe. "It's November. I believe I'd get cold as we walk the streets of New York," her voice reflected Tony's playfulness.

"Perhaps, but if I have anything to do with it, cold is not what you would be feeling." He left her for the shower. It amazed her how he could flip a switch and immediately send her entire body into mayhem. She concentrated on breathing, replaced her robe, and went back to her hair. Her mind, however, was in the next room thinking about Tony's steamy shower and slippery soap suds.

Claire wore her hosiery and dress when Tony reentered the bedroom. His gaze lingered on her. "I think you look stunning." His expression wasn't in complete agreement. He approached her and lifted the hem of her dress, just high enough to expose the tops of the hosiery. His grin broadened. "My! What will they think of next? Very good." He lightly kissed her lips. Claire smiled. He was so predictable - well, sometimes.

By the time they reached the front doors of the building Eric had the limousine warm and ready for their adventure. Once in the back of the car Claire asked Tony about their plans. He would only disclose that their first stop was dinner. The cold crisp night air formed crystals on the windows of the limousine, making the lights of the city shimmer. They seemed to flash rhythmically with intensity mimicking the hum of music coming from the cabin's speakers.

It didn't take long, considering the traffic, to reach their destination—the Crown Plaza Hotel on Broadway, in the heart of New York's theater district. Once inside, Tony directed Claire to Brasserier 1605, a beautiful restaurant bustling with patrons. The hostess immediately ushered them to a romantic table with a stunning view of Times Square. The waiter seemed to know their timetable better than Claire; he provided exceptionally efficient service. Tony ordered a bottle of wine, approved a taste, and the waiter poured two glasses. For their appetizer they enjoyed delicious grilled sea diver scallops with seared Atlantic salmon as their main course. Claire thought everything tasted scrumptious. Along with other sensory organs recently reawakened, she had a newfound appreciation for food. She enjoyed the aroma as the plate appeared in front of her, the taste on her tongue, and the texture as she chewed. Tony watched happily as she delighted in each bite of her seafood.

His mood amused Claire. It seemed different, in a positive way. He talked excessively, yet not about anything in particular. She asked when they were going back to Iowa, and he said he did need to have a few meetings on Friday. So they could leave Friday night or wait until Saturday. Claire felt bad about not being with Catherine on Thanksgiving. She would love to be with John and Emily, but knew better than to ask. Catherine had become her closest family. She hoped Catherine had someone to visit for the holiday.

He wouldn't give hints about their next destination. Being in the Theater District, Claire guessed they were on their way to a show. Smiling, he refused to tell her which one. After dinner Eric appeared to chauffeur them to the Broadhurst Theater. The title on the marquee read "The Merchant of Venice" with Al Pacino. Claire knew it was one of the hottest tickets in town. They, of course, had amazing seats. She'd never been a Shakespearean fan; yet, she became completely engrossed in the play. By the time it ended she'd laughed and cried. The entire cast's performances were riveting, taking her to another world for two hours and completely draining her with the range of sweeping emotions. She was ready to go back to the apartment.

Eric waited for them as they left the theater. Not surprisingly, Tony didn't ask Claire if she wanted to go back or go out. She assumed they would be heading to the apartment, so when Eric went another direction she was surprised. They headed north to Fifty-Ninth Street, and Eric stopped at Seventh Avenue. They were at Central Park.

The cold crisp air awakened her as they moved from the warm limousine to the waiting horse-drawn carriage. The horseman was prepared for the brisk weather with blankets, and Eric supplied them mittens and scarves. They snuggled together under the blankets holding mittened hands and observed the beautiful park with lights lining the paths and illuminating some of the trees. The large strong horse pulled the carriage slowly and steadily around the eight hundred plus acres. The methodical trot rhythmically created a cadence for their dialogue. Their noses and cheeks reddened in the cool air as they cuddled, talked, and enjoyed the incredibly romantic setting.

Gently holding Claire's mittened hand, Tony spoke honestly with love, "Claire, you know I have dated many women." She said she had read about some. "There have been women who have wanted to date me solely for my money, and I admit to taking advantage of that." His honesty had her full attention. "You know I'm a private person. Truly there are few people who have seen the real me. There are all sorts of psychological reasons for why I am the way I am. They probably stem from childhood and traumas early in life. But, the past is that, and the reasons don't matter. What matters is that unlike many of my business associates or acquaintances, you have met the real me." That thought made her feel slightly uneasy. "There are sides to me that need subduing. Honestly, I've never cared to try, but I do now. And I believe it is possible."

Then while tenderly holding her hand and looking into her eyes, he asked, "Claire, the other night you asked if I cared about you. Honestly, with our initial arrangement I never intended to. But, without a doubt, I do. Do you care about me? Do you enjoy being with me?"

Claire considered her answer. Honesty was the best policy, no matter the consequence. "Tony, I do care about you. I want you to be happy, and I would do anything to help that happen. And on a night like tonight, or even a quiet night at home, I enjoy being with you. More than enjoy." She smiled and her emerald eyes glistened in the cold air. "But honestly, there are times I don't. There are times I want you away from me, or vice versa." She maintained eye contact and watched for his reaction.

He smiled, kissed her long and hard. She kissed back. "You are the most amazing woman. I have vice presidents, presidents, and chairmen of boards who have never experienced me as you have. None of them would have the courage to answer that question as honestly as you just did." She exhaled. "It is your strength and determination that have infuriated me. That strength and resilience has also made me fall in love with you."

Perhaps it shouldn't have been a shock, but it was. He said that he loved her. He had her complete attention and yet her internal monologue almost drowned out his voice: *Love, really? He just said he loves me? Do I love him?*

"Claire, I experienced life without you after your accident. I don't want to do that again. But I want you to make your own decision. Tonight I would like to present you with two options: your freedom, you may leave tonight and your debt is paid; or," he removed a diamond solitaire ring from his jacket pocket, "you could agree to marry me and spend the rest of your life with me, not out of obligation or contractual agreement, but because you want to be with me."

Her heart beat rapidly and her lungs momentarily forgot to breathe. She stared at Tony and at the ring. With only the illumination of the streetlamps she saw the brilliant solitaire diamond. It was surrounded by a delicate diamond border with additional diamonds on the platinum band. She'd never seen anything so beautiful, and Tony was offering it to her. Her mind couldn't stop spinning. She knew she should answer, speak, say something, but words failed her. He continued, "You told me yesterday no more black boxes, so I took it out of its box." He grinned. "Could we see if it fits?"

Claire nodded yes, and extended her left hand. Tony smiled at her as he removed the fuzzy mitten and placed the ring on her fourth finger. She was suddenly glad she agreed to a manicure. "It seems to fit." Tony looked into her emerald eyes. "The question still seems to be unanswered. Do you want to keep it on and stay with me? Will you please be Claire Rawlings?"

She weighed her possibilities. He could be the most romantic man in the world. He was incredibly generous with his money, both to her for whatever she needed and others; thus: much philanthropic recognition. He was the most amazing lover. She'd never in her life experienced sensual highs like she had with him. He was the only person she could talk with freely. He knew all about her, because he knew her private information. *But,* that was the word that haunted her. *But,* he could be dark, mean, cruel, controlling, and sadistic. *He* was the reason for that private information. "I . . . I'm so surprised." She stuttered, "Are you seriously asking *me* to marry *you*?"

He smiled. "Yes, this entire night has been leading to this proposal. I've watched you with me, in private and public, with my closest friends, and I want you there always. I love you." Again, internal debate: *Love? He keeps using that word. Love, do I love him? I think I do. When did that happen?* Oh my, Claire needed to think about this. The napkin thing happened too quickly, this needed contemplation. "Please let me think. I promise you an answer soon."

He waited patiently. The carriage steadily moved through the cold crisp air. She saw her breath as she looked at her hand and at Tony. She thought about his patience as she healed from her injuries, about him risking public exposure with Dr. Leonard, about how he made her feel when she saw him walk into a room. Her contemplation took a while. They sat back in the carriage. She rested her head on his shoulder and thought. He didn't say a word, he didn't push. He held her hand.

She could decide to leave and do what? Go back to Atlanta. Did she still have an apartment? He waited. There was a side of him that frightened her, but the idea of living without him, frightened her more. She needed him. He told her that. Most importantly, she loved him, she really did. Sometime during the last eight months he'd become her everything. She couldn't imagine life without him. Finally, she answered, "God help me, yes. Tony, I will marry you. I love you too." He wrapped his arms around her and kissed her tenderly. She laid her head back on his shoulder as the carriage continued through the park. Claire looked again at her left hand.

"If you don't like the ring we can look at others. It's from Tiffany's. We can go Friday and exchange it."

"Oh no! I love the ring. Besides, you chose it. It's exquisite. I'm just so surprised." She thought of something. "Does Catherine know you were planning this?"

Tony said she suspected, but he hadn't told anyone. He didn't know her response. "I never go into a meeting that I don't know the outcome. I'm always prepared for every situation. Tonight I wasn't sure. You asked about your debt being paid a few months ago. I thought perhaps you would take that option." He leaned down to kiss her hair. "I can't tell you how happy I am you didn't. I know Catherine will be too."

When the carriage arrived back at Seventh Avenue, Eric had the limousine warm and waiting. As Tony helped Claire down from the carriage and led her to the car, he told Eric, "My fiancée and I are ready to go back to the apartment."

"Yes, sir. Congratulations Mr. Rawlings and to you too, Ms. Claire."

That night after some of the most wonderful lovemaking Claire ever experienced, she began to consider the reality she was getting married and that meant a wedding. "I don't know how to plan a wedding to someone like you."

"Someone like me?"

"You know what I mean. This isn't your everyday Indiana or Iowa wedding. You are Anthony Rawlings. We can't go to dinner without photographers. A wedding will be a national spectator event."

He chuckled. "My dear that is why there are wedding coordinators and planners. We will hire the best. They will assist in everything." That made Claire feel better. She wondered if the wedding was a catastrophe; wouldn't that be a public failure? "By the way, how do you feel about a Christmas wedding?"

Her mind went into overdrive. "Christmas? As in four weeks from Saturday?"

"I can't wait any longer than that, to have you be my wife, Mrs. Anthony Rawlings."

She knew from experience his mind was made up. With queasiness deep in the pit of her stomach, she said, "I feel that you must hire the world's best wedding coordinator and planner."

Claire tried to sleep but the panic of planning a wedding in four weeks made her suffocate. She lay next to her fiancée and attempted to make sense of everything. Maybe she needed to compartmentalize, one thing at a time: wedding, reception, dress, and maid-of-honor. "Tony, I would like Emily to be my matron-of-honor."

He was almost asleep and his voice sounded far away, "We can discuss it tomorrow. Good night."

"Good night."

This is the finest measure of thanksgiving:
a thankfulness that springs from love.
--William C. Skeath

Chapter 25

They talked into the early morning about the wedding. Therefore, Thursday morning, Claire slept soundly until after nine. Sensing she was alone in the big bed, she focused her gaze on her left hand. On the fourth finger was a spectacular engagement ring. Smiling, she marveled at the reality; it wasn't a dream. She was really marrying Anthony Rawlings. Until last night, Claire hadn't allowed herself to think of Tony in terms of emotions or endearments. She knew she was having feelings, but she wouldn't let herself elaborate. However, when he said he loved her, it opened a floodgate. She thought about her feelings and how she missed him when he was gone. How she enjoyed having him around to talk with. How he could make her feel special, and how she thought about him when they were apart. She realized, to her own amazement, she really did love him! She couldn't contain her smile; this revelation was so astounding!

Claire wrapped herself in a thick long robe and walked downstairs to the dining room. As she approached, the rich poignant aroma of fresh coffee filled her lungs and brought her senses to life. Jan had coffee warm and ready. Tony wasn't there. When she enquired, Jan informed her, "Mr. Rawlings is in his office. Ms. Claire, if I may? Congratulations."

"Thank you, Jan. I'm sorry you have to work on Thanksgiving," Claire offered as Jan poured her coffee.

"It is all right, miss. I'm looking forward to having guests this afternoon for dinner. We rarely entertain here."

"Guests? I'm sorry. If Mr. Rawlings mentioned guests, with the excitement of our engagement, I've forgotten. Do you remember who is joining us for Thanksgiving dinner?"

"I'm sorry. I don't believe he told me names. I know there will be two, and they are scheduled to arrive at one thirty." Jan convinced Claire to eat an English muffin and grapefruit. After breakfast, Claire went to Tony's office.

She could hear him speaking behind the closed door. She may be his fiancée, but interrupting him uninvited in his office didn't seem like a good idea. Perhaps some rules would change, but she knew he would choose which ones. She went back to their bedroom, showered, and thought about how glad she was she'd bought new clothes. If she needed to be the perfect companion for some business associates, she felt better in well-fitting clothes.

She chose a black pair of wool slacks and a pink knit sweater from Neiman Marcus. The black boots she decided to wear had high heels; Tony wouldn't seem as tall. Dreamily, she thought about fuzzy socks and her new hoodie—being Mrs. Rawlings would teach her to keep up appearances.

Actually, being Claire Nichols taught her that.

As she straightened her hair, Claire marveled at the new even lighter shade. The auburn showed through enough to be considered low lights, but she was definitely now a caramel blonde. Although Catherine packed many pieces of Claire's new jewelry, she wanted to wear her grandmother's necklace and the O earrings Tony brought her from Europe. She shook her head; that seemed so long ago. Once she was completely dressed, she relaxed on the bed and let her mind wander.

Internal monologue: I'm going to marry Tony. I'm going to marry Tony in four weeks. I need a wedding dress. I need to call Emily. There are guests coming to dinner. Perhaps after dinner I can approach the Emily subject with Tony. Where will we marry? Who will we invite? Suddenly, a nice destination wedding anywhere, seemed like a good idea.

Her mind went from the wedding to Thanksgiving. She could hardly believe it was truly Thanksgiving. She'd arrived at Tony's house on March 20. Now she'd be eating Thanksgiving dinner with him and some associates and planning her wedding. She imagined drowning in chocolate sauce, too much of a good thing!

As a means of escape she let her mind float to childhood Thanksgivings. They usually went to her grandparents' home, where Grandma made all the traditional foods. She remembered helping her grandma and mother bake pies. At Thanksgiving they usually had pumpkin, apple, and sometimes pecan pie, and always too much food. Even when she lived with Emily and John she baked pies and helped Emily with cooking. Part of her wanted to go down to the kitchen and offer to help. However, she knew that wouldn't be appropriate.

She was somewhere deep in her memories when Tony entered the bedroom. He wore slacks and a burgundy ribbed turtleneck sweater which looked wonderful stretched across his broad shoulders and chest. He wore suits so often. Claire liked seeing him in something other than a jacket and tie. He smiled and joined her. "Good morning, my fiancée." He kissed her lips. "How are you feeling today?"

Claire propped herself up. "Good morning, to my fiancé, I feel well. I was just thinking about Thanksgivings when I was young. Did you eat all the traditional Thanksgiving foods when you were young?"

He sat next to her on the edge of the bed. "Claire, don't talk about the past. We have a future ahead of us, let's look ahead."

"I'm sorry, I guess I'm reminiscing." She touched his arm. "Tony? Who's coming to dinner?"

"First, let me tell you . . ." his voice brimmed with excitement, "I have been on the telephone all morning. Patricia is going to contact Shelly, and a statement regarding our engagement will be released tomorrow. Also, you have an appointment tomorrow at a very exclusive bridal boutique in Manhattan for a wedding gown. They are expecting you, the future Mrs. Anthony Rawlings. They want to meet your every need." He kissed her lips and continued to hold her gaze with his chocolate brown eyes. "I want you to have the dress of your dreams. Patricia will also choose a wedding planner and coordinator to meet with us when we return to Iowa. Since Christmas is on a Saturday, the wedding will be December 18, which too is a Saturday. I hope you don't mind, but with the wedding only three weeks away I decided to have it at the estate. Now we don't have to worry about booking a place, and security is already set. We just need to decide how many guests and where on the estate to hold the ceremony and reception. I did reach Catherine. She is thrilled, and told me to tell you so."

Claire felt inundated, information overload! She laid her head back on the pillow. "Maybe this is all happening too fast." Tony didn't say anything, but his smile subdued. She reached for his arm, "Tony, it isn't that I don't want to marry you, I do. But three weeks, that seems very rushed."

He scooped her into his arms. "I promise you, money can make anything happen. Don't worry about it. We will marry on December 18 and it will be amazing."

"I just worry about disappointing you."

"Claire, this is your wedding. I want you to be happy. I also know you're not back to yourself. I don't want you to overdo. Just enjoy all the things your money can buy and watch the wedding take shape. It will be spectacular."

"My money can't buy us a piece of gum."

He laughed and kissed her. "My dear, in three weeks and two days you will be able to buy a gum factory if you want. I want you to share all that I have. You will have everything the world has to offer."

Claire struggled with the meaning of his words. "Tony, I don't want your money. I have not done anything to deserve part of your fortune. I'm happy to share your name, I don't need any more."

"My love, you have done more than you will ever know. And I'm pretty sure you will do more." He leaned down to kiss her, while his hands busily undid the buttons on her slacks.

"Don't we have guests coming?"

"They aren't due until 1:30. I'm pretty sure we can be successful multiple times before then." He removed her slacks and started removing her sweater. He straddled her legs as he removed his sweater and undid his slacks. His smile was seductive and his chest moved with breaths of anticipation. Claire inhaled his cologne and knew if he bent down she would taste the scent on his neck.

"But, Tony—" He put his finger to her lips.

"Shhh, I have better things for those beautiful lips to do than talk."

They left the bedroom together just before 1:30. As they approached the steps Tony said, "I'm sure you realize, but I'm going to say it for the sake of clarification. Just because we're engaged, divulging private information is still forbidden."

Claire looked up at his eyes and wondered what he possibly thought she would say to his associates. "I promise I know that." They continued to the front stairs. Muffled voices came from the sitting room below. "Now who am I meeting?" As she asked, the voices came into range, her eyes moistened, and she looked to Tony for confirmation. "Is it really them?"

He gently held her shoulders, "Yes, I invited them to surprise you for Thanksgiving, but now you have even bigger news to share."

"I can tell them about our engagement?"

He smiled. "Of course, didn't you say you wanted Emily to stand with you?" She wanted to run down the stairs or cry out, but his grip on her hand tightened. "Claire, follow my rules."

"I will." She replied and obediently fell into step with her fiancé.

When the soles of their shoes hit the marble floor, John and Emily turned toward them. They'd been enjoying the view from the sitting room windows. Her family looked just as Claire remembered: John tall with dark blond hair and playful blue eyes, and Emily with the Nichols brown hair, cut short and sassy, and Claire's sparkling green eyes. Claire ran to Emily and hugged her.

"I didn't know you were coming. It is a wonderful surprise. Oh, Emily, it's so good to see you!" And then she hugged John. "And, John! Oh, let me introduce you to Anthony."

Emily told Claire it was good to see her, too. However, she and John made eye contact, sharing an expression of concern. Claire looked so different. They proceeded politely as Claire made introductions. "Anthony, this is my sister Emily. And, Emily, this is my fiancé Anthony Rawlings." Emily and Tony shook hands. Anthony emitted charm.

"Very nice to meet you, Mr. Rawlings." Her brain made sense of Claire's words. She looked at her sister in disbelief. "Did you just say fiancé?"

Claire continued with introductions, "And, Anthony, this is Emily's husband, my brother-in-law John Vandersol. John, please meet my fiancé, Anthony Rawlings." The two men shook hands and exchanged greetings.

Gracious as ever, Tony said, "Please, we are about to be family. Call me Anthony."

Claire smiled and they all sat down to chat before dinner. Jan entered the room to offer hors d'oeuvres and drinks. Claire showed Emily her engagement ring and told them about Tony's romantic proposal in Central Park. John and Emily were speechless, perhaps in shock. Tony was very attentive, holding Claire's hand, putting his hand on her shoulder or thigh. She rambled on, cautious to not divulge any forbidden personal information.

During Thanksgiving dinner, Claire learned Emily had attempted to reach Tony around her birthday. Emily didn't know what else to do. She had no way to reach Claire, and she saw pictures of the two of them together in magazines. Apparently, it isn't easy to get calls or e-mails through to Anthony

Rawlings. Just recently an e-mail finally reached him and he called. It was during that telephone conversation about a week ago when Anthony invited them to NYC for dinner.

Claire apologized for her inconsiderate behavior. She should have been better at staying in touch. Life had been a whirlwind since she started working with Tony. The important thing was that they were together now. Claire asked her family if they were driving home to Troy or staying in the city. John said they decided to spend some time in the city. After all it was a three-hour drive home.

Tony then surprised Claire again. "Well, Emily, Claire has a reservation tomorrow at a bridal boutique in Manhattan. I'm sure she would love to have you join her to look at wedding dresses."

Claire tried not to stare at him. She looked to Emily. "Yes, I would love to have you join me if the two of you don't have plans."

Emily looked at John. "Of course, I'd like to help you."

"Emily, I would also like you to be my matron-of-honor. Would you please stand with me at our wedding?"

"You want me? Of course, I will." Emily sounded cautiously enthusiastic. "But, did you say the wedding will be the eighteenth of December?"

"Yes, it will. That's all the more reason to find some dresses soon." Claire smiled at her sister. "Hopefully they'll have some bright pink puffy bridesmaid's dresses." Emily laughed.

From her peripheral vision Claire saw Tony's fleeting expression of disbelief. She turned to her fiancée and smiled. "Tony, it's a long-standing joke. Emily made me wear a green dress at her wedding. Since pink is my favorite color, I have long threatened to have her wear the puffiest bubblegum pink dress I could find when I married." He exhaled and smiled, relieved she wasn't serious.

Once they finished eating, Tony invited John to the living room for the four o'clock football game. He asked the ladies if they would like to join them, but Emily said she would rather catch up with her sister. Tony kissed Claire before leaving the room. It appeared very sweet, but Claire saw the warning in his eyes.

Jan poured the ladies coffee and cleared the table. Claire and Emily sat at the table, drank coffee, and tried to catch up. Once they were alone Claire knew the conversation would be more difficult to dodge. Emily was full of questions. How was her little sister, a meteorologist in Atlanta, suddenly engaged to one of the wealthiest men in the country? How did they meet? Where has she been living? Why hasn't she been in contact? Why is she so thin? Why is her hair blonde? Did she really like living this way, being waited on and having house staff do everything? She always liked cooking. Now she says she hasn't cooked, why? What is Anthony like? Why were they marrying so fast? Is she pregnant? Wasn't he much older than her? Did she love him?

Claire did her best to be evasive with some answers and more detailed with others. Above all she told Emily she did love him. It didn't start that way. It was strictly a working relationship. Tony could be a wonderful, kind, romantic, gentle man. She also told Emily Tony was very private and begged her to not repeat anything about their relationship to the media or anyone else. Claire didn't understand at first how tenacious the media could be, but the longer she'd been with Tony the more apparent it became.

She asked again, not for Tony but for her; please don't share private information with others. Emily said she understood. Emily was very happy to hear Claire sound so happy and excited about Anthony and their wedding. However, what about her weight, she was too thin. And what about meteorology? Did she plan to ever work again in her chosen field? Claire was tired of all the questions. Formulating answers made her head hurt. She wanted to hear about Emily and John.

Emily proceeded to tell her stories about John and the law firm and about her class and teaching. She talked about some of their friends in Troy and Albany, people Claire knew when she lived with them. She also talked about some friends back in Indiana. Claire laughed as they remembered stories from childhood. The names were people Claire hadn't thought about in some time. Her mind wandered, thinking about the guest list for the wedding. She wondered if she had anyone to invite other than Emily and John. She thought about college friends, and that reminded her of Meredith. Claire knew Meredith didn't intend for her sneak interview to produce such drastic consequences, nevertheless it did. Perhaps college friends were better not invited.

They joined the men when they thought the game was nearing its end. However, it was far from over, it was getting interesting. Both men seemed to be cheering for the Saints. Claire wondered how John and Tony would get along. They were both incredibly strong willed. Tony was not accustomed to being anything less than the alpha male. John seemed to respect Tony; after all, he was Anthony Rawlings.

Claire loved and respected John. Ever since the death of her father and her grandfather, John was the man of their family, an omnipresent influential part of her life. Now seeing him there next to Tony, she reconsidered her assessment. Tony dominated in structure, probably four inches taller, and in demeanor, more self-assured. They both shouted at the screen as the Saints regained the lead with less than two minutes to go.

Then, the room fell silent when it appeared the game would be tied with a field goal. The Dallas kicker missed the field goal, wide left, and the men simultaneously stood and cheered. Seeing these two men united in a common goal, Claire felt her chest swell with delight. After the game they sat in front of a warm fire and enjoyed the lovely view of the city and delicious dessert. As Claire sipped coffee, forgoing dessert, Emily told Tony all about the pies Claire used to bake. She explained what a great cook and baker Claire was. Tony seemed very interested in this new information.

They discussed the plans for the next day. Tony needed to work, and John graciously agreed to stay at the hotel and do some work also. Eric, their chauffeur, would bring Claire to the Vandersol's hotel and pick Emily up for the bridal boutique. Emily offered to take a taxi, it was no problem, but Claire and Tony insisted. It was settled. Claire would be at the Hyatt Regency at nine in the morning to pick her up. Their appointment was for ten.

Tony then asked if he and Claire could join them for dinner Friday night. They planned to go back to Iowa on Saturday morning. Claire now understood why Tony was so vague about their travel plans. John and Emily agreed.

Before they left, Emily hugged Claire like she didn't want to let go. "I have missed you so much. We're all we have left. Let's not stay out of touch again." Her green eyes shone with sincerity. Claire's began to tear. She wanted to say so much, but knew she was supposed to be elusive.

Before she could speak, Tony injected, "Emily, we have a wedding in three weeks. I bet you will be tired of hearing from Claire after that!" He laughed.

They all laughed.

Tony offered John and Emily, Eric for the ride back to their hotel. John politely declined. After Jan retrieved their coats, John and Emily left. When the door shut, Claire turned to Tony. "Thank you! Thank you so much. This was absolutely the best Thanksgiving ever. I can't believe you surprised me like this."

He smiled but she saw the message in his eyes. "Your sister is extremely inquisitive." Claire agreed, her head hurt from working so diligently on answers. Kissing her cheek, "My dear, you should take an aspirin and retire to our room. I'll be up shortly. I have some pressing matters in my office that I must attend."

First Claire went to the kitchen to thank Jan for her hard work. She really appreciated all she did to make their Thanksgiving special. Jan seemed genuinely touched and surprised by Claire's appreciation. While walking up the stairs, she thought about the estate and the top-notch surveillance, perhaps Tony's work was to review some video footage of her conversation in the dining room. She told herself it would be all right, she'd followed all his rules.

A sister shares childhood memories and grown-up dreams.
—Author unknown

Chapter 26

Friday morning, Tony left the apartment early so Eric could drive Claire and Emily to the boutique. On her way to Emily's hotel, Claire contemplated her fiancé. By the time he came to bed the night before, she was sleeping. She faintly remembered him kissing her, turning out the lights, and feeling relieved. Maybe he hadn't been reviewing surveillance. Maybe he was doing actual work on Thanksgiving night? No matter, when he came to bed, he wasn't upset. That morning, before leaving, he hugged her tight and told her to have fun with her sister choosing her wedding gown. Claire wanted to believe her life was as it appeared.

Traffic to the hotel was crazy. Until Claire saw the multitude of people, she'd forgotten all about *Black Friday*. The department stores were inundated with hoards of shoppers. Seeing the mayhem around her, made their destination of a private boutique all that more appealing.

The associates at the boutique would be totally devoted to them. None of this mad rush she witnessed from the windows of the limousine. Smiling faintly, she fondly remembered Black Friday shopping with her mom and Emily when she was young. To save $25, $50, or $100, they would wake at three in the morning and stand in multiple lines. It sounded unpleasant, but the memories were warm.

Eric approached the Hyatt Regency a few minutes before nine. Emily wasn't waiting. "Miss, would you like me to go to the front desk and inquire of Mrs. Vandersol?"

Claire thought a moment. "No, we'll give her a few minutes, and then I'll go in." Emily hadn't read the *Anthony Rawlings's rules of punctuality* memo. Claire decided she deserved some slack. Five minutes after nine, Emily emerged from the lobby. Eric quickly got out of the car and opened the door. Emily entered the limousine and hugged Claire. She looked around at the leather seats and splendor.

"Seriously, this is how you get around New York?" Claire said yes. "And you don't feel ostentatious? Perhaps you haven't heard, our country is in an economic downturn."

Eric pulled away from the curb, and they entered traffic. It wasn't the stop-and-go traffic causing Claire's neck muscles to tighten, more the sudden onset of defensiveness. "Emily, please don't judge me or Tony. I want you to be part of our wedding. Let's have fun looking for dresses."

Emily exhaled and sat back on the seat. "Claire, I want to. I really do."

Claire could tell there was a "*but*" coming.

Emily continued, "But John and I sat up for hours discussing you and Anthony."

Sitting straighter, Claire asked, "What did the two of you decide?"

"We decided we love you. We are so happy Anthony invited us to get to see you. But here is one of our concerns." Claire raised her eyebrows, Emily inquired, "Why did Anthony need to invite us? Why couldn't you?"

Claire's head almost touched the ceiling. She sat so straight, looking Emily directly in the eye, "Emily, that's ridiculous. I could. I told you things have just been busy. With his schedule, we are all over the place, as I'm sure you've read about in the media. I didn't even know until last week Tony was needed in New York." And then to clarify, she added, "*He* didn't know until last week. He has a lot on his plate."

"Uh . . . hmmm, please know we're just concerned. It seems like you're a different person." The conversation paused and Emily continued, "That isn't necessarily bad, but it makes us uncomfortable." Emily no longer saw her little sister, but a polished, refined, stylish, elegant, and worldly woman. "I've tried to learn about Anthony Rawlings. Everything I found about him on Google is business related. He has an impressive reputation as a businessman, but I cannot find anything about him personally."

"Emily, he is an impressive private man too. But I must emphasize *private*. He asked me to join him in his private personal life. I want you and John there, but you must respect the importance of his confidentiality."

They sat in standstill traffic. "Okay, we can do that. But, we worry about you. Don't you get to have a life too?"

Claire felt her blood pressure rise. She needed to defend the life she'd despised for months. It was time to utilize the compartmentalization, bring out the good stuff. "Just because I haven't contacted you doesn't mean I don't have a life. I do. I have a very full and rewarding life. I live in a beautiful home. We attend a number of events and functions. I've met wonderful friends in the Quad Cities area." She surveyed Emily's reaction. "I'm not doing meteorology currently, but I'm working with Tony. As I said, he is a very busy man with a busy schedule." She didn't need to offer more explanation.

The car moved again. Emily stared incredulously, "Are you living with Anthony? And how long have you been living with him?"

Claire exhaled; as much as it killed her, she knew she couldn't spend her day like this. It was too much work, and although it was early, her head pounded. "Okay. Emily, I'm sorry this didn't work." Claire suddenly pushed the button and opened the window to Eric. "Eric, we have a change of plans.

You may drop me off at the boutique, but Mrs. Vandersol will be going back to the Hyatt."

Emily stared at Claire in disbelief.

Eric answered, "Yes, miss."

Claire shut the window, sat back in the seat, and didn't speak or look at Emily. She should be sad, but truly she was mad. She also realized she'd behaved like Tony. Perhaps she was being too cautious about his rules, but she knew too well, behaviors had consequences. Given the choice, she'd choose to err on the side of Tony.

"Claire, I'm sorry. You're obviously a strong independent woman. I think of you as -- my kid sister, someone who needs us to look out for her. Anthony Rawlings is lucky to have you in his life. I still don't understand how it all happened. I don't care how wonderful *he* is. He is the fortunate one in this relationship. I love you and want to be a part of your wedding. If this is what you want, we will support you 100 percent."

Claire was too emotional to be completely like Tony. Overwhelmed with a sense of relief, she reached over, hugged Emily, and smiled. "Good! Let's put this behind us and have fun looking at dresses!" Pushing the button again, she said, "Eric, we are both going to the bridal boutique." She closed the window.

"One more thing though." Concern showed in Emily's green eyes. Claire exhaled; she didn't want to hear *one more thing*. "John is planning to speak to you tonight about your prenuptial agreement."

"What? I don't know anything about that, he should talk to Tony." Claire thought about that scenario. "On second thought, *no*, tell him not to worry about it. I totally trust Tony, and I honestly couldn't care less about his money. It really isn't an issue. Tell John to forget it."

Emily said she would tell him, but couldn't make any promises. After all, he was an attorney, and Claire was his kid sister-in-law.

The entrance to the boutique was a grand ten-foot door surrounded by limestone. Above the door was a street number but no visible store name. There were no gowns in the window or advertisements evident, a different experience from when they had shopped for Emily's dress. Claire knew from past boutique shopping, to enter the boutique you needed to ring the bell. However, Eric called ahead and as he parked the car and opened the door for Claire and Emily, the door of the boutique opened.

A woman in her fifties or sixties dressed in posh business attire rushed out to welcome Ms. Nichols to their *modest boutique*. She introduced herself, Sharon Springhill. As she ushered the women into the shop, she gushed, "Ms. Nichols, we were so happy to receive Mr. Rawlings's call yesterday. Since that moment we have worked diligently to create a collection especially for you. We truly hope that you, the future Mrs. Anthony Rawlings, will find the dress of your dreams today."

Claire did her best to play the person she'd become. Looking at Emily and sensing Emily's uneasiness, Claire decided this was an opportunity to educate her sister. "Ms. Springhill, I'm very excited to be here today. Mr.

Rawlings told me the wonderful reputation of your boutique. I appreciate you taking the time to personally assist me on this holiday weekend."

Ms. Springhill thanked Claire for the kind words. (*Emily witnessed Claire's ease with the situation.*)

"Now, Ms. Springhill, this is my sister, Mrs. Vandersol. She will be my matron-of-honor. Perhaps Mr. Rawlings informed you our wedding will be on December 18. I'm hopeful you will not only be able to assist me with my dress, but also one for my sister." (*Emily would experience the treatment Claire endured.*)

Emily was immediately met with her own entourage of associates. Claire smiled at her sister as their eyes met. Emily shook her head, it didn't seem real. Mrs. Springfield offered the women coffee, water, tea, and champagne. Next, they were escorted to seats in front of an open area. It reminded Claire of a dance floor in a hotel reception hall.

Ms. Springhill explained how she put together a collection especially for Mrs. Rawlings. It included many of the top wedding gown designers: Vera Wang, Oscar de la Renta, Manuel Mota, Monique Lhuiller, Maggie Sultero, Winnie Couture, and Mieko, as well as others. "Please sit back and relax while models display the most extravagant and stunning wedding gowns you have ever seen. Feel free to make any requests. If you choose, you may see any gowns again, and please touch the magnificent fabrics. "Ms. Nichols, once you narrow the selection you may try on those gowns. We will then take your measurements so that the gown of your dreams will be tailored specifically for you. Also, if you desire a certain gown but would like something changed, the designer can be contacted and every effort will be made to accommodate your desire.

"After the wedding gowns, they will gladly repeat the process for Mrs. Vandersol. Is there anything we can get you to make you ladies more comfortable?" Claire told her they were fine and excited to see the gowns.

The decision proved incredibly difficult. Most of the gowns were exquisite. Actually, some were a little strange, Claire and Emily exchanged glances. However, most were elegant. There were glamorous gowns with bold contrasts in volume, rich fabrics such as lace, organza, or heron, and the finest accessories. Some were covered with drapes bound with precious-stone details, natural folds, pleats, ruffles, or tulle.

There were fashionable gowns with very thin and light materials in fluid, sheer, and mermaid-cut styles. These were made with soft fabrics like chiffon, pleated chiffon, or morbid tulle. They accentuated curves, had impeccable details such as asymmetrical necklines, floral appliqué, feathers, or rich gemstone embroideries.

The Oscar de la Renta and Monique Lhuiller gowns were created in an attempt to recreate a world of dreams and pure fantasy. These wedding dresses had flattering strapless necklines, meticulously enhancing the waist, and skirts with spectacular volume. They included stunning A-line and mermaid styles, lined with thousands of feathers, cascading ruffles, and magical applications. Claire thought they would make Cinderella or Belle proud.

The sisters watched models for two hours, and Claire created a short list of over ten dresses. She felt overwhelmed. Ms. Springhill suggested Ms. Nichols and Mrs. Vandersol enjoy a light lunch while they view the ten dresses again.

While dining on chicken salad on a bed of lettuce with a side of fruit and iced tea, Claire narrowed the race to four. They varied significantly. The first gown had a beautiful A-line neck with a mermaid bodice and a large skirt covered in fine feathers. The skirt could be bustled or left down for a chapel-length train. The next gown, by Oscar de la Renta, was crafted from the highest quality chiffon and a flowing full satin skirt with a mermaid bodice that was accented with intricate hand embellishments and glistening Swarovski crystals. The third was strapless with an empire waist, the underlay made with morbid tulle and a sheer overlay embossed with floral appliqués of lace and gem stones. And the fourth, by Vera Wang, was very creative, classical smooth lightweight silk chiffon designed to hug the bodice, with a full, flowing chiffon skirt. What made this gown different was the embroidered lace off-the-shoulder overlay that created lace sleeves and a chapel-length train. The decision made, Claire would try on the four dresses.

First they needed to see the matron-of-honor dresses. Emily was slightly taller than and not as lean as Claire. The dresses they viewed were mostly black or silver, but Ms. Springhill promised any color that Claire desired. Claire smiled. "That's wonderfu! We will be able to get pink!" Ms. Springhill didn't know she was teasing. The two sisters snickered.

They narrowed it to a satin Oscar de la Renta gown with a tighter skirt, a Valentino gown with a lace overlay, and a Monique Lhuiller gown that would be perfect with Claire's second choice. They realized Claire must choose her wedding gown first and then the matron-of-honor's dress would be chosen to complement.

At two thirty they began trying on gowns. When Claire looked at her watch, she had a sickening feeling the process was taking too long. She worried Tony would wonder where they were. Or perhaps, think they went somewhere else? She would let him know how time-consuming the process was as soon as she got the chance.

Hoping to avoid suspicion, Claire decided to check in with Eric. She wanted him to know it would be a while before they needed to be picked up. She used the shop's telephone to call. Emily offered her phone, since Claire left hers at the apartment. Claire decided the shop's phone would be better. The boutique's number would appear on Eric's caller ID. She worried if she called Eric on Emily's phone her location maybe questioned. And if she used Emily's phone, Tony might assume she used it for other calls. It bothered her that every move needed to be scrutinized for possible misinterpretations. She told herself perhaps they didn't, but better safe than sorry.

"Hello, Eric, this is Claire."

"Yes, Ms. Claire, are you ready to be picked up?"

"No, that's why I'm calling. This has been a very difficult process. I assume we will be here another hour or perhaps two. I'll call you when we're done."

"Yes, Ms. Claire, I will be there when you're ready."

Emily could overhear her every word. Claire wanted to ask Eric to call Tony, to let him know they were still at the boutique. However, she worried it might raise Emily's suspicions. So, instead she said, "Thank you, Eric."

Claire found herself in an uncomfortable situation regarding the measuring for her gown. She had so many things to think about that lack of undergarments slipped her mind. Claire asked Ms. Springhill what undergarments were usually worn with these dresses and told her she would like to purchase some now so the dress would fit as close as possible to how it would on her wedding day. Apparently, this wasn't an unusual request. Ms. Springhill brought her a strapless body-shaper. Once that was on, Claire allowed the attendants to take her measurements. The entire conversation went unnoticed by Emily. She was occupied with attendants measuring and catering to *her* every need.

Claire tried on each gown, entered a large mirrored room, and stood on a platform. She could see herself from all directions. More than anything Claire wanted Tony's opinion. He once said Catherine knew what he liked. Claire wished Catherine was there now, but she wasn't. Instead, Claire had Emily, who repeatedly told her how beautiful she looked in each dress. It wasn't helping. Claire told herself repeatedly: *My wedding will happen in three weeks. I need to make a decision.* The service and choices were fantastic. Spending time with her sister was wonderful. The stress however, caused her head to pound. Claire narrowed the list to two: the chiffon Oscar de la Renta gown and the Vera Wang gown. Perhaps it was the issue of a December wedding in the Midwest, but the idea of the lace sleeves on the Vera Wang gown appealed to Claire.

Ms. Springfield knew Claire's measurements and promised she could produce either gown. Ever so politely, she emphasized the importance of a quick decision. Claire would need to return for additional fittings. She said replied that would be fine, but secretly wondered if Tony anticipated that.

Next, they needed to choose a dress for Emily. Claire decided she really liked the Valentino dress with the lace overlay. It would complement either bridal gown. She took color swatches and promised Ms. Springhill the color decision by Monday. There was a sudden realization that color had multiple implications. The decorations, the flowers, and the invitations usually all contained the same color scheme. Up until now, she hadn't thought about this. Claire felt the impending tears. There were so many things to think about.

At almost four, Eric arrived to retrieve them from the boutique. Claire was exhausted and overwhelmed. She hadn't spent that much time out and away from *home* since her *accident*. Her head pounded violently to the point of nausea and she wanted a nap. True to her new persona, Claire didn't show Emily or anyone the way she felt.

Emily tried to pretend she didn't notice as Claire tipped the staff at the boutique. After models and tailor's assistants, and of course Ms. Springfield, the total was over $1,000. This didn't include the cost of a dress. Once in the car Emily genuinely expressed her elation at their shopping experience. "Claire, that was amazing! I've never been treated like that before." Emily seized Claire's hand, "Can you imagine if some of those girls from high school could see you now?"

Claire smiled. She had thought about that at one time, but it didn't seem important anymore. "It really isn't that big of deal."

"Oh my god, Claire, you just tipped half my house payment!"

"Really, Emily, please, it isn't that important." Emily's reaction made her uncomfortable.

"You know, Claire, the only people who say money isn't important are people who have it." She then asked Claire about her dress, "I want to wear the dress you like. But, I'll be honest, with flying to Iowa, staying there for I don't know how long, and other expenses, I don't know if we can afford a dress from there. I noticed there were no price tags. That isn't a good sign."

The pounding in Claire's head demanded her attention; she wasn't thinking as she answered. Looking into the car's refrigerator for something to drink and eat, Claire replied, "Emily, I don't want you to worry about it. Tony will pay for the dresses. I can talk to him about flying you to Iowa and a place to stay too."

She didn't mean to, but she'd offended Emily. "Thank you, Claire, but my husband and I can afford to pay for ourselves."

"Oh please, Emily, I'm not trying to upset you. I know you can. But we are springing this on you without warning. You can do whatever you want regarding the flight and stay, but please let Tony take care of the dress. He said he wants me to have my dream wedding, so please let him take care of the dress." Then she added with a feigned smile, "And as I remember, you and John paid for my beautiful green dress some years ago."

Emily smiled. "You're right, we did. Of course, it was about $150. You *tipped* almost ten times that today. I'm just not used to this new Claire. Give me some time."

Claire handed Emily a bottle of water and offered her some blueberries as she silently prayed, "Please, let some food and water help my head." The water tasted cool and refreshing. Her mind drifted to coffee, the amazing fragrance, and knew immediately it would make her feel better. She decided she would ask Jan for some coffee when she got back to the apartment.

The traffic flowed much better than it had early in the morning. Before they reached the Hyatt, Emily's phone rang. John wondered when she would be back. She told him they were close and it had been a long day. John reminded her they were supposed to have dinner with Claire and Anthony, did she know any details? Emily said she didn't, but Claire promised to call them as soon as she got back to the apartment.

Emily gave Claire her cell number as she got out of the limousine. She told Claire it was a great day, and she looked forward to their dinner tonight. They hugged and Emily went into the hotel. As Eric pulled away, Claire laid her head against the seat. Tears leaked from her eyes as they closed. Her head throbbed and she felt utterly spent. Somewhere between the Hyatt and Tony's apartment building Claire fell into a sound sleep.

"Ms. Claire, we have reached Mr. Rawlings' apartment." She heard Eric's voice. Claire opened her eyes but was immediately disoriented. She tried to

182

familiarize herself with her surroundings; soon she realized she was in the limousine outside Tony's apartment building. Eric held the door open, and the cool November air helped Claire focus. She entered the building and went up to the seventy-sixth floor. As the elevator opened, Claire's face felt suddenly flushed and her heart rate increased. Standing at the open door to his apartment was Tony.

I think I've discovered the secret of life—
you just hang around until you get used to it.
—Charles M. Shulz

Chapter 27

Seeing your fiancé across the room should make your heart race. Seeing her fiancé standing in the doorway did that to Claire. Instead of accelerated by love though, she presumed it was anxiety. Upon entering the building, her watch read 5:30. Her thoughts churned slowly through her aching head. Obviously, he finished his work. She wanted to get home first . . . but she had Eric. How did he get home?

"Good evening, Claire." His expression indifferent, she couldn't read him.

Mask in place. The nap helped the headache, no longer pounding, only gently aching. "Good evening, Tony." She reached up to kiss him. He bent down to accommodate.

"You look beat. Did you find a gown?" He led her into the apartment. Claire exhaled and tried to explain the complexity of the day. The boutique was wonderful, too wonderful, with a selection that was too large. He helped her with her coat, gave it to Jan, and escorted her up the stairs to the bedroom. Halfway up the stairs, she remembered coffee.

"Oh, just a minute, Tony. Jan?" Claire stopped and went back down the stairs and called, "Jan?" The housekeeper returned to the foyer.

"Yes, Ms. Claire?"

"I need something from my coat pocket please." Still holding her coat, Jan handed it back. Claire removed a small piece of paper from one of the pockets. "Thank you, could you please bring coffee upstairs?" Jan replied affirmatively and disappeared with Claire's coat.

Claire proceeded up the stairs to Tony. He waited patiently, silently watching her. She handed him the piece of paper. He took it, unfolded it, and asked, "What is this?"

"It's Emily's cell number. She gave it to me so I could call her with details of tonight's plans." Tony's expression didn't change. He wadded the paper, put it in the pocket of his slacks, and continued to escort Claire up the stairs. She wasn't sure what his actions meant. However, his lack of response probably meant the end of *that* conversation. "I am sorry I'm so late. I had no idea this would be such a long day."

Tony said that it was all worth it if she found her wedding gown. She told him she had it narrowed to two. The boutique had her measurements, and all they needed was a call to let them know her decision. However, Ms. Springhill emphasized she must do it soon. Claire told Tony she would appreciate his opinion. He said he trusted her judgment.

She sat on the edge of the bed, exhaled, and lay back. The coolness of the room combined with the firmness of the bed helped Claire try to relax. She closed her eyes and hoped the coffee would help her head.

"Eric told me you fell asleep after Emily left the car." He sat next to her on the bed, stroking her hair. Claire breathed a sigh of relief. He didn't seem upset. The tension in her head began to subside.

"I'm sorry if that was bad, but my head hurt so badly I could hardly focus on Emily."

"Of course, it is fine. You were alone and exhausted. I told you, I don't want you overdoing. You are not 100 percent yet." He kissed her head. "I spoke to your brother-in-law and moved our reservations back to eight o'clock. Maybe you should continue your nap for a little while. We don't need to leave until seven thirty."

Claire thought about it. Dinner wasn't for another two hours, but she decided a shower would be more beneficial. Claire already had a nap. They talked as Jan knocked on their door. She entered the room and put a coffee carafe, cream, and two mugs on a table near the windows. She inquired if they needed anything else. Learning they didn't, she left.

The open drapes exposed a spectacular view filled with darkness even though it wasn't even six in the evening. The New York City lights glittered below, evidence of inhabitants racing from place to place. Claire held her mug of coffee, inhaled the rich aroma, and fell silent, mesmerized by the sight. This time of year, with shorter dreary days, had always been a difficult time for her. She loved sunshine; it made her joyful. This year she'd missed most of the autumn sun and now the bleakness of winter was rapidly descending.

To her, dark was contrary to light. Therefore, instead of joy, it brought sorrow. That is why she liked Atlanta. She stood at the window, looked at a magnificent skyline, sipped her warm mug of coffee, and thought about being sad. This made her chastise herself. She should be happy about her wedding and her reunion with Emily. But what she really wanted was to be back in Iowa. She didn't want the pressure of choosing a dress and dealing with Emily's constant questions. She didn't long for the warmth of Atlanta anymore, but for the warmth of her fireplace and lack of pretense.

She saw Tony approaching in the reflection of the window. He stood close behind her and put his arms around her waist as she rested her head against his chest. Tony's voice sounded soft and affectionate, "What are you thinking about? You seem far away."

"I don't want to say. You'll think I'm ungrateful." She put her mug down on the table and turned to face him.

Tony lifted her eyes to his. "I appreciate honesty above all." He wasn't being authoritative, only candid. He noticed how tired her eyes looked as he lightly kissed her lips. "And let me decide what I think."

She continued to look in his eyes. The brown matched the color of her coffee lightened by cream. It gave her strength to be honest. "I want to go home." His expression changed slightly, telling her he didn't understand her meaning of *home*. "Tony, I want to go back to your home, I want to be back in Iowa." He smiled and hugged her.

"Why would that make you ungrateful?" She explained she loved his surprise, seeing Emily and John thrilled her, but things have changed. Emily asked so many questions and seemed so dismayed by Claire's life, it felt as though they weren't connected anymore. Tony had released her chin and her face rested, buried in his chest. The thumping of his heart filled her with security. She closed her eyes and listened. The steady beat made her head feel better. She couldn't see his face or smile of satisfaction.

She continued, saying if she could, she would cancel their dinner plans for tonight. Lifting her eyes again, he said, "You know that isn't an option. We've made a commitment and we will honor it. But, I'm happy to know you want to be home with me, to *our* home. We will be there tomorrow." Claire nodded her head and said that yes, she knew. She picked up her mug of coffee and went to the bathroom for a shower.

Once there she noticed the large garden tub. It wasn't as though she hadn't seen it before, it had been there all along, but it looked very inviting. Starting the warm water she decided to find out where they are going. When she opened the door to ask Tony, he was sitting on the bed with his back to her. He had her purse open, the contents strewn on the bed, searching for something. Perhaps something Claire left in there that she shouldn't have had. Maybe evidence of her being somewhere with Emily instead of the bridal boutique, but there was nothing. She considered saying something, confronting him about privacy, instead she quietly closed the door and thanked God she'd given him the paper with the telephone number.

Eric pulled up to the restaurant on the Upper East Side at approximately seven forty-five. Claire was very pleased with Tony's plans for the evening. First, the quaint, casual seafood restaurant was away from the hustle and bustle of the busy streets and not as elegant as their normal dining establishments. Their reservation had been moved to eight, and although the Hyatt wasn't far, Emily and John weren't there yet. Second, she approved of Tony's choice of attire, they both wore jeans. When they left the bedroom, Claire told Tony again how much she liked him in jeans. He reminded her how much he liked her out of them. Their eyes sparkled.

Since their table wasn't ready, Tony and Claire went to the bar to wait. At the end of the bar stood one unoccupied stool; Tony directed Claire to it. She sat while he stood beside her. He ordered himself a designer beer and Claire a glass of Zinfandel.

186

Sitting at the bar reminded Claire of the Red Wing. Compartmentalize. She felt much better than she had earlier. Perhaps it was the nap, the bath, the coffee, Tony's understanding regarding her long day, or just some time to relax away from questions. Whatever the cause, her spirit felt revived and ready for the evening. They chatted about the different bottles of liquor lining the bar. Claire recalled some of her bartending knowledge. She talked about most of the liquors from a first-person point of view, ones she liked, ones she didn't, and why. It amused Tony she'd tried so many. After all, she'd only been legally drinking for six years. Claire smiled and repeated the word *legally*. They were chatting and laughing when John and Emily approached.

Proceeding with the customary round of *hellos* and handshakes, Emily and John ordered drinks, stood conversing about nothing in particular, and soon their table was ready. John, Emily, and Claire went to the table while Tony stayed back to pay the bar tab.

Once the hostess took them to their table, Claire excused herself to go to the ladies' room. As she exited the bathroom, which was located down a narrow hall, she was surprised to find John waiting for her. "Well, hi. Did you think I was lost?" Claire started to pass him, thinking they were going back to the table, when John stopped her.

"Claire, I really need to talk to you without Anthony present."

Claire suddenly felt uncomfortable. "No, John, you don't."

He spoke soft and fast. "Yes, I do. Tell me you haven't signed a prenuptial agreement yet."

"I haven't."

"Good, I want to review it first. Emily said you don't think it is necessary, and I should drop it, but I'm your brother. I have known you since you were a little girl. Let someone who has your best interests at heart make sure you are represented."

"Thank you, John. I believe Tony has my best interests at heart. I don't care about his money, I trust him, and I . . ." Claire could see the change in John's expression. Oh god! She knew by the tightness in her stomach Tony was behind her. She turned and looked directly at his chest. He was *right* behind her.

Continuing Claire's sentence, Tony said, "And I believe this conversation would be better held in a private setting." Tony's voice exuded displeasure. They, however, stood in the hallway of a public restaurant; therefore, it was not loud, rude, or aggressive. Claire looked up to see his face, wondering how much he had heard. She could see the brown disappearing behind expanding blackness.

"Tony . . ." Claire started to speak. His expression stopped her cold.

"Shall we all go to our table? I believe our waitress would like to introduce herself. John, you and Emily are welcome to join us in our car. We will be glad to drive you back to your hotel following dinner. At that time, *if* you choose, you may continue your legal counsel." Claire prayed he would not choose to continue. She knew from experience, there were some things not worth pursuing.

John looked from Tony to Claire and back to Tony. He sounded strong and defiant. "That would be fine, Anthony. I appreciate the offer. We would be glad to join you." He then lightened his tone. "Emily tells me you have a very nice car." They all began to walk toward the table.

"Thank you, it isn't mine. I lease cars in the city. Too many accidents with all the traffic . . ." And the conversation continued benignly to the table and throughout dinner.

Claire knew Tony and knew he was angry. To the casual onlooker, he appeared fine. He excelled at the art of maintaining appearances. He chatted, listened, laughed, and watched. Every now and then, his and Claire's eyes would connect. She wanted to tell him she was sorry. She hadn't asked for the counsel, but of course, she maintained her mask and didn't approach the subject. Emily didn't know about the hallway conversation. She innocently conversed.

By the end of dinner Emily and Claire decided Claire would wear the Vera Wang dress. She liked the lace sleeves, it would be best for a winter wedding. They also decided on the dress for Emily. Tony had printed off all the contact information for the boutique. Claire gave it to Emily and told her she was sorry, but Emily would need to return to the city one or two more times for fittings. Emily said it was all right.

John asked them what time their flight back to Iowa was in the morning. Claire looked at Tony. She didn't want to say, "Oh, we can go anytime. It's Tony's jet." He answered, "We plan to leave early. This wedding is coming together very fast. Our wedding planner will be at the house tomorrow at two. Luckily, we gain an hour on our way back." Claire sighed, he was good. She also decided he either genuinely started to relax or he could fool her too. Regardless, he appeared very accommodating.

After their appetizers, salads, and main entrée, they all had coffee. Surprisingly, after the uncomfortable hallway confrontation, the dinner went well. Earlier, back at the apartment, Claire shared Emily's comments regarding the cost of the wedding with Tony. He hadn't said much other than to acknowledge her concerns, but apparently developed a plan. "John and Emily, I want to thank you for joining us this Thanksgiving. It means so much to Claire. She told me about the loss of your family, the two of you are important to her." Claire listened intently, as did the two of them. "I can be impulsive. I must admit after so many years of bachelorhood I'm delighted to have met the one woman I want to spend my life beside." He looked at Claire and smiled. She smiled in return. "That is why Claire agreed to such a fast wedding. That can be difficult on those people we hold dear. You may have had plans for that weekend, and I doubt you were planning a trip to Iowa." He had everyone's attention. "Therefore, I would be honored if you would allow me to take care of your travel plans to and from Iowa. I'm speaking for Claire, but I believe she would like you to be there a few days before the ceremony. Our home is not near hotels. Please know you are invited to stay with us. We have room." He sounded gallant and magnanimous.

Claire reached his hand under the table and squeezed. He squeezed back and held her hand. She didn't know how John would respond, but she was exceedingly pleased with her fiancé. "And while I have your attention, I want

188

to give Claire her dream wedding. Please allow me to take care of any wedding apparel and accessories."

At first, Emily and John said nothing. Claire knew it was killing John. He was a successful attorney, but they had education loans they were still paying. They had a mortgage, car loans, probably credit cards. Tony had more money than he could spend in a lifetime. She prayed they would accept.

Finally, John spoke. "Anthony, thank you very much. It's difficult for me to accept your generosity."

Tony had one more ploy, "John, haven't I heard stories about Claire living with the two of you for a year after college?" John said yes, she did live with them. "Perhaps you could justify this as an overdue rent payment?" Tony smiled. Claire wanted to cry. Instead, she beamed at John and Emily. They had to see how wonderful Tony could be.

John and Emily exchanged glances. Finally, it was Emily who accepted, "Thank you. You have our numbers. Please let us know the details." The conversation was done. They all stood to leave and Claire thought about the bill. Apparently, it was taken care of without anyone realizing, one less confrontation. Tony had contacted Eric and he had the car waiting outside. Claire hoped the polite attitude of the dinner would continue into the car.

The women got in first, followed by John, who sat by Emily, and Tony, who sat by Claire. As soon as Eric pulled away from the curb John began speaking. His voice was strong and direct as if he were addressing a jury or judge, "Anthony, I apologize for ambushing Claire in the hallway. And, Claire, I apologize for making you uncomfortable." Emily looked at John with horror in her eyes, completely unaware. Claire exhaled and sat back, thinking only, oh god, he *is* going to pursue this. She deferred to Tony. "But, I've known Claire since she was a small girl. I've done my best to look out for Emily and for Claire, especially since the death of their parents. I love her like a sister."

He smiled at Claire, then back to Tony with all seriousness. "I am an attorney, and I believe Claire deserves rightful representation regarding the legal ramifications of your marriage."

Claire didn't speak, Tony did, "John, I definitely appreciate the fact Claire has someone else who cares about her well-being. I must emphasize, she will be *my* wife and *I* will look out for her. I can assure you, we have an entire team of attorneys who will represent her in any necessary legal circumstance."

John continued undeterred. "With all due respect, your legal team will look out for *your* best interests, as they should. Claire is obviously in love with you and trusts your decisions."

"Are you implying you do not trust my decisions?"

"No, I'm not implying. I am saying as Claire's brother-in-law and attorney I should review the prenuptial agreement prior to her signature."

Claire didn't feel good about this discussion. Maybe she could help. "Thank you, John, for your concern. I do trust Tony—" She immediately knew she shouldn't have spoken. She stopped.

Tony continued, "Your concern is admirable. And your persistence is commendable. As Claire's attorney, not her brother-in-law, I will inform you we do not plan on having a prenuptial agreement. I want Claire to have half

189

of everything. I do not plan on divorcing her, leaving her, or her leaving me. I believe she should be my partner in every way with everything. She will have half of everything I possess as of December 18."

John sat in silence and stared at Tony. He hadn't expected that information. Finally, he spoke. "Have you consulted your team of legal counsel?"

"Excuse me? Are you asking as Claire's attorney?"

"No, I'm asking as your future brother-in-law. I know Claire. I know she is a wonderful woman who is in love. But, as an attorney, a man of your wealth should not enter a business deal without a contract, and you should not enter a marriage without a prenuptial agreement."

Tony smiled, amused. Amusement did *not* imply a good thing. Claire prayed it was all a figment of her imagination, perhaps she was sleeping again and this was a nightmare. Emily sat in awe, dumbfounded by the verbal debate transpiring before her. Tony decided the conversation was over. "John, thank you for your advice. Thank you for your legal consultation. Your care and concern for Claire is duly noted and welcomed. I look forward to more lively debates with you in the future. May I make one suggestion?" John said yes. However, his answer was inconsequential. The statement formed as a question was purely rhetorical. Tony would offer his suggestion either way. "These conversations should and *will* take place in private."

John agreed.

They sat in silence for a while. Finally, Emily broke the uneasy stillness, "Claire, it has been so nice to see you. I'm going to miss you." She reached out for Claire's hand and squeezed, "And I can't wait until we're together again for the wedding." Then Emily turned to Tony. "If we are still welcome?"

His mouth smiled. Claire didn't need to look to know his eyes did not. "Of course, we look forward to your visit." Once the car reached their hotel, Eric opened the door and Tony got out first. Emily and John both hugged Claire on their way out. Emily told Claire to call more, and they both shook Tony's hand as they went into the hotel.

Tony got back in the car and Eric shut the door. He laid his head back on the seat. Claire still didn't think she should speak. She wanted to tell him how pleased she was with all he'd said. She did trust his decisions and she didn't care about the money. However, it was obvious Tony wasn't happy. She chose to remain silent.

As the car pulled away Tony squeezed Claire's hand and spoke, his tone was neither warm nor playful, "I believe it is good you had a nap this afternoon." Eric drove them to the apartment.

Prolonged endurance tames the bold.
—Lord Byron

Chapter 28

During the eight months Claire lived on Tony's estate, she never saw visitors, business or personal. The house remained busy with staff and employees. People who clean, cook, and fulfill other responsibilities filled the house. The grounds often bustled with gardeners and maintenance workers, but there were never *guests*. That was why, as they approached the house, winding up the drive, it seemed strange to see multiple cars parked on the brickyard in front of the main steps.

On the plane and again in the car, Claire received the *rules* speech. It seemed incredibly redundant. She'd heard it hundreds of times, literally. She knew the words by heart. Follow my rules: do as you are told, do not divulge personal information, actions have consequences, appearances were of vital importance, and public failure was not an option. Apparently, being Tony's fiancée didn't exempt her from the rules. As a matter of fact, it made them all that more critical.

Shelly, Tony's publicist, released the prepared statement to the press. It simply read:

Anthony Rawlings, entrepreneur and world-renowned businessman happily announces his engagement to Claire Nichols, originally from Indiana. The two plan a December wedding. Details are not available at this time.

The press release made the engagement public. She now directly represented him. Changing her mind at this point would be unacceptable and a public failure. She didn't plan on changing her mind.

However, if she needed a reason for changing her mind, last night would have been it. Apparently, Tony's newfound gentleness and affection

191

evaporated during his discussion with John. Claire told herself that it was a momentary setback. The discussion upset Tony. John's behavior had consequences. Claire willingly accepted her brother-in-law's consequences in his stead. She knew how to compartmentalize, and even believed she was getting good at it. From experience, she believed with the morning, the new caring Tony would be back. She was mostly right.

When they entered their home, Catherine met them at the door. Her smile beamed from ear to ear, and she hugged them both. Claire truly loved her. She was the heart of their home. Tony obviously respected her opinion, and she his. Catherine's approval pleased Claire. It was probably the one that mattered to her the most other than Tony's.

"Ms. Claire, I am so happy. I have known for a long time that you are exactly what Mr. Rawlings needed in his life." She beamed at Claire as Tony listened.

"Umm, am I what anyone needs?" His tone and face smiled. Catherine hugged him and told him that many people need him. Then she informed him he had guests in his office. Claire suddenly thought about her restrictions regarding his office. Why could others be in there without him, but she couldn't? Walking toward his home office, she debated this in her mind. The answer was painfully obvious. Everyone else in the world had access to telephones, computers, and the Internet—except her.

The double doors to Tony's office stood ajar. The conference table was cluttered with books resembling photo albums and an open laptop computer. Two women and a man arranged the materials and talked to one another. Claire and Tony stood silently hand in hand in the doorway and observed.

Finally, one of the women looked up and acknowledged Tony. "Mr. Rawlings, hello. Let me introduce you to your wedding planner and consultant."

Tony stepped toward her. She was an attractive, tall, professional-looking brunette who looked about the same age as Claire. As she stepped toward Tony, he turned toward Claire. "Patricia, let me finally introduce you to my fiancée, Claire Nichols. Claire, this is my number one assistant, secretary, and right-hand man/woman, Patricia." His introduction revealed his admiration for her abilities.

They both extended their hands. Claire spoke first. "I have heard so many wonderful things about you. It is very nice to finally meet you."

Patricia's greeting sounded less gregarious. "Hello, Ms. Nichols, I have heard about you." Claire definitely detected animosity but chose to wait and let the chips fall. Patricia continued with the introductions. "Brad Clark and Monica Thompson, may I introduce Mr. Anthony Rawlings and his fiancée, Claire Nichols. Mr. Rawlings, Brad is your wedding consultant, and Monica is your wedding planner. They come highly recommended and have some wonderful ideas to share."

Claire and Tony shook their hands and told them how happy they were to meet them. Tony looked at his watch, 12:30. They were due to arrive at two. In Tony's book, they had made bonus points. Claire, on the other hand, had anticipated lunch. She was less pleased, but smiled and preceded with their meeting. Brad and Monica showed Tony and Claire to Tony's conference table.

Brad and Monica began by explaining how honored they were to be chosen to assist with their wedding. Then they presented a very informative Power Point presentation with endless options available to Mr. Rawlings and Ms. Nichols. They also displayed photos of their previous work, examples of decorations, cakes, receptions, etc. They asked questions, both of Tony and of Claire. What did they want their wedding to say? How many guests did they anticipate? Where on the estate would the wedding and reception be held? What would be the time of the ceremony? What colors did they want? What type of food? What type of music?

While the questions were tedious, Claire couldn't help notice Patricia's stares. She was excessively attentive to Tony. "Yes, Mr. Rawlings." "I can get that for you, Mr. Rawlings." "Let me take care of that, Mr. Rawlings." For the first time since John's consequences and the multiple rule discussions, Claire was happy to be the future Mrs. Anthony Rawlings. It even amused her that as an adult, the cattiness of another woman could readjust her attitude. Claire found herself holding Tony's arm, looking at pictures of cakes and lights and tables and flowers and saying all the right things. He smiled affectionately and she radiated happiness. Patricia sat on the sidelines taking notes.

Tony then asked Claire to show Brad and Monica around the main level of *their* home so they could brainstorm. Brad and Monica would get back to them on Monday with possibilities for the ceremony and reception. As she walked them from room to room, she saw the mansion from a new perspective. In their eyes it was a magnificent display of architecture and an exquisite home. It hadn't been that to her, it had been a prison. Tony referred to it as *their* home, both now and last night with John and Emily. She smiled as she thought, *this is* my *home.*

Tony and Claire promised to get a guest list together very soon. They, with the help of Brad and Monica, decided that being a Christmas wedding, red, green, and black would be the colors. The question still remained whether Emily's dress would be green, red, or black. There would be Christmas lights, lots of lights, starting from the gates and going up the drive to the house. The house would be decorated very chic Christmas. The number of guests would determine the setup of the wedding and reception. The music during the wedding would be provided by a string quartet and a harpist. Brad and Monica would put together some demo CDs and Tony and Claire could choose the music.

The reception would be on the grounds, either in the house or perhaps in the backyard. Claire thought that sounded cold. Brad promised a tent, decorated and heated. He even had pictures of previous tent receptions. With the decorations, tables, and people, it didn't appear like a tent, only a reception hall. The next hurdle was the cake. They must have looked at fifty different pictures of cakes. Regarding flavors, Tony said he liked traditional white. Claire went out on a limb and said she liked chocolate. She hoped for some taste testing. Monica smiled and explained they had other options such as carrot, red velvet, caramel, chocolate raspberry, and more. Claire felt once again overwhelmed by too many choices.

The next debate involved the menu for the reception. Since Claire had only chosen two of her own meals in the last eight months, she asked Tony if she could take a break and get something to eat. She didn't feel well, low blood sugar. He kissed her cheek and said she should rest. He could take care of it. Patricia added, "I will be here to help."

"I'm sure you will." She kissed Tony and went to the kitchen to find Catherine and some lunch. They were about done for today. Brad and Monica would return Monday late afternoon when Tony returned home from work. At that time, more definitive plans would be made and others finalized. It was fun talking possibilities without considering the financial ramifications. Tony was right. The wedding would be planned and accomplished by December 18. Money could make anything happen.

Their kitchen was more industrial than cozy. She hadn't eaten in there before, but with people everywhere it seemed like a safe, isolated location. Sitting at a small table near the windows, Claire looked out over the backyard and garages. She was there eating a sandwich when Tony found her.

"What do you think about the plans?" His voice sounded light and brought her back to reality. She'd been letting her mind wander. It hadn't been any place in particular, just a happy place. She was thinking about lights, Christmas trees, her wedding dress, Tony in a tuxedo, and a warm feeling. She remembered the warmth of her visions while she was ill, and her current thoughts were giving her that same feeling. It was a nice change to have reality be her warm place.

She smiled at Tony as he approached. "I think they sound wonderful. I can't believe they aren't freaking out about the deadline."

"What did I tell you?"

She smiled. "We don't have enough time to discuss all the things you've told me."

"You seem happy." Grinning, he stole the other half of her sandwich. "I meant about what money could do to help our wedding proceed as you want." He took a bite of the sandwich.

"You said it would and it obviously does. I'm still slightly in shock." Claire took a drink of water and caressed Tony's arm. Looking into his brown eyes, she said, "It's a good shock." He took her water and started to kiss her neck. "Do you realize you have taken my sandwich and now my water?"

Tony cooed, "I think maybe you have taken something of mine."

He stood by her chair. She put her arms around his waist and looked up at his face. "I did? What did I take?"

He bent down to kiss her. She stood to meet him halfway. His lips softly touched her lips and her neck as his hands became tangled in her hair. "I believe it was my heart." Claire's body forgot the demands of the previous night. Actually, it began to make demands of its own. He tugged her hair with his fingers, causing her face to look up. She considered asking about Patricia, it was a fleeting thought. There was a more pressing issue. "Is everyone still here?" she pressed back.

194

"Brad and Monica left, they will return Monday to give us more information. We can make more definite decisions then." She kissed his neck as he spoke. His voice revealed the effect of her kisses. "And Patricia is collecting names for our guest list. She's still in my office. I told her I needed to check on you to make sure you were feeling all right." His chocolate eyes hid behind closed lids.

Claire couldn't resist. "I'm feeling very good, how do you think I'm feeling?" He murmured agreement as she spoke between kisses. "So explain why I can't be in your office alone and she can?"

He pulled her close. "Because, I said so." His hands caressed the soft skin under her sweater.

"I hated that answer when it came from my parents, I don't think I like it from you either." She wasn't arguing or complaining. On the contrary, she was agreeing with everything.

"Okay, how about because you don't need to worry your pretty head about anything in there? The telephones, Internet, computers . . . All you need to worry about is me."

"Oh, and I do! I worry about you constantly." She nuzzled his chin and listened to his heart pound rapidly in his wide chest. "So you don't worry about Patricia's pretty head?"

His voice sounded gravelly and far away. "Does she have a pretty head? I hadn't noticed." He couldn't have said anything that would have pleased Claire more at that moment. She suggested going to his room or her room, he mentioned the attributes of the kitchen floor, when Catherine made a loud coughing sound.

"Excuse me, Mr. Rawlings, Ms. Claire. Mr. and Mrs. Simmons are here to see you both." Claire looked at Tony with desperation. "What happened to never having visitors?" She smiled and tried to straighten her hair and sweater. Tony suddenly turned away from Catherine and looked out the back window, breathed deeply, and tried to adjust his appearance. Claire decided she should address Catherine, Tony was having difficulty talking. "Thank you, Catherine. Can you please tell them Mr. Rawlings and I will be there in a few minutes?"

Catherine said she would show the Simmons' to the sitting room. Claire went to Tony and whispered in his ear, "Sorry."

He turned to her, grinning, his voice adoring and playful. "You aren't yet, but give me some time." There was a time those words would have terrified her. Today wasn't one of them, the wedding planning, being home, and fanciful foreplay set a stage. The stage felt warm, like her visions.

"I look forward to that promise." She leaned against a counter and waited for him to contain himself. She tried, but couldn't remember one time in the past eight months he'd been in this predicament. Grinning, she found it amusing.

They walked hand in hand to the sitting room. When they reached the archway Brent and Courtney stood to greet them. Courtney ran to Claire and hugged her. Next to Catherine, it was the best response she received from anyone regarding their engagement. She really felt like she was being hugged by a friend. Claire couldn't help feeling happy. It was a real happy, one that suddenly seemed to be recurring. She liked it. Courtney pulled Claire's left hand to see her ring, and led her to one of the sofas. She wanted to hear all about New York, the proposal, and everything! Claire looked to Tony. He and Brent were involved in discussions which led them away from the ladies and toward Tony's office.

Claire curled up on the sofa with her arms wrapped around her knees and chatted with her friend. It wasn't uncomfortable or difficult. She didn't feel threatened by Courtney's questions or the pressure to feign her answers. She didn't feel the need to minimize Tony's extravagant proposal. She felt warm and accepted. Catherine brought them coffee, and Courtney listened as Claire told her about New York City. From shopping for the perfect outfit to the cool crisp evening in Central Park, she retold the entire day. It all was so romantic! She wouldn't repeat his proposal, but it was wonderful. She couldn't believe he really proposed.

Courtney could hardly contain her excitement. "We have been friends with Tony for a long time. And both Brent and I have noticed something different with Tony lately. The way he looks at you, we've never seen that look in his eyes before. It's wonderful to see him in love."

The simplicity of chatting, giggling, and sharing, delighted Claire. Sometime during their conversation she thought she heard voices, loud voices coming from the direction of Tony's office. Courtney heard them too. They shrugged and went on with their chat. Courtney told Claire she would be willing to help her in any way. She would be glad to taste-test food or desserts, listen to music, tie bows for chairs, address invitations, whatever Claire needed. She was officially at her disposal.

The men returned to the sitting room. Their disposition not as jovial as the ladies; however, they acted affable. Courtney finally asked, "Is everything all right?" Tony said it was and Brent agreed. The ladies were having too much fun to let the men change that. Courtney continued to ask about the wedding. Would it really be in three weeks? Did they like the coordinator and planner? When Tony wasn't around she wanted the scoop on Claire's dress. Then she told Tony about her offer to help Claire. She was so excited. They left about two hours after they arrived.

Claire started to go upstairs to her suite when she remembered Patricia. Had she left? Tony said she had, when Brent got there. She took information home and she would bring him a guest list to evaluate Monday at the office. "Can we please eat in my suite? It's been a great day and I'm tired."

During dinner Tony told Claire he and Brent exchanged *words* during the afternoon. Brent was Tony's head legal counsel and his best friend, Claire was surprised. What happened? He explained, Brent borrowed a page from her brother-in-law's advice book. Claire sighed. "The prenuptial agreement again." He said yes, Brent also insisted they have one. Claire agreed. "I don't presume to know anything about your belongings, but if everyone thinks we should have one, let's just do it."

She didn't realize the conversation had become intense, but before she could blink he lifted her from her chair. His tone immediately harsh and his proximity too close. "I am sick and tired of everyone telling me what to do. I have made my decision. That is what I told Brent and what I'm telling you. There will *not* be a prenuptial agreement and do you know why?"

Claire met his gaze. "Tony, please, you said you wouldn't hurt me again." He released her arms and she fell back to her chair.

"And you promised to not give me cause."

She thought about his question, she hadn't answered, yet. Not answering could be considered cause. "I don't know why we shouldn't have a prenuptial agreement other than you don't want one."

"That is part of it." He paced. "The other part is..." and he knelt by Claire, his face once again too close to hers, his eyes shining black, and stared into her eyes. She didn't look away, "I know I won't leave you. And I *know* you won't leave me." His voice slow and malevolent, he asked, "Will you?"

She faced one of those junctures: be frightened by his tone, proximity, and allow his sudden unpredicted change in disposition to ruin a day that she truly enjoyed, or attempt to defuse the situation before it got out of hand. She chose the second. She answered his question with a voice which sounded both calm and composed. "I agreed to be Mrs. Anthony Rawlings just three days ago. It has been a whirlwind since then, and my wedding is in three weeks. We are both overwhelmed. Tony, I would never think of leaving you."

His eyes still flashed, blackness intensified. "Do you have any idea of the consequences if you did decide to leave me?"

Continued eye contact and composure, "I would rather think about the consequences of staying with you and learning what makes you happy," she smiled, "and learning what you want of me, and when you want it." His eyes lightened and flickered brown. "Perhaps you could give me some hints?" He was calming. She watched the tension and fury leave his face. Continuing with the composed but now playful tone, she added, "As a matter of fact, I think you promised me something this afternoon in the kitchen."

It worked. He mellowed. She didn't make the first move, wanting him to believe he was in control. When he didn't speak and stood, she thought perhaps he was leaving her suite and this conversation was done. But he didn't. Instead, he scooped her out of the chair and carried her to the bed.

He wasn't his old self and he wasn't his new gentle self. He was somewhere in between, but closer to gentle than the night before. She did it, she mellowed him. Her response resulted in the consequence she hoped. Claire would figure him out. In the meantime, this was a little thunder but no storm.

Without friends no one would choose to live,
though he had all other goods.
—Aristotle

Chapter 29

T he next two and a half weeks flew by in a flash.

Sometime during their first night home, Claire awoke and heard Tony's breathing in her bed. The drapes were open, and the moonlight illuminated her suite. She looked around and snuggled into the soft covers. She was in her suite in her home, not in New York. In three weeks, it would actually be half hers. The monetary value wasn't what enamored her. It was the fact that he wanted it to belong to her. She possessed memories she refused to revisit. She also possessed a promise of a future. As she cuddled under the fluffy down comforter next to her warm sleeping fiancé, she knew she would hold tight to that promise.

They met with Brad and Monica on the Monday following Thanksgiving. Claire knew they were definitely worth the expense, whatever that may be. Tony told Claire not to worry about it. Their ideas were amazing. The wedding would take place in the grand entry, with Claire descending the staircase. It would be decorated with lights and sheer tapestries. The reception would be in the backyard, in a large floored, heated tent accessible to guests from the sunporch. There would be many Christmas trees and millions of clear lights. There would be evergreens and red flowers. Emily would wear black and carry a red bouquet. There would be an open bar and hors d'oeuvres and then a full sit-down meal of multiple courses. The cake was chic and decorated with real flowers. The flavors would include white, chocolate, raspberry, and carrot. Claire was especially excited about the string quartet from the Quad City Symphony, the place of her and Tony's first night out.

Tony gave them the list of guests Patricia had compiled. He asked Claire about guests over and over. She repeated, she only cared about Emily and John and Tony's close friends. She saw the difficulty Emily had with Claire's new lifestyle and feared her old friends would not feel comfortable. She mentioned Meredith as an example of why her friends from before should not attend. Tony couldn't argue her logic. The guest list consisted of the few people who called Tony, Tony, and 150 of his not so close business and political allies. People, he explained, should be invited whom he liked, needed, or who needed him.

Brad and Monica had a draft of the wedding invitation:

You are cordially invited to the private
wedding ceremony of:
Ms. Claire Nichols and Mr. Anthony Rawlings.
The ceremony will take place at the Iowa City estate of
Mr. and Mrs. Rawlings
on December the eighteenth two thousand and ten,
at precisely five thirty in the evening.
A dinner and dance reception will immediately follow at the estate.

Patricia volunteered to receive and compile the RSVPs. It would all be handled at Tony's Iowa City office.

The string quartet would begin playing at five with the ceremony at five thirty. There would be valet parking and a coat check since winter coats were predictable. The reception would include a live jazz band and dancing. There would not be a DJ, but there would be an MC to make announcements and talk to the guests. Each guest or "couple" would receive a gift basket in appreciation of their attendance from Mr. and Mrs. Rawlings. The baskets would include a bottle of fine wine, two crystal wine glasses, some fine chocolates wrapped in red and green foil, and a note thanking them for their attendance.

Brad asked Claire if her father would be giving her away. She told him her father was deceased. He asked if she had anyone else to give her away or did she plan to walk down the stairs and aisle alone. The question prompted Claire to think of John. She didn't ask; she just looked at Tony.

He sighed and responded to Brad, "She would like to have her brother-in-law give her away." Later Tony told Claire he liked the idea. Perhaps if John gave her away, he would accept she was his wife first and foremost. Tony, Brent, his best man, and John would all need matching tuxedos. Tony liked Armani and said he would contact the men to have the tuxedos tailored. It didn't take Tony and Brent long to reach a mutual understanding regarding the prenuptial agreement. Tony agreed not to have one. Brent agreed to accept Tony's decision.

Once Tony and Claire approved the designs and blueprints Brad and Monica created, the work began. First thing Tuesday morning crews of workers descended upon the estate. There were trucks with cherry pickers putting lights in trees, and electricians connecting wires to ensure illumination. A construction crew worked in the backyard building the large tent, with more electricians for lighting and heating.

There were people in the house putting up decorations. Catherine was uneasy with the multitude of people. She made sure everyone knew she was in charge of the house and everyone answered to her.

Claire did her best to stay out of the way. Tony left each morning for work. He had a wedding in less than three weeks and the pesky challenge of a multibillion-dollar industry which needed his attention. He even needed to make some day trips to places as far away as Dallas, Los Angeles, and New England.

Claire also needed to make a few more trips to New York for dress fittings. Tony hadn't planned for that. It was Courtney's offer of help in any way that reduced his anxiety. He required Claire to be the one to call Courtney and inquire. Courtney sounded thrilled. They would use Tony's jet as long as he wasn't using it. If he needed to travel there would be Rawlings Industries jets available. Eric would accompany them.

Tony also allowed Claire to contact Emily and John after the meeting with Brad and Monica. She let Emily know about her dress, it would be black. Emily sounded elated to learn it wasn't pink. Claire also asked John if he would do her the honor of walking her down the aisle and giving her away. He responded, "Claire, I'd be honored to walk you down the aisle, but know I will never give you away." Of course, Tony was listening as she spoke and rolled his black eyes at Claire. She didn't let her voice falter. She thanked him for his constant devotion. Claire also reminded Emily to contact the boutique regarding her fittings and told them that Tony or his secretary, Patricia, would be contacting them about their travel plans as well as John's tuxedo.

Everything was falling into place.

On their first trip to New York, Claire and Courtney left Iowa early on Wednesday morning, the eighth of December. With an hour time difference, it took three and a half hours to get to NYC. They left at six in the morning, which both ladies said was too early. They arrived before ten East Coast time and went directly to the boutique. The dress was ready and in need of alterations. Claire's shoes were white Mary Jane-style beaded four-inch heels. They looked magnificent with the dress.

When Claire exited the dressing room, Courtney screamed. At first it shocked Claire, but then she started laughing. Courtney was a riot. Claire had so much fun with her. Courtney went on and on about how stunning, beautiful, and stylish Claire looked. She promised Tony would be spellbound from the moment he saw her.

After the boutique Courtney told Eric she and Claire were going to the Astor Court at the St. Regis Hotel, one of the top New York tea rooms, for lunch. She also told him he didn't need to worry about picking them up until after three. They had some shopping to do. Claire tried to argue. She didn't want to discuss her uneasiness, but she knew she'd only received permission for her gown fitting, not shopping. Courtney wouldn't discuss it. With no way to contact Tony, Claire felt increasingly ill.

Once they arrived at the tea room, Courtney sensed Claire's discomfort. She didn't question Claire, she just casually mentioned, "Tony and I agreed when we spoke the other night, you need a new dress for the wedding rehearsal. And this afternoon would be a great time to find one." Claire relaxed. She wished he had said something, but if he knew about it, she felt better.

Without saying all of that to Courtney, she smiled and said, "Well, all right then, let's have some lunch and find the best rehearsal dress in the city!" She'd shopped many times with her credit card, but shopping with a friend and her credit card was much better. Courtney helped her find a beautiful red Valentino cotton tweed dress with an asymmetrical bow. The V neck would show off her journey necklace, and of course she needed new shoes for her new dress. The Salvatore Ferragamo leather peep-toe pumps were a perfect complement. Not only did she look stunning, but the color was also perfect for the whole Christmas theme. Claire enjoyed shopping with someone who seemed comfortable with the higher-end purchases.

The rehearsal would be at Tony and Claire's house, but Courtney insisted the rehearsal dinner be at her and Brent's house. After all, it was the groom's parents' responsibility, and they were Tony's oldest and dearest friends. They would be honored to host this special event. Claire thanked her for her kindness, and told her she would talk to Tony and get back to her as soon as possible.

When Claire returned home that night she was relieved she arrived before Tony. When seven o'clock came and he arrived for dinner, she found herself nervous about the additional shopping and luncheon. He didn't alleviate her unease when he asked about her day. How did she like her dress? Oh, she liked it very much, and Courtney liked it too. Did they come right back to Iowa after the boutique?

Claire hesitated and watched Tony. His expression didn't reveal any knowledge of her activities. She suddenly worried Courtney told her it was okay just to pacify her. She put on her mask, bit her lip, and casually continued, "Oh no, we didn't. Courtney prearranged with you," she added, "to make a day of it."

While Claire answered Tony looked at his plate then moved only his eyes to Claire. "Excuse me?"

Her heart raced. "Why didn't you tell me you arranged for us to shop for my rehearsal dress?" He smiled. Apparently, Courtney drove a hard bargain, he couldn't resist.

They scheduled their final visit to the boutique for Saturday, December 11, one week before the wedding. They planned to arrive at the boutique by ten, have a final fitting, and return at three to try on the dress again with the final alterations and bring it home to Iowa. This trip also had surprises planned. On Friday evening as Tony and Claire ate dinner, his iPhone rang. He answered and handed Claire the phone. It was unusual for her to receive a call, and especially unusual for her to talk on a telephone without it being on speaker. She answered tentatively, "Hello? This is Claire?"

"Hi, it's Cort." Claire understood why Tony allowed her to talk; he trusted Courtney. Her voice comforted Claire. Courtney went on to let Claire know Sue, MaryAnn, and Bev were joining them for New York City tomorrow. Since they had time to spare between fittings, the women planned on taking Claire out for a bridal shower luncheon. Stunned and startled,

Claire was thrilled. She hadn't even considered a shower, after all Tony could buy anything she needed, but it was part of the wedding tradition. She told Courtney it sounded wonderful and asked if she could hold a minute. Claire hit the mute button on Tony's phone and looked at him across the table meeting his intense gaze.

"She wants Bev, MaryAnn, and Sue to join us tomorrow." His eyebrows rose. "They want to take me to lunch for a bridal luncheon." She smiled.

"And do you want to do this?" He tormented her, making her request his permission. She knew Courtney was waiting.

"I do." He didn't speak. "I think it would be nice to have a shower." Still no response. "May we have the shower?" He smiled and nodded. She excitedly hit the mute button, "Courtney, I think that sounds wonderful. Will we all meet at the airport or do they need to be picked up?" When she hung up she thanked Tony. This was wonderful and unexpected. She handed him back his phone.

The plane ride was joyous with talk of the wedding and excitement over Claire's dress. The merriment continued when she exited the fitting room as all the ladies went crazy about the dress and how beautiful Claire looked. A few minute alternations needed to be completed. Eric hadn't been available to join them on their excursion, so they traveled by taxi. Claire liked that. Having all of them pile into one cab reminded her of her past life.

At noon they arrived at King's Carriage House, a wonderfully quaint English-style restaurant located in a brownstone on the Upper East Side. They had reservations and were taken to the second level where the walls were painted a deep rich red and large chandeliers glowed. The intimate tables were richly arranged, very girlie. It exuded the shower feeling and alone would have thrilled Claire, but the real surprise came in seeing Emily sitting at their table. She ran to hug her sister and asked how she knew. She explained Claire's good friend Courtney planned the entire thing. When Claire hugged Courtney, Courtney whispered in Claire's ear, "Tony gave me her number." Claire had a marvelous afternoon!

After the luncheon Emily accompanied them back to the boutique where they all saw her in her matron-of-honor's dress. Claire surprised her with a gift of a pair of black Jimmy Choo satin pumps with a jewel bow. They were perfect for the dress and the wedding. However, it was as Claire came out of the dressing room in the wedding gown one last time, completely altered and ready, that everyone, even Ms. Springhill, applauded. Claire was elated with the final result. She felt so pretty.

The five ladies flew back to Iowa with Claire's gown, shoes, undergarments, including slip and veil. Emily would arrive on Wednesday evening. It was a great afternoon and they ended it with a bottle of champagne and some snacks on the plane home.

When Tony entered the suite that evening, she sprung up and encircled his neck with her arms. "You are awful!" And she kissed him passionately.

Surprised, he replied, "Okay, remind me to be awful more often. What did I do?"

"Only assist in giving me the best bridal luncheon ever, which included my sister!" He looked at her suspiciously. She quickly replied, "Oh, don't start. Courtney told me you were the one who gave her Emily's number. You, who acted like you didn't know anything about others joining us. You're really rotten. And I love you more every day." She kissed him again. He grinned and returned the kiss.

He asked to see her dress. She told him, "No." He expressed astonishment at her denial. "You can't see it until next Saturday."

He conceded to see what she would wear under her dress. Claire grinned. They were alone in her suite. Seductively she began to unbutton her blouse, one button at a time. Tony didn't mind the consolation prize.

Love one another, but make not a bond of love,
let it rather be a moving sea between the shores of your souls.
—Kahlil Gibran

Chapter 30

Emily arrived on the Wednesday evening before the wedding. Tony sent his private plane to pick her up in Albany. John, however, was involved in a hearing and wouldn't be available until Friday. He apologized to Claire for the mix-up but couldn't change the trial date. Claire decided it would be nice to have Emily all to herself. However, as she sat in the back of one of Tony's cars at the airport waiting, she worried about Emily's reaction to flying in a private plane. The interior of the BMW was warm and permeated the smell of leather. It was significantly better than the cold Iowa chill outside the windows.

It snowed the past three days, and everything was brilliantly covered with a beautiful clean white blanket. Once the door of the jet opened and stairs descended, Claire got out of the car, feeling the brisk air. She wore jeans, a furry jacket, and snow boots to stay warm. Keeping her leather gloved hands deep in her pockets, she watched the crew clear the runway and the pavement as the snow continued to fall.

Emily descended the stairs and hugged Claire. "Hi, sis, are you by yourself?"

"Carlos drove me here, but Tony's still at work."

They got into the warm car while Carlos retrieved Emily's luggage and placed it in the trunk. Emily smiled and said, "You know, when you and Anthony offered to arrange our travel plans, I was kind of expecting a ticket on United or something." Claire didn't speak, she waited. "But, I'm not complaining. I am, however, anxiously anticipating your home." Claire sensed Emily's honest attempt at acceptance.

Relieved, Claire excitedly continued, "Good. I can't wait for you to see it. Right now, it is very busy and cluttered. There have been hundreds of workers preparing for the ceremony. But, we can get away from all the people and have some time to ourselves. Have you eaten?" It was seven thirty in Iowa, the sky was very dark, yet the snow, which continued to fall, made it appear brighter.

"I had a few snacks on the plane."

"Good, we will eat when we get home." Claire replied.

The estate looked stately on any given day. In the snow, it appeared splendid. With the addition of millions of white lights lining the drive, the trees, and bushes around the residence, it was grand. Claire was very pleased to have Emily visit. She never would have dreamed of asking Tony to allow her and John to stay. Therefore, his invitation wasn't only unexpected, but remarkable. Of course, there was plenty of room. With Tony, room wasn't the issue— it was privacy.

During the past two weeks, privacy was at a premium. There were workers everywhere. When you turned a corner on the main level, you never knew for sure who you might encounter. For that reason, Tony and Claire spent most of their time hidden away in her suite. Tony even felt the people were too close on the first floor while in his suite or office.

While the car wound up the driveway Emily speechlessly watched as the estate came into view. The house glowed from the decorations for Christmas and the grand event. Carlos stopped in front of the house where a grounds worker busily cleared the walk for Ms. Claire and her guest. Emily reached for her door handle. Claire touched her hand and she hesitated. Carlos got out and went around and opened their door and then opened the door to the house.

Once inside, Catherine greeted them. Claire happily introduced two of her favorite people. Emily sensed an exceptional relationship between Claire and Catherine. Catherine informed them, "Ladies your dinner can be ready at any time. Mr. Rawlings is delayed due to weather. However, he recommended that you eat without him."

Claire thanked Catherine and told her she would show Emily to her room, let her freshen up, and they would return in fifteen minutes.

Emily and John were given a room down the hall from Claire's suite. It was a room with one of the doors Claire was surprised to see many months ago. These bedrooms were rarely used by anyone and kept immaculate *just in case* they may be needed. It was a suite about half the size of Claire's, with a queen-sized bed, bedroom furniture, a sofa and chair, a small gas fireplace, attached bath, and walk-in closet. There were large windows looking out onto the backyard. However, all that was visible now was the top of a very large tent.

Claire showed her the room and told her Carlos would have her luggage there soon. Then she showed Emily to her own suite. It was just a few doors away in the same corridor. Emily tried to be polite, but she could only say "this is beautiful" so many times. She asked about Tony. Was this his room too?

"No. He has his own room on the first floor." Claire smiled. "But, he does visit." She sensed Emily's surprise. The fact she and Tony didn't share a bedroom had just earned Tony a few points in Emily's book.

They ate dinner in the formal dining room. As they finished, Tony arrived home. He behaved as polite and gracious as possible. He kissed Claire and hugged Emily and told her how happy he was she arrived safely in spite of the weather. Luckily, the snow was scheduled to stop tomorrow and the forecast was clear for the weekend. Then he turned to Claire. "But you know those weather reports; you can never trust those meteorologists." She playfully threw her napkin at him and he smiled. When he sat, Catherine brought him his dinner. The ladies sipped coffee while Tony ate.

After dinner Tony offered to take the lead on a house tour. Secretly, Claire was delighted. She had been concerned about the magnitude of a tour. It was much easier to defer to Tony. As they walked from room to room and level to level, Emily told them how much she loved their home and jokingly asked if maps were available at the guest relations desk. Tony and Claire laughed, saying it wasn't that big. She would know her way around in no time.

Tony added, "However, it did seem to take Claire a few weeks before she found her way around." His statement caught Claire by surprise. He however didn't notice Claire's reaction. He was busy watching for Emily's reaction. Her obvious lack of understanding satisfied his unasked questions.

Her mask secure, Claire said, "Well, I finally learned the secret. Everything is connected to the main house, and if you need anything just ask."

Her response received a twinkling eyed grin from her fiancé.

Emily retired after the tour, promising to be more fun tomorrow. However, after a day of work, travel, and the magnitude of her surroundings, she was exhausted.

Claire hugged her sister, "Oh Emily, we're so happy you're here."

It wasn't long after Claire readied for bed that Tony joined her. Claire couldn't help but inquire, "Explain that comment, please."

Tony laughed. "My dear, I was just checking your reflexes."

"Well, you nearly caused whiplash."

Grinning, "Perhaps there are other reflexes we could investigate?"

John's hearing adjourned at noon on Friday. He offered to fly commercial, but the earliest he would make Iowa City would be after 10:00 p.m. Tony graciously provided a company plane which allowed him to arrive in Iowa City by three thirty. Emily prepared him for the house and its amenities. He repeatedly expressed his gratitude to Tony and Claire for the flight and told them their home was stunning.

It was a beehive of activity with people everywhere making last-minute adjustments and preparing for the event. There were even people in the kitchen beginning to prepare the food. The tent had been transformed into a picturesque banquet hall.

Claire and Emily readied themselves for the rehearsal and rehearsal dinner. Tony accepted Courtney's kind invitation and agreed the rehearsal dinner could be held at the Simmons'. The rehearsal was scheduled to begin at six thirty, with dinner at eight. It was late, but everyone had to get to the

Rawlings home after a long day of work. The intimate guest list for the rehearsal included the minister, musicians, Brad, Monica, Patricia and a guest, the Vandersols, the Simmons' and their children, the Millers, the Bronsons, Elijah Summer, and MaryAnn Combs. Of course, these guests would be at the wedding tomorrow, but this informal private gathering would allow them more relaxed friendly conversation than would be possible at the big event.

Everyone congregated in the grand hall by six fifteen. This group of friends respected Tony's affection for punctuality. Claire waited for Tony in her suite. He wanted to *make an entrance* with his fiancée. "Ms. Nichols, you are stunning this evening." Just before entering the hall, he beamed and whispered, "Tomorrow at this time you will be Mrs. Anthony Rawlings."

She kissed her fiancé and smiled. "I can't wait."

There was a brief discussion by the head of security about some issues for the wedding. In an attempt to limit pictures, all cellphones, iPods, cameras, and any recording equipment, visual or audio, would be confiscated at the door. They would be returned on leaving the ceremony. The only recording of the wedding would be done by the hired photographer and cinematographer. Those photos would be reviewed by Shelly prior to release. However, as Tony and Claire's personal friends, the head of security asked them to be observant, and if they noticed any prohibited recording notify security personal immediately. They would be everywhere. Claire felt like she was back stage at a rock concert.

The minister took a few minutes to discuss the important meaning of marriage and its significance. "Many people enter into marriage in this day and age without the understanding of eternity. When two individuals are joined in the sight of God, those two become one. They are one for eternity."

Claire turned to Tony. She was in awe. How did she end up in the grand foyer of Anthony Rawlings's estate, holding his hand, looking into his chocolate eyes, and listening to a minister talk about *their* marriage?

The minister continued, "And after speaking with Anthony and Claire, I believe they are fully aware of the commitment which they are about to make, a commitment to God, to friends and family, and to each other. So to you, the intimate group of friends who Anthony and Claire have chosen to share in their special day please join me in a prayer. Let us ask God to provide for Anthony and Claire, not in a monetary way. Let us pray that God will provide them with love, understanding, and patience. That He will provide each of them with the qualities necessary to take what they begin tomorrow and continue it into eternity. Let us pray." Claire closed her eyes, Tony tenderly squeezed her hand, and a tear trickled down her cheek.

Brad and Monica then took control. They told Claire, John, and Emily to go upstairs. Tony, Brent, and the minister went to Tony's office. The string quartet began to play. Brad and Monica wore earphones and microphones. They directed the participants. First, they instructed the men to leave the office and walk to the back of the grand hall. A raised platform surrounded by sleek Christmas trees and lights had been constructed in front of the large windows. The only decorations on the trees besides the white lights were deep red crystal globes. The windows behind the platform exposed snow covered trees with more lights. The quartet was positioned slightly off to one side of the platform and the harpist was on the other. Once the men were in place, Emily was directed to descend the stairs and make her way down the aisle to the platform. After she arrived at her destination, the quartet concluded and the harpist began the traditional wedding march. Although it was the rehearsal, Claire and Tony's friends rose to their feet and Brad motioned to Claire and John to descend the steps.

John offered Claire his arm, kissed her cheek, and began to take her down the stairs. Before they reached the first step he stopped, leaned near, and whispered, "Claire, we love you. We only want you to be happy. Tell me he is good to you and that he makes you happy."

With tears in her eyes, she said, "John, he can be. He does." He tried to smile and patted her hand. They descended the stairs and made their way to the platform. After another song by the string quartet and a verse from the minister, he asked, "Who gives this woman to be wed?"

John spoke loud and clear, "With great love and respect, her sister and I agree to share this magnificent woman." He kissed Claire's cheek and gently lifted her hand from his arm and placed it in Tony's hand.

Shit, was the only word that came to Claire's mind. She looked up at Tony. He was looking at her, but his face didn't register John's words. He apparently had a mask too. Claire was certain if he was a cartoon character there would be smoke coming from his ears. She mouthed, "I'm sorry." He squeezed her hand gently and they both smiled. The minister continued speaking.

They all four rode together in the limousine to Courtney and Brent's house. Claire explained to Emily how in the late morning there would be a masseuse, manicure technician, cosmetologist, and hair stylist all coming to do miracles on them. Catherine and Courtney would be in Claire's suite to assist them both with their dresses.

Tony upheld appearances much more proficiently than John. He remained polite and friendly to both Emily and John and was loving and attentive to Claire. Once they reached the Simmons' house, Tony was the totally devoted bridegroom and the man of the hour. John was friendly but quiet. His unhappiness made Claire uneasy. She privately begged Emily to do something. "Don't let him ruin my special day." Emily promised to try.

Courtney provided a wonderfully delicious Italian dinner with antipasto salad, bread and oil, red wine and pasta. The festive mood and atmosphere filled Claire with hope and joy. Tim and Sue were chatting with Tony, as Claire walked up and overheard them discuss Tim's role during Claire and Tony's honeymoon. At first, she stood politely by Tony. But when they paused, Claire tried to be sneaky. "Now, Tim, tell me again how long you will need to be at the helm?" Tony laughed and pulled her close.

"Good try." Tony said. Then addressing Tim he continued, "You are one of the few privileged individuals to know where we will be in case of an emergency. Most people, including my beautiful new wife, do not know our destination. So do not let her try to worm it out of you." He smiled. "Or you, Sue, if Tim has shared."

"Oh, you are so mean. How will I know what to pack?"

"Another 'A' for effort, Catherine has taken care of it for you." Claire smiled at the Bronsons. They smiled and put their fingers to their lips. They wouldn't spoil Tony's surprise.

The dinner party began to wind down about ten thirty, at which time the gentlemen announced it was time to celebrate Tony's last night of freedom. They headed to the lower level for cognac, cigars, and some serious poker. Brent announced Tony should be prepared to lose more than his freedom. He would be losing some serious money during their tournament. "Ladies do not wait up."

It was MaryAnn who replied, "Don't worry about us. We're doing our own celebrating back at Claire's house. My driver is ready and Catherine has martinis waiting at the indoor pool and hot tub."

Tony and Claire kissed good night and were told they couldn't see each other again until the ceremony. While getting their coats, Emily whispered to Claire, "I'm sorry. I was wrong. You really do have a life and wonderful friends." Claire hugged her sister.

The ladies all went back to the estate, put on bathing suits, and partied in the hot tub. Claire decided Courtney and MaryAnn were teenagers in adult bodies. Tony worried so much about appearances, yet watching these two reputable women dance and sing in their bathing suits Claire believed a little *cutting loose* was acceptable. Just because she believed it, didn't mean she felt comfortable enough to do it. The reason her bachelorette party was at *her* house wasn't lost on her. She didn't want Tony watching her dance and sing inappropriately when he reviewed his surveillance. Claire enjoyed watching and sipped her drink.

Late into the night the subject of sex came up. It was Emily who after consuming a few too many martinis asked Claire, "Are you really okay with marrying a man so much older? What if he can't keep up?"

Claire smiled bashfully, "I don't think that's a problem." She tried desperately to change the subject.

Emily slept that night in Claire's suite. John returned to the estate after staying at the Simmons' home with the men for the bachelor party activities. He slept in their room, but Claire and Emily wanted some *sister time*. It was like being little girls again. They giggled until early morning. At almost eleven Catherine came into the suite and woke them. She brought lots of coffee and breakfast. After they each showered the parade of pampering began.

The forecast was correct. The sky was a brilliant sapphire blue with reflective colorless snow covering everything. The grounds crew diligently worked to clear the drive and plenty of parking spaces. The temperature was cold, in the mid-twenties, yet the sun shone all day.

Claire didn't want to risk seeing Tony and chance *bad luck*. Therefore, she didn't leave her suite until it was her time to walk down the aisle. She and Emily received massages, manicures, and facials. While the beauticians worked tirelessly on their hair, Catherine brought them more food. Claire said she was too excited to eat.

Catherine wouldn't listen. "Ms. Claire, I will not be responsible for you fainting during the ceremony. You must eat." Emily smiled, happy that Claire had Catherine to take care of her.

By four thirty Catherine, Courtney, and Emily began to help Claire get into her dress. First was body shaper, then, the long slip which provided the fullness necessary for the satin gown. The gown went over the slip. The bodice was fitted and altered to perfection for Claire's slim, petite figure. The dress was strapless. However, the accessory which persuaded Claire to choose this dress was the intricate lace overlay which created transparent three-quarter-length sleeves and a long train. The lace of the veil complemented the overlay. The beautician created a sweeping hairstyle that made the perfect niche for the veil to attach.

The lace overlay created an off-the-shoulder look which truly didn't need jewelry. However, Emily had a string of pearls. They were the pearls which belonged to Shirley, Emily and Claire's mother. Shirley wore them in her wedding to their father, as had Emily when she wed John. It was the *old* and the *borrowed* of the wedding tradition. After Claire dressed, the photographer entered her suite to take some special photos of her and her ladies. She wore a *blue* garter and supposed her dress was *new*.

Prior to the ceremony there was a knock at her door. Courtney went to the door. Claire could hear Courtney, "Tony, you are incredibly handsome but you cannot be here." The first thought that ran through Claire's mind was *Tony knocked. He never knocked on her door.*

She heard his voice and every nerve in her body electrified, realizing she would really be his wife. "I have a special gift for Claire, it is her something *new*. Please be sure to tell her the box is blue velvet on purpose." Courtney looked quizzically at Tony. "She will understand, I promise."

Claire smiled, thinking, *I really do love him!*

Somehow he knew she would wear pearls. Perhaps he'd expected her grandmother's necklace; nonetheless, she opened the blue velvet box to beautiful dangling pearl earrings hanging from platinum earclips covered in small sparkling diamonds. With her hair style and the veil, the earrings were perfect. The ladies in her suite went crazy. The consensus was the earrings were perfect and so was Tony. At that moment, Claire believed so too. She wanted to believe it, with all her heart. And her heart did, but it was her mind that held too many memories, ones that she'd successfully compartmentalized away—*away,* not *gone.*

It wasn't for lack of trying.

When Brad knocked on the door of her suite, Catherine and Courtney hugged her and sped off to their seats. Claire looked at herself one last time in the full-length mirror. She liked what she saw and prayed Tony would too. She and Emily proceeded down the hall to the main stairs. She could hear the music from the quartet.

They heard a rumbling of whispers. Suddenly, Claire thought about the guests. Who were they? She really didn't know any of them. She'd heard names and some she recognized. Some were political figures, some were business people she'd met at benefits, and some were names she'd heard in

210

the media. Then she remembered their friends, the people who made last night incredibly memorable. Their friends were the people who supported both of them and were not solely present because of Anthony Rawlings. It was the others, the ones she didn't know, that scared her. She felt like they were all judging her. She wanted to be perfect for those people so Tony would be proud. The multiple acetaminophens helped to keep the headache at bay.

Brad listened to his ear piece and waited for the deviation in music. The hum of voices disappeared. Claire couldn't see the guests or the men exiting Tony's office, but she knew that was what was happening. Emily kissed John and Claire before she descended the stairs. John took Claire's arm, kissed her cheek, and said, "I will not disrupt your day. You look amazing, and I want you to know how much I love you. You aren't my sister-in-law, you are my little sister. Please remember you can always count on Emily and me." He squeezed her hand. "Just always know you are loved."

Claire kissed his cheek and thanked him. Brad gave them the signal, and they started down the stairs.

When John was asked who gives this woman to be wed, he replied, "With great love and admiration, her sister and I."

The next thirty-five minutes passed as if a dream. Claire saw faces. She saw the smiles of her new friends and of her sister, but what she noted above all else was Anthony Rawlings. When she reached the aisle and beheld him, he was watching her and waiting.

He had eyes only for her. He stood incredibly handsomely in front of the guests, hands resting casually at his sides, shoulders broad, impeccable Armani custom tuxedo, a gratified smile, and eyes encircled in chestnut brown yet, still absorbed light. Standing next to him in front of everyone, she felt drawn into the darkness and searched for light and warmth. As his eyes sparkled, she felt weak. Internally, she was saying, "I am marrying him. He is marrying me. I am now *his* wife." At that moment she realized this was a contract now recognizable by the world. It wasn't two signatures on a napkin, but a real legal marriage contract. He owned her.

There was nothing she could do about it. He gave her one chance to escape, and she didn't take it. She made a decision, and that decision would have consequences. Now the world watched, and public failure wasn't an option. The world saw the most amazing wedding money could buy with a stunning woman happily marrying a handsome man. In contrast, Claire saw a napkin. She knew too well appearance meant everything. As the music played and the minister spoke, she worked desperately to re-compartmentalize the flood of thoughts and emotions beseeching her mind. She smiled lovingly, answered the minister obediently and behaved appropriately. The kiss at the conclusion of the ceremony was romantic, and the minister's announcement of "Mr. and Mrs. Anthony Rawlings" was met with loud applause. Everything appeared perfect.

The reception was an equally flawless exhibition. Brad and Monica thought of everything, the ambiance was romantic, with impeccable decorations. Claire and Tony dutifully greeted each guest and thanked them for attending their special day.

Throughout the entire evening Tony was wonderful. He told Claire he loved her. He told her how beautiful she was, how honored he was to have her as his wife, and how he couldn't wait for the reception to be over so he could show her. Under it all, Claire continued to have an uneasy feeling. She worked diligently to keep it buried under layers of makeup, hairspray, crinoline, slips, satin, lace, pearls, and pretense.

Everyone enjoyed themselves. Claire even saw John and Emily laughing with Tom and Bev. Once the first course was served, Brent stood, lifted a glass of champagne, and offered a toast to the newlyweds. "May I have your attention, ladies and gentlemen? I want to take this opportunity to welcome Claire Rawlings to our world. Claire, Tony has been my friend, my confidante, and my boss," the crowd giggled, "for a very long time. I have watched him as he has succeeded in business and failed in love," another snicker, "but recently Courtney and I have watched as Tony has experienced success in the area of love. Claire, when you are present his smile is brighter and his eyes have a spark. Perhaps you haven't noticed, but sometimes Tony's eyes can seem dark. That isn't the case when he is with you. You are the light of his life. You have given Tony the part of his life that was missing. And as we look around, it is obvious that not a lot was missing." There were smiles and agreement all around. "Now with you by his side, I believe my good friend is truly a man who has everything. Thank you, Claire. We are so happy to welcome you and we look forward to an eternity of a happier Tony Rawlings."

This precluded a standing ovation, lifting of glasses, and claps of agreement. After they cut the cake and gently fed each other a bite, Claire chocolate and Tony vanilla, the conductor fired up the jazz band. The music resonated soulfully, rhythmical and lively. The lights of the tent dimmed and the dance floor glittered with intensified brilliance. Tony led Claire onto the dance floor hand in hand. His eyes, soft as crushed velvet, beheld his beautiful new wife. She was lost in his gaze of complete love and adoration. Swiftly, her doubts and fears faded away. He had the most amazing ability to dissolve her heart and soul. Gallantly he took her hand, encircled her small waist with his strong, powerful, yet tender embrace. Her body immediately molded to his. They moved in sync. He turned, twirled, and spun her around the floor. The bustled wedding gown swayed to his slightest inclination. They had only danced together a few times, but their bodies moved together on numerous occasions. She became lost in his stare, and without thought or consciousness he had complete control and dominance over every aspect of her being and every movement of her body. With each crescendo of the music, Claire's heartbeat accelerated. The guests surrounded the dance floor to watch the newlyweds waltz. Tony tall and dark, Claire petite and light, their contrast intensified the beauty and sensuality of the moment. Claire didn't notice the gathered crowd until the music reached its final *fermata*. Up until that moment, her brilliant emerald green eyes could only see her husband. When the music stilled, he gently kissed his bride and the guests applauded. Claire blushed and smiled.

212

The band began again and Tony charmingly bowed and asked Emily to dance. John nodded to Emily and extended his hand to Claire. Whispering in Claire's ear, John said, "You are beautiful in love." The four of them danced for a few minutes until the MC asked the guests to join them. Promptly, the floor burst with couples.

Sometime after eleven Claire and Tony, no longer in their wedding attire, kissed their friends and family goodbye and said adieu to the others. They left to begin their honeymoon adventure. Once again, Claire was being led by Tony to an unknown destination.

After their flight reached its cruising altitude Tony began to seduce his wife. He caressed, kissed, and tantalized her. He told her in a raspy, sensual tone he loved her, how amazing she had been and she was. He also told her what she already knew, "Mrs. Rawlings, you are now mine, completely. You belong to me."

Tomorrow is a mystery. Yesterday is history. Live today,
it's a gift, that's why they call it "present."
—Unknown

Chapter 31

Claire awoke to the sensation of their plane decelerating on a runway. She'd been somewhere in a dream as her body lay upon the leather sofa wrapped in the soft cocoon of a luxurious blanket. The sudden increased roar of engines combined with the screech of brakes transported her to the present. She wasn't sure how long she'd been asleep or if they'd reached their mysterious destination. But, she remembered the excitement in Tony's eyes as he talked about their romantic journey. Willingly, she continued to allow herself to be taken to places unknown.

Looking down at her left hand, she saw the familiar engagement ring now with its new mate. Her wedding band glistened with embedded diamonds matching the circle around the large solitaire. They were truly beautiful. Pondering the past nine months, it boggled her mind to think she was wearing such an amazing set of rings and more importantly their meaning—she was married. She was married to Anthony Rawlings.

Slowly, she turned to see her husband. His bare feet elevated as he lounged in a reclining chair. Watching him, she marveled at his relaxed pose, a stark contrast to how he usually looked when they flew. His attention was focused on the laptop resting on his long legs. Her cheeks and the tips of her lips moved upward as she noticed his jeans. They were the ones he worn when they left the reception. It seemed they were both wearing what the other preferred—he in his jeans, and her out of hers. She snuggled into the soft blanket and closed her eyes. The engines hummed as she felt the plane taxi toward its stop. Claire recalled the past twenty-four hours. Tony was right. Brad and Monica created the perfect ceremony and reception. She remembered the estate and decorations. Even the snow obeyed as if requisitioned to complement the final product. She thought about their friends, her family, and the guests. She recalled John's kind words and Brent's welcoming toast.

Smiling, she remembered Tony, incredibly handsome in his tuxedo and incessantly complimentary of her and her gown. Cinderella at the ball couldn't have felt more special. Like Prince Charming, he only had eyes for his bride. That admiration continued onto the jet. Once the cockpit door closed and the lights dimmed, his devotion grew to fervent passion.

Suddenly, Claire realized the implication of her blanket. If they'd reached their destination she needed to dress and quickly. "Are we at our honeymoon?"

He turned from his computer and smiled. "You didn't need to wake. You look so beautiful and peaceful."

Keeping the blanket wrapped around her, she went to him and knelt beside his chair. "I think I was worn-out." Her emerald eyes glowed as she put her arms around his exposed midsection. Looking into his milk chocolate eyes, feeling his warmth, and inhaling his scent, she thought to herself, *He is really my husband.*

Tony's eyes met hers then scanned toward her blanket. Smiling, he said, "It was a busy day, Mrs. Rawlings." The *Mrs. Rawlings* made Claire's eyes sparkle. He gently kissed his wife and playfully attempted to see under her blanket.

"And an eventful night, Mr. Rawlings."

"It isn't over. We're just stopping in LA to refuel. We have much more flying before we reach our destination."

This made Claire think. "So, are we going to Hawaii?"

"Would you like to go to Hawaii?" Claire said she would, she'd never been. He loved to make her squirm "Well, we'll have to find out where we end up, won't we?" He kissed her again.

The plane was now standing still. Eric and the pilot entered the cabin and bid hello to Mr. and Mrs. Rawlings. Apologizing for the interruption, they promised to be airborne in less than thirty minutes. Tony told them it was fine, just please do whatever was necessary as soon as possible. They had a honeymoon to get to. The two men promised they would and opened the outside door to the cabin. The rush of fresh air was no longer cold. They definitely weren't in Iowa.

Tony placed the laptop on the floor and invited Claire to his lap. She climbed up, resting her head on his strong chest and listened to the beat of his heart as he spoke about Los Angeles. His hands tenderly explored under her blanket, gently caressing her soft skin. He asked if she'd ever been there. Claire said no, she'd been to northern California, San Francisco when she was young on a family vacation. She remembered going to Alcatraz. Her dad, being a policeman, thought it was neat. But she didn't. She recalled during the tour actually going into cells. There were audiotaped voices and sounds of cell doors closing, she didn't like it at all. He hugged her. "I promise not to plan a visit to Alcatraz in our future. How old were you when you went there?"

"I think I was twelve." Claire looked up at his face. "Why do you ask?"

"Oh, I was just wondering." Tony went on to tell her about Eli and MaryAnn's home in LA, actually in Malibu. Tony said he'll need to bring her to one of their parties. He wasn't much into the whole Hollywood scene, but even he had to admit, Eli and MaryAnn could throw an awesome party. Eli's guests usually included people Claire had seen in movies or on TV. Eli could be an ass, but he was great at what he did, and there were multitudes of people who would kill to attend his parties. Tony described MaryAnn and Eli's house as an architectural marvel situated on Malibu beach, hanging off a cliff overlooking the Pacific Ocean.

"I would love to see it sometime. Do you stay with them when you travel to LA?" "No, I—I mean, *we*," he smiled, "we have an apartment in Hollywood, not far from Malibu."

Claire smirked. "Maybe sometime you could tell me how many apartments *we* have?"

"*We* have many residences. It'll take time to familiarize you with all of them."

She couldn't wrap her mind around the idea. She had places in Iowa, New York City, Chicago, Hollywood, and other locations.

"They are not all as grand as New York and Chicago. I spend more time there."

"Yeah, well you never saw my apartment in Atlanta." Claire replied, "I'm pretty sure compared to it, they're all palatial."

Claire and Tony were talking and laughing when the door reopened. She quickly closed the blanket as the pilot announced they were ready to leave. She began to stand when Tony pulled her toward him. "Umm, don't you think I should be in a seatbelt when the plane takes off?" Reluctantly he released his hold, but not before opening her blanket and grinning. Claire kissed him, moved to the other chair, situated herself, her blanket, and buckled the seatbelt. Within minutes they were airborne, and she drifted to a fitful sleep.

Still at cruising altitude Claire awoke with Tony sleeping soundly in the neighboring recliner. Finding her air legs, she eased her way to the back of the cabin, which held a small shower and dressing room. From twenty thousand feet the view out the window held only blackness separated by a scattering of stars differentiating sky from sea. She found an overnight bag, undoubtedly packed by Catherine. It contained shower, hair, and cosmetic supplies, as well as a black negligee and a summer blouse with capris. She smiled. The negligee would have been nice, but Tony didn't seem to mind the blanket.

After a quick shower and fresh clothes she felt more alert. Her watch read eight twenty, but a glance out the window told her it was still dark wherever they were. They'd been traveling over eight hours. They should be in Hawaii soon. Finishing her makeup she smiled, thinking of sunshine and beaches. She didn't know how long they would be in Hawaii or on which island. The idea sounded wonderful and Tony enjoyed surprising her, but she wistfully thought about being involved in the planning.

Walking unsteadily back into the cabin, Claire found Tony sitting at the table with his laptop and coffee. He turned to watch her enter. "Good

216

morning, Mrs. Rawlings, you look beautiful. I wish you would have awakened me, I could have joined you in the shower." He grinned over his cup.

"I don't think we both would fit. Besides, you looked too peaceful." She sipped the warm auburn liquid and allowed its robust aroma to revive her senses. Tony explained they would be landing on Oahu in Honolulu in an hour. It would only be about three in the morning, but they would deplane, find some breakfast and walk around before continuing their flight. "Continuing, we aren't staying in Hawaii?" She sounded disappointed.

"No, Hawaii is just a fuel stop, but we will need to revisit sometime for you to sightsee. It is a lovely place." His eyes taunted. "But, not as lovely as where we're going."

"And we are going where?" Claire asked, intrigued. Tony's eyes sparkled, the black almost completely overtaken with the soft brown hue. His grin mischievous, he didn't answer. "And how much longer until we get there?"

"Mrs. Rawlings, you are very inquisitive. What if I told you that we won't reach our destination until tomorrow?"

Claire thought about that. *Twenty-four more hours of flying?* She realized he wasn't talking about twenty-four hours. "Well, Mr. Rawlings, I would say it sounds like we are crossing the International Date Line." She smiled smugly.

He looked at her with admiration, and addressed Eric, who was refilling their coffee cups. "My wife is not only beautiful, she is also incredibly intelligent." He kissed her head as he stood. "I believe I will freshen up before we begin our descent."

With that, he disappeared behind the wall at the back of the cabin. Claire noticed his laptop open on the table. The screen was, of course, locked. A quick Google search of land west of the International Date Line would've been beneficial. She would just need to rely on her memory. But then she wondered if they were staying in the northern hemisphere or heading south? Sighing, she sipped her delicious coffee. She would have to wait, she didn't have a choice.

Before they left the plane Tony told Claire to get her purse from her overnight bag. Jokingly she asked if she needed it to pay for breakfast. No. She needed her passport. "When did I get a passport?" He reminded her they'd discussed it months ago and Brent had filed the necessary paperwork. Apparently, this all happened while she was recovering from her accident. She couldn't remember any of it, yet there it was: her picture, her signature, and her name *Claire Nichols*. Tony promised to apply for a new one with her real name, *Rawlings*, as soon as they returned, and a new ID. He smiled. Her new credit cards had already been requested.

Hawaii was anticlimactic. She smelled the humid sea air as they descended the steps to the solid ground. The gentle tropical breeze enticed her skin. But they didn't see anything other than the inside of the Honolulu International Airport as they searched for and found a restaurant that served breakfast.

After eating they needed to pass the TSA desk. Eric handled the inspection of the plane and bags, Tony and Claire needed to show their passports. When they were with the TSA agent she asked their destination.

Claire didn't know. Tony answered, "Fiji. Nadi, Fiji." Claire remembered Fiji was a group of islands, she wasn't sure how many, in the South Pacific. As they walked back to the plane she squeezed his hand and smiled. He wasn't pleased his surprise was spoiled, but she knew where they were going and it made her happy. They had six more hours of flight.

They landed in Nadi, Fiji at ten thirty in the morning Monday, December 20, after flying over eighteen hours. As their plane approached Nadi, Claire watched out the window, mesmerized by the turquoise water and sparkling white beaches. If Tony were upset about the TSA agent, witnessing Claire's anticipation returned his own excitement.

Once they landed, Eric loaded their luggage onto a small plane with a propeller and pontoons. He wished them an enjoyable honeymoon and promised he would be waiting when they returned. Apparently, their final destination could only be accessed by air.

Tony and Claire then took a forty-five-minute flight to a private island. Their altitude was low, allowing them to enjoy the sights: dolphins swimming, gorgeous secluded white sand beaches, palm trees, and tropical rain forest vegetation. Outside the open windows of the plane was a true paradise, an oasis away from the rest of the world. Claire had never seen anything like it, and told Tony over and over how amazing it all looked. Her childlike delight amused him. They landed on a crystal-clear aquamarine lagoon lined with a horseshoe of pristine white sand.

Waiting on the beach was their personal staff: two chefs, maid, hostess, and boat captain. Claire had become accustomed to being waited upon, but these individuals *lived* to please Mr. and Mrs. Rawlings. The staff gathered their luggage, and they all walked a winding path to their *bure*, a Fijian word for *straw hut*. The humid tropical breeze blew Claire's hair as her sandals sank into the white sand. Holding her husband's hand, they approached their temporary dwelling.

It was the most luxurious straw hut Claire had ever seen. Situated on a cliff above the water, they had stunning views of the ocean. First, they entered a gracious living room with a cathedral thatched ceiling, woven bamboo covered walls, and polished mahogany floors. Each room of their bure contained ceiling fans as well as the possibility of air conditioning. Claire couldn't fathom why anyone would possibly want air conditioning. There were huge bi-folding doors which opened the entire frontage to private decks overlooking the water or tropical vegetation. Each deck contained lounge furniture for relaxation. The front deck even had a private infinity pool. As they stood in the living room and looked, the pool appeared to extend into the lagoon and beyond into the ocean below. The staff took their luggage to the large master bedroom complete with a four-poster king-sized bed. Roaming from room to room, Claire found a luxuriously designed bathroom which opened to a private outdoor lava rock shower and generous soaking tub designed for two. Thankfully, surrounding the outdoor shower and tub were lush tropical plants. After the tour of their temporary home, their hostess, Naiade, asked if they were ready to dine. Claire was famished. Tony informed Naiade they would be pleased to dine on the deck.

The only thing missing from their bure was technology, which was just fine with Claire. She was accustomed to the lack of connectivity. Tony, however, was relieved once he learned he had access to the Internet with his laptop. He explained he needed to stay in contact with Tim, Brent, and others from his businesses. He reminded Claire, "You my dear, only need to stay in contact with me." Pulling her close, he added with a grin, "I promise to help."

She pressed herself closer and kissed his neck. "I think I can handle it."

"Be careful, Mrs. Rawlings, we may miss our meal."

Claire smiled. "I believe we have plenty of time for that. Right now, I'm hungry!"

Apparently, they could make suggestions to their chefs at any time. They decided for the next ten days seafood would be the entrée of choice. They both enjoyed trying native dishes. Naiade told them about some activity options, including: unlimited access to a boat with a private captain, where they could enjoy a ride to watch marine life, island hop, or snorkel. A living barrier reef was nearby. They could also kayak or hike into the jungle.

From the dining deck they enjoyed an amazing view of the ocean, with a wonderful sea breeze. The chefs prepared yellow fin tuna, fresh fruit, organic vegetables, and freshly baked bread. It all smelled and tasted scrumptious.

It was early afternoon locally when they finished their meal and Claire was exhausted. She'd just traveled over eighteen hours, lost an entire day crossing an imaginary line, and gotten married. It was enough to tire anyone. Tony recommended relaxing in the outdoor soaking tub which opened to the endless blue sky. Over the next ten days they would discover it was even more enticing under the stars and moon.

Tony may have suggested the tub as a place to relax, but Claire anticipated he had other plans. The tepid tub water, gentle sea breeze, sound of the waves lapping the beach, and romantic atmosphere combined to help increase Claire's energy level. Tony understood they'd been traveling a long time, but to him it wasn't tiring, it was confining. He wanted to release some penned up energy. Appreciating the amorous setting, Claire knew she would've been disappointed with anything less.

Tony didn't disappoint. Soaking in the warm water with him behind her, she rested her head against his wide chest. He began by massaging her shoulders, relieving the tension of the trip. As his hands moved, Claire felt the energy she'd thought gone begin to build inside of her. His lips found the nape of her neck and ignited goose bumps upon her arms and legs. Between kisses he whispered, "Thank you for being my wife. I love you."

He held her in his arms and caressed her skin. She in turn stroked his arms. Looking down she saw her rings sparkling under the water. When his hands discovered her breasts, they throbbed in anticipation; her nipples became hard and needy. His touch moved to her stomach and below causing Claire's energy to return with a vengeance. She couldn't control herself anymore. When she turned to face him, the warm water lapped the sides of the tub. Their mouths heatedly nibbled at one another's as their tongues intermingled. Every action was consensual.

219

Claire wanted him as much as he wanted her. As the breeze rustled the orchids and surrounding vegetation, he filled her with more than energy. Like on the dance floor they moved together, their bodies became one like their names. The exuberance of his sensuality carried Claire beyond revitalization to ecstasy.

As his fingers instigated passion, his lips alternated between suckling and asking questions, did she like her honeymoon destination? She did, very much. Was she happy with the way their wedding turned out? She was. It was perfect. Was she happy to be Mrs. Anthony Rawlings? She was. How happy? How pleased? How grateful? Eventually they made their way to the king-sized bed. Even with the ceiling fan and sea breeze they both dripped with moisture.

Before Tony joined his wife in midday slumber, he watched her sleep. She was exhausted, yet she had just gone with him to the other side of heaven. After all of the sex they'd experienced, it was difficult to believe it could get better, but it did. Lying on the bed she emitted warmth and the most amazing scent. He gently moved her hair from her moist shoulders and revealed her sensuous neck and beautiful face. Tenderly he kissed her lips, tasting her sweetness. Even in slumber he saw her smile.

That night they dined on the deck by torchlight, overlooking a magnificent horizon, and watching the sun settle into the ocean. The chefs created an amazing dish from fresh seafood, organic fruits, and vegetables all from the islands. This dish included green pacific lobster and fresh snapper. They also chose wine from an extensive list.

After dinner they strolled hand in hand along the beach, feeling the soft powdered sand beneath their feet. The humidity decreased with the setting of the sun as the breeze created the perfect temperature. Their only light came from the moon as its rays glistened off the water. Others had been on the same beach and stayed in the same bure, but it felt as though they were the first.

The days merged together; waking to the sounds of tropical birds and sea breezes, going onto one of the decks, drinking coffee, and eating breakfast. Next, they would dress in bathing suits, walk the beach, and swim in the lagoon. Or perhaps lounge by the pool or in the pool. They would eat lunch and then resume their busy relaxation schedule. The mornings and evenings would have cool breezes, but the middays were steamy and tropical.

They discussed their options for activities and decided *together* how to spend their days. They utilized the boat and captain on multiple occasions. He took them snorkeling and they learned that different times of day brought out different aquatic life. One evening, at sunset, they floated while all around them dolphins jumped and played. If the captain hadn't warned them, Claire may have tried to touch one. They seemed so close and tame. The captain told them to be careful, appearances can be deceiving. That seemed like good advice.

On a few occasions the captain took them to uninhabited islets only accessible by boat. The chefs would prepare a special lunch complete with fresh fruit and wine. And on the completely secluded beach, with a blanket and their picnic basket, Tony and Claire would find some way to spend the hours before the captain returned. Claire looked at all the clothes Catherine packed. She literally spent her days in bath robes, bathing suits, beach covers, and a sundress for dinner. There was no need to wear clothes or any occasion to do so. Actually, they spent a great deal of their time without any clothing. Situations wouldn't usually start that way: a swim in the lagoon, sunbathing on the beach, or a night swim in the pool; but would often conclude that way.

The sun brought back Claire's bronze skin from summer. It started to subside with the beginning of autumn. Her *accident* accelerated the process, leaving her complexion pale. Tony told her she looked beautiful, the fair complexion made her eyes standout, the emerald green more intense. Seeing herself now, she believed the tanned skin with the blonde hair looked healthier. Her eyes still looked prominent. If she needed to be blonde, she liked herself better with a tan. Unlike her tan during the summer, this one lacked lines.

Other than the staff, Tony and Claire didn't see anyone during the entire ten-day stay. They were completely secluded and tucked away from the world. Christmas came and went. They wished each other a merry one, but there were no evergreens or snow. To Claire that was wonderful. She would take warmth and sunshine over cold and snow anytime. Besides, there were plenty of decorations at home for the wedding. Tony apologized for not having a gift for her on Christmas morning. She told him it made her happy. He had given her too many gifts; besides, the honeymoon was her gift and she loved it. She repeatedly explained she didn't care about monetary things. The more she protested the more Tony pointed out the advantages. He wanted her to realize she had it all and the ability to get anything else. The world was hers for the asking.

The tropical climate was well known for its fruit, and the chefs made it available at all times. There were papayas, pineapples, bananas, avocados, pears, mangoes, and limes. They prepared them in salads, side dishes, entrees, and constantly available fresh. Together the newlyweds learned how incredibly sensual fruit could be.

Tony teased Claire's lips with the sweet aromatic juice of a freshly cut pineapple or papaya. Gently placing it on her tongue, closing her eyes, she would suckle the juice from his fingertips. Often as the fragrant fruit passed her lips, the juices dripped down her chin. Gallantly, Tony would attempt to remove the sugary nectar with his tongue. At times he'd *accidentally* drop the sticky fruit and it would fall on Claire's breasts or stomach. He'd then eat it directly from her bare skin. The result was sultry and exhilarating. The outdoor shower was an excellent steamy setting to wash away the tacky, clammy sweet liquids. However, it always began a new adventure.

On more than one occasion he tested her endurance. His encouragement was always gentle, affectionate, and sensual. At times his physical touch caused such erotic convulsions she felt she would never experience such a high again. And, then she would. Claire contemplated Emily's question the night before her wedding. If he was this unquenchable at forty-five, she shuddered to think how he had been at twenty-five.

Tony mentioned on multiple occasions he was thrilled to have Claire as his wife, but with this title came responsibility. She had done well *most of the time* in the past. Now, it was different. She was no longer an enigma or a rumor; she was Mrs. Anthony Rawlings. Her actions, words, and appearance reflected directly upon him. He loved her and wanted her as happy as she was here in paradise, but the real world was coming. He wanted her prepared.

For ten days of complete togetherness, no possible threat of the outside world, chance of public failure, opportunity for breaking rules, or risk of negative consequences, Claire enjoyed the light hue in Tony's eyes. She gave herself freely and keep him satisfied. She found a place of contentment with her situation and happiness in her decisions.

Sometimes while lounging, she would think about the *out* Tony offered in Central Park. She wondered would she be happier? Where would she be? And the biggest unanswered question, would he really have let her go? Then she would open her eyes and see a lush tropical paradise, incredibly handsome generous husband, and recognize her decisions led her to this consequence.

Thursday afternoon, December 30, Mr. and Mrs. Rawlings rejoined Eric at Tony's plane in Nadi. This time they traveled back in time, arriving back in Iowa City Thursday night. Glistening under a blanket of white snow, the house looked regal as they approached. The decorations were gone, but the houselights shone upon the brick and river stone facade. It was magnificent and welcoming. Paradise was just that, but now they were home.

There is a wisdom of the head, and a wisdom of the heart.
—Charles Dickens

Chapter 32

Samuel thought it a farce, the nightly meal with everyone present, his parents, wife, and son. Yes, they lived in the same house, but the formal meals seemed pretentious. It reminded him of the TV show *Dallas* with Nathaniel the reigning omnipotent patriarch.

Amanda looked to her husband as the dinner concluded. Samuel leaned over and affectionately kissed his wife's cheek. "I need to speak to my father for a few minutes. I'll be upstairs in a little while."

She smiled. "All right, I'll be waiting." But her eyes questioned her husband.

"I won't be long." Then he whispered, "I'll fill you in later, I promise." Amanda's eyes smiled as she looked into Samuel's face. She knew the rules. You don't question anything in front of Nathaniel. Dealing with her father-in-law was worth it; Amanda adored her husband.

"Anton and I will be upstairs."

Their son, home from boarding school, watched his parents. "I'll be up in a minute, Mother, I need to do something." Amanda smiled at her husband and son. Anton had grown so much during the past semester. Only fifteen, he stood half a foot taller than her and was still growing. His eyes could shine, but she also saw his grandfather's darkness. More than anything, she wanted to keep that blackness away.

"All right, maybe we can watch a movie when we all get to our suites? I have some new videos." Amanda began the ascent up the grand stairs. Samuel straightened his neck and walked down the corridor toward his father's office. The double doors stood as a barrier to the inflexible man within. Inhaling deeply he formed a fist. Respectfully, he knocked on the grand double doors. He listened for the words from within. "Come in." This wasn't going to go well. His father knew his displeasure with the recent direction of Rawls Corp. Now the recent *positive slant* and the unexpected shareholder acceptance were too much. These ideas from Jared Clawson had to stop.

One idea reaped Rawls millions. The next cost them millions. Currently, the balance sheet was in their favor, but the risks and the possible legal repercussions weren't worth the benefits. Stepping into the large office, Samuel silently prayed he would be able to make his father see his point of view.

The man behind the desk sat bold and defiant. "I wondered how long it would take you to confront me."

"I didn't think we needed an audience." Samuel closed the double doors, unaware they were slightly ajar.

"Always worried about others' opinions." Nathaniel grinned. "Obviously, a trait you received from your mother. I don't give a damn what others think."

"Perhaps you should." Samuel offered.

"Speak your mind."

"You know my thoughts. You need to get rid of Jared Clawson. You need to stop these alternative means of financial gain."

Nathaniel's laugh rumbled through the office, "I *need*?"

"Father, I'm sorry, maybe *need* isn't the best word. You *should*."

"You are *sorry*? You are a weak piece of shit!" Nathaniel stood and walked around his grand desk, facing his son. "Haven't you learned anything? Don't apologize! Apologies are for cowards, they make you appear weak."

Standing tall, Samuel continued his mission. "This situation is getting out of hand."

Nathaniel laughed again. "Out of hand, like we are making millions upon millions, and this is bad?"

"We were doing well before, and it was legal."

"So what part of these monies don't you like? Your wife is enjoying the money and your son is enjoying the best education. You, your wife, your son will never know what it's like to be without. Tell me again what you don't like."

"I believe they would've been happy with our earnings before. Amanda and Anton do not need excess. Neither do I." Samuel watched his father turn back toward his plush leather chair. "Neither does Mother."

Changing directions, Nathaniel abruptly turned and struck his son's left cheek. "Don't you *ever* tell me what your mother needs. You have no idea what she's been through. *You* have never lived as we did. Money is good for one thing. It buys what you need, what you want. And because of my decisions, you and Anton will never worry about money. *Do not* ever tell me what to do with my business and don't apologize. I raised you better than that!"

Samuel knew there wasn't an answer for his father. He turned to walk away.

"Where are you going, boy?" Nathaniel bellowed.

"I am going upstairs to my wife. Do you have a problem with that?"

"You are going upstairs, to the upper level of *my* house. No. I don't have a problem. Do you?"

"No, Father, I do not." Samuel exited the office and briefly saw Anton's face. The teenager witnessed the entire scene. Samuel hoped when they were up in their suite, they could talk about it. *His* son would know discussions were welcome.

God, grant me the serenity to accept the things I
cannot change, the courage to change the things I can,
and the wisdom to know the difference.
—Reinhold Niebuhr

Chapter 33

The view through the windshield of Tony's new Mercedes-Benz CLS-Class Coupe reminded Claire of space movies. The snowflakes were like stars being passed at warp speed. The snow, wind, and subfreezing temperature accentuated the reality they were no longer in paradise. She settled into the heated seat, rubbed her leather gloved hands, and watched the snow covered terrain. The glistening sparkles would've been pretty if not for the blowing and accumulation. Tony didn't mind. He was enjoying his new car, which had arrived at the estate while they were gone. To Claire's relief, it handled amazingly well on snow.

Although almost eight at night, she felt as though she was finally waking; the jet lag was difficult to navigate. Both she and Tony slept late following their arrival back to reality. Now as they headed to Tom and Bev's for a New Year's Eve celebration, she thought about their return.

When they entered the estate, Catherine's welcoming smile was the best sight Claire could imagine. They immediately embraced. The peaceful stillness of the mansion, barren of decorations and workers, was comforting. She and Tony ate a light dinner and fell sound asleep.

It was this morning, while more awake, they discussed their bedroom situation. Now that they're married, should they move into one room? When Tony asked her opinion, a benchmark moment, she replied she liked maintaining two rooms. The most important thing was sleeping together, the location was irrelevant. Claire said she liked her suite. Truth be told, she did. Yes, she knew it had surveillance and memories, but it was also where she felt safe and at home. Maybe she'd come to terms with the recordings. She felt . . . well, secure. If Tony could watch her every move, he wouldn't question her actions. She also mentioned, "Besides, my suite doesn't match yours in terms

226

of technology." His had the big multifaceted screen and God knows what else. "And you wouldn't be able to access all your stock market data from here."

Since their big storm last summer, Claire hadn't been required, or asked, to watch any more videos, but she believed Tony did. She also believed he could access his videos and anything else he wanted from his office, bedroom, movie theater, or anywhere else he chose. This hadn't been confirmed, but somehow she suspected it was true.

His reply was why, even now as they drove Claire was still stewing. "I think that sounds reasonable, I don't believe we will be running out of room anytime soon." As Claire watched, the honeymoon hue of Tony's eyes faded into darkness and he continued, "However, regarding the technology you mentioned, I believe it would be prudent to maintain the past restrictions involving my office and bedroom. I do not think you need unsupervised access to computers, Internet, or telephones."

"Tony, I'm your wife. What do you think I'll do?"

"I think it's best to avoid possible *glitches*." He lifted her chin. "Do you agree, or would you like to discuss it further?" He'd closed the conversation.

Claire stared into his eyes, squared her shoulders, and straightened her neck. "I agree. Excuse me. I need to take a shower." He released her chin and she walked away. She'd learned months ago she didn't like glitches and pursuing a closed conversation wasn't prudent. However, every bone in her body wanted to pursue it. She really didn't care about the technology. She didn't want to access it. Claire wanted the *ability* to access it!

Ten hours later, as they rode to Tom and Bev's party, she contemplated the closed conversation. Now that she was Mrs. Anthony Rawlings, didn't that give her some kind of clout? Some perks? Could she possibly revisit the subject without fear of retribution? As she debated this internally and watched the glistening flakes sparkle in the illumination of the Mercedes' beams, she wondered if her life had changed.

She was Mrs. Anthony Rawlings, but was that really different from being Ms. Claire Nichols?

"What do you think?"

Tony's question pulled Claire from her thoughts. "I'm sorry. I didn't hear your question."

"I asked if you prefer the view in Fiji over the frozen splendor of Iowa."

Claire laughed. "I don't think you need to ask, do you?"

"Probably not, but I'm trying to get you to talk."

"I'm talking."

"Yes, you are. But you haven't really been talking since this morning. Would you like to discuss it before we get to Tom's?"

Claire thought about the question. Yes, she wanted to revisit the subject, but should she? "I don't know." Her feet were cold and the fashionable boots weren't helping. She tried to get them under the blow of the Mercedes' heater. "If I say yes, am I opening a closed subject?"

Tony appreciated the fact his wife was thinking this through. "Yes, I guess you are. Is it worth it to you?"

The interior of the car was warm, yet Claire pushed her gloved hands deeper into the pockets of her fur jacket and considered the implications. Did she really care anymore about technology? Was it worth pushing this discussion? She knew immediately the answer was *no*. "I think my decision is to not reopen the conversation. However, I want you to know it isn't the technology I long for. It is the *ability* to access it."

Tony smirked. "Claire, your talents were wasted in meteorology. You would've made a wonderful businesswoman. You just said you didn't want to pursue the subject, yet you managed to enlighten me about your motivation. I am, once again, impressed."

His condescension didn't help her disposition. The snow was coming at the windshield with enough velocity to make her feel as though they were flying thought space at *hyperspeed*. Her lips pressed tightly into a line. Finally, she asked, "What kind of response do you expect?"

"Honest, as always."

"Okay. Seriously, who do I have left to contact? I don't understand why you feel the restrictions are still necessary. God knows I know the rules." The branches of the pines lay low with inches of heavy accumulating snow. Keeping her gaze to her right, Claire saw them through the side window. They were nearing the Millers' home and the sound of soft music filled the air. Tony didn't respond. After all, this discussion was closed. The familiar sense of powerlessness filled Claire's chest. She wanted the conversation to end. "I love you. I will do whatever you want or expect of me. I admit I'm not pleased by your verdict, but I'm okay. Let's spend tonight with our friends and welcome the New Year." At least she'd explained her view. That was something.

The Millers' home was magnificent. Beverly had fantastic taste in decor. It was ultramodern yet amazingly inviting. The unique style was a combination of stone, brick, and wood, accentuated with glass and chrome. Despite the numerous windows, the house was warm. They could watch the snow and wind and stay snug inside.

Perhaps it was the fire in the fireplace or the wine in their glasses, but the gathering radiated warmth. Their friends happily celebrated their return. They wanted to know all about the honeymoon. Claire told them that it had been wonderful. Tony literally took her to paradise. Everyone complimented their wedding. They were a beautiful couple. Sue mentioned how beautiful their pictures were in the press release. Claire had forgotten about press coverage until that moment.

"I haven't seen the released pictures. Do you have copies?" Bev said she didn't but would be glad to pull them up online. Claire glanced at her husband, he didn't speak, but his eyes did. Claire knew she shouldn't, but she agreed. "Thank you, I'd love to see them."

Instead of bringing out a computer, Bev removed a remote from a drawer and pointed it at the large television on the wall. The New Year's countdown from Time Square changed to a homepage. Bev entered "*Anthony Rawlings*" into the search engine. Nine months ago, the procedure would've seemed mundane, but now it fascinated Claire. She would've loved to take the time to read the multitude of pages which appeared as options. Bev reduced the search by entering "*wedding*." Claire briefly saw an accompanying article;

but within seconds, Bev clicked, and the pictures appeared on the screen. Claire stared. There *they* were in their wedding attire. There were three different pictures: a head shot, a full-length frontal view, and one of them dancing. Everyone watched Claire as she beheld herself on the screen. She looked at Tony and her. They looked like models. Tony was tall, handsome, and buff, dark hair, dark eyes, and dark tuxedo contrasting dramatically with Claire. She looked petite, blonde, and striking. Her hair was so light she assumed some of her friends from before may not recognize her. Next to Tony, she seemed small. Tony was right about her eyes. In the head shot, her green eyes shined vividly. She'd seen her dress in the mirror. But seeing it on the television screen and looking at it from afar, it was obviously eye-catching, elegant, and spectacular. She smiled. It had been a good choice.

Claire realized everyone in the room was watching her, especially Tony. Most were happily awaiting her response. Tony seemed less pleased with the entire situation, but she knew he wouldn't say anything there. It would be a matter better discussed in private. Finally, Sue put her hand on Claire's knee and asked, "So what do you think?"

Claire giggled. "I just can't believe my wedding is news." Everyone snickered. What did she expect? She married Anthony Rawlings. Claire looked up at him. He had eyes only for her – dark eyes. Daringly, she got up and walked to her husband. Lifting herself by her toes, she reached his cheek and gave it a kiss.

He obliged, bending down to allow his cheek to meet her lips. Addressing the group, Claire nonchalantly replied, "I guess I just forget who he is. But, I have a lifetime to remember." She kissed him again.

They toasted the New Year with champagne. Brent, Tom, and Tim especially wished Tony a profitable year. If his year was lucrative, theirs would be also. It was after one in the morning when the party broke up.

The coldness of the leather transcended Claire's slacks. She wanted the heater to warm the seat as well as the interior of the car quickly. The roar of the defrost in the stillness of the night told Claire the poor Mercedes was trying its best. Tony scraped the snow from the windows and talked with Brent and Tim as they did the same. Everything was blanketed with several more inches of white. Thankfully, it had stopped falling. Absently, Claire wondered how often Tony needed to scrape his own windows. She knew she was trying to divert her thoughts from the reprimand she was about to receive.

Her husband remained pleasant and attentive during the party, but his expression as he opened her door let her know that *this* subject wasn't closed. Claire pondered that thought. Wasn't it really the same subject as earlier? So shouldn't it be closed?

Each time she exhaled she noticed the faint white crystals which formed and hung in the air. She straightened her posture and squared her shoulders; she was ready. The windows were clear and she could hear Tony and Brent's voices, his door would open at any moment. With each passing minute her demeanor moved from anxious to indignant.

All she had wanted to do was see *their* wedding pictures. Why was that such a big deal? After all, it was *her* wedding. The fact the pictures were available online shouldn't matter. Once on the road, the only sounds were those of the tires on the snow and the hum of the heater. Claire waited. After a significant silence Tony spoke. "Do you remember I told you I received e-mails from Emily and she would like you to call?"

"Yes, and you said I could call her tomorrow." Claire felt a sudden panic.

"I was just wondering. Your memory seems to be failing you."

"May I still call my sister?"

"Yes, *I* keep my word."

Claire exhaled. This Tony was more indirect than the one she was accustomed to. Maybe that was the advantage of being his wife. She'd been looking for that *perk*. "Thank you." She glanced toward her husband, his jaw muscles defined as he clenched. He was waiting for her to approach the subject. Reluctantly she did. "What did you think of our wedding pictures?"

"I think you were absolutely stunning and I'm a lucky man."

That wasn't the response she anticipated. Yes, she was annoyed that this was a big deal. However, her intuition told her to back off. "I'm sorry about encouraging Bev. My curiosity got the better of me." Apologizing seemed like the best option, even if it only sounded sincere.

"It isn't just what you did. It is what you said."

Claire couldn't remember what she said, so she asked. "What did I say?"

"You said you forget who I am."

"I forget that marrying you is newsworthy, I love you for you. I forget that you are Anthony Rawlings. To me, you are Tony."

His grip intensified on the steering wheel and she felt his tension radiating through the interior of the car. "I have told you over and over, you must remember who I am. If you forget who I am, you will forget who you are, and the significance of your behavior." It was a different version of the *appearance speech*. He was right. He had said it over and over. She listened, replied at all appropriate times, and was thankful it was only the abridged version.

Tony returned to work on the first. He did so from his home office. He had a lot of things to do. Apparently, he had tried to keep up-to-date while in Fiji, but *someone* kept him distracted. With him working in his office and her free to do as she pleased within the house, Claire soon realized how event filled the last month had been. She was suddenly overwhelmed with the sensation of solitude.

Claire arrived at Tony's office before lunch to make her call. She expected the *limitations lecture*. Surprisingly, he didn't give it. He dialed the telephone, turned his back and worked on his computers while Claire waited to speak. John answered. She prayed John wouldn't say anything to upset Tony. "Hi, John, it's Claire, is Emily there?"

"Hi, Claire. Welcome back to the United States. You are back, aren't you?"

"We are, we returned on the thirtieth." She was sending out mental signals, *put Emily on the phone!*

230

"So was it as beautiful as the article described?" Tony turned to Claire, she needed to conclude with John and move on to Emily. She looked at him pleadingly, she knew.

"I didn't read the article. But it was amazing. Tony definitely took me to paradise for our honeymoon. Hey, is Emily there?"

"Oh, yes. She's right here. Good to talk with you. Please tell Anthony I said hello."

She made eye contact with him, *hi*. "I will, thanks, John." She heard Emily take the receiver. Apparently, they weren't using a speaker phone.

"Hi, Claire, how is my jet-set sister?" Claire smiled. Emily was trying her best to accept Claire's life.

"I'm wonderful, glad to be home. How are you?" Tony turned back to his work. Emily explained that she and John were well. They wanted to thank Claire and Anthony again for the transportation. A Rawlings Industries jet took them back to Albany on Sunday following the ceremony. She also thanked them for allowing them to stay in their home, it was amazing! She asked Claire more questions about the honeymoon. Claire made it sound magical but not too over the top. Tony politely kept his back to Claire during her conversation. She knew he was listening to every word but appreciated the gesture.

After ten minutes Claire's internal clock told her time was running out. "Well, it sure was good to see you two and to talk to you—"

Emily interrupted, "I wanted to let you know John's been offered a job with a different company."

This shocked Claire. She didn't know he'd been looking for a different job. Emily said he hadn't. It was a surprise to them too. Claire asked if it was in Albany. No, it was either in New York City or Chicago. The company had offices at both locations, as well as others. Claire knew that meant Emily would have to leave her teaching job. Emily said she knew that. They were weighing the pros and cons. Financially, if he took the job, she wouldn't need to work. It was a tremendous increase in pay. Claire was happy to hear that, but she knew how much Emily loved teaching.

Claire also added the *pro* that Chicago was much closer to her and Tony. She asked if John would be doing the same type of law? Emily said it was international corporate. He'd studied it. But for the last four years he has practiced mostly corporate within the United States. Tony pointed to his watch.

Claire told Emily she was interested and she would try to call again to see how things were going. She also warned, "Please think it through. Don't just jump for the money."

Emily said, "That's easy for you to say."

Claire understood, but wanted them to be happy first and foremost. Emily asked when she would hear from Claire again. And if there was a better way to contact her than Tony's private e-mail?

Claire told she was still trying to understand the whole *Mrs. Rawlings* thing. So many people trying to interview her and the like, well she was sure Emily understood. So yes, Tony's private e-mail was best. They bid each other goodbye and Tony hit the disconnect button.

Claire thought about the call as she stood to leave his office. "Thank you. I appreciate the chance to talk with her." She turned to let him work.

"Claire, wait a minute." Her first thought was that he expected some sort of gratitude. She turned back to him with fire in her eyes. He casually leaned on his desk.

"She was fishing."

Confused, the fire still flickered. "Fishing for what? Information about our honeymoon? Honestly, Tony, she's my sister. Maybe she's just interested in learning about me from me, not a magazine."

He looked impatient. "Are you done?"

"Yes." He indicated for her to sit. She did.

"She was fishing to find out if you knew about John's job offer."

"That doesn't make sense, how would I know . . ." She looked at Tony and her heart rate increased. "Why? Why would you offer John a job? I can tell you don't like him."

"I don't like his strength and determination. He pursued the prenuptial agreement in *my* limousine even though he knew I didn't want him to. He even had the balls to offer me advice. Then during the rehearsal, he stood in front of me and our friends and had the audacity to *not give you away*."

"I knew that upset you. We just never discussed it before now." Tony nodded. "Then please explain why you would offer him a job?"

Tony smiled a devious grin. "I didn't. Tom did. He contacted John while we were away. They have had two meetings in New York. John does have an amazing résumé for someone who went to law school in Indiana."

"It is one of the top twenty-five law schools in the country." Claire immediately regretted defending John.

"Yes, thank you, Mrs. Rawlings. I will let Tom know that he may contact you if a cheering section is needed for Mr. Vandersol." Claire apologized and asked Tony to continue. "He graduated *magna cum laude* from Indiana University School of Law and was hired by an East Coast firm that predominately hires from within the Ivy League. He has worked very hard, and after only four years is an associate on the fast track for partnership consideration."

Claire wasn't sure if it was Tony or Tom, but someone had done their homework. "All right, he has a good résumé, but you just said you don't like him."

"Actually, Mrs. Rawlings, I said I don't like his strength and determination, or more accurately, they infuriated me." He smiled again. This one wasn't devious, more mischievous. Claire suddenly experienced déjà vu and smiled back.

"Tony, John isn't me. He doesn't know you as well as I do."

"That is good. I would prefer to keep it that way."

"I mean, I don't want you to be upset if he refuses your offer." Tony lifted his eyebrows. Claire continued, "John has worked very hard to achieve what he has in life. He may not accept your offer as being based on his résumé, but as being based on a familiar relationship."

232

"You know him better. But Tom made him a very impressive offer. Those student loans, mortgage, and other debts you mentioned would no longer be an issue. Emily would not need to work, and they could live anywhere they wanted."

"Emily likes her job. She loves teaching. Our mother was a teacher up until the day she died. Emily enjoys doing what she does." Claire realized she wasn't facilitating the conversation. "But, I'm sure the loss of debt would be appealing. Emily could always find another teaching job. She does have over six years of experience. I just don't want you to be disappointed if he refuses."

"It is interesting the lengths some people will go to reduce their debt."

Claire chose to ignore that comment. "Has Tom given him a deadline? And what was the point of me talking with Emily but not knowing about John?"

"Tom has asked for an answer by the end of January and I was curious." This time Claire raised her eyebrows. "I wondered if Emily would come right out and ask you about the job. And I figured if you knew about it, she would think you persuaded me to offer it to him. Or more accurately, persuaded me to persuade Tom."

Claire thought for a moment. "Well, I can honestly say it never occurred to me to ask for such a thing. And obviously Emily doesn't realize I don't have that kind of influence over you."

His smile flashed, but more unscrupulous this time. "Why, Mrs. Rawlings, I believe you've been known to be quite persuasive." The enlightening conversation was done. Claire had a lot to consider. She didn't feel good about the probability of John being employed by Rawlings Industries. However, she was honest, both to Emily and Tony. That's all she could do. Honesty was always the best policy, right?

Part of the happiness of life consists not in fighting battles,
but in avoiding them. A masterly retreat is in itself a victory.
—Norman Vincent Peale

Chapter 34

The new year began, and the routines of the past year continued. Tony left in the morning for work. Claire stayed home swimming in the indoor pool, working out in the gym, reading books, watching movies, and waiting for his return. She still relied on Catherine to inform her each evening of Tony's plans. One change was if he were in town, he *always* came to her suite. She may even be asleep, but he slept with her. Another change was that he personally informed her of any events, gatherings, or activities they would attend as a couple. Claire felt this was an improvement from Catherine's last-minute information.

Together they attended two formal events in January. The University of Iowa held a banquet, preceded by cocktails and hors d'oeuvres, to recognize platinum donors. Mr. Anthony Rawlings, of course, was one of them. They also attended a political fund-raiser for the Iowa City District Attorney's Office where a speaker spoke about the role of private industry in the nation's financial recovery. Claire played her part well. She remembered all the rules of her first outing at the symphony. Now, as Anthony Rawlings's wife, she didn't need to be the perfect companion—she needed to be the *perfect wife*. She projected the persona well: beautiful, polite, contented, and appreciative.

Claire had been a newlywed over a month. And most of that time was spent wandering around her home. The continual snow and cold even restricted her from getting outside into the woods. She wondered about Courtney or Sue. Perhaps they didn't want to see her. She hadn't seen or talked to anyone since Emily, the first of January. The walls of her beautiful home were closing in upon her.

When Tony worked from home, Claire joined him in his office. It wasn't a requirement; she thought of it as a getaway from her normal routine. He mostly worked from Iowa City, but he also went out of town a few times. He said he wanted her with him on these business trips, but things were too busy. There would be no time for social activities, and she would be bored. He decided it was better for her to stay home.

She felt increasingly claustrophobic, and Tony seemed completely unaware of her plight. Claire decided perhaps this qualified as one of those *I am a busy man. If you want something, you need to ask me* situations. One night after Tony returned from a short stay in Chicago and the two lay in his dark suite, Claire decided to ask, "I would like to go with you on your next business trip."

"I told you, things are busy. You would be bored."

"I'm bored now. I've barely been out of this house since our honeymoon. I'm going crazy." She expected some realization, an apology for being so involved in business that he'd neglected his wife, perhaps some sweeping request for forgiveness. That wasn't what she received. Abruptly, he turned. Sensing his face above hers, she felt his breath on her face.

"Really? You are bored?"

Resilient, "I am."

"And you didn't catch the end of the conversation?"

"I'm sorry, I didn't. I'll stay out of your way, and we don't need to go out on the town. I just want to get out of this house."

"You have received many invitations for outings." He remained inches from her face.

"What? What kind of invitations? And why didn't I know about them?"

Tony explained, "You didn't know about them, because I chose not to pass them on to you." Claire waited while he continued, "During our wedding preparations you were extremely busy, sometimes you weren't home when I returned. I didn't like that." His cadence slowed. "Besides, on New Year's Eve you seemed to have memory issues. I decided going out as Mrs. Rawlings alone was not something you were ready to do."

Claire felt the anger building within her chest. She feared if she spoke her words would fan her husband's fury, not subdue it. Therefore, she concentrated on keeping her lips pressed together as he continued, "And I like knowing you are home, safe and out of trouble. I have too many things on my plate right now. I don't need to worry about you having an *accident*."

She had remained silent as long as she could. "From whom?" Claire asked assertively.

"Excuse me?" Tony understood her tone. He wanted clarification on her meaning.

"The invitations I've received, who are they from?"

"I believe your ability to understand has diminished with your memory. I said I chose *not* to forward them to you. *I* decided you will stay home, safe. Good night." Tony lay back on his pillow.

She lay still for what seemed like hours. His breathing slowed and became rhythmic. For the first time since he'd proposed, she didn't want to be with him. Claire decided since they were in *his* suite, she could go to *hers*. She waited until she felt certain he was asleep, and then gently lifted the covers. Feeling for her robe she heard his booming voice rip through the darkness. "What do you think you are doing?"

"I'm aware the conversation is done and that I have no control in my own activities. It is all in your hands. But at this moment, I'm also aware you do not consider me a spouse or a partner. I'm going to my suite to ponder this information."

"No, you are not." A conclusive statement. At a little over six foot four, Tony's arm span was immense. Perhaps if she hadn't been tying her robe and putting her feet into slippers she might have had better balance. Nevertheless, in less than a second he grasped her arm and her world tilted. She was once again lying on his bed. The weight of his upper body pinned to the mattress. Memories of their wedding pictures came to mind; she felt small and defenseless.

"Tony, remember your promise." Her voice sounded falsely formidable.

"Which has *always* been contingent upon yours." Her chest suddenly became heavy, not from the weight of his body, but his words. He continued, "You are right." She didn't speak, unsure of her correctness. "The conversation *is* done and I *am* in total control of your activities, including where you will sleep, and which invitations you will accept." The tears began to pool in her eyes. "However, you are also mistaken. I don't *consider* you a spouse. I *know* you are *my* wife. You belong to me."

His forearms pushed against her shoulders causing them to ache. His words weren't a revelation; Claire knew she was his possession. He continued moving his face closer. "You are staying *here* tonight. You are not leaving *me, my bed, or my presence.*" The tears flowed. "Now it is time for you to respond appropriately." His weight shifted slightly.

Claire remembered times in the past when she hadn't replied quickly enough or to his liking. She focused her energy on keeping her body from trembling. However, she couldn't concentrate on that and tears, so her words became muffled sobs. Swallowing hard, she tried to strengthen her voice. "I will not leave you. Even if I left your bed tonight, it would have only been because I'm upset, not because I want our marriage to be over." She took a ragged breath, imagined his dark eyes, and thanked God that the room was too dark to see them.

"Continue."

"I will not leave your bed. I've agreed in the past, I agree now and forever to submit to your authority. I'm sorry if I've given you cause to break your promise."

Inhaling, she tried desperately to defuse his temper. "If you recall, this entire incident started because I asked to be with you when you went away. I don't want to leave you. I want to be with you."

"Your ability to respond appropriately has benefited you on multiple occasions."

He released her shoulders and laid his head on his pillow. She stopped sniffling and tried to regulate her breathing.

"Now take off that robe." As she obeyed he added, "I believe we will experiment with some other forms of response." He rolled back toward her. "But you *are* my partner. I don't want you to do anything you don't want to. So perhaps you would rather go to sleep?"

236

Claire knew this was one of those *offers you can't refuse* her grandmother used to talk about. She answered, "No, I'd rather respond to you." She successfully avoided the trembling and almost stopped the tears. The end result was that her head pounded to the beat of her heart, currently too rapid.

"This time it will not be verbal." His hands seized her petite frame as his domineering tone claimed her spirit. "As you may recall, this conversation is over."

Claire closed her eyes and nodded. She did her best to ignore her headache and respond to her husband. Just before they drifted to sleep, Tony offered more information. "Courtney and Sue have called multiple times, I will think about their invitations. Emily has called and e-mailed. John called, he respectfully declined Tom's offer. I believe Emily can wait."

Claire's heart sank. This new information no doubt influenced Tony's temperament. She wanted to believe Tony's offer to John was made in good faith based on John's credentials. John's refusal didn't surprise Claire, though she was sure it did Tony. He didn't often experience rejection. This wasn't the first time she received the consequences of John's actions.

What concerned Claire the most was her relationship with her sister, would she be allowed to speak to or see Emily? She kissed Tony and sounded as compliant as she could muster. "Thank you, I would really like to see Courtney and Sue." Claire wanted to move away from him, to the far side of the king-sized bed, or better yet, upstairs, but instead she rested her head on his chest. "And I promise my memory is better."

"I am glad to hear that." He slowly embraced her shoulder as his voice softened.

"I need to be in Phoenix next week. It has been in the seventies there. Perhaps you can join me."

She nodded her head. "Thank you. That would be nice." They fell asleep.

The next day, using Tony's iPhone, Claire was allowed to call both Courtney and Sue. She didn't utilize the speaker phone, and although present, Tony didn't question the content. Both the ladies wanted to catch up and hear all about *married life*. Claire said she would love to, would check her calendar, and get back to them. She also apologized for not returning their calls sooner, things were just so busy.

Much earlier than normal, the sound of Tony's alarm woke them on February 1. Their flight to Phoenix was leaving at seven. The trip was only planned for one night, but Claire didn't care. They were leaving the estate and that was enough to propel her from bed to the shower. She would stay at their apartment while Tony met with associates; if all went well they would dine out tonight. He described this apartment as one of their smaller ones. As she showered, she wondered what *small* really meant.

Steam filled the bathroom with a muggy fog. She secured the luxurious lavender towel around her body as Tony entered. "We aren't going to Phoenix."

Her shoulders slumped. "Why? Did I do something?"

Tony hugged her warm body, her hair dripped onto her shoulders and the floor. "No. We can't go anywhere. Eric just called. We should have looked out the window."

He took her to the tall French doors leading to her balcony. When he moved the drapes she could only see white. At least twelve inches of new snow had fallen on the ground, trees, balcony rail, everywhere. With the addition of the eight to ten inches of old snow, there was now almost two feet, and it continued to fall, accompanied by wind. Barely seeing beyond the balcony, she saw drifts transforming the backyard into an ocean of white waves. Heaven knows how deep the snow was in the bigger drifts. Claire sat on the bed with large droplets gliding down her back, discouraged. She sighed.

Sitting next to her, Tony rubbed her leg. "Think of it as a snow day. Didn't you like those when you were a kid?"

"Yeah, because I didn't want to go to school, but now I want to go."

He hugged her shoulder. "You want to go to school?"

Exhaling loudly, she said, "I want to go *anywhere*."

Tony lifted some of her hair. "Well, I'm afraid you will catch pneumonia if you try to go somewhere." She laid her head back on the bed, pressed her lips into a tight line, and looked up at the ceiling. If she opened her mouth she would scream. She was trapped!

Leaning over her, he said, "How about we celebrate our newfound *free day*?"

She knew what he was thinking and didn't want to celebrate. Telling him *no* was supposed to be her option. However, it hadn't been tested and Claire didn't think she was emotionally strong enough for the trial.

Despondently, she asked, "How do you want to celebrate?"

Still leaning over her, he said, "How about you take me to your lake?"

"What?" Claire's thoughts spun. The lake would be frozen and was about five miles away. Would they freeze? It was out, out of the house! "Are you serious?" Her eyes sparkled as she tried to read her husband's expression.

"If it makes that spark come back to your emerald eyes, I'm serious." He kissed her forehead. "We have boots, coats, and gloves, everything needed to ski. It was one of our honeymoon options. So let's get you dry, us fed, bundled, and find this lake I've heard so much about."

"It's about five miles away. Don't you need to talk to the Phoenix people, let them know what happened?"

"Are you trying to discourage me? I will contact the Phoenix office. We can communicate later in the day. It is still very early there. And I know I am older, but I really think I can make five miles." He smiled with milk chocolate eyes. "Besides, we also have cross-country skis. Do you think you can get us there on skis?"

In the midst of a Midwest blizzard, Claire was filled with more warmth and excitement than she'd felt in sometime. Their *discussion* a week ago left her uneasy. She didn't like the way he'd treated her, or the way it made her feel. But once it was done, she hesitated to revisit the subject. Now he wanted to go to her lake. "I bet it's prettier in the summer, but I'd love to get

238

out. I know I can find it." They ate breakfast, and Catherine made them thermoses of coffee. She chided both of them for even thinking about going out in the snow. However, with Tony by her side Claire knew it didn't matter. She was going to her lake, a place she hadn't been since her *accident*.

They dressed in layers, wrapping themselves head to toe, complete with hand and foot warmers, and were out of the house before eight. The wind had subsided but the snow still fell.

It had been many years since Claire cross-country skied. However, the motions swiftly returned as the long slender skis and poles allowed them to glide over the twenty plus inches of snow. At first, she worried about navigation. But with most of the ground level obstacles covered, it wasn't difficult. Skiing was much faster than walking. They reached the clearing in less than thirty minutes. Claire told Tony all about the flowers, butterflies, and animals present in the heat of the summer.

They wore tinted goggles to shield the brightness of the snow, but she sensed his serenity as he listened to her stories. They arrived at the lake shore approximately forty minutes later. Claire wasn't cold. She was exhilarated from the fresh air, exercise, and scenery. Green leaves and blue waters were her preference, but the snow covering the evergreens and ground glistened beautifully. The frozen lake, covered with peaks and valleys of drifts, reminded her of a large flat cake with vanilla frosting. She felt as warm as if it were August.

Tony was completely enthralled by the glistening vista before him. He'd never taken the time to experience his own property. It wasn't something he cared about or gave much consideration, until now. As they stood and watched, three deer, one six-point buck and two does, galloped at full speed from left to right across the lake. Tony and Claire stared. If the deer could do it, they could too. Skiing on the lake was effortless compared to the woods: no hills, valleys, or trees -- only open space. The wind and snow had ceased. They were gliding on a white dreamland. Claire imagined that this was what it would be like to ski in the clouds. The farther west they traveled, the more of the shoreline they could see. Everything looked virgin, completely unspoiled.

After the snow ceased, other animals ventured out of their warm homes. They saw foxes and multitudes of squirrels and birds. Tony said he thought all birds went south for the winter. At first, Claire thought he was joking, and then she explained not all birds migrate. She told him in Indiana the cardinal was omnipresent. She remembered always being excited to see one in winter, it looked so red and vibrant in contrast to the stark gray of winter. Tony continued to ask questions and listen to his wife.

It was almost one when they arrived back at the house. Catherine was elated to see them. She'd been worried. She promised she would send lunch, but first wanted them to get warm. Entering Tony's suite they found his large fireplace roaring with flames and radiating tremendous heat. Claire laughed as Tony removed his ski hat. His hair was messier than she'd ever seen and his cheeks were pink and frigid. Her giddiness amused him. He offered to help remove her winter gear. It didn't take long to realize Fiji had been a better honeymoon destination. Snow activities required too many clothes.

When their food arrived Tony covered Claire with a blanket from his bed. She lay on the rug in front of the fireplace with the soft down comforter and Tony wore only a pair of gym shorts as Cindy wheeled in their lunch. Cindy started to put the warm foods and drink on the table, when smiling at Claire, Tony told Cindy she could leave. Cindy thanked him and left the cart.

Claire smiled at her husband, bare chested, setting their lunch on the table. "Sometimes I think you are the most amazing man I've ever met."

He poured two cups of coffee and carried them to his wife. Joining her under the comforter he prompted, "And other times?"

Answering honestly, she said, "Other times, I don't like you." He looked at her with astonishment. She kissed his lips. "Today is definitely a *like* day." He smiled and told her he was glad.

While eating lunch Tony asked her about the *don't like* days. She thought about playing it off, lying, or telling him she was joking. Then she decided to be truthful. "I love you. I really do. I sometimes feel like the luckiest woman on the planet, but other times I feel like a five-year-old." She waited. Did he understand what she was trying to say? His eyes weren't darkening; he was listening. "I know you may not think so, but I really don't have any intention of causing you harm. Why would I? You told me your grandfather trusted the wrong people. Was your grandmother one of them?"

Tony seemed slightly shaken by the mention of his grandfather. "No. Why do you ask?"

"Because I'm going to assume she loved him and he loved her. If they didn't they wouldn't have married." Tony nodded. He understood where she was going. "I realize there are people who may try to hurt you or your business, but I'm not one of them." She wasn't sure how she could explain her feelings to him. She looked directly into his eyes. The mention of his grandfather minutely darkened them. "I don't have a problem with you being in control of our lives. I trust you. I just wish you trusted me, so I could feel like a wife instead of a child or a possession."

She'd been happy, but this conversation was making her sad. "I'm sorry. I'm ruining this wonderful day." She looked down at her lunch and her cold soup. Closing her eyes she heard his chair move. Claire didn't want him to see the tears escaping her lids. She didn't look up.

Anthony Rawlings gently took his wife's hand and helped her rise from her chair, then tenderly lifted her chin. As he saw her tears he said, "Claire, it seems to me that you apologize a lot." She started to say she was sorry, but snickered at herself instead.

"See? See that smile you have? You can't, but I can. It is beautiful, even with your hair a mess, which it is. And your smile doesn't stop at those perfect lips; it extends to your pink wind-burned cheeks, and most dramatically it extends to your bright emerald green eyes." He was bending with his nose was millimeters from hers. "I apologize for not causing that smile to come out more." Claire felt her resolve melt as her knees weakened. Thankfully, she was being supported by his strong, steady arms.

Tony continued, "You are right about so many things. Listening to you talk today about the different trees, snow, a blizzard, animals, and birds --

240

you know so many things I have never attempted to learn. And you know me better than anyone. I have tried to keep my past that, the past. But you have managed to take the bits and pieces I have offered over the course of a year and weave them together into some psychological basis for your comprehension of me. I must reluctantly admit you are correct." She wanted to say something, but he kissed her tenderly and continued, "You have not intentionally given me reason to do anything but trust you. And yet, I know I have not always behaved well. This may come as a shock, but I have issues with control." She couldn't help but smile. "There's that smile."

Tony led her to the sofa in front of the fire. Wearing a soft bathrobe she sat in front of him and leaned her head on his T-shirt covered chest. They both faced the fire. She heard his heartbeat and the sound of his breathing. The fire radiated warmth and his skin the aroma of exercise. She felt safe and secure. But at the same time, she had the feeling of living in a house of glass. The security could crash into broken pieces at any second. He asked her what she was thinking, she answered. He didn't respond for a long period. She was apprehensive to turn and see into his eyes.

Finally, he spoke again. "Perhaps I'm afraid of losing you, afraid if you truly know me you will not want to stay with me."

She wasn't sure. But due to his voice and breathing, she wondered if he was having difficulty staying composed. She wanted to alleviate his discomfort, tell him it was *okay,* he didn't need to say anything else. She didn't turn around. "Tony, I'm pretty sure I know you. I'm also sure I'm still here."

"Because you haven't had the opportunity to leave." His arms were tenderly wrapped around her.

She caressed them gently with her small hands. "No, not because of that, and not because of the gifts or the trips or the money, I'm still here because I made a commitment to you. I did that in Central Park and again in our home, because I *love* you and *want* to be with you."

He hugged her. "Mrs. Rawlings, I love you too. And I want to trust you more and be less controlling. But what I don't want is to ever hurt you like I did. If you are kept safely away from the world, there is less of a chance that anything will happen which could cause me to react as I did before."

"I used to feel that way, like I wanted to stay here and not risk the chance of upsetting you. I do not *want* to upset you. But, Tony, that isn't a life. Having me home waiting for you because I have no choice, and having me home waiting for you because I want to be, are two totally different things." She waited but he didn't respond, so she continued. "If you would trust me, I will do my best to follow your rules. I will discuss things with you prior to doing them. I will check with you before I go anywhere. I understand the importance of appearances and the significance of consequences. I don't want to upset you. I do want the *opportunity* to upset you." Claire decided this conversation was easier without looking into his eyes. She could imagine small black irises with large velvet borders. However, she was certain her imagination and reality differed.

"Tell me what you want. What freedoms have I taken that you would like returned?"

She told herself, here is your chance, respond appropriately. "I would like access to my own invitations. I will not accept or decline without speaking with you, but I would like the knowledge there are other people out there who care about me. I would like to be able to speak to my sister without being afraid you won't let me, or be upset by my conversation. I would like the ability to leave the estate—just because. And again, it wouldn't happen without your consent, but just to know I can." She listened to his breathing, the only alteration occurred when she mentioned Emily. "And I would like you to be able to contact me directly about our evening plans, not to be told by Catherine. It makes me feel juvenile." She'd done what she could, been as honest as she could. Now, she exhaled and relaxed against his sturdy chest. She couldn't think of anything else to say; she'd wait.

The outdoor adventure was exhilarating, cold air, brilliant snow, and muscle exertion from skiing. The warming up process had been remarkable, crackling fire, soft rug, and tender lovemaking. The lunch was warm: soup, *panini*, and hot coffee. Now they had shared, talked, and been totally honest with one another. Claire's body melted against his; she felt drained. She waited for his response, knowing her fate didn't rest in her own hands. She had no choice but to trust the man who had her wrapped affectionately in his arms. Closing her eyes she listened to his heart, his breathing, and drifted off to sleep.

Nobody can go back and start a new beginning
but anyone can start today and make a new ending.
—Maria Robinson

Chapter 35

Grandma Nichols once said, *"The only constant in life is change."* Claire prayed those changes would be good. After their *heart-to-heart*, she began to see small signs that gave her hope.

The afternoon of their talk, she awoke on the leather sofa in Tony's suite. Hugging the warm comforter, she gazed around. The diminishing daylight accentuated by the glow of the crackling fire illuminated the room. She was alone. At first, she assumed her husband was in the adjoining bath or dressing room, but open doors and silence soon told her otherwise. This had never happened. His suite had technology. She'd seen him use it. The large framed screen could access the world at a click of a remote.

Tentatively, Claire rose and walked to his bureau. The top left drawer contained that key to accessibility. She didn't want to point and click. She needed to know if she could. The internal monologue began: *Can Tony see me? He'd never talked about cameras in his suite. Did they exist? Is this a test? A trap?* She asked for the ability to upset him. Claire decided she needed to know if she'd been granted that chance.

Her hand trembled as she gripped the slender handle. What if the drawer was locked or the remote was gone? Calling upon her courage and strength, she pulled. Through the darkness and into the cavernous depth, she saw it—silver with black buttons. The remote was there, available to her. Emotions swept through her: relief, she was getting the chance she requested. Happiness, he was trusting her. Sadness, she couldn't touch it. Fear, would he catch her? She listened for the sound of footsteps, or worse, doors opening. The only sound came from the fireplace. Claire carefully closed the drawer, walked back to the sofa, and collapsed onto the soft cushions. The flames flickered as the scene melted before her moistening eyes. She pulled her knees into her chest and watched the blaze before her. Fear and sadness pushed relief and happiness away. Summoning the happiness, she told herself this was a good thing, and attempted to regain her composure before she left his suite.

About a week later she sat perched on a high stool with her Gucci heeled boots teetering on a wooden rod, listening to her friend's voice -- more evidence of progress. Claire loved Courtney's company. She could talk enough for the both of them, making Claire laugh in the process. Today Courtney was talking about the Red Cross, the amazing job it did responding to natural disasters and helping the citizens of Iowa and the United States. She explained the financial problems facing the organization with donations decreasing and needs increasing. Courtney was the fund-raising chairman for the Quad City Chapter. She asked Claire to help with her committee, believing they had the connections to individuals and businesses who were surviving the economic slowdown. They could use those connections to help raise money. She asked Claire which fund-raisers she thought would be most profitable. They discussed the pros and cons of an auction, banquet, sports tournament, or raffle. There were so many possibilities. Courtney wanted to exceed last year's goal.

The pub where they sat was electric with energy. Located on the University of Iowa's campus, its tables overflowed mostly with students coming and going. The hum of voices combined with the sound of moving chairs caused Claire's toes to move with excitement. She hadn't been around this many people in so long. She wanted to absorb all the vitality. Claire told Courtney with a degree in meteorology, the idea of assisting with a charity which aided with the disasters she used to forecast, appealed to her.

Courtney gave her a folder of information. It contained a calendar of scheduled committee meetings and a list of committee members' names, e-mail addresses, and telephone numbers. As Claire ate her salad, she scanned the contents. This volunteering would be more time consuming than she'd realized. That was great. Of course, she knew she would need to run it all by Tony. But how would it *appear* if Mrs. Anthony Rawlings wasn't willing to help charities? Besides, he'd allowed this outing, knowing Courtney intention. More evidence.

Courtney stood to get them both more coffee, and Claire looked around the restaurant. She couldn't believe her exhilaration at being out with a friend. Between Courtney and the surroundings she feared her chest would pop. The people at the other tables looked so carefree. They probably took their freedoms for granted; Claire knew she used to. Exhaling, she thought about her husband. He *was* trying to consider her requests. She smiled as she remembered him telling her to call Courtney.

Everything seemed normal as he entered her suite and talked about his day. It was as he entered the bathroom for a shower that his words stunned her. "Claire, I almost forgot, Courtney would like you to call her. My iPhone is on the bookcase. Her number is in the address book under Courtney S., help yourself." Then he turned and closed the door. Claire stared. Was it really him? The other times *she* called from any phone he'd dialed. She worried perhaps she imagined the whole scene. Her legs wobbled as she walked toward his iPhone. Slowly, she picked it up and went through the address book. She scrolled until she saw Courtney S. There were many names. She continued to scroll and saw Emily V., John V., and John V. home. She scrolled back to Courtney S. and hit the *dial* icon. The screen indicated the call was *in progress*. It didn't last long and Claire believed her clammy hands and shaking knees weren't detectable on the other end. Most excitedly, she'd made a call which led to this lunch.

When Courtney returned, she set the mugs on the table. Their salads were gone and the Red Cross had been thoroughly discussed. It had been fun. Now they were having some more coffee and chatting before returning home. Gently, Courtney reached out and held Claire's hand. Suddenly, Claire felt uneasy. With as much practice as she had maintaining eye contact in difficult situations, she looked away from her friend. Courtney's pale blue eyes showed too much concern.

"I am so glad you have agreed to help me." Courtney spoke softly and slowly.

Claire's uneasiness made her want to pull her hand away. Instead, she smiled. "I'm happy I can help you and others."

"Claire, you don't need to be perfect all the time. You don't need to say everything perfectly, look perfect, and be perfect. Life isn't a test you must continually pass." Claire stared silently at her friend, afraid her voice might crack. The energy of the room evaporated. "I just want you to know Brent and I have known Tony for a long time . . ." Claire swallowed. She'd heard this speech from everyone who knew her husband and entitled it the *Great Man Speech,* usually accompanied by *He works so hard.* "And he can be a pompous, condescending, controlling ass."

Claire's eyes grew wide and her head dropped. She didn't cry. She laughed, suddenly and uncontrollably, bordering on hysteria. It wasn't good for appearances. Apparently, her laughter was contagious because Courtney started laughing, too. People looked at them. Fleetingly, Claire didn't care. After a few moments, she regained enough composure to ask, "Excuse me? What did you just say?"

"Honey, you heard me. And I'm pretty sure you know exactly what I said." Courtney squeezed Claire's hand again. "Don't get me wrong, I love your husband. But let me be honest, sometimes I hate him too." Claire nodded. She completely understood. "It's all right. However, it's not all right for you to feel alone." Claire listened. "Your husband loves you. I see it in his eyes when he looks at you. I've never seen him look at another woman the way he looks at you. But he has demons, ones I don't even begin to understand. And he has serious issues with control. He can drive Brent crazy sometimes."

"Courtney, I think maybe we shouldn't be having this conversation." Claire's uneasiness returned.

"Tony would say we shouldn't be having this conversation. What do *you* say?"

Claire didn't know what to say. Part of her wanted the conversation to end, it made her uncomfortable. The other part of her wanted to talk, open up, and feel connected to someone in this world besides Tony. "I think maybe it would be better not to speak about Tony."

"All right, Claire, I respect you. I respect you for marrying Tony and for your inability to talk." Claire tried desperately to maintain her mask. "I have tried my very best to make you comfortable. I want you to feel relaxed with me."

"I do Courtney. I consider you my friend."

"Honey, I am your friend. You are my friend. And Tony is a dear friend, too. But that doesn't mean I don't worry about you."

"Thank you, but you don't need to worry about me. I'm fine."

"Yeah, I recognize fine. And sometimes when you're with us, you are fine. Other times you only seem fine." Claire didn't know what to say. "It must be difficult to suddenly be thrust into Tony's world. He puts a lot of significance on appearance. Well, maybe he hasn't mentioned that to you." Courtney started to stand to leave.

Tears began to escape down Claire's cheeks. Her voice barely an audible whisper, "Courtney, please sit back down." Courtney did. "If Tony knew we were having this conversation, I wouldn't be able to have lunch with you again, and perhaps it could affect Brent's job. I know they're best friends, but with Tony, I'm not sure there are boundaries." Courtney was at least twenty years Claire's senior, yet she listened earnestly, recognizing the sincerity of the younger woman's tone.

"So my intuitions aren't unwarranted." Claire shook her head *no.* Courtney spoke softly. "Claire, are you all right?"

"Courtney, I think we need to go back to your SUV. I'm uncomfortable having this conversation and I'm definitely uncomfortable having it in a public place."

They stood, put on their warm coats, gathered their purses, and walked to Courtney's SUV. The break in the conversation and fresh cool air gave Claire time to regroup. Alarms sounded in her head. If she chose to continue this discussion she would be breaking rules: number one, do as you're told. She'd been told on multiple occasions the importance of appearances and not divulging private information. This was her first time out alone as Mrs. Anthony Rawlings. She wanted to be involved with the Red Cross and wanted more freedoms. Breaking rules would *not* facilitate those goals. They walked to the car in silence.

Sitting in the passenger seat, Claire buckled her seat belt and straightened her posture. She knew what she would say, "Courtney, thank you for your support. You're right. I've been overwhelmed by the responsibility of becoming Tony's wife. He has been supportive and understanding and is helping me recognize the significance of and the obligations accompanying that title. I'm sure he'll be happy to know you're willing to help me, too."

Courtney understood, Claire had just ended the conversation. She didn't want to push, only to let Claire know she was there. "I'm glad you're feeling better about it. Just know that sometimes women pick up on things men don't, even *very observant* men. I hope it'll help you to know I'm quite perceptive and I'm here for you whenever you need me."

Claire thanked her again and asked her a question about the Red Cross. While driving, Courtney asked if Claire and Tony had special plans for Tony's birthday this weekend. Claire was taken aback. She didn't know it was her husband's birthday. However, he hadn't known it was her birthday either.

"I don't believe we do. Tony seems to be very low-key about birthdays."

Courtney declared it was settled, they would do something together. She told Claire about a bar in Rock Island with live music, good food, and a fun atmosphere. Courtney thought it would be good for all of them. Claire promised to discuss it with Tony and let her know. They debated the best day; Tony's birthday was on Saturday. Either Friday or Saturday would work for the Simmons. When Claire got out of the car she invited Courtney inside, Courtney declined. Claire leaned over and hugged her.

"Thank you for everything." She looked directly into Courtney's caring blue eyes. "I'm looking forward to helping you and you helping me." She grabbed her Prada handbag and the charity information.

Catherine let her know Mr. Rawlings would be home for dinner in her suite at seven. *Suite* meant casual, but Claire decided she wanted to make the night special. She wanted him to know how grateful she was for the small freedom. She also knew she'd experienced an excellent opportunity to upset him and avoided it. She wouldn't share that information, but in her mind it gave them more reason for celebration.

Tony was pleasantly surprised by Claire's appreciation and enthusiasm. When she showed him the schedule of committee meetings he said it would be a week-by-week decision. Circumstances can change. However, he didn't anticipate any glitches. She didn't either.

During dinner she mentioned she learned a secret about him. Intrigued, he said, "I wasn't aware I had any secrets from you."

Claire smiled. "I learned Saturday is your birthday."

His eyes darkened and his jaw clenched. "I thought since I missed your special day, we could miss mine."

"Well, Courtney thinks we should all go to the Rock Island Brew Company." He knew the place, he'd been there. She waited for him to agree to the celebration. Finally, she asked, "I promised Courtney I'd get back to her about it, would you like to go Friday or Saturday night?" His agitated expression made her uncomfortable. "Or would you rather I told her we will celebrate on our own?" She realized this was a subject he didn't want to continue.

"*I* will think about it and get back to Courtney." The discussion was done and Claire didn't know their plans.

The next evening Claire sat surrounded by papers when Tony entered her suite. Dressed and ready for dinner, she was completely absorbed in the financial information of the Iowa Red Cross. He looked at her mess and placed two large leather-bound photo albums on top of her papers. Claire looked at the albums and then at her husband. "Good evening, what are these?"

He bent to kiss her and the tips of his lips moved upward. "These are the proofs of the most beautiful bride I've ever seen." Quickly, forgetting the mounds of paper she began looking through the albums. The only pictures she'd seen were the ones on New Year's Eve. The first album began with prewedding poses. The estate, the men, the women, everything and everyone looked beautiful. Then ones of Claire and John prior to walking down the aisle. Tony watched as she turned each page, she was afraid to linger on the photos of John and Emily, she would look at them later. The next were a series of Claire approaching Tony and him waiting. She had to admit -- she looked beautiful. Tony added adjectives: stunning, amazing, gorgeous, and striking. They both appeared to be brimming with love and adoration. There were photos from multiple directions, some very artsy.

Their food arrived and they still had a full album to view. After dinner they spent the entire evening on the sofa in front of the fire, going over and over each photo. They talked about the people, decorations, and ceremony. There were numerous posed photos of the two of them in the grand hall and at the base of the stairs. She laughed at ones where the photographer put her up a few steps, trying to make her taller. "You know, if you had married one of those models you dated they wouldn't have had to do that."

He kissed her tenderly and gazed at her with soft brown eyes. "I didn't want to marry any of those women. I have never wanted to marry anyone but you." He could melt her heart so easily.

The next photos were of the reception. They both agreed the guests seemed to enjoy themselves. Then pictures of them dancing -- Claire remembered her overwhelming desire as Tony directed her around the floor. "I love watching your eyes sparkle as you look at these photos." She told him how much she enjoyed their reception, especially the dancing. "Well, it won't be the same, but we can try to relive that dancing on Saturday for my birthday."

Claire smiled, they were going to celebrate. "I don't know how I can possibly choose which pictures I like best."

"Then don't. Get them all." Placing one arm around her and flipping the pages back, he added, "But this one of you on the stairs with your gown all around you, I want that one. I want it enlarged over the grand fireplace in the sitting room."

Claire wrinkled her nose. "That's silly. I don't want to see me great-big every day."

"I don't care. I want to – and I will. Actually, I think I'll contract an artist to paint it." He leaned back and smiled. Claire just shook her head, stopping him from doing something he wanted to do was beyond her ability.

Next, she saw the *family* photo of her, Tony, and the Vandersols. "Tony, can we have copies of some of these made for Emily and sent to them?" She only said Emily on purpose, but the *them* should have been *her*. He sighed and conceded. She knew to drop the subject, but sometimes she couldn't stop herself. "Has Emily tried to contact me anymore?"

248

"Yes."

Claire didn't reply. He knew what she wanted. If she persisted it would be arguing or pleading. If he changed his mind, he would let her know. Besides, they were having a nice evening with the wedding pictures; she directed the conversation back to the album. "Look at this picture of MaryAnn and Eli. They were hilarious!" The Vandersol conversation ended.

Trust not too much to appearance.
—Virgil

Chapter 36

T he birthday was a success. Tony and Brent joked that with late-night partying they shouldn't drive an hour home, so everyone rode together in the limousine. The Brew Company was vibrant with music resonating from multiple sections of the large warehouse style building. The main stage had a "Tribute to Jazz" performance. Courtney reserved a premium table and told the restaurant they were celebrating a birthday. The people at the Brew Company didn't know his name, only that Tony was the guest of honor. Claire, Courtney, and Brent laughed as the singer acknowledged him with a rendition of "Hey Big Spender" and wrapped him in her feather boa. Watching Tony's tolerance, Claire decided she could learn a lot from Courtney. He seemed to accept things from her Claire wouldn't dare to attempt.

A week later, Tony invited Claire to Chicago for two nights. Even though she needed to cancel a committee meeting, she wanted to go. It was even her idea to go to the spa and lighten her dark roots. Brent and David Field, whom Claire met what seemed like a lifetime ago on her first trip to New York, were with them as they flew to Chicago. Claire sat on the sofa while the three men discussed their impending meetings. To pass the time, she looked through her purse and was pleased to have her new ID and credit card. Claire didn't care about their money, but shopping was one of the few pass times Tony granted without hesitation.

Her old driver's license was a Georgia-issued ID. She thought it was interesting to see the difference in different states licenses. She soon realized the variances didn't stop with the issuing state; the new one contained her name, Claire Rawlings, and printed at the top was *VALID IDENTIFICATION*. Her Georgia ID had said *VALID DRIVER'S LICENSE*. She hadn't noticed it before. It wasn't something she should bring up with Brent and David present but decided it was worth discussing when they were alone.

Claire spent the afternoon at the spa lightening her hair and receiving a manicure and pedicure. When she arrived back at the apartment, Charles informed Mrs. Rawlings, Mr. Rawlings would be detained until after nine. He could happily serve her dinner at a more appropriate hour. She declined, "Thank you, Charles, I'll wait for Mr. Rawlings."

While dining, Claire sensed Tony multitasking. He was eating and conversing with her, but his mind was elsewhere with Brent and David on some big deal. He talked about the next evening. Hopefully, they would be able to go out to dinner and perhaps to a show. It all depended on his meetings. Claire said it sounded great, but she understood if his work went late. She planned to spend the entire day shopping and knew they were scheduled to go home on Thursday.

As Claire contemplated the best way to bring up her question, Tony did it for her. "You are going shopping tomorrow? Did you see your new ID and credit card? They should be in your wallet."

"I did. I was wondering, why is my new ID not a driver's license?"

Tony momentarily stopped eating and looked at Claire as if she'd asked *why is the sky blue or why do birds fly?* It seemed as though the only word missing from his next sentence was *Duh.* "Because you don't drive." His tone wasn't cruel, perhaps cold.

She thought carefully about her response. "I haven't driven since I've been with you, but I used to drive and enjoy it."

"You now have access to a driver. You didn't before, correct?"

"Correct. However, you have a driver, and you still drive. The Simmons have a driver and Courtney drives."

Tony's annoyance with this conversation came through loud and clear, his words were flat with restraint. "Claire, this is a ridiculous conversation. You have a driver or you are with me. You have no need to drive."

"Tony, you are obviously busy with work. We can discuss this later."

Throughout the past year there were numerous instances when Tony purposely baited Claire. He liked to observe her reactions. Initially, it was done maliciously. It intrigued him to see how far he could push. Lately it had become a private game. He found her self-control and resilience incredibly sexy. The restraint she demonstrated to refrain from arguing, when clearly her body language screamed fight, was stimulating.

This evening Tony was not playing a game. His mind was set, Claire would not be driving. The fact they were even discussing the subject seemed absurd. "Let me help you. It *has* been a long day and this discussion is over. It does not need to be revisited."

She thought about saying, "Fine – I'm going to bed." However, before she could, he continued, "I would offer you the opportunity to decide on your own if it is worth continuing, but I have decided not to take that risk. It isn't."

Her chest expanded and contracted as she released a sigh. Looking at her husband, she kept her lips together and remained silent. He watched her neck stiffen and eyes flash. He waited. After a prolonged silence, confident of her compliance, he continued. "Now tell me about your day at the spa."

Claire did her best to feign enthusiasm and replied, "It was very nice. They always do a great job and make me feel special." Thinking, *as opposed to how I'm feeling right now.*

A wall of glass extended from ceiling to floor behind Tony. Through the night sky Claire saw the head and tail lights of vehicles moving around the windy city. Somewhere deep in her soul she wondered, *Will I ever drive again?*

Chicago was uneventful. She shopped without accidentally providing an interview. They dined at a steak house not far from the Tower and went to the Cadillac Palace Theater for *Les Miserables*. Claire saw it many years ago from the *nosebleed* section. It was one of her favorite live musicals. A winner of seven Tony Awards, she didn't mind seeing it again. It amazed her they could get such exceptional seats. The night before Tony didn't know if they would be attending a show. "Les Miserables" had been sold out for months. Now they were seated in a premium box enjoying the outstanding performance.

Apparently, Tony's dealings were successful because they and Brent were able to go back to Iowa as planned. David stayed behind to finalize some contracts. Reading her book, Claire observed Tony with Brent, sensing a difference from the accustomed friendly casual interaction. Watching and listening to them discuss business issues reminded her of Courtney's comment, "He can drive Brent crazy sometimes." She hadn't seen it before, but understood it now.

Tony's repertoire of personalities included an overpowering domineering force which apparently was reserved for those closest to him. Claire had plenty of personal experience with this personality, but she'd never had the opportunity to observe it directed at someone else. Today she witnessed Tony's manipulative rule being unleashed on Brent. It wasn't pretty. She understood how Brent could relay things to Courtney, because that's what real couples do, and Courtney could hate and love Tony at the same time. Pretending to be absorbed in her book, Claire didn't want to be included in the conversation, or for her presence to make Brent uncomfortable. It obviously wasn't affecting Tony.

The last week of February, Claire and Tony prepared for an interview with *Vanity Fair Magazine*. Shelly, Tony's publicist, made a point to come to their house and explain to Claire that this interview was important to Mr. Rawlings's public relations. There were many speculations in the media about the two of them, their fast wedding, and lack of prenuptial agreement. This would be their way to shape and control the information. Claire thought it was a nice gesture. Truthfully, if Tony told her to do the interview, she would do it. What surprised Claire was the extent of planning and preparation which went into it.

Shelly agreed to *Vanity Fair* because of their willingness to work openly. They gave her a list of questions. She deleted, added, and tweaked them until both parties were satisfied. Then Tony and Claire were given the questions and time to work on their *spontaneous* answers. Next, with Shelly's assistance, they practiced and modified their answers. She arranged for cosmetologists, beauticians, and clothing designers to assist them before the photo shoot. Shelly promised to be present throughout the entire interview and photo session. She would step in and stop any unapproved questions. This was better than Mr. or Mrs. Rawlings refusing to answer a question or appearing unaccommodating. The article would then be reviewed and approved prior to publication.

Claire thought the whole thing was hilarious. Did all people go through this before an interview? There was a time in her life when she read a celebrity interview and assumed it was as it appeared. Being Mrs. Rawlings continued to teach her so much.

The day of the interview finally arrived. The people who came to make Claire and Tony beautiful arrived early, before seven thirty. By the time Shelly arrived they both looked like models. *Just another day sitting around the house!* Claire thought as she looked in the mirror at her professional makeup and styled hair.

Catherine assumed the challenge of the house. It sparkled. Even the weather received the perfection memo. Not realizing it was late February, the sun shone through a sapphire blue sky, and a fresh layer of snow blanketed the gray dingy ground, adding luster to the outdoors.

Anne Robinson, the reporter from *Vanity Fair,* arrived promptly at nine accompanied by a photography crew. The Rawlings were only introduced to the lead photographer, Shaun Stivert. The plan commenced with photos first, while Claire and Tony looked fresh and beautiful. Then they progressed to the interview. The whole process was more work than Claire imagined.

Shelly was true to her word and omnipresent. She didn't hesitate to say, "No, I think this would be better," or, "We went over this. You know that will not be discussed today." Claire studied her lines well, knowing what to say and how to say it. Tony practiced too. Claire thought they both sounded sincere and spontaneous. The *Vanity Fair* crew finally left after one in the afternoon with Shelly not far behind. "I think that went very well. I will let you know as soon as I have an approved copy." Once she left, Claire relished the quiet house again, her head pounded behind her eyes. The headaches weren't as frequent as they were right after her *accident.* However, when they struck they could be debilitating. Sleeping in a very dark room was the best remedy.

Claire accompanied her husband to his office following the interview. Driving into Iowa City would be counterproductive this late in the day, he hoped to accomplish as much as possible from home. Mr. and Mrs. Rawlings sat silently as Cindy brought them their lunch. Claire closed her eyes and enjoyed the peacefulness as Cindy placed their food on the long shiny table. After pouring their coffee she asked Mr. Rawlings if they needed anything else.

"No, you may go." And then he spoke to Claire, "How do you think it went?"

She opened her eyes to focus. "I really think it went well. It was more draining than I'd expected. I can't wait to see the final article."

"Shelly said we should have a draft by next week. It's supposed to be the cover story for the April publication, so it won't hit the newsstands for a while." Claire shook her head. She couldn't believe her marriage would warrant a cover story for anything, much less *Vanity Fair*. The food and coffee helped her head, but she suspected it'd gone too far. A nap was the real remedy. Once they finished eating, Tony walked over toward his desk.

"Do you need me? I would like to go upstairs. The morning wore me out," Claire asked as she stood to leave.

He picked up a manila folder and handed it to her. "I would like you to stay here while you look at these." She took the folder to the sofa and sat down. The content of the folder was a mystery. She suddenly had visions of Tony with the Meredith Banks interview. Sometimes compartmentalized memories would sneak out.

She opened the folder to find over an inch thick stack of papers. They were printed e-mails. Her mind moved slowly, exhausted from the interview process and dulled from her headache. Confused, she asked, "What are these?"

"Your invitations." Granting her another freedom, he watched as she read. She looked at the top e-mail:

To: Anthony Rawlings, anthrawl265@rawlingsind.com
Date: February 25, 2011
From: Courtney Simmons, courtsim768@rawlingsind.com
Subject: For Claire, attachment
Please let Claire know that our meeting is scheduled for next
Wednesday at noon, but I would like to get together before that so
we can brainstorm. We need to get the fund-raising calendar set by the next
meeting. Attached is a file she needs to review. If one of you could let me know
when a good time to get together is I would appreciate it. Courtney
          (Paper clipped to the e-mail was a five-page report)

Claire didn't know what to say, finally she weakly managed, "Thank you." He didn't reply. He watched and continued to evaluate her response. She went back to the stack. The e-mail under Courtney's was from Emily. It too was dated February 25, 2011. However, it was a series of correspondences.

February 25, 2011
Hi, it is me again. I realize that Claire is busy with her new
responsibilities, but I would like to talk to her. I'm usually home most
evenings. It has been almost two months. I have sent many e-mails and tried
numerous times to call. Thank you, Emily.

February 11, 2011
Mrs. Rawlings is unable to respond to your request at this time.
Patricia M.

February 9, 2011
Hello, this is Emily Vandersol, again. Could you please inform Mrs.

254

Rawlings that her sister would like to speak to her? Thank you.

February 2, 2011
Mrs. Rawlings is unable to respond to your request at this time.
Patricia M.

February 1, 2011
Hello, Emily Vandersol here. I'm the sister of Mrs. Rawlings. I'm not
sure who is replying to these e-mails. I have attempted to reach Mr. Rawlings to no
avail. Please inform Mr. Rawlings or Mrs. Rawlings that my husband and I would
like to talk with them. We would be happy to meet them if they plan a trip to New
York, or a telephone call would be acceptable. I look forward to your response.

January 23, 2011
Mrs. Rawlings is unable to respond to your request at this time.
Patricia M.

January 22, 2011
Hello, Anthony, are you receiving my e-mails? I know that you have
learned of John's decision. I would like to talk to you and Claire. We need
to be sure this job thing doesn't affect our family relationship. Let me talk
to you about John and his reasoning. Please pass this on to Claire. I will be
home all weekend, she can call anytime.
Thanks. Em.

January 17, 2011
Mrs. Rawlings is unable to respond to your request at this time.
Patricia M.

January 15, 2011
Hi, Anthony and Claire, I had hoped we could talk, but I haven't been
able to reach you. John is meeting with Tom on Monday. It would be nice
if I could talk with Claire and settle a few things before John's meeting. I
hope you check your e-mails on the weekend. I will be waiting for your or
Claire's call. By the way, I saw some of your wedding photos in the grocery
store this morning. You two looked wonderful. Please call.

January 4, 2011
Mrs. Rawlings is unable to respond to your request at this time.
Patricia M.

January 3, 2011
Hi, Anthony, I need to speak to Claire again. I'm not sure if she told
you, but I brought up John's job offer the other day. I've been thinking about it, and
feel guilty. It wasn't fair of me to talk to her about it. I know you all have a lot going
on. John wanted to know if she had anything to do with your offer. I could tell she
really didn't know about it. I need to tell her I'm sorry for putting her in a difficult
position. I appreciate what you are offering John. I am trying to stay out of his

decision process. But I would like to talk to Claire some more; it was so nice to see more of her during the wedding. Please ask her to call me, and tell her I love her. The photos of you two on the news were amazing. Thanks again for the transportation and the stay in your home. It was beautiful. Thank you, Emily

This history was stapled together. Claire's eyes were wet by the time she finished Emily's last or first e-mail. She looked up at Tony. He still didn't speak; his dark eyes glared. Claire wondered what she was supposed to do with this information. Perhaps it was her head, but she truly didn't know how to respond, so she asked, "Thank you for giving me my invitations, now what am I supposed to do with this knowledge?"

"Tell me what you want to do." His tone hard.

Claire rose and approached his desk. "I want to call her." She could see the deliberation on his face. She remembered not being able to read his expression. Her ability wasn't comforting. Claire tried desperately to modulate her voice. "I will do it here on the speaker phone. I don't care if you listen to every word and tell me what to say, I just want to call her." He still didn't speak, but the intensity in his eyes multiplied. "Tony, may I please call her?"

"It is almost three, which would be four in Troy. Would she be home?" It wasn't an answer but it wasn't a denial.

Claire thought about it. School finished at three fifteen, at least it used to. "She might." As if thinking out loud, she added, "And as a plus John won't be."

He didn't respond to her last statement, instead he began to talk about her e-mails. She sat. He explained the folder included multiple e-mails from people she didn't know. Since their marriage many people have attempted to contact her for various reasons. Patricia replied to everyone, "Mrs. Rawlings is unable to respond to your request at this time."

Tony continued, "Your preparation for the *Vanity Fair* interview and execution today impressed me. I also appreciate you made requests a month ago and have been patient. I believe you deserve to be rewarded. Therefore, regarding your e-mails, from now on, before Patricia replies you will have the opportunity to review them. We will discuss them. Together we will decide responses. Of course, I will have the final say. However, I believe you have earned a voice."

Claire realized Tony believed he'd presented her with a freedom. She couldn't help think it was, instead, only a glimpse of what she was missing. The forbidden opportunities would now be staring her in the face. "Thank you, I understand."

He turned to his computer screens, and she watched the back of his head for what seemed like hours. He knew what she wanted. She'd made her request. Now he was making her wait. How would she respond? He'd provided a token of his approval. Would she submissively accept or would she pursue the idea of calling her sister?

Claire closed her eyes and tried to stop the pounding in her temples. Perched on the chair's edge near his desk, she refused to budge. The folder, the gift he'd given her, sat closed on her lap. She didn't care about people she didn't know, and her head hurt too much to read anymore. She waited as his fingers flew between the keyboard and mouse. Sitting silently and expressionlessly she remembered Courtney's kind words, *Life is not a test you must continually pass.* Claire absentmindedly rolled her shoulders and straightened her neck. If the only way she would be able to call Emily was to pass this test, then by God she wasn't moving from this seat. Finally, he turned to face her.

"Why have *you* not called until now?" He presented his question with harsh overtones.

Thinking out loud, she said, "I've been busy. I can tell her about the Red Cross and preparing for our interview."

What followed were not suggestions, they were orders. "You *will be* apologetic and explain that *you* have been meaning to call. Seeing her recent e-mail reminded you, *you* haven't. Your reasons sound valid. I'd prefer you don't discuss the job situation. It is done. And of course there are no hard feelings."

The directives should have been upsetting, but she'd played this game before. They were the means to her goal. "Yes, I promise."

He dialed the phone, put it on speaker, and didn't bother to turn away. The phone rang three times. Claire's hopes began to sink when finally Emily answered.

"Hi, Emily, it's Claire." Emily's voice brimmed with excitement. Claire's sounded happy and apologetic. They spoke for about ten minutes. On a few occasions Tony indicated that the subject needed to be changed. Claire attempted to keep the discussion away from the job, but Emily was determined to discuss it, explaining how John was currently very close to being named partner. He didn't feel right abandoning the firm which had taken a chance on him when he first graduated. He'd worked hard to get to his position and didn't feel right working for family. However, he was very honored Anthony would consider hiring him. They also discussed Emily's class, and she asked about the interview Claire mentioned. Before they hung up Claire promised to do a better job responding to Emily's e-mails.

It amazed Claire how one phone call could make her both happy and sad. Maintaining her *happy* voice during the call almost reduced her to tears on its completion; her energy was totally depleted. "If it's all right with you, I'll take the folder upstairs and look through it. We can discuss the e-mails after dinner."

"That is fine, you may go." He had work to do.

Once upstairs, Claire decided to nap instead of looking through the folder. It'd been a long day. The contrast between the interview and her reality intensified the pounding behind her eyes and more recent nausea. She took some acetaminophen, crawled between the soft cool sheets, and allowed the tears from the phone call to flow. Sleep was a welcome escape.

However, it wasn't long after she fell asleep when Tony woke her. He wanted to thank her again for her performance during the interview. He also believed she wanted to thank him.

This only is denied even to God,
the power to undo the past.
—Agathon

Chapter 37

On March 15, Tony brought the official final copy home. It had been approved by Shelly and was scheduled to be published at the end of March, officially the April 2011 issue of *Vanity Fair*:

"Anthony Rawlings Introduces the World to the Love of his Life,
His Wife Claire Rawlings—Let the Rumors Cease and
Learn how She has Changed His Life"

By: Anne Robinson Photos by: Shaun Stivert

You don't marry someone you can live with, you marry the person who you cannot live without.—Unknown author

On a beautiful snowy day in the Midwest Mr. and Mrs. Anthony Rawlings sat down with *Vanity Fair* and addressed the questions, rumors, and realities of their acquaintance, courtship, engagement, and marriage. The exceedingly private man and his beautiful new bride graciously opened their home to our photographers and interviewer. (Photo of Tony and Claire dressed in casual elegant slacks and sweaters, sitting on a sofa in their gorgeous sitting room.)

The home of Anthony and Claire Rawlings is a stately 6,000 plus acre estate near Iowa City, Iowa. Most of the land is wooded, uninhabited, and unspoiled. Animal activists will be happy to know it is home to many indigenous woodland animals. Their residence is a spacious elegant home secluded within the private gates of this countryside.

Built by Mr. Rawlings approximately sixteen years ago, it resembles a 1940s Romanesque-style mansion. The exterior has exquisite asymmetrical facades of river stone, limestone, and brick accentuated by round arches over windows and entryways. There are thick, cavernous entryways and window openings, thick masonry walls, and rounded towers with conical-style roofs.

The main house is centered upon a round brick drive. Projecting from the main structure are wings of additional corridors and rooms. Upon entry you may feel you have entered a museum; however, the warmth and love radiated by the newlyweds soon help you to realize you have entered a family home; a quality Mr. Rawlings states was missing until recently.

It was late May of 2010 when Anthony Rawlings first introduced the city of Davenport to the then Claire Nichols. They attended the Quad City Symphony. Mr. Rawlings was asked to attend the event because of a generous donation made to both the Quad City Symphony and the Support the Arts Foundation. Mr. Rawlings has long been known for his generosity and pursuit of philanthropic endeavors. He is a firm believer in the arts and continues to support endeavors that promote artistic pursuits. As a local celebrity, Mr. Rawlings is often seen attending functions in and around the Quad Cities (as well as in cities like Chicago, New York, and Los Angeles).

It was his companion on that evening that was unfamiliar. He has been seen on various occasions with different women, some with names we recognize, such as Cynthia Simmons and Julia Owens. Truthfully, throughout his forty-six years he has been seen with many beautiful women. However, it was apparent to those present on that evening in May, that this was different. Many on-lookers reported "glances" and "hand holding" that were not witnessed before.

When discussing their first public "date," *Vanity Fair* noted that the new Mrs. Rawlings couldn't help look at her husband with blushed cheeks and a bashful smile. She stated that she recalled the standing ovation he received and how handsome she thought he looked. But she hastily added that at that time, neither of them was looking for a "long-term" relationship.

Anthony said that he recalls seeing Claire when he picked her up for the symphony. He even recalled her outfit, a black dress with a beaded bodice, and that her hair was up with curls. (Anthony gently played with his wife's hair as he described the style.) He remembered that she was stunning and he was proud to accompany her to the event.

VF: Now, ladies, ask your husband if he remembers what you were wearing on that first date! I had to think that Mr. Rawlings should have realized at that moment his heart was lost. I wanted to know how the two of them got to that first date. How did they meet?

Anthony told the story of meeting Claire in Atlanta, Georgia. She had worked at a local television studio as an assistant meteorologist. Due to a recent buy out of the station by TTT-TV (according to Mr. Rawlings's publicist this article is a strictly personal view of Mr. Rawlings, no Rawlings Industry holdings are to be discussed), Claire was working at the Red Wing, a well-known dining establishment in Atlanta. Anthony just happened to be meeting some business associates there one evening. After his meeting was complete, he began talking to the most beautiful bartender he'd ever seen. He said one of the assets of Ms. Nichols was that she did not know him. Claire reiterated, "I really did not know who he was, even after he told me his name. I don't watch much television or read business journals."

The two newlyweds seemed to get lost in each other's eyes while they reminisced. "I thought I had heard the name Anthony Rawlings before, but I had no idea why."

Anthony said the rest is history. He knew he needed to know her and know more about her.

VF: Was it "love" at first sight?

They smiled at one another. Claire shook her head. "Probably not," and she added, "Anthony is a complicated, private man. You can love the wrapping paper, but with him it takes some time to find out what is inside. I wouldn't give my life to someone without knowing what is inside the package."

"What is love? Love is when one person knows all of your secrets, your deepest, darkest, most dreadful secrets of which no one else in the world knows. And yet in the end, that one person does not think any less of you."

Mrs. Rawlings added she has seen the inside of the package and loves it more than the wrapping paper. Anthony, on the other hand, related his journey to that of Romeo, who said, *"Did my heart love till now? Forswear it sight. For I never saw true beauty till this night.* Perhaps I had waited much longer and knew when I met her that my wait was complete."

VF: Mrs. Rawlings, can you share some of your findings with our readers? What have you found under that amazing wrapping paper?

Blushing slightly at the inference, she quickly recovered. "Well, he isn't exactly how he appears." Anthony seemed to be interested in what she was about to reveal. Claire continued, "For example, he has been known to hold webinars and web conferences from home in a shirt, tie, suit jacket, gym shorts, and sneakers." She smiled at her husband, who playfully shook his head. He responded, "Great. Now I'm going to have to stand before each webinar to alleviate the participants' curiosity." He smiled broadly. When asked if anything else surprised her about Anthony, after some reflection she answered yes. He is a Vikings fan. They both grinned. Being originally from Indiana, Mrs. Rawlings said she couldn't imagine she would marry anyone who isn't a Colts fan. Anthony made a comment about real football teams that play outdoors, and Claire was quick to mention two recent trips to the Super Bowl. Their playful banter was enjoyable to observe.

VF: Have you two had any arguments, disagreements, or fights?

"No!" They answered simultaneously and laughed. Anthony took the lead on this question. "Of course. I can't imagine spending quality time with someone and always agreeing. That is not what I want in my life. There are multitudes of people in my life that will agree with my every thought. Claire has 'stood up' to me in ways that captains of business have not. Her strength and determination are what I fell in love with." Tenderly wrapping his arm around her shoulders, he added, "As well as her beauty and intelligence."

After smiling at Anthony, Claire added, "I have been told that some of those qualities can be infuriating." This reporter enjoyed Anthony's dismissal of that comment.

VF: Will either of you share the story of the proposal?

Claire volunteered, "Oh, I will. He was amazing. First it was dinner in Manhattan. He took me to the theater district. We dined at the Crown Plaza Hotel and our table had a view of Times Square. I had no idea what his plans were for the evening, he enjoys surprises. After dinner we went to see 'The Merchant of Venice' with Al Pacino, fantastic by the way. Afterward, I was honestly tired and ready to go back to my hotel. But instead we went to Central Park." Laughing she recalled, "It was very cold that night, the night before Thanksgiving. It hadn't snowed, but it was very cold. However, he planned for that with mittens and blankets". After each sentence she looked into his eyes. Even this reporter saw the twinkle in her green eyes as she recounted his proposal. Claire went on to say, "I did not expect a proposal. I was completely shocked. But there he was, in a horse-drawn carriage in Central Park, under the lights, with a diamond ring."

Vanity Fair will add that her "diamond ring" is actually a designer original Tiffany & Co. 4.3 carat brilliant center stone bordered by a delicate diamond bead set in mil-grain detail in platinum. The matching wedding band is also platinum, with delicate inset diamonds. While actual value would not be released by Mr. Rawlings or Tiffany & Co., New York, where he is said to have purchased the set, due to the size, clarity, and unique cut, it is estimated above $400,000.

VF: Did you say yes immediately? (Now come on, ladies, think about what you would have done.)

Claire sat back. "No." At this Anthony smiled and put his hand on his wife's knee. He goes on with the answer, "No, she didn't. She made me wait for what seemed like an eternity." But leaning over to kiss his bride, he added, "She finally relented. And I was elated."

The worst thing you can do for love is deny it; so when you find that special someone, don't let anyone or anything get in your way.

VF: Now some people have questioned the quickness of your nuptials. What do you have to say to those critiques?

Anthony answered, "I guess they have never been as in love." Claire continued, "We didn't want to wait. We made our decision. We wanted our family and friends to share in our happiness."

VF: The personal accounts were extremely complimentary. How did you pull off the wedding of the century in less than a month?

Mrs. Rawlings replied, "With the best wedding planner and

coordinator in the world! They were amazing. We never worried about a thing."

According to the press releases the wedding was magnificent. The bride was gorgeous in an exquisite Vera Wang gown, reportedly from an elite Manhattan boutique. The groom was dazzling in a custom Armani tuxedo. The estate was impressively decorated with a Christmas theme. Lights and evergreens were everywhere, with deep red accents. The guest list was limited and exclusive, but was said to contain some powerful business and political individuals, as well as personal friends and family of the bride. The groom's only family is now his wife. (Photo of Mr. and Mrs. Rawlings in wedding attire standing at the base of the grand stairway, decorations can be seen behind them. Note: multiple wedding pictures and decorations can be seen in a collage of pictures at the end of the article.)

VF: Addressing Claire Rawlings, how has it been to be thrust into the public eye? It seems that the stigma that accompanied the death of Princess Diana has begun to fade and reporters are once again brazenly pursuing celebrities.

Claire blushed and glanced at Anthony. "May I say first I do not feel that I am a celebrity? I have done nothing to warrant celebrity status. That is why when you ask your question, the first response I think of is, it has been unreal. I still find it amazing that anyone would think my clothes, shopping habits, or hairstyle newsworthy. It is something that I am learning to handle. Anthony has been superb at buffering the media as much as possible."

Claire added, "*You* can be overwhelming at times." Addressing this reporter, she continued, "*You* meaning the press," smiling a lovely smile, "not *you*. However, if being married to this marvelous man means seeing myself on an occasional magazine," she leans toward his protection, "it is more than worth it." Mr. Rawlings included that he desired to shelter her from too much unwanted exposure. After all, he prefers to remain as private as possible.

A s the couple walked hand in hand to share a tour of their home it wasn't hard to imagine that a splendid wedding ceremony could easily occur within these walls. The grand hall is breathtaking on this February afternoon. The two-story winding staircase ascended to a railed landing which appeared to extend down various hallways. The ceiling, at least another story high, holds a magnificent chandelier that illuminates the foyer.

The intricate marble flooring extends behind the stairs to a window-lined sitting room. These areas were all utilized during the ceremony. Beyond the sitting room, which also contains a magnificent fireplace, is a comfortable sunporch that Mrs. Rawlings says is one of her favorite rooms in their home. She enjoys reading and sunlight very much. Even in the winter months, if it's not too cold she can enjoy the sun's rays on the porch. However, it is in the summer with the windows open and the fresh breeze that the room is ideal.

Not far from these exquisite rooms is a grand dining room that the newlyweds claim to utilize regularly. Mr. Rawlings commented that just being with his bride is a special occasion worthy of formal dining. Beyond the sunporch this reporter could see the expanse of their backyard. Apparently, during the wedding it contained a large tent that created the hall for their reception. On this day it was snow covered and pristine. The yard is encased by trees. Currently, the trees are bare and one can see into the depths of the forest, but Anthony explained that within months the green leaves will obstruct the view and the lawn will appear an oasis in itself. He also pointed out the deck, pool area, and patio. He is proud of the house. He offers that he helped design it from memories and ideas from other dwellings. He believes the result is exquisite, and this reporter agrees wholeheartedly.

Mr. Rawlings also showed *Vanity Fair* his home office. As an entrepreneur who began his fortune with the Internet, it seems only appropriate that his home contained high-tech electronics. Not only does his desk contain multiple computer screens, but behind his desk on the wall was also a collage of screens, second only to the ones this reporter has seen in television studios. His office is decorated in a masculine tone of wood and leather. When asked if he often works from home, Anthony responds that he does when he can. It gives him an excuse to be close to Claire when she is not out and about. (Photo of Mr. Rawlings behind his impressive desk, working on his computer with screens illuminated behind him.)

Mrs. Rawlings took that opportunity to tell *Vanity Fair* a little about her recent philanthropic endeavor. While working as a meteorologist, Claire saw the damage and devastation that natural disasters can wreak upon our country. She never imagined that she'd be in a position where she could make a difference to people, but now she is. Claire has recently begun to work with the Red Cross of Iowa, the Greater Quad Cities, and of the United States. She's been diligently working to facilitate their fund-raising efforts. The economy has had a dreadful effect on the Red Cross's reserves. These are essential for the organization to be able to continue their efforts on a daily basis and especially in case of disaster. The sad reality is that the reserve is dwindling. With Anthony's connections and her understanding of disasters and the resources needed, she hopes to be of help to the organization. Anthony's admiration for his wife's endeavors is evident in his expression as she discusses the work the Red Cross can do, if adequately funded.

The tour continued to the lower level of the main house, where a large welcoming entertainment/ recreation room exists. There's a pool table, game table, comfortable sofas and chairs, a large flat-screen television with four smaller screens surrounding it, and a handsome handcrafted mahogany bar with intricate tile in the mini kitchen behind the bar. Adjoining this room is a theater room complete with plush seating for six, and a screen large enough for twenty-six. The other direction from the recreation room leads to an exercise gym, with every piece of exercise equipment you would want or need. Mr. Rawlings explained that he likes to workout. He finds himself needing to burn off energy after a day of business dealings, which usually occur while seated. *Vanity Fair* notes that he appears fit, as does Mrs. Rawlings. She, however, leads our crew to her favorite workout, an indoor lap pool complete with spa and sauna. Claire Rawlings said she prefers the outdoor pool, but during the colder months, which are numerous in Iowa, the indoor pool is an ideal alternative.

Back in the sitting room, *Vanity Fair* tries once again to learn more about this stunning couple. (Photo of the couple with warm coats standing on the front steps of their home and another of them sitting on the floor before a roaring fire in a grand six-foot tall fireplace. Note the portrait of Mrs. Rawlings in her wedding gown above the fireplace.)

VF: Mrs. Rawlings, how do you feel about living in Iowa after living in Atlanta, Georgia?

Rubbing the sleeves of her soft cashmere sweater, Claire responded, "I would gladly live any place with Anthony. However, if he chose some place warmer it would be all right." They both smile. "Seriously," she continued, "I grew up in Indiana. Iowa isn't much different. The Midwest is a beautiful area. I love sunshine and warmth, but the change of seasons and newness of each spring is in my blood. From my short experience with Iowa, I think it is a wonderful state with wonderful people."

VF: It was rumored that you, Anthony, wanted to surprise your wife with your honeymoon destination. Is that true?

Smiling with a smirking grin, he answered, "Yes, I tried diligently to surprise Claire for our honeymoon. And I almost succeeded." VF had to ask, "Almost?"

Anthony looked at his wife, she continued the story. "He would have succeeded had it not been for the TSA agent in Hawaii." Mrs. Rawlings was obviously amused by the story. "I wasn't the least bit upset. I'd sought to learn the destination for some time. No one would betray his confidence, no matter how much I tried. So after arriving in Oahu, Hawaii, all I knew was that we had farther to fly and we were crossing the International Date Line."

Anthony chimed in, "Actually, she figured that out from a hint," and he winked at Claire.

She continued, "So when the agent looked at our passports and asked our destination, I wasn't able to answer." Smiling, she added, "But Anthony had to. And it was then I learned that we were going to Fiji." (Photo released by the Rawlings of the two of them dining on a torch-lit deck with a magnificent sunset and the ocean in front of them.)

VF: Mrs. Rawlings, were you pleased with your husband's destination choice? Some women would want to be more involved in the planning.

"That may be true, but my husband planned ten days in paradise. It was amazing. I've never experienced anything like it. It was a tropical oasis. I know we have pictures for your publication, but honestly photos can't do it justice. The climate, atmosphere, cuisine, beach," and leaning close to Anthony, smiling into his big brown eyes, "his company, all made it a dream. I'm not sure heaven can compare."

VF: So you did not mind not being involved in the planning?

"If all his decisions are as amazing as our honeymoon, I do not mind at all." He kissed her cheek.

I've learned that people will forget what you said, people will forget what you did, but people will never forget how you made them feel.

Anthony added, "I have had many years of living on my own, making my own decisions, and doing everything for my benefit. I have learned that people remember most how you make them feel. I try to work my business with that in mind. When I negotiate with someone, they will forget what I say or what I do, but they will not forget how I make them feel. Do they feel important to the deal? Do they feel central to the transaction? I wanted our honeymoon to be special because it would benefit me." His smile looked mischievous to this reporter. "However, I wanted it to be special so that Claire would feel special and know how important she is to me." He no doubt had her full attention during his statement, and this reporter would guess during their stay in paradise. Mr. Rawlings seems to have the gift of making everyone feel special. Claire agreed he has made her feel special since they first met.

VF: *Vanity Fair* would like to thank you for taking the time to allow us into your home. Now is it true you have other homes besides this one?

Anthony answered, "Due to my multiple business sites and intensive travel schedule we do own a few apartments here and there. It makes traveling much easier." (Insert text box of real estate holdings of Mr. and Mrs. Anthony Rawlings.)

VF: Mr. Rawlings, your answer about "we" owning brings VF to another more controversial subject. May I ask about the debate regarding the lack of a prenuptial agreement prior to your marriage?

"I would prefer you didn't. However, the only way to stop the rumors is to address them. First let me say there was no debate. We did not consider a prenuptial agreement, much less debate one." Taking his wife's hand in his, he continued, "I'm elated to have the world get to know my wife. Mrs. Claire Rawlings is an amazing woman. She did not know who I was when we met. She has told me exactly what she thinks of me or of my actions and not always in a complimentary manner. She did not anticipate a marriage proposal on that *cold*," he smiled at Claire, "night in Central Park. I trust her implicitly. I have worked my entire life to build a business empire. It means nothing without someone with whom to share. I did not feel it was fair to ask her to sign a piece of paper that would restrict her partnership with me in any way. She is my wife and I am her husband. It may not be PC to say this today, but we believe in forever, in trust, and in love. A piece of paper is not going to matter when we are old and gray. We decided together that our commitment to one another is stronger than any legal agreement." Mrs. Rawlings squeezed his hand. "Like it is said in a movie, *she completes me*."

VF: Thank you again for the brief glimpse into your life. Below is a quote that was recited during your wedding ceremony. To our readers, it was meant as a dual statement to both of them, from each of them.

I love you not only for what you are, but for what I am when I am with you. I love you not only for what you have made of yourself, but for what you are making of me. I love you for the part of me that you bring out. —Roy Croft

(Photo collage at the end includes photos of home: grand hall, sitting room, library, office, dining room, recreation room, exercise room, theater room, and indoor pool. Also included are wedding photos: of ceremony, reception, with cake, talking with guests, and dancing. There are a few of Fiji, the private island where the couple stayed, the beach, infinity pool, lounging decks, and outdoor shower.)

Claire read the copy and imagined the photos which would be inserted. It truly *appeared* perfect.

Three days later, on the eighteenth of March, Tony surprised Claire with a long weekend getaway to Lake Tahoe. The beautiful snowy mountains filled with skiing, roaring fires, and hot coffee made for a great escape. The ski resort, literally a mile above sea level, had crystal-clear air that permeated deep into their lungs. The mountains provided the most amazing skiing with over a hundred inches of base and freshly fallen powder. The tall majestic evergreens bowed to the weight of the snow which layered each branch. Their small, private chalet held amazing views, warm fires, and no cook. For the first time in a year, despite limited supplies, Claire managed to keep them from starving. With the intensity of their exercise, both indoors and out, she was pleased he liked her cooking. A while ago she'd heard some advice. *Eating is important to keep up their strength.*

Warm, naked, and covered with a soft blanket, she rested her head against his chest. Claire contemplated the significance of *this* weekend as they rested in the afterglow of their love and the glow of fireplace. Three hundred and sixty-six days ago she'd been a different person in a different life. It wasn't that her life now was bad. It was just that the transition had been unplanned, unwanted, and well, brutal. She needed to hear her husband's answer to the question which lingered in her mind. "Tony, why are we here *this* weekend?"

They both watched the crackling blaze as his strong arms encircled her petite body. He took a deep breath and replied, "I didn't want you home in your suite this weekend. I wanted you outside in fresh air." He felt her chest lift, then drop, and heard the soft sniffles. Damn, the crying was what he'd been trying to avoid. Nuzzling his face in her hair, he kissed her head. "If it hadn't happened, we wouldn't be here now. There is a reason for everything."

He tenderly turned her to face him and then rolled her over onto her back. Her blonde hair fanned out onto the rug like a halo. He looked down at her angelic face. Even with the moisture, her eyes were stunning. The tears only made the green more intense in the firelight. Tony couldn't help himself, she was beautiful, sensual, and he wanted her. His bare chest pushed against her supple breasts. He tenderly caressed her pink cheeks and soft shoulders as he looked into her eyes. "I'm not sorry we are together, but I'm so sorry when I think about . . . remember the things I—"

Claire stopped him. Shaking her head *no*, she put her hand to his lips. He stopped talking and kissed her hand, gently sucking the tip of each finger. "Please, Tony. Don't. I don't want to remember or think about that." Her voice sounded amazingly steady despite the tears which now streamed from the corners of her eyes. "I want to think about now."

"But you should know—"

"All I know is that I love you today. I hated you then. It is too much of a contrast for my mind to comprehend. I want to concentrate on today."

"I love you today, too. Tell me what I can do to help. Claire, anything you want, it is yours."

He couldn't take away her memories. That was what she wanted more than anything. "I want you. I want you to love me and fill me with so many good memories that I don't have room for the others." She kissed her husband. "Tony, fill me completely."

Claire wasn't thinking. Her body was in control; more accurately, out of control, moving in sync with desire. She didn't think, because she feared if she did, it would be about the past and not the present. Instead, she surrendered her body and her mind to her husband. There was a time she'd tried to keep her mind, but no longer. He possessed both.

His lips found her soft skin and watched as her eyes responded. He wanted to see the spark, to have it be there. Briefly, he thought about the saying *the end justifies the means*. If that were true, then he wasn't sorry. In his arms, beneath his body, responding to his touch was the woman he'd watched for so long. He suckled her hard nipples, and she moaned deeply, wanting—no, needing *him*. At that moment in time, sorry was not his most prominent thought.

ALEATHA ROMIG

Nothing improves memory more than trying to forget.
—Unknown author

Chapter 38

I t was happening again. The satin sheets dripped with sweat as Claire gasped for breath. Trembling, she concentrated on inhaling and exhaling, convincing herself that she *could* breathe. This was only a dream or a nightmare. Once over, she never remembered the scenes, just the terrible feeling of helplessness. It always ended when she heard the beep and woke. It was the same damn beep she'd heard when she first arrived. It meant her suite was locked. When the dreams first started, she could roll over, find her sleeping husband, curl up next to him, and fall back to sleep. Now regulating her breathing, she knew that wasn't possible. Like so many times before, she needed to get out of bed and complete her new routine.

The steady breathing from a few feet away told Claire Tony was sleeping peacefully. Quietly, she lifted the covers and eased out of bed. Her hands shook as she tied her robe and tiptoed to the hallway door. "This is dumb," she whispered, as her feet crossed the lush carpet. However, it was now her reality. She knew sleep wouldn't be possible without completing this new drill. Gripping the metal lever, she pulled, and the door easily opened. She closed it and proceeded to the balcony. Moving the draperies aside, the French door opened without hesitation. The rush of fresh air filled the room and her lungs. She walked through the opening, gently closing the door behind her.

Her perspiration-drenched body relished the cool night breeze. Standing at the rail, she inhaled the spring air and lifted her hair to dry the moisture from her neck. It wasn't that she wanted to remember the feelings of a year ago. Truly she didn't. When she stepped onto a patio, terrace, or into the backyard and memories would start to resurface, she could stop them. It was at night while she slept that the compartmentalization of her internment would come rushing back. Then in the minutes or hours which followed, she would attempt to calm her lingering fear. It was the one she tried to keep away, the terror that at any moment, without warning, history could repeat

273

itself. The sickening realization that she would be completely helpless to stop it was what robbed her of sleep.

The cool cement under her feet brought her back to present. She shivered, pulled her cashmere robe tight, and wished she'd grabbed slippers. But her trembling wasn't caused by the cold. She knew it was her dream. Looking up she noticed the clear black velvet sky peppered with stars. Absentmindedly, she thought, *that's why the temperature dropped.*

Sighing, she fell into a chair. This knowledge would never matter again. Her job was her name, Mrs. Anthony Rawlings -- Meteorology was gone— forever. She'd left the suite in such a panic she hadn't looked at the clock. It really didn't matter, sleep was out of reach. Pulling her legs into her chest and covering them with her soft robe, she began her mental therapy session. Her still rapid heart rate told her tonight it would last hours instead of minutes.

Self-therapy consisted of a mental list of reasons her nightmares were ridiculous and she had no basis for her fears. Claire believed if she could convince her conscious self, her subconscious self would be forced to agree. When she allowed her mind to go back to the spring of a year ago she could rationalize that now her life was significantly dissimilar. She now had more liberties than she'd experienced since her arrival.

Tony stayed true to his word about her e-mails. He even decided she needed her own address, clarawl1084@rawlingsind.com. This made printing easier. He was also correct about the numerous requests for interviews, money, and endorsements she received daily from people she'd never met. Having Patricia respond to those requests was easy. She also received personal e-mails. And now she had a voice in the responses. Overall, when asked, Tony agreed to requests regarding Courtney, Sue, Bev, or MaryAnn. If he had other plans for the day in question, as occurred from time to time, his plans trumped. But the act of requesting was the crucial portion of her negotiations. If she wanted to reply to someone or to go somewhere, as he had said many months ago, she simply needed to ask. She'd become accustomed to this component. It was a daily reminder of Tony's authority.

Regarding that authority, it did not assert itself as it had a year ago. She reasoned perhaps it was because her behavior didn't warrant that type of implementation. No matter the cause, life was undeniably better.

Watching the moonlight on the budding trees, Claire reminded herself of the outings she'd recently enjoyed. They'd included lunches in Iowa City, Red Cross meetings in Davenport, and shopping in Chicago. A few weeks ago MaryAnn suggested a catch-up day in New York as she and Eli were there for business. Tony reviewed all of the e-mails before Claire, and she didn't expect permission to spend the day in New York, but she asked. Surprisingly, he acquiesced. Smiling and feeling her pulse slow, she remembered flying off to a beautiful April day in NYC in a Rawlings company jet with Courtney and Sue. All of the women had a marvelous time, and Claire made it home before seven. He was home first, but she was home for dinner. He wasn't unhappy.

Calming, as the gentle breeze blew her hair she listened to the voice in her head and remembered a recent unexpected freedom. Secretly coveting the chestnut hair which kept trying to return, she informed Tony she needed an appointment to maintain her blonde. He said they had no overnight plans in the near future, so she should just go. If he had the private plane she could take one of the company jets, just plan to be home before dinner. Shocked, she remembered questioning, "Are you saying I can go by myself?"

"My dear Claire, is there any reason you should not?"

She assured him there was not. He or Patricia arranged the appointment, and Claire went to the airport and boarded a company jet by herself. She landed in Chicago, took a waiting cab to the Trump Tower where she spent the rest of the morning being pampered. Then she ate lunch and shopped for a few hours and came home. Blushing in the cool night air she thought about being back in her suite before six and how she did her best to show her husband the meaning of a statement she'd made months earlier: *coming home to a wife who wants to be home is better than coming home to a wife that has to be home.* He caught on pretty quick, the first indication was the spark in her emerald eyes and the next clue involved a black satin robe and a warm waiting tub of water. Truth be told, she couldn't remember eating dinner at all that night.

Claire's eyelids reminded her she should be sleeping. Slipping back into her suite and under the warm blankets, she thought about the man lying next to her. He continued to be a paradox. The man Claire met when she first arrived hadn't shown his personality since her *accident*. She knew he was still here, that knowledge alone was motivation to obey his rules. She'd been told too many times his promise to keep that personality away was contingent on her ability to behave appropriately. The stress of that reality and unpredictability loomed omnipresent.

The man who worked to court her, to convince her she was important, desirable, and loved, still existed in a muted form. He was still attentive, present, and always sexual, but he was busy with work and often preoccupied. That was understandable. He was a successful man with many fires to tend.

It was his need for complete supremacy over *every* aspect of her life that felt stifling and unbearable. Claire theorized this was the cause of the suffocation which usually accompanied her nightmares. He had companies, peoples' jobs and livelihoods on his list of responsibilities. The fact he controlled her comings, goings, e-mails, hair, and often attire seemed ridiculous.

Attempting to stop the rise in blood pressure, she reminded herself that no matter what, she loved him. He could infuriate her one moment and make her feel less than human. And the next, he could make her feel like the world spun only because she mattered to him. It was just that those two contradictory emotions could come too close together and in any order. As Claire reminisced, she recognized that similar to a year ago, her mood, liberties, and sense of self-worth seemed to have a common denominator -- Anthony Rawlings.

As that realization struck, he rolled toward her, wrapped her in his arms; and though still sleeping, murmured, "My love, you're so cold. Come closer." She melted against his warm chest. At this moment in time, he made her feel safe and loved. She closed her eyes and fell asleep.

As the spring blossomed into summer, their biggest source of dissension continued to be her family. Though she loved to hear from Emily, seeing her name on an e-mail made her stomach turn. It almost always came accompanied by dark penetrating eyes.

She would sometimes choose to have Patricia reply instead of herself. There were days and circumstances when the communication wasn't worth the conflict. It depended on Emily's words, some motivated Claire's determination more than others. Her calls with Emily were always monitored. It was a reality she didn't dispute. If she did, it would result in loss of all communication. He didn't need to spell that out for her. She knew it as well as she knew that her *freedoms* lay vulnerable to his whims.

Since the call following the interview, Claire spoke with Emily about every three to four weeks. She heard from Emily at least once a week via e-mail. After Claire had her own e-mail address, Emily's notes were more informative. Claire would hand-write her response. It was approved or edited and then sent by Patricia. If Emily questioned Claire's *ability* to do anything, she would profess her freedoms as Tony evaluated every word.

That same Tony was the one who surprised Claire with the long weekend at Lake Tahoe. And over Memorial Day weekend he arranged for a getaway to San Francisco. While there, they met Eli and MaryAnn for dinner at an exclusive nightclub with a glorious view of the bay and bridge. The next day, after a romantic drive down Highway One in a leased convertible, they strolled hand in hand on the beach at Big Sur. The force and spray of the waves pounding the huge rocks along the ocean shore astonished Claire. It wasn't like the Gulf of Mexico or even the tranquil waters of Fiji. Instead, it reminded her of the beach scenes in movies. During these excursions, he made her feel like a star. Their final day in San Francisco they went sightseeing; no trip to Alcatraz was planned or even discussed.

He also had a two-week business trip to Europe planned for the end of July. This time he wanted her with him. Uncharacteristically, he asked her to help make the sightseeing plans. They would visit Italy, Switzerland, and France. He had meetings but promised free time for his wife. Claire spent hours in their library looking at books on destinations, museums, and points of interest. The Internet would have been easier but she found incredible pictures and information in the resource books.

The work with the Red Cross slowed. Their calendar was planned and their goal set. It was now a matter of implementation. Courtney had other members on her committee. They divided the events: Claire was chairman of a silent auction scheduled for October. She drafted letters requesting donations, and Patricia sent them out to prominent associates of Mr. Rawlings. The letters requested donations from *Mrs. Anthony Rawlings*. Tony had already brought many positive responses home. Claire secured a ballroom in Bettendorf where the auction would be held simultaneously with a wine-tasting event. She even arranged for the wine and catering to be donated, believing a little wine might help increase bids. Courtney seemed genuinely pleased and appreciative of Claire's help.

The summer heat created the climate Claire enjoyed the most. She contentedly spent many of her days at home by the pool or at her lake. When summer began Tony hesitated to approve her journeys to the lake. He'd been there. He knew how far it was from the house. What if a real accident occurred? At first, she relented to his decision, but then she decided it *was* worth the struggle. Her lake had been her refuge. She wanted it back.

Determinedly, one Sunday in early June, Claire pursued the liberty to hike. Tony finally acquiesced, saying he wanted to be mad but it was the memory of her excitement during their February visit that made him relent. She asked him to join her. He had other plans for their day, but agreed. They brought a blanket, a picnic packed by Catherine, and water. When they reached the shore Tony seemed to understand why she loved the site. It was nothing like it had been in February. The colors of the summer starkly contrasted the whiteness of their last visit. The lake sparkled and glittered with hues of blue created by the reflection of the sapphire sky. The trees surrounding the lake were lush, full, and green.

The ones in the woods had been also, creating a maze Tony hoped Claire could truly navigate. He listened to the sounds of the lake shore. In forty-six years he'd never stopped to listen to waves lap the earth. The consistent beat, swoosh, swoosh, swoosh, combined with the gentle breeze of the trees soothed him in a way he couldn't describe. He laid out the blanket on the shore under the shade of a tree and invited Claire to join him. She unpacked their lunch and they sat in silence.

At first, Claire worried -- afraid he might be upset by her impudence. Then she stopped worrying and looked at him, really looked at his face; he was peaceful. She thought about who she saw: Anthony Rawlings, multibillionaire tycoon and entrepreneur, a man in complete control of everyone and everything. Claire hoped perhaps she was witnessing this lofty man seeing himself as part of a grand picture. Maybe for the first time he wasn't seeing himself as the center. Not wanting to break the spell, she let him sit undisturbed.

Sometime later (Claire had lost track of time) Tony finally spoke, "This is beautiful. This is here on our property and I've never seen it, not like this." The sun sparkled and shone as prisms of light and color danced off the water. Having taken the sandwiches out of the basket, Claire broke off a piece of bread and threw it into the water. Tony laughed as minnows swam to devour their newfound feast. She smiled at her husband. Her smile radiated into her eyes, she could feel it. His milk chocolate eyes looked from the water to her. He leaned toward her. "Thank you."

"For what?"

"For showing me what I have been missing. I've been so goal oriented, so driven, I've missed so much." She scooted closer and offered him his sandwich. "I'm really not hungry yet, are you?" His hands were exploring her collar bone, causing goose bumps to rise on her arms.

"I think I can wait."

The soft blanket, soft sand, and gentle breeze created the perfect bed. Their actions weren't hard and rough, but tender and thorough. Keeping rhythm with the waves Tony took Claire beyond her refuge to a place of ecstasy.

The hours of daylight almost reached their peak. The summer solstice was near. Between exploring the lake, shore, wildlife, and one another, they found themselves still on the shore as the sun began to set. It was all right. Claire knew this time there would be no punishment or *accident*. This time she was safe. They sat and watched the crimson ball as it bled a cherry glow across the sky, slowly fading behind the line of shadowed trees at the far end of the lake.

There is only one way to happiness and that is to cease worrying
about things which are beyond the power of our will.
—Epictetus

Chapter 39

Claire's education regarding the responsibilities of Mrs. Anthony Rawlings continued during the summer months. She now had the responsibility of entertaining Tony's business associates. As a bachelor, these gatherings weren't expected. However, now with a wife by his side, Shelly felt this personal touch benefited Mr. Rawlings. "They" hosted multiple dinner engagements. On the Fourth of July, they held a large barbeque/pool party for many of Tony's associates at the estate in Iowa. Guests included those she'd met briefly at her wedding and those that she'd never met. Tony introduced her to everyone, and she remembered names and faces remarkably well. Her job description remained the same as fourteen months earlier: be perfect. To accomplish her goal, she needed to be beautiful, polite, contented, and appreciative. Now there was another requirement: be a most gracious hostess. Surprisingly, Claire didn't find these new duties difficult. For most people to pull off a dinner, barbeque, or pool party would require planning, cleaning, cooking, setting up, and tearing down. For Mrs. Rawlings, that wasn't the case. Everything happened without her input. Invitations went out, RSVPs counted, meals planned, house or apartment cleaned, food prepared, tables and decorations set, the food served, and miraculously everything cleaned by the next day. She needed only to be present, ever attentive to her guests, and most importantly, attentive to her husband.

The first entertaining experience occurred at their New York apartment. *They* hosted an intimate dinner party for ten. It was true, Claire's nerves were shaken prior to the hors d'oeuvres. Perhaps it was Tony's pep talk about appearances, responsibility as his wife, and the unacceptability of public failure. However, wearing the clothes he chose, hair styled as he suggested, and appearing as dutiful as she could muster, the evening progressed surprisingly well. Her talent for remembering names, faces, facts, and the intuition to know when not to interrupt *business* talk, yet understand when to augment small talk, succeeded in making everyone feel comfortable. After the guests left, Tony gently wrapped his arm around her waist and whispered in her ear, "You were magnificent."

It made all the difference. From that point on, when she learned of an impending gathering, she had but one solitary goal—to please her husband. On some occasions they would be at opposite sides of a room and she would look up from a conversation to observe his eyes. The presence of brown rimmed pupils would strengthen her resolve to perform her role to perfection. On those occasions she would discover the black voids, she would excuse herself from her current activity and attempt to learn the source of his unhappiness. Once discovered, it became her responsibility to right the wrong. Assuming this responsibility of Mrs. Anthony Rawlings, familiarized her with many of his associates and made her feel less alone. She met the people Tony dealt with on a daily basis. In reality she may have been a beautiful accessory, but she believed she provided an important asset to his public relations. The added bonus was that she continued to amaze Tony by excelling at any obstacle put before her.

A week before they needed to be in France for Tony's meetings, he informed Claire they would spend a few nights in New York City before their trip. He could work from the NYC office and it would decrease their travel time to Paris. Claire's research discovered many sights she anxiously anticipated seeing in France. They would arrive in Paris where he had two days of meetings. She wanted to see the Eiffel Tower, the Louvre, Muse'e d'Orsay, Notre Dame Cathedral, and the Arc de Triomple among other places. She told Tony multiple times how excited she was being involved in planning their activities. Next, he promised her two nights in the south of France, one of his favorite destinations. He had special plans for this destination. She read about Cannes, the French Riviera, and Monaco, but willingly trusted his decisions.

Next, they would be off to Italy. His meetings there were in Rome and Florence. They would have the opportunity to visit museums and monuments in both cities. Her two requests were the Vatican and the Galleria dell' Accademia, the museum which housed Michelangelo's David. Tony promised that David didn't have anything she hadn't seen before.

He wanted her to see the island of Sicily. The water, he said, was beautiful. The blueness rivaled Fiji. He mischievously smiled and let her know how nude sunbathing was acceptable in the Mediterranean.

"I don't think I like the idea of nude sunbathing among multitudes of people."

With a naughty smirk Tony agreed. "I believe you're right my dear." He slowly unbuttoned her blouse. "Besides, I don't believe I want others seeing what is mine, and I have the pleasure of seeing whenever I chose."

His last meetings were in Switzerland. He needed to be in Genève and Interlaken. He explained if she enjoyed the beauty and splendor of the Rocky Mountains at Lake Tahoe, she would marvel at the Swiss Alps. They were magnificent. He knew she would love all the nature had to offer in Switzerland.

As Tony spoke about their trip he expressed his desire to spend more time in Europe. "I want to show you so many places. We aren't even planning for Venice. A gondola ride is one of the most romantic adventures. And what about London, don't you want to see Buckingham Palace?"

"We have forever to visit those places."

As he spoke about cities and sites, his eyes danced with enthusiasm. His excitement to share something with her meant more than the trip itself.

The Tuesday before their scheduled departure they sat in her suite with Claire reviewing e-mails and Tony working on his laptop. She only needed to discuss e-mails she felt deserved personal follow through of any kind. She read each one and eventually came to one from Emily. She'd expected to see it. The last one had been about a week ago. This one contained new information. It wasn't just the "I want to see you" text.

> To: Claire Rawlings clarawll084@rawlingsind.com
> From: Emily Vandersol johnemvan@aol.com
> Date: July 19, 2011
> Re: Hi.
> Hi, Claire, How are you and Anthony? We are doing very well. I'm on summer break, which you know. Would be great to see my little sis, but anyway, know how busy you are. How have those dinner parties been going? Still cracks me up. You being the one hosting parties! Would never have guessed it. Anyway, didn't you say you two were going on vacation? I heard something on the television about you being on another private island. Really? Have you been gone? I never know what to believe. But I wanted to let you know John and his associate just had a big win in court recently. They made a huge impression on the partners. Not to mention some big money for them, too. We've been invited to multiple dinners and John has had some "lunches" with a few of the partners recently. It is looking like all his hours and hard work will be paying off soon. Would love to hear from you. Please give Anthony our love. How is Iowa? I have some time, maybe you and I could visit in person? Or are you too busy for your big sister. (I'm trying guilt.)
> Love ya, Em

Claire read it, sighed, and wrote on the top: "Patricia, please respond," then moved on to the next. She sensed Tony's eyes penetrating her consciousness. He'd read it. She didn't need to discuss the contents, she wasn't requesting anything. Lifting her gaze she saw his eyes and answered, "I don't want to deal with it, okay? I'm too excited about our trip."

He shrugged his shoulders. "Well, that's fine. I just thought you might want to see her and John while we're in New York before our trip. It sounds to me like a celebratory dinner for your esteemed brother-in-law is in order."

Claire looked at Tony in disbelief. "Are you suggesting we meet them this weekend before we leave for Europe?" She watched for his reaction.

There was none. He continued reading on his laptop and making notes on his iPad. "Please don't tease me."

His smile appeared genuine. "I'm not teasing. If it will make you happy as we head out on our European adventure, I can suffer through a few hours of *Mr. Wonderful.*"

She got up from the table and went to him on the sofa. "Really? Can I please call her and see if they're available?"

"Yes," his hand touched the hem of her light pink sundress, "however, I can think of something I'd like to do first."

Claire reached for his laptop and set in on the floor. Climbing on his lap she giggled, "Really? I can't think of anything..." Her world tilted as he pushed her onto the sofa and followed on top of her. The rest of her sentence would wait. Dinner and the phone call would need to wait.

They arrived in New York on Thursday night and planned to leave Sunday for Paris. Tony thought Claire might need to shop before their trip, but she assured him she'd done enough research to learn she could do plenty of shopping in Paris, Italy, and Switzerland.

Tony laughed. "That even scares me, Mrs. Rawlings. I believe you're getting too good at this shopping thing."

They arranged to meet John and Emily Saturday afternoon at a restaurant in Newburgh, a scenic little city on the Hudson River, midway between NYC and Troy. Tony said their apartment could lend itself to a longer visit than he wanted. Claire knew this was difficult for him and appreciated his honesty. Besides, she liked the idea of a public setting. Tony would never do or say anything in a public place to jeopardize his image. She knew no matter how the dinner progressed, she would reap the consequences, negative or positive. However, seeing Emily and John for the first time since their wedding was worth Tony's chosen aftermath. She could endure the night. Tomorrow they were leaving for Europe.

When they stepped outside their NYC apartment, the air between the tall buildings hung heavy and moist intensifying the July heat. Automobile exhaust filled their lungs as the motionless air refused to transport the odors away. The summer sun penetrated the dark lenses of her sunglasses, causing Claire to squint after exiting the dim cool lobby. She used to like the city, but now she thought pensively about the tranquility of the Iowa countryside.

During the hour and a half drive, Tony worked on his latest project while Claire appreciated the tinted windows and air conditioning of the limousine and tried to read. She packed many books for their trip. Between flights, drives, and waiting for Tony, she anticipated significant amounts of downtime. The words on the page didn't make sense. She read and reread, but her thoughts were miles ahead at the restaurant. It had been seven months since they had been together. She wanted it to go well. However, she overwhelmingly feared it would not.

Trying desperately to ignore the onset of another headache, she anticipated problems. What if John said something? What about the job topic? What if Emily pursued her earlier concerns? Her mind raced through

282

these situations and more. She contemplated possible solutions. It didn't always work, but having contingency plans made Claire feel better.

They were an hour out of Newburgh when Tony broke the silence. "Claire, please stop."

Shocked she turned to him, "Stop what? I'm reading."

"No, you're not. You are sighing, fidgeting, and stressing about things over which you have no control."

"I'm sorry. I just want this afternoon to go well."

"Are you planning to do or say something wrong?"

"Of course not."

"Let me tell you about this current project."

She really wasn't interested, but he rarely offered to share. She closed her book. "All right."

"These are perspectives on a company. Actually, a family owned business in Pennsylvania. At one time it employed over seventy-five people. Today it employs forty-six. I don't care about this company or the employees, but I am significantly invested in their major competitor."

Clare definitely didn't see the connection to their lunch, but she nodded and replied, "Okay."

"When founded, the original president made wonderful decisions. In the past five years, the reins passed, and the decisions have been less fortuitous. The chairman is now seeking to sell the company, recognizing the economic climate. They need money to continue; banks aren't lending money. If he doesn't sell, the doors will probably close in the next two years." Still lost, she maintained eye contact and nodded. He went on. "I'm considering a very low-ball offer. The benefit to me is to reduce the competition. If my offer is accepted, the doors will close immediately. According to my accountants, the company in which I'm already invested is projected to increase sales by over 18 percent immediately upon the close of this company. This means I reap benefits. They project my venture in this company will be recouped in profits in less than two years. The long-term benefits are increasingly fiscally rewarding. What do you think the employees of the Pennsylvania Company are hoping will happen?"

"They either want their company to go on as it is, or to be sold to someone who'll keep it running."

Tony said, "Good, why?"

"So they will keep their jobs."

"The people on the manufacturing floor, custodians, secretaries, and other auxiliary employees played no part in the decisions which will now have direct consequences on their lives."

"Yes, but they have families, debts, and responsibilities." Claire thought about Tony's daily decisions and their far-reaching impact. "And I'm sure they're all worried."

"Exactly, just as you're worried about this afternoon. What can the people in that plant do to help their situation?"

Claire thought about it. "Nothing. I isn't in their hands." The reality made her sad. Not for her -- her situation suddenly seemed trivial, but for those forty-six people.

"Correct again. You have done all you can do." He was now talking about this afternoon. "You have done much more than I ever imagined. Continue to behave as you have. If Emily or John do or say anything, it's their doing, not yours."

She thought about John's words in the past and how she'd experienced consequences, just like those people were about to receive. Tony started to read again, but Claire had questions, "Tony?" He looked at her and raised his eyebrows. "Sorry, but I have some questions."

"Go ahead."

"So are you saying the actions of the people who do not have control, have no consequence?"

He closed the screen of his laptop. "Are we talking about Pennsylvania or here?"

"Let's start with Pennsylvania."

"No. Their actions may have great impact. A lot depends on the goal of the person who has control. Let's say someone else with capital decides they're interested in this company. More than likely, they will either personally visit, or as I did, send an envoy to investigate the company. If those employees are hardworking, loyal -- *and* if this investor is interested in keeping the doors open, their actions will be an important piece of the equation when decisions are made. Their attitude could actually determine if their company will remain open. On the contrary, if the employees are dissatisfied and disgruntled, investors interested in maintaining the company will shy away." Momentarily lost in thought, Tony continued. "One of the issues which affect these situations is the knowledge of the employees, or the people seemingly out of control. It is interesting how many people live their lives completely unaware of decisions unfolding around them." Claire listened as Tony went on and worried about these forty-six people and their families. "Now if they are aware and proactive, they may try to recruit investment on their own. I have controlling interest in a few such companies, funded by Rawlings Industries yet run and invested in by the employees. They now benefit from not only paychecks, but also dividends. It creates a wonderful incentive for hard work and dedication."

Thinking out loud, Claire said, "So if I decided I was tired of shopping for clothes and wanted to shop for companies, I could go to Pennsylvania, offer them a little more than your low-ball bid, and keep the company going, assuming the employees are hardworking, loyal, and want to keep the doors open." She smiled as she spoke.

Smiling in return, he said, "Well, yes, Mrs. Rawlings, I know you have the capital. However, if you use my bid as a baseline, you'll end up arrested for insider trading. You cannot make an offer based on the offer of a competitor, unless it has been made public. Mine has not."

With nothing more than concern in her voice, she asked, "How can you make a deal without considering the people and lives it affects?"

"It is called business. It is how we have what we have and will have much more." He wasn't gloating or harsh, just stating facts. "Closing that business is my concern, the people are not. If my bid is accepted, their presence is no longer needed."

"So there are times when innocent people reap the consequences of others due to no fault of their own." Claire spoke from experience yet now seeing the principle from a different perspective.

"Yes. It happens all the time."

"All right, tell me about our situation. You were comparing the two. You were saying my actions have no effect on the outcome of this afternoon so not to worry about it?"

"No. I said not to worry about it. Your actions have already had a great effect on this afternoon."

Claire saw his eyes, brown and genuine. She wanted more information. "Please, Mr. Rawlings, tell me what I have done to affect this afternoon."

He sighed. "Claire, why are we going to Newburgh?"

"To see Emily and John."

"That isn't the entire answer." He waited.

"We are going because of me?"

"Of course, do you on *any* level believe this is my first choice of a Saturday afternoon activity?"

She knew it was not. "But it was your suggestion. We wouldn't be going if you hadn't allowed it."

"You're right. But we are going because *you* want to. We are going because you have patiently accepted every challenge, every test, and every ordeal which has come your way. And for the record, not all have been my doing, merely a byproduct of being Mrs. Rawlings. Apparently, it can be a difficult role." She knew that too and smiled. He continued, "You have not just accepted, you have conquered."

She didn't know what to say. He complimented her regularly but she was never certain of his sincerity. He reached out, squeezed her hand, and continued, "You have exceeded any and every preconceived idea I have ever had about you. The one limitation I've placed on you that I recognize has caused you anguish is your sister. Truly I have no ill feelings toward Emily. She can be excessively inquisitive, but you two share a bond." He watched her eyes. "I told you months ago I would try to be a better husband. I have spent most of my life only concerned with myself. I'm truly trying even if it does not always appear so."

She prayed her smile radiated into her eyes, but she could feel the moisture, too. "Tony, I love you. I know you are trying. I'm contented with the strides you've made. That doesn't mean I don't hope for more. That may make me ungrateful, but I do. I think you're amazing. That is why I want you, Emily, John, and me to be a family. I want them to know the remarkable man I married." She kissed him and he kissed her, too.

She still wasn't confident in the outcome of their family reunion, but her expectations improved, as did the feeling in her head; the ache subsided. When they arrived, Emily and John were already seated at a private table with a wonderful view of the Hudson River. They greeted one another with hugs and handshakes. Tony watched as Claire's eyes sparkled when she talked with her family.

Tony was civil, refined, and mannerly. To the unknowing observer he may have even seemed cordial and friendly. Claire was glad John and Emily qualified as unknowing. He was a master at appearances and was even the first to extend his hand and congratulate John on his accomplishments. "We are still sorry you didn't decide to join us at Rawlings Industries. I believe that despite what your sister-in-law said, you would have been a real asset."

Claire smiled and shook her head at John. "I didn't say a word. I was as shocked as you when I learned of the offer. Tony and Tom did their homework. But we definitely respect your decision and are thrilled with your success."

John respectfully thanked them both. The job offer was a huge compliment and he was honored. He also accepted their congratulations on the result of his trial, but as far as partnership, nothing was currently set. He added with a grin, "The jury is still out."

Tony's comment pleased Claire. It cleared the air, allowing her to breathe easier. The four of them had a nice dinner. Claire told her sister and brother-in-law about their upcoming trip to Europe.

Emily said she spent a long weekend in Fishers, Indiana, visiting some old friends. She named a few and told Claire how they all sent her their best. The mention of her past life darkened Tony's eyes a few shades. Claire didn't pursue the subject, only smiled and nodded acceptably. Emily also commented on Claire's hair, did she like it so blonde? Of course, it looked beautiful. Emily actually said that she looked *stunning,* but so different. Some of their old friends asked if it was really her in the pictures; the name was right, she just didn't look the same. Claire wondered if that meant she wasn't stunning before.

Claire asked how they liked the wedding pictures she sent. They both said they liked them very much. Emily even said she bought some new dresses to wear with her wedding shoes. She's never owned shoes like those and planned to get Anthony's money's worth out of them.

Tony smiled at Claire and commented, "What a great idea. Maybe Claire could decide to wear some of her shoes more than one time." They all laughed. The mood was jovial. The dinner tasted delicious and catching up was fun.

In the car on their way back to Manhattan Claire told Tony, "Thank you, but I'm glad that's done. It's too much stress for me. Besides, I'm too excited about our trip!"

His eyes lightened again.

If that night needed to qualify as a type of consequence, Claire would call it positive. The next day, they flew east across the Atlantic.

*Believe that life is worth living and your belief
will help create the fact.*
—William James

Chapter 40

In Paris, Tony booked their suite—more like an apartment—in the Second Arrondissement located in the heart of Paris. Many of the major attractions Claire wanted to visit were within walking distance. Tony gave her complete freedom to roam the city while he was in his meetings. At first, she worried about the language barrier; after all, he spoke French like a native. However, unlike the rumors she'd heard, as long as she attempted to speak their language, the French were polite and fluent in English.

She did her best to frequent the shops along *Rue de Faubourgs Saint Honoré*, but she found the styles too bold for her liking. After his business was complete, they experienced Paris together. They took romantic walks along the Seine and in the Tuileries Gardens. They also dined on amazing cuisine. The cultural differences fascinated her. Dinner didn't begin until 8:30 p.m., but earlier than that, they could experience *l'apéritif* (from 6:00 to 8:00 p.m.), where cafés and bistros offered their best cocktails or wine by the glass. Tony's understanding of the French was not limited to their language. He was also well versed in their wines. Apparently, the French consider wine to be an adjunct to each meal and snack. It reminded Claire of college.

Paris claimed to be capital of romance, but Claire would suggest the Côte d'Azur or the French Riviera seek to take the title. Located in the southeastern corner of France on the Mediterranean coastline, it boggled her mind to think she was actually there in the *playground for the wealthy*. She didn't realize Tony planned this portion of their trip with no business obligations, no meetings, commitments, or other recipients of his attention. He was totally devoted to her.

The French Riviera was a major yachting and cruising area. Unbeknownst to Claire, they reserved a private one-hundred-foot luxury sailing yacht, complete with their own captain and first mate. It would be their *hotel* for two nights. They boarded *their* yacht in *Beau lier-sur Mer*, a beautiful Mediterranean resort village.

They spent the next seventy-two hours lounging on the sea decks, enjoying the interior cabins, and cruising up the coast toward Italy. Some of the ports they viewed from their deck, others they stopped and explored. Cruising on a private yacht in the Mediterranean was amazing. Claire's favorite port was Monaco. The entire experience seemed surreal. Being the second smallest independent state in the world, the entire city-state was less than one square mile. They were able to walk the hilly streets and enjoy many attractions. There were museums and palaces, as well as shopping. Tony relished Claire's unabashed enthusiasm for Monte Carlo. Claire believed that *Le Musée Oceanographic* or the palace above the sea was one of the most beautiful places she'd ever seen. She didn't want to leave. However, *their* yacht was docked in the scenic harbor and waited to take them north to Italy.

The last port before Italy was Menton. It was nicknamed the *Pearl of France* and was famous for its gardens. Tony's zeal at sharing nature with Claire amused her. His research told him that *Jardin Serre de la Madone*, often known as the *Serre de la Madone* (Hill of the Madonna), was a garden noted for its design and rare plantings. It wasn't difficult for Claire to show the enthusiasm Tony expected.

Next, they flew to Sicily for the weekend. Landing at a small airport in Catania, Sicily, Tony arranged to have a *Maserati Gran Turismo* waiting. Actually, it was the *Gran Cabrio*, the open-air version of a small dynamic sports car. The rag top allowed them to tour the countryside and see everything as it came into view. Driving around Sicily and driving around Iowa proved dramatically different. Claire learned very quickly speed limits exceeded those found in the United States and didn't seem to be strongly enforced. The one-lane winding roads always had someone wanting to pass or needing to be passed. Tony loved the challenge. Riding around the island with him that weekend made Claire feel like she truly put her life in his hands as never before.

The desire to drive never occurred to her the entire weekend.

Their hotel was in Taormina, located on a plateau below *Mount Tauro* on the east side of Sicily, on the coast of the Ionian Sea. Their suite rested high on a cliff with a splendid coastal view from their private glass railed balcony. It was known for its ancient Greek splendor, medieval charm, and unique views of Mount Etna. Tony was right about the water. The shades of blue and green were comparable to the waters in Fiji.

There were beaches nearby which offered the sunbathing Tony mentioned. However, Claire suggested they spend their time seeing other attractions. They spent hours walking the endlessly winding medieval streets and tiny passages. Thankfully, most were inaccessible by car. They discovered garden treasures hidden behind stone walls and terraces overlooking the coast. The Greek Amphitheater built in the third-century BC offered breathtaking views of Mount Etna and the sea. The history and age of the amphitheater had Claire talking about the youth of America.

288

Tony listened to her enthusiasm and watched her energy as she held his hand and walked through miles of history. The sightseeing was new to him. He traveled for business, not pleasure. Claire's presence made all of this new and fun for him too. One of his goals for their trip was making her happy. Another was creating *good* memories.

The evenings in Taormina were enchanting. Together, they strolled the illuminated streets and indulged in delicious cuisine. They watched in awe as lava left a stream of steam and light in its wake as it flowed along the snow covered slopes of Mount Etna.

Hesitantly, granting Tony the pleasure of driving, they drove to Mount Etna, where they hiked. Claire was fascinated to learn ancient Greeks believed the mountain was home to the one-eyed monster known as the Cyclops. Her father loved mythology. He'd read stories of Cyclops to her as a child. It astounded her that she was actually walking around the foothills of a mythological site. With Mount Etna being an active volcano, the height of the summit changed with each eruption. The lava created beautiful solidified structures. These structures were called gorges, and at *Alcantara Gorge*, Claire and Tony walked around and touched the basalt gorges and columns which were formed after thousands of years of rushing waters. They waded in the *Alcantara River* and experienced the coolness of the water coming from the snow topped peaks.

On Sunday night they flew to Florence where Tony had more meetings. Not reading any of her books, Claire kept busy with museums and sidewalk cafes. While sitting and enjoying a coffee at a sidewalk café, Claire noticed the signs advertising Wi-Fi. She saw people with their laptops and the wall of available computers. This vacation had allowed her more personal freedom than she'd experienced since originally arriving at Tony's. He hadn't mentioned any restrictions. Yet, he had mentioned restrictions to Internet use thousands of times at home. Claire decided she would spend her time in Italy seeing Italy. She could access the Worldwide Web from Iowa and hoped someday that would be an option. Today, she would enjoy Florence.

While wandering the *Galleria dell' Accademia*, the museum housing Michelangelo's David, Claire lost all track of time. The museum was large with a magnitude of amazing exhibits. The art fascinated her. She lingered at the impressionistic paintings. The greatness of the exhibits caused her to forget about everything except the treasures she was seeing and experiencing firsthand.

When she realized the time, an immediate rush of panic nearly knocked her off her feet. It was four thirty and she was supposed to be back at their suite by five. Her minute recollection of Spanish did little to help her navigate the Italian street signs. She'd walked to the museum, stopping at others on the way. The sidewalk cafés and narrow streets all looked the same. Normally she had an uncanny sense of direction, but seeing the minutes tick away on her watch made her lose any navigational skills she'd previously possessed. She practically ran the streets filled with people, trying desperately to find her way back to their hotel. At five thirty she reached the *Relais Santa Croce*. Entering the exquisite lobby, she did her best to regain her composure.

With only twenty-four rooms, the staff excelled at name recognition and attention. The concierge immediately greeted her in broken English, "Good evening, Signora Rawlings, your husband he awaits you in your suite. May I carry your baggage?"

Claire's heart sank. She knew Tony's meetings were nearby. Now her fears were realized. At first, she told the concierge no, thank you. Then she decided perhaps having someone enter the suite with her was a good idea. She handed him the few bags she carried and they proceeded to the Rawlings suite. The concierge assisted her by using her key to unlock their door. The double doors opened to the sitting area, complete with fireplace and windows overlooking the historic center of Florence. Tony wasn't there.

The concierge placed Mrs. Rawlings's bags on the sofa and thanked her. She reached into her purse for a tip when Tony appeared from the bedroom. He smiled gallantly at the concierge, thanked him, and handed him a generous tip from his money clip.

Thanking Signor Rawlings, the concierge bowed and left.

Claire's heart began to pound in her ears as she and Tony stood silently for what seemed like an eternity. She'd used all her resolve maintaining her facade with the concierge. She hadn't witnessed the *other* Tony in quite a while. She worked diligently day and night to keep him away. But now she was late, she broke his punctuality rule, and there was no need to explain. She knew her reasons wouldn't matter. So she stood, tall and resolute. Her eyes weren't full of fury, they brimmed with tears. He just watched and said nothing. The pupils of his eyes were taking over, yet his expression wasn't keeping up. Claire waited.

Tony watched her. He'd been worried. What if something happened to her? He didn't even know where to begin to look. When he heard her arrive his immediate feeling was relief, she was okay. But then he saw her, knew she was safe, and relief faded into displeasure. It wasn't conscious, but he felt it happening, and he didn't want to give in to it. Her expression looked so frightened. Yet she stood so strong and proud.

There was a time he would have enjoyed quelling her resolve; but right now, all he wanted to do was make her feel safe. Finally, without speaking Tony indicated they sit on the sofa. Claire sat and waited. He broke the silence. "Tell me what you saw today and what caused your delay." He didn't yell or strike. The relief led to Claire's sudden loss of control. Tony reached for her and she started to tremble. It happened involuntarily. "Claire, it is all right." His tone comforted her as he pulled her close.

"Tony, I'm so sorry. I was at the *Galleria dell' Accademia*, which was amazing, when I realized the time. I immediately left the museum, but I couldn't understand the signs and the streets all look the same." Her words ran together with small sobs between. "I knew the hotel was within walking distance -- but I suddenly couldn't remember the direction."

At first, he didn't speak; he held her. Then he said, "It's a foreign city, mistakes happen. I was worried something happened to you. I didn't want you to have an accident." His voice was tender, yet his words . . .

290

Their discussion continued to the bedroom. She finally regained her composure. He tried his best to show her she was safe and loved. She showed him her relief at his reaction. Later after they'd soaked in the large marble tub, they dressed for a romantic dinner and walked through the streets of Florence. Although the streets were packed with people, as they walked arm in arm it felt like their private journey. The romantic city, beautiful structures and tepid night breeze combined to enhance the evening.

It wasn't long until they arrived at their next destination, Rome. Tony had meetings scheduled for one of their two days. They stayed at Rome Cavalieri-Waldorf Astoria, in a luxurious suite with a magnificent view of the city highlighted by the dome of Saint Peter's Basilica.

Claire was relieved to learn her tardiness in Florence didn't cause the loss of her *roaming pass*. Although Tony continued to allow her to sightsee alone, he reminded her multiple times to keep track of time. She spent the day walking and busing around the city while Tony attended to business. The ancient history that accompanied everything in Rome fascinated Claire.

She visited the Coliseum, the Forum, and the Pantheon. She enjoyed a latte in *Piazza Navona* and watched as couples threw coins into the *Trevi* Fountain. The sights were breathtaking and remarkable, but the entrenched fear she felt in Florence affected her. She enjoyed everything, but now it felt tarnished. She didn't want to feel that way, but sometimes memories and emotions would overcome her. Not wanting Tony to see the change, she dutifully put on her mask and performed to the best of her ability. The sights were still amazing and spectacular.

The next day, at Vatican City, they walked hand in hand through the atrium of Saint Peter's Basilica. They viewed the Vatican grottoes, Saint Peter's Treasury, Saint Peter's Square, and the Vatican gardens. As they walked the steep road back to their hotel, Tony confessed, "With all of my traveling, I rarely sightsee. Today, when you said you wanted to spend the entire day at the Vatican, I thought you were crazy. I expected to be done in an hour or two." Claire watched as he spoke. "But it was incredible. I just want you to know I understand how you lost track of time in Florence. I get it." She didn't speak; she squeezed his hand. Something from her past came to mind and she smiled. He once said she was *trainable*, perhaps he was too. It just took longer with him.

The last country on their journey was Switzerland. Tony had meetings, first in Interlaken and then in Genève. They spent one night in Interlaken. The Swiss Alps were the epitome of pure unsullied nature and grandeur. The small town of Interlaken was surrounded by crystal-clear lakes, sparkling streams, and waterfalls. And ever present were the *Monch* and *Jungfrau* mountain range of the Swiss Alps. Claire felt like she was in the middle of a postcard.

While Tony met with investors, Claire chose to relish the relaxing scenery and take in the atmosphere. She wandered the streets, enjoyed the cafés, and rested in the beauty of the tranquil landscape. Their two weeks were action packed. She could have spent her time any way she chose, the options were numerous. However, she enjoyed some downtime to reflect on all they'd seen and to relax in the natural splendor.

Her memories overflowed with sights and sounds of ancient cities. She could close her eyes and recall the amazing art and architecture. Inhaling the sweet Swiss chocolate as she sipped her coffee and nibbled on the *candy bar*, she remembered the amazing cuisine and delicious wines. She thought about her husband. He'd spent the entire two weeks open and understanding. She never anticipated the freedoms she'd been granted. Her stack of books remained unread. Even when she was late, his voice and expression were more of care and concern than of anger. Her thoughts moved from his voice and expression, to his strong, safe embrace. They'd made love at every stop.

She recalled the yacht with the rhythmic rocking from the sea. Smiling, she thought lustfully about wanting him -- how on many occasions it was her who initiated their carnal encounters and he who responded appropriately. Claire slowly realized he was doing what she'd asked, filling her with good memories. She finished her chocolate and smiled contentedly.

Early Saturday morning they boarded a train to Genève. Tony had one more meeting. It was his last obligation of their trip. After it concluded, they'd spend the last night in Genève and fly home in the morning. Claire couldn't believe how quickly the fourteen days had passed. She felt completely exhausted and yet exhilarated. The first time she remembered Tony traveling to Europe he'd stayed for eight days. Claire remembered when he arrived home he had said he was tired. She understood. Being absent from Iowa for over two weeks, she was ready to get home. Their destinations were spectacular; however, Claire longed for the serenity of her own bed and suite.

Before they went out for their final night in Europe, Tony insisted they take some time to visit famous boutiques and shops on *Rue du Rhône*. Claire repeatedly told him she needed nothing. As if unable to hear or comprehend, he led her to an exclusive jewelry store. He wanted her to have something to remember their *time*, so he purchased a sparkling diamond watch. She wondered about a possible double meaning.

After a nine-hour flight, they arrived home. She couldn't remember being more tired. Their flight from Fiji was longer, yet they predominately rested in Fiji or at least spent time horizontal. She felt like she had been literally sightseeing, walking, and hiking for the past seventeen days. Their dinner in New York seemed forever ago, still she knew it was not.

Before they went to bed, Tony brought Claire a large stack of e-mails from his home office; she chose to not look at them. She'd do it tomorrow. They both collapsed into her bed. She thanked Tony repeatedly for the trip of a lifetime and the wonderful memories. She drifted into a dreamless sleep with her head resting on his shoulder, listening to his breathing.

Though exhausted, his arm embraced the soft warm body that nestled against his side. Her steady breathing told him she was sleeping. Closing his eyes he could hear her voice thanking him for the memories. Inhaling the scent of her hair he recalled their unforgettable trip and marveled at the intense satisfaction blooming within his chest.

Before he drifted off to sleep, Tony whispered, "I plan to go into the office tomorrow."

Stirring only slightly, Claire murmured, "All right, I'll see you tomorrow evening. I plan to sleep through your alarm." He smiled at her honesty as they both floated into blissful slumber.

It's not a question of enough, pal.
It's a Zero Sum game, somebody wins, somebody loses.
Money itself isn't lost or made, it's simply
transferred from one perception to another. Like magic.
—Gordon Gekko

Chapter 41

Anton stood silently outside the grand doors of his grandfather's home office. Even though the double doors were tightly closed, he could hear the voices from the other side. His father insisted Anton be excluded from the conversation within. As far as Anton was concerned, that was ridiculous. Something big was happening, and it had to do with *his* name and the company he'd been told would be his. Samuel could shelter him from the discussion and knowledge of the business dealings, but Anton wasn't ignorant. He could read a NYSE ticker. Rawls Corp. stock had plummeted from 79.8 to 56.4 at the close of trading. The news release proclaimed *rumors* of wrongdoings within the corporation. The four men within the office weren't drinking beer and playing cards; this was deadly serious. It felt like everything was crashing down around them. Someone opened a dam and the water couldn't be stopped.

Inside the cherry-paneled, regal office, Nathaniel questioned Clawson. "You said *no one* would ever know. What the hell happened? Where did these allegations come from?"

"Mr. Rawls, I don't know. We've covered our tracks for almost ten years. You've made a bloody fortune. Maybe the feds got nervous because you were making too much profit."

"What the hell is that, *too much* profit?" Nathaniel couldn't sit. He paced every inch of the plush carpet. "Have they investigated Trump or Gates? I'm nowhere close to those men."

"It doesn't matter who else has been investigated." Samuel tried to bring the men back to the task at hand. "What matters is that we get our ducks in a row and meet the investigation head-on."

294

Clawson gazed over to his assistant, Cole Mathews. Mathews was busy organizing stacks of paper and utilizing a shredder to reduce the paper overload. Clawson addressed both Rawls men. "Cole and I are making sure there is no evidence linking Rawls to any of the allegations."

"You said no one would know. Why is Mathews shredding papers? There shouldn't be anything that needs to be shredded." Nathaniel watched as Mathew's green eyes briefly met his. He seemed to be working as fast as the shredder would allow.

Samuel spoke above the grind of the shredder, "Instead of shredding, we need to be open to the investigation. Be honest, take our fines and penalties and move on." He might as well have been talking to the walls. His father and Clawson were devising a strategy as Mathews shredded without pause.

Cole Mathews entered their inner circle about two years ago. He didn't talk much, but was a whiz at research. Tell him a stock or a company, and bingo, he would have more insider information than one would believe humanly possible. Suddenly, Nathaniel regretted not having Clawson and Mathews sign some kind of power of attorney or non-disclosure statement, a way to distance him from them.

These two men helped make him mega-wealthy. At this moment, if possible he would hang them both out to dry to save himself and his family. Hell, Samuel wouldn't even meet his eyes.

Briefly, Nathaniel thought about the recent news. The space shuttle "Challenger" had blown up during takeoff. That was a damn shame. Just maybe that news would overshadow the unfortunate *false* allegations regarding Rawls Corp.

*The sudden disappointment of a hope leaves a scar which the
ultimate fulfillment of that hope never entirely removes.*
—Thomas Hardy

Chapter 42

O n the day following their return, Claire woke late, relishing the
large empty bed. After Cindy brought her coffee and food, she sat
on her balcony, ate breakfast, and enjoyed the summer day, truly
contented to be home. August in Iowa reminded her of Indiana, and even
though the temperature and humidity continued to increase, the summer's
climax was rapidly approaching. Before long, the balminess would diminish
and evidence of autumn would materialize.

Claire intended to appreciate the remaining days of summer. She took
the folder of e-mails to the pool. Knowing that Tony read them before
delivering them, she decided to separate the ones she felt needed responses
and expedite her evening request session. Eighteen days' worth of e-mails
took quite a bit of time. She started by removing the ones she didn't intend to
answer. Next, she reread the ones from acquaintances. What did they want?
Could she help in any way? If not, they went into the *"Patricia, please
respond"* pile. If she believed there was something she could do, she put them
in a pile to discuss with Tony.

Next was the pile of friends and family. It was considerably smaller.
Most of them knew she and Tony were out of the country. Most of her friends
wanted to know about the trip and schedule get-togethers. Courtney wanted
to do lunch as soon as Claire recovered from her traveling. MaryAnn's e-mail
apparently went to both Tony and Claire. She invited them to a movie
premiere party at their home in Malibu in October. Claire checked her
calendar. It was the weekend after the Red Cross silent auction. She added
those to the *"discuss with Tony"* pile. The last few pages were from Emily.
She definitely preferred sitting in the sun, drinking iced tea at her pool, in her
bathing suit, and reading Emily's e-mails to doing it under Tony's glare.

The first one was a note about their get-together. Emily and John enjoyed seeing them and thanked them for dinner. Apparently, John spoke to the waiter about paying the bill prior to their arrival, but somehow it never came to the table. This caused Claire to smile; she hadn't noticed. Emily wished them a good time on their trip. She anxiously waited to hear all about it. The second came a week later. It began with, "I know you are still in Europe, but I wanted to tell you . . ." The firm set an arbitrary date of November 1. At that time, there would be a review of the associates' production, hours billed, and fees recovered. She was optimistic about John's final numbers. He spent every waking hour working. But cautiously, she said if he didn't make the cut, it wasn't the end. He would still be an associate and considered for partnership during the next review process. She asked Claire to call when she got home. The third e-mail was dated yesterday. It began, "Are you home yet?" She asked multiple questions about their trip and talked about her impending school year. Apparently, the economic state of the country was affecting the finances of her school as well as others everywhere. Even though she worked for a private school system there were severe budget cuts which would affect her classroom directly. It made Claire wonder if she could use some of her *capital* to make a donation. She decided to put these in the *Tony* pile. She wanted to call and perhaps pursue the donation.

Lunch arrived at the pool. Settling into the lounge chair, with a book that made the trip to and from Europe but never opened, Claire was filled with comfort, peace, and contentment. She was home. Jet lag settled in and soon she fell into a deep sleep, sleeping through most of the afternoon. Catherine woke her at four and she went to her suite to prepare for Tony. At five o'clock, Catherine informed her that they would dine on the back patio. Her life's routine had resumed.

August faded into September, and before she knew it October knocked on the door. Claire and Courtney were very busy finalizing their efforts for the silent auction. The donations, facility, caterers, and wine distributors all confirmed; the guest list approved and invitations mailed. Excited about the impending event, Claire felt it was her debut to the philanthropic world. Tony not only participated in this world, he excelled. She wanted Mrs. Anthony Rawlings to be equally synonymous with charity as Mr. Anthony Rawlings. It was the first time Claire informed Tony they would be attending an event. He smiled and told her he would check their calendar.

During the auction planning her hostess duties didn't cease. Various dinners occurred at various locations. They also attended functions and events together. Her biggest decisions involved wardrobe and hairstyle, and often those choices were made for her. That made the Red Cross function all the more important to Claire. She knew she had more to offer.

Not long before the auction, Tony and Claire attended a forum in Chicago where Tony was the keynote speaker. He was asked to give a speech about *success*. The theme of the conference was "Risk verses Failure in the World of Business." He never practiced his speeches or ran ideas by her. So as Claire sat next to her husband at the head table and he addressed the audience, his words were new to her, too.

When she first met him, really met him, she didn't like the *business* Tony. He was the one who used to visit her suite; always professionally dressed, impersonal, methodical, detached, and other adjectives not as complimentary. But now she enjoyed watching and being beside Anthony Rawlings, esteemed businessman, while he shined in his element. He radiated an aura that said *I am successful*. By some it might have been perceived as conceit. Claire probably thought of it that way at one time, but now she found it attractive. In the past, she disliked or hated his ingrained confidence and authority, but now she could look at it differently. It was sexy. Watching and listening to him, she comprehended the importance of her role.

Many times following the dinner and speech, the organizers would schedule a question-and-answer symposium. These were informal, with various people approaching Tony and asking him questions. Many of the attendees were young entrepreneurs looking for advice. According to Shelly, Tony's participation was essential for public relations. According to Tony, his participation was hell. Claire's duty included politely interrupting participants, so he could move on to the next and eventually leave.

During these Q & A sessions, multiple people approached Tony. Claire tried to appear attentive, yet unobtrusive, until it was time for her to interrupt. She didn't pay attention to the individuals. They blended together in her mind. During this particular conference, a question came from one of the participants which caught them both off guard. A man, younger than Tony closer to Claire's age, dressed in an expensive suit approached Tony.

"Hello, Mr. Rawlings, I'm pleased to meet you. Your speech was remarkable and inspiring." Tony shook his hand and politely thanked him, and then the blond man with big soft blue eyes continued, somewhat timidly, "I have an unusual request. May I speak with your wife for a few minutes?"

Claire hadn't looked at the man until that moment. She was gazing into the crowd. His words made her turn, first to Tony, seeing his surprised expression, and then to the man. Her mask momentarily shattered. She recognized him immediately and suddenly wondered why she hadn't recognized his voice. The mayhem in her head tied her tongue until Tony's eyes brought her back to reality. Placing her hand gently on Tony's arm, she hesitantly spoke, trying desperately for a sturdier voice.

"Oh my, Anthony, Simon." Tony watched as she stuttered through introductions. "Anthony, may I introduce Simon Johnson. Simon and I were students together at Valparaiso a million years ago." Her speech flowed too rapidly. "Simon, may I introduce my husband, Anthony Rawlings."

The two men locked eyes and shook hands again. Tony was polite. Claire watched his eyes, as if a switch had been flipped from light to dark. Turning to Claire, he responded, "I believe that is Mrs. Rawlings' decision."

There were other people waiting to speak with Tony. Claire excused Simon and herself, allowing Tony to speak to the others. She and Simon walked away. As they walked, Simon absentmindedly put his hand in the small of her back; she immediately stepped away from his touch. They sat at an empty table.

Simon spoke softly, "Claire, I apologize if I've put you in a difficult position. It is just that I have wanted to speak to you for a long time."

"Like eight years?" Even she was surprised by her unfriendly tone.

"This is the third event I've attended where you and Mr. Rawlings have been present. I finally summoned the nerve to speak to you."

Remembering a previous reunion, she said, "First, Simon, tell me you're not a reporter or talking to me for a publication of any kind."

His blue eyes looked startled and then softened. "No, Claire, I just want to talk to you. It must be difficult not knowing who you can trust."

She breathed easier. "It is. I've made a few mistakes I don't plan to repeat."

"It is a mistake I made that I want to talk to you about, too."

She looked at him. He hadn't changed since their freshman year of college. But alas he had, he was older, more mature, and more confident. His blond hair still needed trimming and his gleaming eyes were still as bright. She couldn't forget the passion she'd witnessed in those eyes.

"I've seen your picture so many places recently. I felt that I needed to talk to you at least once and explain what happened during the summer of '03."

They met at Valparaiso their freshman year. Simon's major was computer programming while Claire's was meteorology. Living in the same dorm, they ran into one another often. Their mutual attraction blossomed into young infatuation and rapidly into romance. They were each other's first love. The new, unfamiliar emotions overwhelmed them both. Simon proposed to Claire daily. She had other plans for her life, plans of a career and national success which didn't include marriage. During the summer they visited each other's hometowns, met the families, and did all the things young lovers do. Claire's mother commented how plans can always be modified. She liked Simon. Their sophomore year was to include Greek life, parties, studying, and time together. But somewhere between meeting the family and classes resuming, Simon disappeared. He called a few times, wrote a few letters, and vanished. Claire knew college had been a financial strain on his family. That was why when out of the blue, during the summer, Simon had received an offer for a dream internship and he had, had to accept. An opportunity like that was unheard of for a sophomore. His computer talents exceeded many of the older students. The internship was in California, and he couldn't miss the opportunity. It was supposed to be just one semester. She waited for him to return, he didn't. Their correspondences became less frequent and then nonexistent.

She moved on. Forgetting him wasn't possible, but successfully compartmentalizing him was. Over the years life's challenges and routines filled her consciousness, only sometimes in unconsciousness did he return.

"That isn't necessary. We have both moved on with our lives." Claire began to rise. "But it was nice to see you."

He touched her hand gently. "Please, Claire, I need to tell you." She timidly sat. "Do you remember that I went to California?" She nodded. "At first, it was an internship, but then they offered me a job. I'm not sure you remember, but college was difficult for my parents to afford, and the offer was too good to pass. I wanted to go back and finish my degree, but there I was, twenty years old, being offered my dream job."

Claire remembered the letter she received saying he wouldn't be returning from California. It broke her heart. She wanted to join him, but he didn't ask. "I'm glad it worked for you. Are you still living in California?"

"Yes, I am. And the company I went to work for interestingly is a subsidiary of Rawlings Industries."

Claire's heart started to race. If Tony knew, Simon would lose his job. She saw the darkness, she wanted to protect him. "Are you still there?"

"No." She sighed with relief. "I was with them for over five years, but I left long before you met your husband. I read the article in *Vanity Fair*." She smiled. "I have my own company now."

"That's great, I hope you're happy."

"With business, I am. I should thank Mr. Rawlings. The start I received from his company made a big impact. Today I create some of the games people play on their phones. I'm doing well."

"I'm truly happy for you." She glanced nervously back at Tony. "I do need to get back to Tony."

"My mother has been keeping up on you, relaying information to me. She liked you a lot."

"I liked your mom, too. Please tell her I said hello and to not believe everything she reads." Claire's eyes saddened with memories.

"Before you go, I wanted to let you know, even now with my success, I regret not coming back for you." Claire didn't speak, she couldn't. "I thought about it constantly, but the job required a lot of travel. I was in China when your parents died. If I had been Stateside I would have been there for you. I just had to tell you. I didn't leave you because of anything you did or said. Claire, you have remained perfect in my memories. I wish things had been different." She felt a rush of sadness at what may have been. But Simon continued, "I even followed your career. I knew you were in Albany and then in Atlanta. I remembered you wanted a career and I thought maybe after you achieved that success we could try again." Claire looked at the table. This was making her uneasy. She needed to go back to Tony. "But I want you to know I'm happy for you. And I'm happy you are happily married."

The increasing feeling of anxiety made her stand. "Thank you, Simon. I wish you continued success. Please give my best to your family. I must get back to my husband."

"Do you have your phone?" Claire's expression became confused. Simon smiled.

"I'm making you sad, which wasn't my intention. I wanted to show you my latest game, it is fun and I hope it will make you smile. Do you remember staying up all night playing video games?" She did, but it seemed like another person, in another life.

"I created this most recent game with someone from my past in mind. Kind of a tribute, I guess."

300

"I don't have my purse, it's at the table." She silently berated herself. He was being so open and honest, and she was lying about a phone!

He reached into his pocket, pulled out a smart phone, and started touching the screen. "Here it is, you can download it for $1.99." Smiling, he added, "Which I believe is within your price range." Claire looked onto the screen. The goal of the game seemed to be to find something. But in order to accomplish this goal, you had to rummage through clothes, old pieces of pizza, pizza boxes, soda pop cans, etc. She smiled and he explained, "Each level has a new item to discover. It's very popular with the college and post-college demographic. It's made me millions." She really smiled at him. He actually made that kind of money with games. "I'm glad I saw your smile. Claire, you are beautiful, but I miss the brown hair."

"Bye, Simon. Good luck to you." She nodded. He looked like he wanted to hug her or shake hands, some type of contact, but she turned away. Immediately, she made eye contact with Tony. He'd been watching. She resumed her position beside her husband.

Acknowledging her return, he flashed his charming smile, nodded, and greeted her, "Mrs. Rawlings."

When they stepped out onto the sidewalk, the Chicago lights sparkled in the clear September night air. Tony's hand gently rested in the small of Claire's back. The temperature was still warm, but she felt a shiver. Eric opened the door of the limousine and Tony helped his wife into the car.

Lost in her thoughts, Claire watched as the lights of the city passed the windows. Her mind was back at college. The memories of the messy dorm room, the clutter, and now the game brought a warm feeling. She was happy for Simon. He succeeded in accomplishing his goals. She remembered his aspirations, not of wealth, but happiness and family. She recalled he wanted to be able to help his parents. She hadn't asked if he was married. She hadn't even looked to see if he was wearing a wedding ring. But with all her soul, she hoped he was.

"Mrs. Rawlings," Tony was addressing Claire. She turned to face him. He was uncomfortably close. "What is your name?"

Bewildered she just looked at him. He reached for her chin and held it so they were looking at one another. "Your name, what is your name?"

Annoyed and alarmed, "Tony, what are you doing?"

He didn't loosen his grip. "I am asking you a question, one that you seem to be unable to answer."

Mystified by his behavior, she answered his question, "My name is Claire. Claire Rawlings."

Slow and deliberate, "Explain to me, Mrs. Rawlings, how you can be sitting with me, your husband, wearing the rings I purchased, in the limousine paid for by my hard work, and thinking about another man."

He still held her chin. "Tony, please let go of my face. You're hurting me."

He let go of her chin. His hand slid behind her neck, tightly holding her head and the hair hanging down her neck. He continued, "Do I need to repeat every question or do you think you may be able to answer at least one the first time?"

Flashing, her green eyes spoke alarm and the stiffening of her neck spoke resolve, "Seeing Simon caught me off guard. I have not thought of or heard from him in eight years. Do you not think that deserves some reflection?"

His grip tightened. "No. I believe the past is just that. It is done and now it is time to concentrate on the present." Her neck hurt. He had her head positioned so their eyes made contact, his shone black. Hers weren't apologetic, but full of fury. She didn't respond. He continued, "At present I believe you need to concentrate on showing me *my* wife is first and foremost concerned with pleasing her husband."

He used his other hand to shut the window between them and Eric. Next, he unzipped the slacks of his tuxedo. Shocked and repulsed, Claire started to protest. She soon found speaking impossible. Holding her neck, he silently directed her head, resting his head on the seat, his fingers entwined in her hair. Claire tried to push away with her hand. Tony seized her hand and twisted it back. He did not release the pressure and movement on her head until he was finished.

As they walked through the lobby of the Trump Tower, Claire did her best to appear composed. Tony placed his arm around her waist and tenderly whispered in her ear, "I have more ways you can demonstrate your devotion, Mrs. Rawlings. We will review when we reach our apartment."

The last thirteen months dissolved into nothingness. She wasn't Claire Rawlings, wife. She was Claire Nichols, whatever *he* wanted her to be.

Any idiot can face a crisis,
it is day to day living that wears you out.
—Anton Chekhov

Chapter 43

The silence within the limousine intensified with each mile as Tony and Claire rode from Bettendorf toward home. The silent auction unofficially raised over a half of a million dollars *net*. The cost of the event had been less than $10,000 due to Claire's clever procurement of donated services and goods. The noiselessness of the ride was a stark contrast to the convention center.

Before they left the conference hall, Courtney spoke ecstatically about Claire's ability. "This turned out so well! I just can't believe the final figures. Honey, together we are going to raise money for every organization west of the Mississippi."

Although she felt uneasy regarding her future philanthropic activities, Claire hugged her friend and wore her smile. "Oh goodness, we'll have to see."

"Well, enjoy this success for a little while because I have plans!" Courtney's enthusiasm was contagious. Claire smiled and nodded her head.

Mrs. Rawlings' more recent hostess duties aided her efforts. She shrewdly mentioned the auction, both for donations and possible attendance, whenever possible. She found it interesting how Tony's business associates were willing to participate in one or both when personally approached. The fact that they were in her home, eating her food, and receiving her attention didn't hinder her efforts. The current president of the Red Cross of the Greater Quad Cities thanked Mrs. Rawlings and Mrs. Simmons profusely.

Many of Tony's associates from out of town attended the event. Claire hadn't realized when she invited them that this had an additional impact on the Quad Cities. These important people needed places to stay and food to eat while in Bettendorf. According to Courtney, the media estimated their event reaped over a quarter of a million dollars windfall to the Quad Cities. Claire hadn't seen the coverage. She didn't like television, and any other form of communication was still forbidden.

As a matter of fact, since the Chicago Symposium Claire had lost many of her newfound freedoms. She still saw e-mails, but only after responses had been sent. No longer a *freedom,* they were merely a blatant illustration of what was now prohibited.

During the final preparations of the auction, it was undeniable Claire and Courtney needed to communicate and see each other. However, contact and endeavors with others had dramatically decreased. Tony decided that Claire needed *time* to decide what was really important to her.

The night in Chicago was reminiscent of her first encounters at the estate. Tony was excessively domineering, controlling, and demanding. Even the sadistic, cruel sexual tendencies from before her accident reappeared. Once back at the apartment, Claire tried to reason with him. "Please think about what you are doing." It was as if his black eyes couldn't register her voice. She pleaded, "Tony, remember your promise. I am your wife. Think what you are asking me to do."

"You are my wife. However, I am not asking." Unaffected, his demands continued.

When she awoke the next morning, feeling the too familiar aches from a year before, she dreaded his presence. Lying silently, she listened for his breathing. Relieved, she heard the sound of his shower in the adjoining room. Slowly, she sat up and thought about her options. Up until seeing Simon, things were progressing well. Even in Italy when she broke his rule, he responded with kindness, not cruelty. But as she listened to the running water Claire debated leaving him, the apartment, everything.

She didn't know how. Where could she possibly go where he couldn't find her? She fell back against the soft pillows and allowed herself a few tears. Momentarily, she had difficulty filling her lungs with a sufficient amount of air and remembered her nightmares. This wasn't a dream, it was her reality. She didn't want to see or talk to him. However, she recognized the helplessness surging through her veins. Her only way forward was through the man in the next room. Slowly, she eased back the blankets, squared her shoulders, and walked toward the mirror. The steely determination propelling her feet didn't come from courage, more from a sense of powerless necessity. The reflection before her had been worse, it'd been much worse. Yet seeing the red and blue markings made her stomach twist. She reached for her robe and covered the evidence.

Minutes later he stepped into their bedroom. The man before her seemed completely ignorant of the previous night's events. He casually kissed her cheek and said, "The shower is all yours." She just stared. *Who is he?* He grinned. "I would have stayed longer if I knew you were awake." Later that morning, he helped her prepare to leave Chicago and kindly discussed daily pleasantries.

The incident forced Claire to recognize she'd deluded herself into believing the other Tony was gone. He wasn't gone. In fact, he was incredibly close to the surface. That morning she had no idea with whom she was flying or even with whom she shared a home. Every night she would wait as her stomach twisted into knots, wondering who would walk through the doorway.

Claire expected the recent events to increase the frequency of her nightmares, surprisingly they diminished. Her theory: her consciousness now shared the stress that only her unconscious had endured.

After the repercussions and some passage of time, she tried to talk to Tony about Simon. He didn't care or want to hear her perspective. His only notion remained: at a public event she left his side, her husband, to spend *time* with her ex-lover. To Claire that was a ludicrous observation. Her interpretation went more like, at a public event, to allow Tony the ability to be accessed by fans, she escorted Simon aside and discussed issues with him for a sliver of time. The dissimilar interpretations didn't have common ground presently or in their future. The subject was closed.

As they rode home from Bettendorf, Claire wondered what Tony thought of the silent auction and what consequences she would endure now that her presence wasn't required in a public venue. It wasn't until they were almost home until Tony finally spoke, taking her from her thoughts. "Congratulations."

"Thank you."

"The auction was a complete success."

"Thank you. I'm pleased. Courtney is happy. I wanted to make you happy, too."

"And now you don't?"

"No. I do." She was sincere.

"I've told you before. You continually surprise and amaze me with your abilities." And, as an afterthought, he added, "Some more than others."

Claire didn't react, that was what he wanted. Instead, she sat dejectedly and thought about the date, October 8. Her thoughts went many different directions. She thought about the auction, someone bid $70,000 for the two-day use of Tony's plane and pilot. It was a great donation. He'd thought of it. Other donations like stays in resorts, entertainment packages, NBA, and NFL tickets helped in surpassing their goal.

She also remembered they were supposed to be in Malibu the following weekend for Eli and MaryAnn's party. She'd been looking forward to it since they received the invitation. The Simmons and the Millers were all going. The film was a thriller. Claire knew of the actors, but she mostly looked forward to seeing their home.

Another thought was her family. John's deadline was less than a month away. She hadn't spoken to Emily since before *Simon*. So many other freedoms had disappeared. The idea of talking to her sister seemed preposterous. Claire didn't have the resolve or strength to follow through on such a request.

Selfishly, she thought about her upcoming twenty-eighth birthday and contemplated the truth of her life. She rode in her limousine to her estate with her wealthy, handsome husband. Amused, she decided that was the *Vanity Fair* version. For the unabridged version: she was secluded in Tony's limousine, she would have liked to drive her own car, to his house, her prison on multiple occasions, with her husband who was handsome and cruel, sadistic, manipulative, and controlling. Even Tony's success as a businessman lost its luster since talking to Simon. Tony ruined lives, futures, and dispensed consequences to make money. Simon had fun and made games. People spent less than $2 for one of his games, but with enough people, that added up. The reality saddened her. She didn't know for sure, but predicted there were forty-six people in Pennsylvania without jobs.

Her life wasn't worse than that of many others. On the contrary, it was better in many ways. She realized injustice was a widespread problem, yet many of the same questions remained: how did she end up here? How had her life's goals been so radically modified? When she took the time to think about it, none of it made sense.

On October 14, in a company plane Claire happily flew across the continent with the Simmons, the Millers, and Tony. A week earlier she would've considered the likelihood of their California trip occurring improbable. However, she'd spent the last week at home with her devoted husband. Each evening the man she married returned home from his office.

The stress of his unpredictability was making her insane. Since the auction, he'd been attentive, loving, and caring. With the weather turning cooler, the days shorter, and the stress of the dual *Tonys*, Claire believed she was teetering literally on the edge of sanity. A strong wind was all it would take to blow her one way or the other. Iowa had its share of storms, strong winds, and tornadoes, they were all unpredictable. It made an ironic parallel for her life.

Courtney remained true to her observant promise. She *knew* something was askew with Claire and Tony. She didn't know what. Claire thought the less she knew the better. Tony didn't understand their connection. Claire tried to facilitate his misconception by complaining about Courtney, "She is fun, but she talks so much . . ."

It was a ploy she prayed would work. She really needed Courtney in her life. Their plane touched down in Los Angeles on Friday night. The party was the following evening. During their flight they shared wine, laughed, and shared stories of Eli's previous parties. Apparently, the sky's the limit regarding behaviors with the Hollywood scene. Claire waited anxiously to experience it for herself. The Simmons and Millers were dropped off at a five-star hotel. The Rawlings went to their apartment.

The LA housekeeper met them at the door while a driver took their luggage to their room. Tony explained they would like a light dinner as soon as possible. Claire wasn't hungry, her head ached. She only wanted to unpack and go to sleep. Once alone, Tony assumed his alternate persona. "Tomorrow evening we will be in an overtly public arena. It wasn't long ago when a *glitch* occurred in a setting such as this."

She didn't want to hear him. "Tony, please don't start this again." The flight, wine, and aching head contributed to Claire's irritability. Her insolent retort stunned him momentarily. Recovery didn't take long. As she carried clothes to the dresser, he seized her arm and turned her to face him.

"Claire, I do not appreciate your flippant attitude. There will be many more journalists present than you have ever been exposed to at one time."

His grip hurt. She looked directly into his eyes and stood tall as he glowered over her. "I assure you my attitude is not flippant. It is just that you are increasingly repetitive. I know the speech and I know—" She didn't get the chance to finish her sentence. It was the first strike since her *accident*. She remained standing but temporarily dazed, more by disbelief than pain.

He spoke again as if he hadn't just shattered his promise and her security. Her house of glass now lay in a pile of shards. "You have a responsibility and I expect you to behave appropriately." He let go of her arm, walked to the suitcase, and pulled out Claire's hiking boots. "By the way, would you like to know why these are packed?"

Her mind wheeled as he changed subjects. She was having difficulty keeping up. Refusing to cry, she exhaled and took the bait. "Why do I have my hiking boots?"

"As a surprise for your birthday, I made reservations for Sunday and Monday night in the presidential suite of a very exclusive hotel inside Yosemite. I thought you would enjoy the Sierra Nevada Mountains and National Park. After last year, I didn't want to miss celebrating your birthday." His tone became stern. "However, instead of surprising you like I hoped, our romantic birthday getaway now rests in your hands."

Claire tried to follow his words, her hands? What did he mean?

"If your memory isn't failing, if you can remember my concerns and rules, and if you can obey the few requests I have made, then we will be able to keep the plans for your birthday. If, however, you are unable to handle your responsibilities, I will have no choice but to cancel the reservations and we will concentrate on ways to help facilitate your memory for the future." He stared at his wife as she sank to the edge of the bed. "What is your choice? You want to be a partner. Tell me what you want to do, go to Yosemite or go home and review appropriate behavior?" This was another of those *offers you can't refuse* type questions.

God she hated the dance. A blow to the cheek one minute and discussing a romantic getaway the next. It was the one step forward, two steps back waltz. She wanted to scream. Sitting on the side of the bed, Claire allowed herself tears and swallowed. Her voice revealed her distress, yet she tried to sound composed. "I've never been to Yosemite. I've heard it is beautiful. That sounds like a wonderful birthday."

Unmoved by her tears, he stood waiting for a response to his question. Seeing her husband's stare, feeling a too-familiar twinge of panic, Claire realized she hadn't answered his question. "I'd like to go to Yosemite. I'll do as you say."

He moved closer, took her hands, and helped her stand. Their chests touched as she looked up at his still too-dark eyes. She didn't look away. "Claire, I do not want to break my promise, but at the risk of sounding repetitive, public failure is *not* an option."

"I understand. I'm sorry for making you break your promise. I'll do better."

That night while lying in bed next to his sleeping wife, Tony remembered a scene from his childhood. It was one of many that shaped so many of his decisions. His grandfather's booming voice, "Boy, you will not be joining us at dinner this evening." Surprised, he noticed the absence of his place setting. Tony asked why. His grandfather didn't speak but removed a letter from the breast pocket of his jacket. Tony retrieved the letter and unfolded the page. It was his grades from the last semester of classes. He'd taken seventeen credit hours, a very full load for a freshman. There were five A's and one B+, in Calculus. That seemed good to him. He remembered still not comprehending his grandfather's tone. "You plan to succeed in this world, boy?"

"Yes, sir, I do."

"Then don't let this happen again, failure has consequences. Perhaps some time alone eating in your suite will help you remember perfection is the minimum requirement for success." His grandfather then turned his eyes away and took a drink of wine.

"Nathaniel, perhaps he did his—" His grandfather's dark eyes stopped his grandmother's plea. She looked down at her plate. The subject was closed. Tony looked at his parents, they too were looking down.

He remembered walking out of that dining room vowing to make Nathaniel proud, it wasn't easy. But today he believed he had seized opportunities and created others. If his grandfather were alive, which he should be, Tony believed he would be proud.

The following morning, Tony left the apartment early to golf with friends. During her morning shower, Claire noticed tenderness on her right arm. While drying, she saw a large purple hand print. Claire's concern wasn't that she endured her husband's wrath; it was that the physical evidence was visible. She felt relieved to find Catherine had packed blouses with sleeves. She rationalized if the purple bruise was seen it would break multiple rules: appearances and private information. Most importantly, Tony wouldn't be happy. Thinking ahead, Claire checked her party dress, sleeveless.

Once the ladies were all together, Claire summoned her brightest smile and asked, "So is anyone up for a little shopping on Rodeo Drive? I think a new dress for the party is in order!" It didn't take much convincing to entice the others to join her on three blocks of the most famous and expensive shopping in America. Apparently, her mask wasn't without cracks. Courtney tried on multiple occasions to isolate Claire and ask her what was happening, she said she felt something amiss.

Claire smiled brightly and looked her friend in the eye. "It's just newlywed stuff. We're both new at this marriage thing. We're working on it." Sensing Courtney's disbelief, Claire continued, "Really, everything is fine."

Tony mentioned Claire's shopping talents had improved, he was right. She found two dresses that her friends adored, one from Armani and the other Gucci from Saks. Of course, each needed shoes and a bag. She reasoned, that two would allow Tony to make the final decision. Claire laid the dresses on the bed, with their shoes and handbags, and enthusiastically asked Tony which one he wanted her to wear. He liked that she shopped with her friends. The reason was never questioned. However, a decision would be difficult without a fashion show. Claire obliged. Tony chose the Gucci deep-blue long-sleeved classic wrap dress. He particularly liked the ease at which it *unwrapped*.

The six of them arrived at the party to a crowd of celebrities and press. Claire stayed by her husband's side as they chatted with people she'd only seen on screen. She was surprised how normal they seemed. Perhaps a few were boorish or narcissistic, but as a whole they were unpretentious and humble and treated Tony with respect. Claire didn't realize until listening to his conversations that he also capitalized in forms of entertainment: television stations, news stations, and movie studios. This connection was the impetus for his friendship with Eli. She'd thought they made unlikely friends.

Now it made sense.

Claire hadn't anticipated the grandeur of Eli and MaryAnn's home. Bev's design house had been instrumental in the decor. Every inch screamed *California*: open spaces, stunning views, clean lines, and affluence. Being built into a cliff with a spectacular ocean view, Claire wondered if they ever worried about earthquakes. She decided not to ask.

Aside from a few excursions with Courtney or MaryAnn, who was determined to introduce her to the Hollywood "A" crowd, Claire stayed dutifully at Tony's elbow. He amiably included her in his conversations and introduced her to everyone. Anthony Rawlings and his bride, how cute they were, still honeymooners and inseparable, it was the talk of the party.

Following a Sunday brunch with their friends, Tony and Claire flew to Fresno. He arranged for a rental car. She wondered how many people *rented* cars valued at over $100,000. He said it wasn't quite the Maserati Gran Turismo, but he liked driving the Corvette ZR1. The man who delivered it claimed it could go from 0 to 100 mph in seven seconds. Claire said, "Seriously, I believe him. We don't need to test it."

Yosemite was as beautiful as she'd heard. The famous stone mountains, waterfalls, lakes, and giant sequoias thrilled her. Her love of nature overpowered her recent unsettled sentiment toward her husband. With the stunning surroundings and his amorous temperament, she could forget his other persona. Or at least, she could compartmentalize it away and focus on this Tony.

On her birthday after climbing a steep trail to the base of Nevada Falls, Tony surprised Claire with a picnic lunch he'd hidden in a backpack, complete with blanket and bottle of wine. She wanted to hate him, his behavior and rules. At times she could. But other times he could be so romantic, tender, and affectionate.

After eating he handed her a burgundy velvet box, "Happy birthday, Claire." Displaying his devilish grin, "I remembered no black velvet boxes."

She shook her head, thinking, *damn, he's good.* She accepted the box and opened it to discover a stunning pair of diamond stud earrings. She had a fleeting memory of earrings long ago. Her parents gave her diamond stud earrings for her high school graduation. They weren't near as big or impressive. Momentarily, she wondered where they were.

"Thank you, Tony, they're amazing." Her words were sincere and appreciative. The diamonds glistened in the rays of sunlight. They were truly the prettiest diamond earrings she'd ever seen. The only prettier diamond would be the one on her left hand.

Tony tenderly kissed her. "Happy birthday, Love, I am glad we are here."

She nodded; so was she.

On Tuesday afternoon Tony's plane and Eric waited for them in Fresno. They arrived home late Tuesday night. The time difference worked better traveling west.

Although the clock read after ten, Claire decided to press her luck. "Tony, I've had a wonderful birthday. Yosemite was beautiful and my earrings are stunning." She wore the earrings, her journey necklace, and her new diamond watch from Europe. "I have one more birthday request."

He hugged her close. "And that would be?"

The past few days had been *good.* She momentarily hesitated, but decided to proceed. "I would like to talk to my sister." She looked up into his eyes, what color were they?

He sighed. "Let's go to the office and call before I change my mind."

She lifted herself on her toes and kissed him. "Thank you." She was barely able to contain her excitement at the ability to call. The fact it was on speaker was expected. When Emily answered, she sounded sleepy. Claire apologized, told her she had just gotten home from out of town, and wanted to call. Emily quickly recovered. They chatted for nearly fifteen minutes before Claire realized her time had expired. Claire apologized for not calling sooner. Things were so busy with the auction. She told Emily about the Hollywood party and about Tony's surprise birthday trip.

Emily thanked them for the donation to the school district. It'd been made anonymously, but she guessed it was from them. She also told Claire she was worried about John. As the deadline approached he spent too much time at the office. He was currently there even though it was after eleven. He would probably be gone before Emily woke in the morning. Apparently, some auditor reviewed their information: their hours worked, hours billed, fees recovered, etc. John hadn't disclosed everything to Emily, but she had a bad feeling. Something didn't feel right. She promised to keep Claire informed if she got the chance to talk to her. Claire told her she would try. She said goodbye and Tony hit the disconnect button.

Hugging her husband she whispered, "It's been a great birthday. I might not be as tired as I thought." Both of their smiles were genuine.

Perspective is the most important thing to have in life.
—Lauren Graham

Chapter 44

Claire straightened the three stacks of papers. She once again had a voice in her e-mails. Besides the *"Patricia, respond"* and *"Ask Tony"* piles, she sometimes made a *"Correspondence"* pile, her written answer to someone's correspondence, or like today, an unsolicited outgoing e-mail. Sometimes they were sent as she wrote them; other times *they* made changes. It was all part of the deliberation and negotiation process. Today's unsolicited e-mail was to Emily. It'd been written and rewritten about six times. Pacing around the suite, Claire wondered if she worded it well and, more importantly, if Tony would allow her to send it. John's deadline was November first. Today was the fourth and she still hadn't heard anything. Claire was hopeful that the note could be sent. After all, Tony was the one who suggested she call on the first. She, of course, jumped at the chance, but no one answered. The last two nights she continued to try; still no answer. She was worried.

With her revelation that her subconscious and conscious were sharing the same concerns, and her newfound *time* around the house, Claire practiced self-therapy sessions continually. Perhaps her concern about John was a defense mechanism, worrying about someone else for a change. Mostly, she concerned herself with the man she'd married. The loving persona was back in many ways: complimentary, caring, and compassionate. Control was always an issue. He expected obedience and submission. As long as she complied, no consequences occurred. She spent endless hours spinning that into a positive paradigm. If it were truly positive, would spinning it take hours?

Having little else to do, she dressed for dinner and read a book while awaiting Tony's arrival. He was expected home at seven, but he surprised her by entering her suite about five thirty. She smiled but immediately recognized something amiss in his expression. Her heart raced, wondering, *what have I done?*

He didn't speak, put some papers on the sofa, and knelt before her. The papers reminded her of Meredith's interview, but he wasn't enraged. *Distressed* would be a better assessment. "Tony, what is it?" He was as shaken as she'd ever seen him. He lowered his head to her lap. Lifting his face, she said, "Seriously, you're scaring me. What's the matter?"

"I came home as soon as I saw the news release. I knew you would want to know. You probably don't believe me, but I *am* sorry."

Claire looked into his eyes: sincerity. With trembling hands she reached for the papers. She had no idea what she was about to read, but it didn't take a psychic to know it was bad.

Tragic Accident Claims the Life of Young Gaming Phenomenon
Simon Johnson, 28, of Palo Alto, California died Wednesday,
November 3, 2011, after a tragic accident.

Claire put the papers down and ran to the bathroom. She was suddenly ill. She hadn't seen Simon in eight years, hadn't consciously thought of him. Now he was gone. Vomiting caused her to tremble. She turned to see Tony standing in the doorway, watching *his* wife. She sank to the floor not knowing what he would say or do regarding her response. He probably thought it inappropriate. Unexpectedly, too weak to defend herself, Claire didn't care. The cool bathroom tile soothed her pounding head as she wept. Claire closed her eyes and surrendered to whatever was coming her way.

Tony knelt down, helped her up, carried her back to the suite, and gently laid her on the sofa. He then sat with her head on his lap. They didn't speak for a long time. Claire cried. She cried for Simon, not a lost love. She was married to someone else. She cried for a life lost too young. The article said he was twenty-eight. She was twenty-eight. That was too young to die.

Finally, she managed, "How did he die?"

"The article said his plane went down in a remote area over the mountains." The sobs resounded. "The authorities found the crash site, no survivors. It came across my news feed and I rushed home."

Claire regained enough composure to sit. "He was a friend. I'm not upset because he and I were involved. He was just too young to die."

Tenderly hugging her, Tony said, "I really understand. I overreacted before." He gently moved her hair away from her face. "It said he was recently engaged." That news restarted Claire's tears. She wanted him to be married and loved by someone.

When she calmed, he brought her tissues and she read the rest of the news release:

Officials found the crash site of Mr. Johnson's personal aircraft in the upper elevations of the Sierra Nevada Mountain range. Mr. Johnson's flight plan indicated he was on his way home to Palo Alto after a meeting with investors in the Los Angeles area. Mr. Simon Johnson, self-made millionaire, was best known for his gaming creations. His creative start occurred with Shedis-tics, a Rawlings Industries subsidiary in Northern California. Mr. Johnson began his own gaming company, Si-Jo, in 2005. Mr. Johnson, originally from Indiana, was scheduled to wed Ms. Amber McCoy of Palo Alto, California, on April 21, 2012. Information regarding services has yet to be released by family.

Claire put down the pages and laid her head on Tony's chest. He put his arms around her and she drifted between sobbing, crying, and dreaming. When she awoke, her head pounded and her eyes ached swollen and tender. Tony was still there, holding her. She got up and went to the bathroom, washed her face, and came back out. "I think I'm done. Thank you for being so understanding."

He motioned for her to return to the sofa. She did. He put his arm around her. "Did you know he worked for one of my companies?"

"He told me that in Chicago, saying how strange fate can be. He said he wanted to thank you for the great start."

"You didn't tell me."

"I didn't have the chance."

Tony didn't respond. What could he say?

The next day, Tony worked from home. Claire rested on the sunporch, feeling her emotions teetering between sad and empty. Despite the recent drop in temperature, merciful sunshine made the porch comfortable. The trees were bare and the grass resumed its winter gray cast. She thought how the entire situation seemed unreal and wondered about Amber McCoy and Simon's parents. She couldn't imagine what they were going through.

Hoping the sunlight would improve her mood, she lay on the loveseat and contemplated life and death. Death seemed peaceful and predictable. She hadn't thought that way for over a year. Tony found her staring into space and spoke sympathetically. "There is a private memorial for Simon on Sunday in Madison, Indiana." Claire turned to her husband. Her makeup was done and her hair styled, but her eyelids were swollen and her eyes seemed distant.

"Okay." She weighed his words. "We should send flowers."

"No, we should attend."

Claire sat straight. "No! We shouldn't. Tony, I have not been to a funeral since my parents died. I can't go to Simon's." Her eyes brimmed again with moisture.

For the second time in two days Anthony Rawlings knelt before his wife. His tone was incredibly sweet and supportive. "I have his parents' number. I really think you should call. I'm not telling you to, I am saying it would be a good idea. The service is private. If they invite you or us, we should attend." Claire shook her head no. Speaking without crying wasn't an option. He handed her the telephone number, kissed her gently, and went back to his office.

It may have been half an hour. It may have been three hours. Time had temporarily lost its meaning. Eventually, Claire knocked on his office door. Together they made the call. The person who answered hesitated before putting Mrs. Johnson on the line. "This is a difficult time. May I ask who's calling?"

"My name is Claire, Claire Rawlings." She remembered Simon having a younger sister and wondered if that was who was speaking. The voice asked her to hold. Soon Simon's mother was on the line. "Mrs. Johnson, I'm not sure if you remember me."

She said she did and thanked Claire for calling. Claire offered their condolences. Mrs. Johnson invited them both to the memorial service. Claire had prayed she wouldn't extend an invitation. Before the conversation ended, Mrs. Johnson added, "Simon and I were very close. I know how much you meant to him. If possible, could you and Mr. Rawlings arrive early?"

Claire looked at Tony, who raised his eyebrows and shrugged his shoulders. "If you would like us to, we will."

"Thank you. The service will begin at two but the family is having a private viewing at noon. I would appreciate it if you and Mr. Rawlings could arrive at one."

Claire said they would and Tony hung up.

The flight to Louisville, Kentucky, was quiet. Incredibly supportive, Tony didn't work or read his laptop or do anything not directed toward Claire. It added to her discomfort. A driver took them from Louisville to Madison, a small quaint town on the Ohio River. It was the first time Claire had been in Indiana in years.

The funeral home resembled a colonial mansion, brick with large white pillars. They arrived early and sat in the car. The entire scenario was unnerving. Claire knew she was fidgeting. Finally, Tony grabbed her hand and squeezed. Claire exhaled and looked at her husband. Astounded by his sensitivity considering this was Simon, she vocalized her thoughts without considering the ramifications. "Why are you being so supportive?"

Perhaps doing the same, he replied, "Because I wasn't able to support you when your parents died."

"What? I don't understand."

He held her hands. "Claire, you had to go through your parents' deaths alone. Emily had John but you didn't have anyone. You said you haven't been to a funeral since then. I couldn't comfort you then, please let me do it now."

She did. Not because he wanted her to, but because she needed him to. She needed the feeling of love and support he described. She melted into his embrace. When the time came, they walked into the funeral home hand in hand.

Claire recognized Mrs. Johnson immediately, a lovely blond-haired woman with Simon's big blue eyes. Realistically, she wasn't much older than

314

Tony. Claire tried to act resolved, but her emotions were too fresh, too near the surface. The two women embraced and wept. Mrs. Johnson then directed them to a private room, where they were joined by Simon's father, sister, and another woman. Claire assumed the slender pretty brunette with brown puffy eyes was Amber McCoy.

Being incredibly resilient, Mrs. Johnson asked them to sit and spoke. "Thank you for coming today, Mr. and Mrs. Rawlings, I know Simon would be pleased."

They both acknowledged her with pleasantries. Claire immediately added, "Please, call me Claire."

"Claire, Simon told me he spoke with you a few months ago. I asked you here early because I wanted to let you know how important that was for him." She held Claire's hand. Claire nodded as Mrs. Johnson continued, "You had no way of knowing how much and how long he pined for you. There was a time he believed if he left you alone until you achieved your career goal, you would be ready to see him again. But seeing you, talking to you, learning that you aren't what they say . . . well, just learning you are still the Claire he remembered, and most importantly, that you are happy, he was finally able to move on."

Claire listened, both with concern for Simon's mother and Tony.

Mrs. Johnson motioned toward the slender brunette. "This is Amber. She and Simon were recently engaged." Claire and Tony both said hello to her. "Simon loved Amber very much, but he had to let you go. I want you to know, you will always be special to our family because our son loved you." Claire's chest heaved as she silently wept. Tony comforted her. "You had no way of knowing his feelings, he didn't convey them. Don't ever think we have ill feelings toward you. How could anyone hold something against someone when they didn't even know it was happening?" She squeezed Claire's hands. "I just thought you should know the importance of your short talk. He walked away knowing you were happily married, he knew he could move on. Thank you."

Claire tried to smile. "I'm thankful we had the opportunity to talk." And for the first time, she truly was.

Then Mrs. Johnson addressed Tony. "Mr. Rawlings, God is so funny."

Tony replied, "I'm sorry, I don't follow."

"Mr. Rawlings, if there was one man my son idealized besides his father it was you." Tony's eyes reflected the appreciation she sent his way. "He received his start at his dream job in one of your companies. When he first started working there, you made a few visits to their office. You probably don't remember, but on one occasion you spoke to Simon about one of his projects. He talked about it for months. He aspired to be like you. Now you and Claire are happily married. I just think God has a sense of humor." She looked lovingly at both of them, introduced them to the rest of the family, and added, "Please sit up toward the front, it would mean a lot to Simon, and it means a lot to me." They did.

Throughout the memorial Tony held Claire's hand. Later when she tried, she couldn't remember the service. Between Mrs. Johnson's words and memories of her parents' funeral her energy went to appearing composed, fighting the pounding in her head, and not fainting.

On the flight home she thought about Mrs. Johnson's words: Simon aspired to be Tony. She thought about her assessment of Tony: ruining lives with his business decisions. Maybe there was more to her husband. If Simon aspired to be Tony, maybe there was something there to aspire to. With her head on his lap, she looked up at him and recognized his expression: thoughts in a million different places. She watched his strong jaw that clenched and unclenched, his dark brown eyes, furrowed brow, and perfectly combed hair. Maybe he helped lives, too. Mrs. Johnson believed he did. Claire just needed a different perspective.

Grandma Nichols said, "Sometimes you can't see the forest for the trees." Perhaps she was too close. She knew Tony, intimately knew his flaws, maybe he was a different man from a distance. The voices in her head debated. Other people thought Tony was a kind, wonderful, generous, benevolent businessman. She knew he could be loving, tender, sensual, and lavish. She also knew a side of him that didn't fit either description. Looking up, she saw her husband absently stared into space as he continued to stroke her blonde hair. Claire appreciated his efforts over the last few days, he was trying. She exhaled deeply and closed her eyes.

Tony remembered her expression during the funeral, so much overwhelming grief. That kind of emotion was only visible with the loss of someone you love dearly. Of course, she lost *two* someones. He remembered the church overflowing with people.

Even though his death was not in the line of duty, Officer Jordon Nichols received full police honors. There were uniformed police everywhere. Apparently, Shirley Nichols had many bereaved friends and students. Blending into the crowd wasn't difficult. Now as he stroked Claire's silky hair he realized his plan took a turn that day. Originally, he had different designs, but watching her flanked by her sister, he knew he had to know her. Actually, reminiscing, he knew before then that he didn't want anyone else knowing her.

The internship was an easy ploy to rid her of Simon. Watching the sadness from Claire and his family today, there was a part of Tony which hated what happened. But it was Simon's fault. He should have just left Claire alone, but no. His actions in Chicago resulted in the consequences today in Madison.

Tony beheld his wife's sleeping face on his leg. That day so many years ago she'd been all alone. Today, he did what he wanted to do then. It was him, not Emily, not John. She needed *him*. This wasn't an occasion for smiles, but knowing she was asleep, he grinned.

As they landed in Iowa he gently woke his wife. It was only about six in the evening but the sky was dark and spitting snow. They hurried from the plane to the warm waiting car. Tony asked Claire a question, "Where would you like to go for our anniversary?"

"Some place sunny and warm." The desire she didn't say aloud was *alone*.

Anyone can give up. It's the easiest thing in the world to do.
But to hold it together when everyone else would understand
if you fell apart, that's true strength.
—Unknown

Chapter 45

November fluctuates between autumn and winter. Technically, winter doesn't begin until after the winter solstice. But as it approaches, the days dramatically decrease in length and the darkness increases. Some days in November include brilliant blue skies and crisp, intense sunshine. The contrast and fluctuations in weather and life created the unpredictable pressures defining Claire's existence. She stressed when Tony was *good* because she knew it may not last. She worried when he was *bad* because she knew how bad he could be.

During a private girls' lunch, Courtney approached the subject again. Since the completion of the silent auction, the frequency of their lunch dates had decreased. Claire desperately missed them. Therefore, following Simon's memorial, she was elated to receive another invitation accompanied by Tony's eagerness for her to accept. He said, "I think you need some fun." She couldn't have agreed more.

They spent the afternoon in Bettendorf eating, shopping, walking, and talking. Courtney knew about Simon. She knew an old friend of Claire's had approached her at one of Tony's speaking events and that Tony wasn't pleased. She didn't know the entire story. She also knew about Simon's sudden death and Tony's remarkable support.

Courtney made Claire laugh, and that was monumental for Claire's precarious mental health. Courtney talked about the impending holidays. She expectantly waited for her children to return home from their points of interest and settle in for holiday celebrations. Claire liked the Simmons children, who weren't really children. They were in their twenties—one still in graduate school, the other beginning a career as an investment banker in St. Louis. Neither married, but their son Caleb had a steady girlfriend. Courtney liked her and hoped Caleb would pop the question soon. She and Brent wanted to be grandparents. It seemed strange Claire was only two years older than Caleb, and Courtney was her best friend.

Another exciting topic for Courtney was her impending trip. Tony finally recognized Brent's hard work and awarded him a substantial Christmas bonus. He told Brent before the holidays so Brent could plan some nice surprise for Courtney. Brent didn't want to risk Courtney's disapproval, so he included her in the planning from the beginning. They were going to Fiji, similar to Tony and Claire's honeymoon. Refusing to miss Christmas with their children, they wouldn't go until after the first of the year. Courtney asked Claire lots of questions. Her excitement was contagious. Claire told Courtney everything she could remember. Mostly the destination equaled paradise and don't worry about packing too many clothes, they didn't seem to stay on in paradise.

Courtney understood Claire's privacy issues. Most of their confidential discussions occurred while walking or driving. Claire couldn't risk someone overhearing. "Honey, I'm really worried about you. I know losing a friend is hard, but it just seems like you have been going down since before Simon's death."

Claire didn't even try to act fine. "I just don't know. I feel empty and tired all the time."

"If there is *anything* I can do for you," she squeezed Claire's hand, "I'll do it."

"I think afternoons like this are the best medicine." Courtney agreed laughter would help. So they laughed. They walked in shops, read funny cards and plaques, and had fun.

When Claire returned that night she felt lighter. She tried with all her might to continue the feeling into her home and her suite. The fact Tony tried to help, wasn't lost on Claire. He immediately showed her an e-mail from Emily, volunteering, "She wants you to call early before John gets home. I think you should call before dinner."

They went to Tony's office and Claire tried again. She'd been trying to reach her for almost two weeks, since the first of November. This time Emily answered on the first ring. "Hello?"

Talking on the speaker phone, Claire replied, "Hi, Emily, it's Claire. We've been worried. Is everything all right?"

"I don't think so. I asked you to call early before John got home."

"I was out with Courtney today. I called as soon as I got your e-mail." That was all true.

"He isn't home yet. Is Anthony there?"

Claire hesitated, should she lie or be truthful? "He is. Do you want to talk to him?"

"I don't know, maybe he can help." Tony looked at Claire and raised his eyebrows.

"I could put you on speaker phone so he can hear too." Emily said that would be a good idea. Tony pushed a button to create an audible change, and said hello. Emily said hello. They heard her voice crack. Claire asked her sister, "Emily, what's wrong?"

"You know the deadline for partnership decisions was the first?" Claire said she did, Tony acknowledged her audibly too. "Well, it has been extended."

Claire broke in, always the optimist, "So that isn't necessarily bad, they're still undecided."

"But now the auditor, the person verifying all the accounting information, is questioning John, a lot. John has been asked to verify everything. He is rummaging through old records and spending hour after hour documenting and authenticating his previous work." Claire and Tony were engaged in concerned eye contact.

Tony responded first. "Emily, I'm sure it is some kind of formality. John works for a very prestigious firm, they just want every *T* crossed and every *I* dotted."

"Anthony, I hope you're right." They could hear her sniffles. "He pretends to be unconcerned, but I can tell that isn't the case."

"He is probably sick of the controlling procedure and stress." Claire could relate, trying to rationalize and validate every move you make can become tiresome.

"I believe he is offended. Claire, you know John. He would never do anything that wasn't completely honest and honorable."

Claire debated about adding to *John's fan club.*

Tony responded first. "We did our research prior to offering John a job. I know he is one of the most honest and honorable attorneys anywhere." Claire scanned her husband's expression. She only saw sincerity.

"I second that, Em. It will be okay. Let them scrutinize John's records, there's nothing dishonest or deceitful to discover."

"Thank you, really, both of you. John didn't want me telling you. That's why I haven't answered your calls, but I really wanted you to know."

Claire felt her internal time clock ticking. "Emily, please keep us posted—"

Tony interrupted. "If I can be of any assistance? Perhaps we can get together for Thanksgiving again this year." Claire watched her husband with astonishment as he spoke. "We could meet in NYC or maybe closer to Troy if it would be easier for you."

Emily thanked them both. She would think about Thanksgiving. She appreciated Anthony's offer of help. It was nice to just talk with them. "I promise to keep you updated. I better go in case John gets home soon. Thank you." They hung up.

Claire had been upset with Tony for almost two months. She despised him for his reaction in Chicago. His behavior that night had repulsed her. She detested the way he treated her in California. On some level she even loathed the fact Simon idolized him. Yet, he had tried on numerous occasions to make amends. Only superficially had she accepted his pleas. Those shallow recognitions were mainly a form of self-preservation, a ploy to pacify him. But at that moment, as he disconnected the line, she overwhelmingly appreciated and cherished her husband. The realization almost immobilized her. Every ounce of her being had been opposed to him, similar to like ends of magnets. Her self-therapy suddenly realized all of her energy had been consumed continually fighting the repulsion and forcing herself to be near him. No wonder she was so drained. But as he hung up the phone, her magnet flipped; suddenly, instead of repulsion she felt attraction. The relief engulfed her, her mask evaporated, and her expression became sincere. "Thank you, Tony." She went to him and hugged him.

He recognized the difference in her touch. Looking down into her green eyes, he said, "I need to keep working."

She didn't understand, thinking he was saying he had work to do. She pulled away to let him have his office. He gently pulled her back into his embrace. She looked up into his soft brown eyes.

"No, Claire, I need to keep working to be a man you are proud to be married to." She buried her face in his chest. There would be mascara on his very expensive suit. He lifted her chin. "I need to work to be the man Mrs. Johnson thinks I am."

Later that night they laughed, cuddled, and talked. Their interaction hadn't been playful for months. Claire was giddy from the release of tension and stress. For the first time in ages her head didn't pound. She wasn't worried about John; he was beyond reproach. Everything would resolve itself there. The looming question had been *here*. Unexpectedly, she believed it too had been resolved. Realistically, the resolution wouldn't be permanent, but she would enjoy the reprieve.

Emily e-mailed them the following week to decline Tony's Thanksgiving invitation. She sincerely appreciated his offer, but John barely took time to eat. He worked continually to rectify the inquiry.

Tony saw Claire's disappointment and offered a *trip* anywhere for the holiday. Claire decided she would rather stay home and celebrate an old-fashioned Thanksgiving together. She wanted to cook him a traditional Thanksgiving dinner. He looked concerned but agreed as long as she would allow him to plan a getaway for their anniversary and Christmas. She agreed.

Giving the entire staff the day off, they lived through Thanksgiving dinner and even survived the carbohydrate overdose. Claire cooked turkey, stuffing, mashed potatoes, gravy, yams, yeast rolls, pumpkin pie, and vegetables. Tony obligingly ate some of everything, saying he liked it all. However, the exorbitant amount of calories contained within the meal far exceeded their usual diet. They both feared they would explode before the pumpkin pie with whipped cream was served.

Although she enjoyed cooking, Claire forgot how much she disliked cleaning. Tony encouraged her to leave it. The staff would take care of it the next day. Somewhere in the recesses of her mind she heard her mother and grandmother, leaving it for someone else was unacceptable. She told Tony to watch football, and she would take care of it. To Claire's surprise, Mr. Anthony Rawlings joined his wife in their kitchen and scrubbed pans, counters, and stove tops. Watching him, Claire decided he was even sexier washing dishes than he was in blue jeans.

After Thanksgiving, the house burst with Christmas decorations. Catherine told Claire prior to her presence there hadn't been any decorations. Claire found that hard to believe. She didn't ask for them, but did enjoy them. It wasn't as extreme as it was for the wedding, but it was festive. They entertained friends and some of Tony's business associates. Claire was happy to open the house for others to see its merry charm.

On the Saturday before their anniversary, they boarded Tony's plane and flew west. This time Hawaii was their destination. On their trip to Fiji, Tony had promised Claire the opportunity to enjoy the Hawaiian Islands. They had ten days. Reminiscent of their honeymoon, they stopped in Los Angeles to refuel and continued another six hours to the island of Oahu, landing in Honolulu.

The difference with this trip was Claire knew her journey's end. She understood that when they landed in Honolulu they needed to board an inter-island flight to take them to the island of Lanai. It was a romantic getaway, not as secluded as their private island in Fiji, but an island paradise nonetheless. Tony had asked her what she wanted, and she had said sunshine and warmth. He delivered. She hadn't told him she wanted to go alone, but Lanai was as secluded as you could get, and she was happy to have her husband with her.

This time they had a suite in a resort. An exquisitely spectacular suite complete with panoramic views of the Pacific Ocean. Claire's favorite amenity was the large private lanai. It included a daybed, dining table for two, and lounge chairs. Tony explained they would have the suite for the entire stay, but they would also spend a few nights on other islands. Tony now understood how Claire enjoyed sightseeing, so he planned excursions for Kauai, Oahu, and the Big Island.

Kauai's spectacular cliffs, canyons, rainforests, and picturesque beaches took them two days and one night of exploration. Claire treasured being on Lumahai Beach, the place where "South Pacific" was filmed. In her mind she could see Mary Martin singing. Tony arranged private sea tours. They saw spinner dolphins, monk seals, green sea turtles, as well as natural wonders, the Na Pai Coast, open ceiling cave, and Honopu Valley Arch.

The day they spent on Oahu, they arrived early on an inter-island plane, rented a car, and Tony drove them around the island. They reverently visited Pearl Harbor, walking hand in hand and reading plaques and names. Tony drove them up Pali Highway through trees and dense forest vegetation until the city below disappeared, and they found themselves in the clouds. It was Nuuanu Pali Outlook. They could see the Koolau Cliffs, amazingly lush coastline, and mountain peaks all from the stone terrace one thousand feet above the Oahu coast. The view was spectacular.

That evening, they returned to Lanai for more private and sensual explorations. Neither of them moved fast or needy. Instead, they both were thorough, sensual, and loving. The sea breeze and sound of the surf provided the ultimate aphrodisiac, and their lovemaking went on and on.

On the Big Island they enjoyed a two-hour helicopter tour of Volcano Park. This was a first-time experience for both of them, and they found the process of creation and destruction thrilling. Claire couldn't help remembering the volcano on Mount Etna in Sicily, also active. In one year she had witnessed two active volcanoes erupting violently, yet without peril. Something told her she was pushing her luck. The pilot explained to them that Pele, the Volcano goddess who lives in the volcano, was very unpredictable. It could continue to erupt for another one hundred years or it could quit tomorrow. Claire nodded; she understood unpredictability.

After the helicopter tour, they spent a few hours hiking trails which took them directly into volcanic craters, scalded deserts and rainforest, and a petroglyph. She had read about them but to be in a volcanic tube exhilarated her. Another Big Island activity Tony insisted they complete was to walk on the Black Sand Beach. Claire didn't think she would like *black* sand, sand, after all, is supposed to be white, but it was unusual and magnificent. Removing their shoes, Claire felt the warmth of the black sand under her feet. She'd expected it to be hot. Actually, she'd experienced hotter white sand in Florida, another unpredictable conclusion.

Christmas day they spent on Lanai in their suite. Claire was prepared for the holiday this year. She had a gift for Tony, an exquisite d. Freemont Swiss watch which she'd purchased on Rodeo Drive in October. If he had seen the bill, he hadn't said a thing. On Christmas morning, he acted surprised and delighted. Claire knew how he appreciated punctuality.

Also planning ahead, Tony had a gift for Claire. However, his gift wasn't as extravagant. Actually, it was very basic and left her speechless. He placed it in a slightly larger black velvet box, the kind that might contain a necklace. At first, she thought he forgot, but his grin indicated a scheme. "It isn't jewelry, so I thought I could use a black box, but if you don't want it . . ." He started to take the box back.

Smiling, she said, "No, I want it." She pulled the box toward her, her curiosity getting the better of her. She lifted the lid to reveal a basic calling and texting only cellular telephone. Previously, she had opened velvet boxes to lavish diamonds and gold which hadn't moved her like this inexpensive cellular phone.

Watching her emerald eyes glisten, Tony decided the accompanying lecture could wait. Claire felt like she received the milestone of liberties. It was a wonderful Christmas. That night, lying on the daybed under the stars, they listened to the sound of waves in the distance. Completely relaxed, spooning against her husband, Claire's mind went back to a snowy afternoon in Tony's suite. That afternoon she made requests. She also made a request as they lay upon a rug in Lake Tahoe. Tonight, she realized, they'd all been granted. As her mind started to slip into sleep, she heard Tony say, "Merry Christmas, my love." She hugged his strong arms. He asked, "What are you thinking?"

Claire turned to face him. "I was thinking that I have everything, everything I asked for. Thank you." She kissed his lips. "I love you," and drifted off to sleep.

They arrived back at Iowa on December 28. Snow blanketed the estate and the decorations glistened. Tony had a meeting in Chicago on the twenty-ninth. Worn-out from their trip, Claire decided to stay home. She told Tony she would try to appreciate the Midwest winter until he returned.

Sometimes it's the smallest decisions
that can change your life forever.
—Keri Russell

Chapter 46

Tony's lecture regarding his gift came on the plane ride home. It started as operational instructions. Claire considered this futile. She received her first cell phone in middle school and knew how to dial a number, answer a call, send a text message, and receive one. However, his lesson did contain useful information. Her telephone linked to his computer and iPhone. If she received a call or text, he received a notification. If she sent a text or made a call, he received a notification. He even had an application allowing him to access telephone numbers and the entire content of text messages. Claire told herself to compartmentalize. She had a cell phone.

He instructed her to only answer calls from numbers programmed into her phone with an asterisk. Examples: *Tony Cellular, *Home Private, *Eric. There were other numbers programmed into her phone: Emily cell, John V. Cell, Vandersol home, Courtney S., MaryAnn F., etc. They could leave voice mails or texts. Together they would listen or read and decide responses. Claire obediently listened and sighed, thinking, *this is ridiculous!*

"You asked for me to be able to contact you directly. This will accomplish what you asked."

She pressed her lips together and thought, *he is right, I did and it will. I want more!* Deciding to capitalize on the *Christmas spirit*, she pushed, "Maybe I could at least text Courtney and Sue back immediately. I mean, after all, didn't you say you can read the texts in real time from your iPhone?" Her husband made a fortune with the Internet, he had technology which allowed him to watch, listen, and monitor her every move. She knew that.

He contemplated his answer. "We will start with my rules. After a time, we can revisit them." She submitted. He hadn't closed the subject. It was a minor victory or a minor defeat. Either way, it wasn't the end of the war.

They celebrated New Year's Eve at their home with friends: the Simmons, their son Caleb and his fiancée Julia, Tim and a six-month pregnant Sue, and Tom and Beverly. They all had a wonderful time. They spent most of the evening in the lower level, playing cards and pool, drinking champagne, talking, and laughing.

Courtney couldn't contain her enthusiasm regarding their son's engagement. Julia appeared overwhelmed by her overly zealous future mother-in-law. Claire couldn't help herself. She offered Julia some advice, "Smile and give in. It makes life a lot easier." They hadn't set a date yet. Courtney told Claire she may have more charitable responsibilities this year. She planned on helping Julia as much as possible with the wedding. Claire read Julia's expression and whispered in her ear, "I promise to talk to her later."

Julia smiled. "Thank you."

Tim and Sue's baby was due March 20. All the women "*oowwd*" and "*ahhhed*" at her growing midsection. It made Claire think, she and Tony had never discussed children. About six months before she met Tony, she had the birth control insert implanted. In hindsight, that'd been fortuitous. However, considering Tony's age, maybe this was a subject they should discuss.

Together they all welcomed the New Year with enthusiasm. "To another great year for everyone and for Rawlings Industries," everyone tapped glasses. Claire and Tony both told the Simmons how fantastic Fiji would be. Claire added, "We can't wait to hear all about it." Then she smiled. "Well, not all."

Courtney blushed. Tony embraced Claire, she'd filled him in on her *packing advice,* and they kissed. Brent looked at Courtney questionably. She grinned, "I'll explain later." That made them giggle some more. The year began with a bang.

Although Tony contacted Claire directly each evening, she didn't feel like she'd gained any liberties regarding communication. Emily had her number and would leave text messages and voice mails. Claire could read them or listen to them, but she couldn't respond until Tony's input was added. She learned deleting texts or voice mails was strictly forbidden, it implied hiding. She didn't ask, but wondered why. If Tony had access to every text why did he need to see it on her phone before she deleted it?

The Simmons left for Fiji and Tony missed Brent. Claire found it amusing. He would never admit Brent's full worth, yet his absence left Tony lacking. She planned to share this secret knowledge upon their return. Courtney asked Claire to fill in with her multiple charities during her absence. Being January, the heart of her winter blues, Claire happily agreed to the additional tasks. Unfortunately, Claire agreed to help Courtney without first conferring with Tony.

"I agree they are admirable charities. I don't think you need to be gone that much."

"It is only for two weeks, and I already said I would help."

"You agreed without discussing it. Did you forget about your responsibilities here? I certainly hope you are not having memory problems again."

"I didn't forget and I'm sorry. I just wanted to help a friend. I promise nothing will go undone here."

"You are right, because you won't be going. Or do you not feel taking care of your husband is important?"

Claire knew her pleas were useless. "Tony, I'm sorry."

She called each organization. "I am truly sorry I won't be able to attend your meeting. It seems that I have double booked my calendar. If you could e-mail the information, I will forward it to Mrs. Simmons." Those calls were made on the speaker feature of her new phone with her husband present. Suddenly, her calendar was open to Tony's whims.

Claire believed these consequences resulted more from Brent's absence than from her insubordination. Tony would never admit that. Her attraction toward her husband was waning. Experience taught her it was a cyclical process. It would wane and then it would wax. She encouraged herself to be patient for the wax.

This January was less snowy than the last, which helped Claire's disposition. Less snow meant fewer clouds, more sunshine. The Iowa air still registered below freezing, but the view from her suite wasn't of frozen white tundra. The winter, combined with the feeling unpredictability was predictably returning, gave her the *teetering on the fence* sensation from before. Continuing her personal self-therapy, Claire reminded herself Courtney would be back in another week and spring was only three months away.

Admittedly, more of an attempt to pacify than an act of devotion, she tried desperately to alleviate Tony's concerns. She obediently waited for him each evening, dressed appropriately for his arrival, attentively listened to his day and concerns, discussed her e-mails, texts, voice mails, and expressed her undying affection. She even chose to not pursue the e-mails and text messages from Emily. That was, until she heard a recent voice mail. The distress in her sister's voice was unnerving. She respectfully asked Tony if they could call her.

They did from Claire's telephone. Having her cell phone saved the long walk to his office. They tried three times and didn't receive an answer. Tony willingly agreed to try again later. They finally reached Emily and the information from the call was difficult for Claire to fathom. John had been accused of fraudulent billing. The Vandersols were devastated.

The next morning, Claire opened her eyes and realized she was waking in Tony's bed. The feeling of disorientation came more from her concern over her family, than from the dark surroundings. She rolled toward him, but he was gone. The clock read 7:03 a.m. If she hurried to the dining room, she might catch him before he left for work. She wanted to thank him again for the ability to talk to her sister during this difficult time. Truth be known, she hoped her gratitude would facilitate her opportunity to support Emily in the future. She put on slippers and her cashmere robe and walked to the dining room. The rich aroma of coffee met her halfway down the corridor. Tony was at the head of the table, drinking coffee, his plate empty, and his laptop open. When Claire entered the room, he looked up. "Good morning, my dear. You look beautiful this morning."

She made a face, "I think you need an eye exam," and gave him a kiss. "I just wanted to catch you before you left." Claire sat down at the table and Catherine poured her coffee. "I wanted to tell you how much I appreciate talking to Emily. This is a difficult time for them." She added some cream, watching the ivory liquid swirl into the black abyss. Then she looked up into his eyes, wondering if they were the color of the coffee with or without the cream, and added, "And I wanted to let you know I'll miss you." She smiled at the cream filled eyes as she spoke.

"Good news, I'm working from home today."

Claire's heart sank, she really wanted alone time to contemplate the *John thing*. However, her smile never faltered.

Tony continued, "So you will not need to miss me."

"That's great! Do you have a lot of work?"

"A few web conferences and phone calls, but don't worry, I know your schedule is free. I have some ideas for us too." The smile and the way his eyes shone made Claire question his ideas. She would be glad when Brent returned. This Tony made her uneasy, detesting the dual personalities.

Sipping her coffee, "All right, I need to work out and clean up. I came down here in a hurry to see you."

"When you're dressed come to my office," he said, as he stood to leave. He paused to touch her shoulder.

Obediently she replied, "I will be there as soon as I can."

He kissed her cheek. "Or you could visit before you dress?" his tone suddenly playful.

She touched his hand. "If I do that, you may not get your work done." He reluctantly agreed and went to his office. She smiled at his attire: shirt, tie, NYU sweatpants, socks, and slippers. *That* comment to *Vanity Fair* had been truthful.

Claire's thoughts wandered as she sipped her coffee, ate her breakfast, and looked out the tall windows. For January, the sky was an amazingly clear sapphire blue. Suddenly, she longed to be outside and in the sunshine. The John situation had her heartsick. Maybe some fresh air would give her a new perspective and some ideas to help her family. The beautiful scene outside the window beckoned her to walk, roam, and get away, if only for a few hours. The snow of the last few weeks melted, yet today it was cold enough to keep the ground solid. Perhaps she would have time for a hike before Tony's ideas. Maybe she could entice him to walk, too. He might have some ideas to help John.

Thinking about her walk, Claire finished her shower and left her bathroom considering the appropriate clothes: jeans, a sweater, hiking boots. Her plans didn't matter. She saw her clothes were laid out. She hated that. This attire assistance occurred without predictability since her *accident*. There were jeans, dressier than she would have chosen, and a blue snug-fitting V-neck sweater—not exactly perfect for hiking, but with the addition of a coat and scarf it could work.

Then she noticed her jewelry on the dressing table. Her internal monologue: *Seriously, it is morning, who needs diamonds in the morning?* Avoiding an unnecessary confrontation, she did as she was bid, dressed in the clothes, and put on the diamond journey necklace, diamond stud earrings, and diamond watch. Her new watch from Switzerland was beautiful, but it sat on her wrist as a constant reminder of punctuality. She'd been late twice. She didn't need a watch to remind her of Tony's appreciation. The first time taught her a lesson she would never forget.

Luckily, there were no shoes set out. She could put on the hiking boots and hope for the best. She was pretty sure Tony's ideas didn't include shoes, but hers did. Maybe he could find his hiking boots, too.

It was almost ten by the time she reached his office. She knocked and waited for his permission to enter. She didn't hear him, but the door opened, and she entered, seeing him seated behind his desk with a shirt and tie, looking so professional. She smiled and quietly sat on the leather sofa away from the webcams and waited for the web conference to finish. It had something to do with a company in Michigan that was losing money. The local government wasn't willing to give more tax breaks. Were they going to close it or keep it open? The discussion revolved around the potential for future profits. It would probably result in more unemployed people. Claire didn't want to think about it. She picked up a magazine and began quietly ruffling through the pages.

Ten forty-five he finally finished. She waited for him to complete whatever he was doing on his computer. Once he was done, she heard his chair turn toward her. "Ahh, blue, my favorite color," he said eying the sweater, as she walked toward him. "You are beautiful in any color." His eyes were appreciative of what he could see and what he couldn't, "or in no color." And he smiled and reached out to put his hands around her waist. "I have one more web conference at eleven, then two lunch phone calls. I would like you back after those." It sounded like a request, it wasn't.

"It is so nice out. I would like to go for a hike while you are working." Wording was such an intricate part of her negotiations.

"No, the phone calls may need to be postponed depending on the outcome of the next web conference. I would like you here if I'm done earlier. We can lunch and discuss our possible afternoon activities." He'd turned back to his computer screen to read while he spoke.

Claire took a breath, leaned down, and gently kissed his neck. She'd been good, he knew she was upset about her family, and she hoped she could press a little more. "Well," exhaling purposely on his neck, "then may I just go out back? The sky is so clear and I could really use some fresh air."

He was obviously engrossed with his computer, but her approach earned her a seductive grin. "Okay, just be back by noon. And could you get me some coffee before you go?"

Claire started to ask where Catherine or another member of the staff was, but deciding that it could delay her trip to the backyard. She kissed his neck. "Yes."

In the kitchen she found coffee still warm in the pot. She added cream, carried it back to his office, and waited. It was now ten fifty-seven.

Tony rummaged through some papers and simultaneously spoke on his iPhone. Hanging up, he said, "Tell Eric there are contracts at the Iowa City office. I need them here *before* one o'clock. He needs to get them immediately." Claire thought about how he was trying to keep her busy at home. She really didn't mind, but she wanted to go on her walk. He saw the question in her eyes. "And after that, go for your walk, just be back by noon."

She smiled and kissed his cheek. "Okay. I'll tell Eric and be back." She hurried to find Eric. Claire asked Catherine about Eric's whereabouts and explained she would be in the backyard if Mr. Rawlings needed her before noon.

Catherine directed Claire to Eric's apartment attached to the main garage. Claire started back toward the garages, a walk she rarely took. She didn't drive, and when she went anywhere, Eric or Tony picked her up at the front door. The walkway between the main house and garages was beautiful. The windows on both sides continued the full length of the hall and were so clear they seemed invisible.

She looked at the sky and thought about her sister and brother-in-law. Emily sounded so distraught on the phone last night. The fact Tony reminded her to call was a miracle in itself. The fact she spoke on speaker phone was expected. Claire couldn't believe John was actually in jail. The charges of embezzlement and fictitious client billing were ludicrous. John would never cheat on a test; much less do any of these things. That was what made John such an amazing attorney. He was honest, beyond honest. Claire tried to reassure Emily. She wanted to go to her and help. However, Tony would never allow that. Perhaps she could send money for John's defense. After all, wasn't Tony telling her all the time how much capital she possessed? If money wasn't good for accomplishing what you want, what good was it?

Her thoughts quickly changed to the beautiful cars as she entered the garages. Tony definitely liked his cars. Claire knew they had multiple new ones since her arrival. It was too bad she didn't drive. Sighing, she thought, *it has been almost two years.*

Light filtered from under the apartment door as Claire knocked. Eric immediately answered. What she could see of his apartment looked like a nicely decorated living room with an attached dining area.

"Yes, Mrs. Rawlings, may I help you?"

"Eric, Mr. Rawlings said there are some contracts at his Iowa City office that he must have by one o'clock. If you go immediately you'll be back in time." As Claire spoke, Eric grabbed his coat and hat. He unlocked a cabinet on the wall which contained keys to all the cars, took out the keys to the BMW 7 Series, and shut the cabinet.

Hurriedly, Eric looked at his watch. "Ma'am, tell Mr. Rawlings I'll be back before twelve thirty." He got into the car.

"I will, drive safely." Claire figured it could wait until she saw him at noon. As Eric pulled out of the garage, Claire noticed the key cabinet. It did not shut properly, revealing the keys to multiple cars. Suddenly nervous,

330

Claire contemplated the keys. She should shut the cabinet. Then she could go out to the backyard for *air*. Or she could take a set of keys and drive to as much *air* as she wanted. She wasn't thinking *air* for a lifetime, only enough *air* to breathe.

The decision took only seconds, yet it seemed like an eternity. She reached in, grabbed the first set she touched, and hit the clicker. The lights on the Mercedes Benz flashed. In the midst of unpredictability she did her best to be stable and obedient. This sudden impulsiveness filled her with excitement and fear. Before she could talk herself out of it, she sat in the car, smelled the *new car* aroma, felt the leather steering wheel, and turned the key.

Her motivation was not to leave Tony, forever. She just felt smothered. The constant monitoring, censoring, and controlling added to her sense of psychological instability. And the *different Tonys* added another dimension to her suffocation. A brief reprieve, or a momentary freedom, would help her sanity. Besides, she told her husband a year ago she liked to drive. That was all she wanted to do, drive.

Do not bite at the bait of pleasure,
till you know there is no hook beneath it.
—Thomas Jefferson

Chapter 47

The dashboard in front of her looked more like something from a helicopter, dials and lights came to life. Claire tried to remain calm. Driving hadn't changed in twenty-two months. She just needed to put the car in gear and push the accelerator. Trembling at the prospect of the simplistic task, she almost ran into the garage door. However, she remembered to push the button, waited for the door to lift, and concentrated on breathing—slowly inhaling and exhaling. The door opened, and cautiously, she proceeded down the driveway. Claire prayed if anyone saw the car, they would assume it was Eric. At the gates, she again pushed a button, the one she'd seen Eric push many times. At first, the gates seemed to hesitate, but then the iron fence swung wide.

She drove toward I-80 and inhaled. It was the sweetest air she'd smelled in almost two years. The clock on the dashboard read 11:16. In forty-four minutes, Tony would expect her in his office. She reasoned perhaps the web conference would go long, and he wouldn't notice her absence. Or, maybe the phone calls would start, and he would be preoccupied. She knew the truth: Tony could do ten things at once. Come twelve and one second he'd be irritated, by twelve fifteen he'd be fuming. Feeling her heart rate intensify, she wondered what would happen when they reunited. What kind of punishment would he decide was appropriate for this behavior? Feeling her wet palms slide on the leather steering wheel, she chose not to linger on the possibilities. The Mercedes was now heading east on I-80. Her mind searched for possible destinations. *Courtney—no, she was out of town. Emily—no, that would be the first place Tony would check.* Utilizing her therapy skills, she convinced herself this was a deserved break. She also instructed herself to relish the overpowering sensation of freedom, a feeling she hadn't known in twenty-two months. Slowly, she felt her senses awaken:

the countryside looked brighter, the leather seats emitted a stronger aroma, the wheels on the pavement created a soft hum, and the vibration responded to *her* movement of the wheel. It all invigorated her.

The brilliant dash indicated a full tank of gas. Silently, she thanked Eric, momentarily worrying he would suffer because of her actions. She concentrated on the majestic world outside the windows and watched the traffic which consisted mostly of semi-trucks. At first, this made Claire uncomfortable, but the Mercedes could weave and pass easily. Before moving to Tony's, she drove a Honda Accord. It was a good car, but the Mercedes felt like driving a cloud. Then, the clock caught her eye, 12:11. She started to wonder what was happening at home. Would he be looking for her or sending someone else to look? All Claire could do now was drive and think. She loved him, *but* the constant pressure was wearing on her. She just needed a break.

Taking the bypass around Davenport, she decided to go south on 74, away from NYC. At 3:30 she passed Peoria, Illinois. The emptiness in her stomach reminded her she hadn't stopped since she left the estate. She desperately needed a restroom and some food. In the distance she spotted golden arches. French fries sounded wonderful.

She hadn't eaten fast food in almost two years. Claire turned the wheel and eased into the McDonald's parking lot. Contemplating her order, she realized she didn't have money. Oh well, the restroom was free. If she had planned this excursion, she would have grabbed a coat and her purse. More than likely Tony had her ID and credit card, but for appearances she usually had cash in her wallet.

The overpowering aroma of fries lingered on her clothes as she got back into the car. Wondering about money, she saw her wedding rings. Of course, she wore hundreds of thousands of dollars' worth of jewelry. She just needed to sell some. How does one sell jewelry? And where?

Back on the interstate Claire decided to take 155 South to 55. That wasn't a good decision, 155 traveled slowly. When she finally reached 55 the signs said *to Springfield* and *to St. Louis*. It had been so long since she actually made decisions. She was lightheaded with independence or perhaps hunger.

Time passed. The sun started to fade and dusk loomed on the horizon. The loss of sunlight produced a similar effect on Claire's mind. Her lightheadedness dissolved into reality. She knew without a doubt she needed to turn around. Tony would be upset and there would be a punishment, a consequence for this action. But, she couldn't keep going. First, she needed cash. Second, what would the press say? Tony wouldn't be happy if her leaving became public. Trepidation filled every ounce of her being as she watched for a place to turn around. According to the sign, there was another exit two miles ahead.

Suddenly, questions swirled through her mind. Was there enough gas to get home? What will Tony do? Whatever punishment he chose, she decided, she deserved. She'd been impulsive and broken his rules. The small break was exhilarating, but it was time to face the consequences. There wasn't another choice. If she had her cell phone, she would call and tell him she was on her way home. She planned to beg for his forgiveness and plead temporary impulsive stupidity.

Lost in thought, she didn't see the flashing lights until they were directly behind her. Once she noticed them, Claire assumed they would pass. She wasn't speeding. But the police car didn't pass. Did Tony send them after her? How did they find her? Pulling over, she remembered the GPS. Had she really thought she could go unmonitored? She appeared casual as the policeman approached her window.

"Ma'am, please show me your registration, proof of insurance, and driver's license."

"Officer, I believe I left my purse at home by mistake. I can show you the registration and proof of insurance." She handed him the documents from the glove compartment.

"Ma'am, your name please?" the officer asked while reading the registration and insurance card.

"My name . . . my name is Claire, Claire Rawlings."

Handing her back the registration and insurance card, the officer said, "Ma'am, I need you to get out of your car."

Claire didn't want to get out of the car. She wanted to go home, her decision was made, and she needed to get home, soon. "Officer, was I speeding?"

"Ma'am, get out of the car, now." The policeman stared at her as he mumbled into his shoulder.

"Officer, I'm in a hurry. I don't have my purse, but I do have this watch. Perhaps your wife would like a very nice diamond watch." She was desperate to return to Iowa, to Tony, but *not* in a police car.

Retrieving his gun from its holster, the police officer repeated his demand, "Mrs. Rawlings, I need you to get out of the car, and keep your hands where I can see them." Holding his gun in one hand, he leaned toward her door. "Unlock your door. I will open it. Let me see your hands." Claire couldn't believe this was happening. She just wanted a moment of freedom and this policeman was treating her like a criminal. Had Tony accused her of stealing his car? That didn't seem like Tony. He wouldn't want the public scandal.

Claire unlocked the door and swung her legs out. Officer Friendly roughly grabbed her wrist and pulled, handcuffing her wrists behind her back. It made her shoulders and wrists ache. "What are you doing? Why are you doing this? I didn't steal this car, it belongs to my husband. I have every right to drive it!"

"Ma'am, I have orders to take you into the station for questioning." He walked her to his car, steering her with her hands.

"What about my husband's car? He will be very upset if anything happens to his car." Claire's voice sounded as desperate as she felt.

"Another officer is on her way, she'll drive your car to the station. It will be kept in impound until it is picked up or you are released." He kept listening to his shoulder.

"The other officer will be here in a few minutes."

"We better not leave until she gets here. I'm serious about my husband. He can become very upset. You don't want to be the person he gets hold of if anything happens to his car." She didn't want to be that person either. Sitting in the backseat of the patrol car, she heard the door slam and felt the sensation. A balloon popped, once full, now completely deflated... Freedom was sweet and gone.

When they pulled up to the Illinois State Police Station 56, she watched the Mercedes drive around the building. Worrying about the car was silly. But she didn't want to give Tony more ammunition for his punishment. The officer directed her into the station. Multiple uniformed and plain-clothed officers met them at the door. She was then directed to a dingy room where the smell of stale coffee and perspiration filled her senses. The only furniture was a steel gray table with two metal chairs. Claire sat in one of the cold chairs as the officer removed the cuffs. Rubbing her wrists, she looked at him and sounded convincingly resilient. "Sir, I am Mrs. Anthony Rawlings. I am sure you have heard of my husband, or at least had contact with one of his companies. I recommend you release me right now and I won't tell him about this incident."

He didn't respond and left her alone where she waited. Feeling the twisting within her stomach, she knew what was coming. Tony was probably on his way. Flying would get him there in less than an hour. The next time the door opened, she would see his dark eyes. The only sound within the small room was that familiar pounding within her head. As she waited, she resolved herself to the consequences she would face at home.

She broke the most important rule, many times, and now it was public. There was no way this wouldn't be on the news. She waited. The door opened. A female officer entered. "Mrs. Rawlings, would you like a drink, water or diet soda?"

"Thank you, I would like some water." Then she waited, some more. The next time the door opened, she looked toward the table. Enough time had passed, this had to be Tony.

"Mrs. Rawlings, I am Sergeant Miles and this," pointing to the man on his left, "is FBI Agent Ferguson."

"Hello. I'm confused, why is an FBI agent here?"

"We would like to ask you some questions about today." Claire nodded. "Ma'am, you must speak. Our conversation is recorded and movements can't be heard on an audiotape."

Claire hated recordings, audio or visual. "Yes, please go ahead and ask me anything. I was just driving my husband's car and forgot my driver's license."

"Ma'am, what time did you leave your residence outside of Iowa City?" Agent Ferguson asked as Sergeant Miles took notes.

Claire wondered if the audio recording wasn't thorough enough. "I left at eleven fifteen AM." That was easy. She'd looked at the dashboard clock.

"Did you see your husband before you left?"

"Do you mean did I ask my husband if I could leave? No."

"No, ma'am, I meant what I said. Did you see your husband before you left your residence?"

"Yes, I saw him just before eleven. He was in his office about to start a web conference."

"A web conference?" Sargent Miles asked.

"It is a conference that is live on the Internet, you know, on the 'web.'" The officers continued to ask questions about times and people. Claire told them the house staff were all present, except for their driver, Eric. He left before her, going to Mr. Rawlings's office to retrieve some paperwork for her husband. Had Claire told anyone she was leaving the house? She shook her head no, then remembering the audio tape she answered, "No." Why would she drive over five hours without her purse or telling anyone where she was going? She really didn't have a good answer. She couldn't tell them she didn't have access to her own ID and she wasn't allowed to go out by herself. If she did, she would be breaking his rules, and when Tony arrived he would be livid. Suddenly, she realized he was probably watching from behind a window right now. She felt her stomach twist. Her only choice was ignorance. "I don't know. The sky was so pretty and Iowa can get so gray. I guess I just wanted to go somewhere warmer."

"Mrs. Rawlings, you should know your husband will survive." Agent Ferguson's tone was flat.

Claire didn't understand, *survive?* Like he would crumble because she left him? "I'm not sure what you mean. Why wouldn't he survive?"

"Mrs. Rawlings, someone tried to kill your husband today. He was poisoned at approximately eleven fifteen this morning." Agent Ferguson answered as Sergeant Miles observed Claire.

She shook her head, trying to make sense of his words. But they didn't make sense. Tony was fine when she left, same as always. "You are mistaken. Mr. Rawlings had a web conference at eleven, where he was speaking with many people from his corporation." Her speech quickened as did her heart rate.

"Yes, he was supposed to be. However, after the web conference began, his associates witnessed him take a drink from a mug and suddenly slump to his side. Many of the viewers attempted to reach him via cell phone, but he didn't move. Luckily, one of the house staff heard the phones ringing and entered the office. They were able to fly him by helicopter to a hospital in Iowa City. His vitals are good, although he has yet to regain consciousness. The doctors believe he will make a full recovery. I am here representing the FBI because this is an attempted murder investigation which has crossed state lines." Agent Ferguson spoke as if he was addressing a suspect.

"I need to get to him immediately." Claire stood as she spoke. Sergeant Miles directed her back toward the chair. She was dumbfounded. "I'm sorry, are you accusing me of murdering my husband?"

"No, ma'am. Your husband wasn't murdered. You are being questioned regarding an *attempted* murder investigation."

She was stunned. "You are accusing *me* of hurting *him*? You should know, no one hurts Anthony Rawlings. If anything he has hurt me, numerous times."

"So are you claiming self-defense?"

336

Claire's neck stiffened, her voice became defiant, "I am not claiming anything. I did nothing that needs claiming."

"Mrs. Rawlings, do you have any idea what was in the mug that your husband drank from?" She knew exactly what was in that mug: coffee, made by her.

"Yes, officer, I would assume the mug contained coffee. Just before I left, I took him a cup of coffee." Her stomach was now a tangle of knots.

"You and your husband don't have household servants who usually prepare the food and drinks?"

"We do. But he asked me to get him coffee." Claire definitely didn't like how this was going. "I believe I need an attorney."

"Ma'am, you haven't yet been charged. However, asking for representation is your right. Be aware your husband's legal staff has sent word that representing you would be a conflict of interest. You will need to secure your own counsel."

"I would like to call John Vandersol, my brother-in-law." As the words left her mouth she remembered, "No, wait. I can't."

Another officer entered the room and began to talk with Sergeant Miles. After the two whispered, Sergeant Miles spoke. "Mrs. Claire Rawlings, my commanding officer has informed me the prosecuting attorney of Iowa City believes there is enough circumstantial evidence to hold you in this facility overnight and transport you back to Iowa City in the morning. The chief prosecutor of Iowa believes he will have an official warrant for your arrest signed by the judge by the time you arrive."

Claire heard the words but couldn't comprehend their meaning. Her internal voice tried to replay the day: *I dressed in what I was told, was in Tony's office at the time he told me to be, and asked like a five-year-old if I could go outside. This morning I poured my husband a cup of coffee, the coffee he asked me to get. Now, I am about to be charged with attempted murder?*

Another officer directed Claire to a cell. It was small, clean, and had a door that locked. She couldn't sleep. She worried about Tony. There was no one at home that morning except the two of them and the regular staff. Everyone had been with Tony for years, and he implicitly trusted them. None of them would hurt him. She worried, had he regained consciousness? Was the poison in the coffee in the pot? Maybe it was in the cream?

She wanted them to try to find the *real criminal* before he tried to hurt Tony again. Claire knew, when he regained consciousness, he would tell them she didn't, couldn't do this, and take her home.

No one can make you feel inferior
without your permission.
— Eleanor Roosevelt

Chapter 48

Yesterday, Claire drove in a luxurious Mercedes Benz all the way to St. Louis. The trip back to Iowa City wasn't as comfortable. She rode in the back of a police wagon, wearing handcuffs and accompanied by a uniformed officer. The county courthouse steps were filled with reporters and photographers. She tried to shield her face. People were taking pictures from all directions and shouting questions: "Why did you try to kill your husband? Did you do it for the money? Did you think you would get away with it?" The police rushed her through the crowd and into the building.

She heard their words with disbelief. How could they possibly be asking such questions? Claire worried about Emily. First John, now her, what must she be going through? Claire reassured herself, once Tony woke, he would take care of everything.

The officer took Claire to another room with a table. Marcus Evergreen entered. She recognized him immediately. He attended her wedding and she accompanied Tony to one of his fund-raisers. Claire thought Tony donated to his campaign. "Mrs. Rawlings, I'm Marcus Evergreen, chief prosecutor for Johnson County."

"Yes, Mr. Evergreen, I believe we've met." Claire held out her hand. Mr. Evergreen didn't accept it.

"Yes, I believe we have. This, however, is a different situation. Mrs. Rawlings, I am currently holding a warrant for your arrest recently signed by Judge Reynolds. Just so you know, before we reach the district courtroom for your arraignment, you are being charged with the *attempted murder of your husband, Anthony Rawlings.*"

"I want you to know I didn't do such a thing. I wouldn't do such a thing. How is Tony?" When Claire added the last question, Mr. Evergreen's eyes dropped to the table. Claire's heart sank. *Oh my god, he's dead! No, then he would have said "murder," not "attempted."*

"He is awake and conscious. He has given a statement to the police but will not be here today."

Claire was relieved to hear he was conscious, but she *needed* him to be here. He would help her and take her home. She wanted to explain things to him. He would be upset about the leaving and driving. There would be consequences, but he would know she would *never* try to kill him.

"I am very happy he is better. Can you tell me what evidence there is against me?" Claire didn't know how this worked, but she thought she needed to find out.

"It will be discussed with you and your attorney after the arraignment." He left the room.

With her wrists once again in handcuffs, Claire was led into the courtroom. She watched the proceedings from a distance, seeing it all, yet not comprehending it as reality. Judge Reynolds spoke, asking questions of Mr. Evergreen. He explained how *the state* believed it had sufficient evidence to *prove beyond a reasonable doubt* that Mrs. Claire Rawlings did willfully and maliciously attempt to murder her husband, Anthony Rawlings, in an effort to profit financially. Furthermore, Mrs. Rawlings fled the scene of the crime and was found near St. Louis. Mrs. Rawlings has access to a passport and the financial ability to flee. Mr. Evergreen asked the judge to suspend bail.

Judge Reynolds said, "Mrs. Rawlings, do you understand that you are being charged with a felony, attempted murder? And if convicted you could be sentenced to a federal penitentiary for a length not to exceed 162 months?"

"Yes, Judge, I understand." That wasn't true—she didn't understand.

"Are you aware that you have the right to an attorney? If you cannot afford one, one can be appointed for you. You also have the right to a trial by a jury of your peers. You also are presumed innocent. It is the burden of the state to prove your guilt. Do you understand your rights?"

"Yes, Judge, I understand." Claire maintained eye contact with the bench. She had a lot of practice maintaining eye contact in difficult situations.

"Mrs. Rawlings, do you have an attorney?"

"No, Judge, I do not. And I cannot afford one."

"The court will appoint one to you following the arraignment." Judge Reynolds reviewed the file before her. "Due to the publicity and significance of the victim, I am setting bond at 5 million dollars. I am also scheduling a preliminary conference for eleven days from today, Tuesday, February 1. Next case . . ." Her gavel struck the bench, echoing throughout the courtroom.

A guard escorted Claire to a holding cell. She sat in the ten-by-seven cube waiting for her attorney. The seclusion should have upset her, but she was too confused to focus. They told her once her attorney arrived, her bond could be posted, and she could leave. Claire knew that wasn't going to happen. She didn't have enough money for a sandwich at McDonald's, much less 2.5 million dollars for bond.

It was after 3:00 p.m. before she was once again taken to the small table room. A short while later, the door opened and a young man, Paul Task, entered, carrying a briefcase, laptop, and wearing a cheap suit. Claire's first thought was that he looked more like a high school student than an attorney. "Hello, Mrs. Rawlings, I'm your attorney Paul Task. I just want you to know that I'm so honored to work on your case. Mr. Rawlings has long been an inspiration to us in Iowa City. Everyone has so much respect for him. Why did you try to kill him? Was it because you don't have a prenuptial agreement? I mean, for the money?"

"*No*! I didn't do this. It is a terrible misunderstanding. I know once my husband is better he will help me. He knows I wouldn't do this to him."

"Yes, of course, Mrs. Rawlings—"

After Mr. Task informed the court that Mrs. Rawlings wouldn't be able to post bond, she was officially charged with a felony. They took her personal property, her jewelry and clothes. They took her picture, her fingerprints, and did a chemical test on her hands. A female officer offered her a prison jumpsuit, underwear, and a bra. Claire accepted it all.

For the next five days Claire waited and responded appropriately to her counsel. She met daily with Paul Task and his associate Jane Allyson. They asked questions and she maintained her innocence. She told them repeatedly the events of the morning in question. She never broke Tony's rules. When he came to save her, she would be able to tell him she maintained his confidence. She would explain to him -- she drove away. But she had decided to turn around. She hadn't *left* him, but only *left* the estate, for a while. She would apologize, accept his punishment, and life could resume.

She wondered who poisoned Tony. That answer could save her from 162 months in prison. Unfortunately, the evidence pointed to Claire. She gave Tony the mug of coffee at approximately 11:00 a.m. In plain view of fifteen people via a Rawlings Industries web conference, he took a drink and suddenly lost consciousness. The video footage from their home security showed Claire pouring coffee in the kitchen and carrying the coffee to his office. The desk area wasn't covered by cameras, but Claire was seen walking away from the desk without the mug.

To make this evidence worse, there was video from the garage of Claire telling Eric to go to Iowa City to get paperwork from Mr. Rawlings's office. Anthony's secretary, Patricia, provided a sworn statement that she didn't have contracts for Mr. Rawlings, and furthermore, she hadn't spoken to him that morning. Being Tony's primary source of transportation, having Eric gone would help ensure that the poison would have time to work. The same camera in the garage captured Claire taking the keys to the Mercedes and hurrying to the car. The significance of *this* car is that it was the only car in the garage registered under the name *Claire Rawlings*.

Claire was shocked. "It can't be registered in my name. I don't drive." Paul showed her a copy of the registration. The same one she handed to the policeman but hadn't read. According to the dealership, Mr. Rawlings came in himself last December and paid cash. It was his wife's Christmas present and had less than a thousand miles on it.

340

Her statement regarding *no valid driver's license* also proved erroneous. Apparently, she did have an "identification card" with the name Claire Rawlings, but her "driver's license" from Georgia under the name Claire Nichols was still valid. Paul couldn't understand how Claire wouldn't know.

She tried to explain, "Tony did everything."

Paul didn't understand. He told her that a jury would also have difficulty.

The state of Iowa furnished Claire with clothes for the preexamination conference. The court ordered preliminary conference remained six days away. This meeting would set the tone and direction for that conference. It was usually attended by the prosecuting attorneys, the defense attorneys, and the defendant, Claire. However, unbeknownst to the defendant, the victim requested to make an appearance. The judge agreed. The goal of this meeting was to determine if a trial could be avoided, and an agreement made. The victim convinced the judge, he could help facilitate that end.

Mr. Evergreen and two of his associates sat opposite Claire and her team, Paul Task and his co-council, Jane Allyson, at a large table covered in documents and laptops. The conference was about to begin when her heart skipped a beat. She saw *him*, through the window of the door. She saw his profile: strong, handsome, and inflexible. She watched as he spoke to someone in the hall, turned the door handle, and entered.

Mr. Evergreen and Paul were talking, but as the door opened, everyone became silent. The entire room turned to acknowledge the entrance of Mr. Anthony Rawlings. Mr. Evergreen stood. "Mr. Rawlings, I thought we discussed this, and you were not to attend this conference."

"Mr. Evergreen," the two men shook hands. Claire involuntarily trembled. If only she had known he was going to be there. "I appreciate everyone's concern for my safety. I will repeat what I told Judge Reynolds, I don't believe my wife is a threat to my well-being. I believe if we can have a few moments alone, we can save the taxpayers of Iowa the cost of a lengthy trial, and this court, some time. Judge Reynolds has agreed to my request." Tony's command of this situation was obvious. It sounded as though he just asked the others to leave the room, but in reality it was a mandate.

Mr. Evergreen and his team began to move their chairs and stand to leave. Paul and Jane whispered to one another as Paul stood. He leaned to Claire. "I will confirm that this has been approved by Judge Reynolds." Then speaking to Tony and doing his best to appear professional, however, obviously intimidated by Tony's mere presence. "Mr. Rawlings, I will need to confirm that Judge Reynolds has indeed approved this visit. In situations such as this—" Tony's height loomed over Paul as he interrupted and handed Paul a paper from his breast pocket.

"Of course, Mr. Task, I would have expected no less. Here is the good judge's written approval." Paul took the paper and scanned its contents.

"Mrs. Rawlings, it appears to be in order." The men started to walk toward the door. Jane didn't move. She was the only member of either team to notice Claire's physical reaction. She sat, looking at her notes, at Claire, and at Tony. The silence intensified.

Finally, Jane rose and met Tony's eyes. "Mr. Rawlings."

"Ms. Allyson," they nodded.

"Mr. Rawlings, this is unexpected. I would like to speak to our client for a few moments and determine *her* desire regarding this meeting. If you would please step into the hall with Mr. Evergreen and his team, Mr. Task and I will discuss this new situation with Mrs. Rawlings." Tony started to speak, but Jane continued with conviction in her tone. "And then, *if* Mrs. Rawlings agrees to your meeting, it may proceed under her conditions." Claire felt a newfound appreciation for her young co-counsel.

Mr. Evergreen placed his hand on Tony's arm and nodded. Tony looked directly at Claire. His dark eyes took her breath away. She hadn't seen those eyes in almost a week. They filled her with intense emotions, both love and hate. He slowly agreed with a broad smile. Everyone else left the room. Paul, Jane, and Claire were alone. Claire remembered to breathe.

Paul started, "Claire, you don't have to do this. But if you don't, it will look like you are not interested in the taxpayers." She wasn't. "It isn't just that. The fact he is willing to talk to you, the person accused of his attempted murder, makes him appear honorable and forgiving. If you refuse . . ." Claire listened, but her mind whirled. She believed Tony knew she wasn't guilty. Maybe he wanted to take her home, drop the charges, and forget the whole thing. If she left with him today, she would be out of that cell. She would be home!

Jane touched Claire's arm. Claire turned to her attorney's concerned expression. "Claire, I think it is completely up to you. Everything Paul said is true, but none of it matters. You started to shake when he walked in the room. If you want, Paul and I," she looked at Paul, who didn't appear as strong as Jane, "or just me, would be willing to stay in here with you."

Claire found her voice. "That isn't what he said. He wants to talk to me alone."

"Claire, what *he* wants is not the issue." Her voice was supportive and strong. "What do *you* want?"

"I want this to be over." She looked into Jane's eyes. "I didn't do it." Jane didn't speak, but lifted her brows. Claire straightened her back, stiffened her neck, and lifted her chin. "I want to talk to him."

Paul said he would get him. Jane leaned close. "Do you want me to stay?" Claire exhaled, she had kept his secrets, she hadn't told people what she went through, and she needed him to know that.

"No, I want to talk to him alone."

Jane smiled and squeezed Claire's arm. "It will be all right. Just know you need to discuss any deal with us before it can be initiated. We will be right outside the door."

Claire said she understood and suddenly thought about her appearance. Her defense counsel exited as Tony entered. They nodded to one another. Tony shut the door and turned to Claire. She watched as he walked to the table. He looked handsome, fit, and healthy. Relief filled her soul, seeing that the attempted murder hadn't caused him harm.

"Tony, I'm so glad you are all right." She reached across the table. He took her petite hands in his. Claire continued, "You know I would never hurt you?" His eyes showed the smallest amount of brown.

"It certainly appears you did." She shook her head and felt tears. He continued, "You handed me the coffee. There was poison in the coffee."

"You told me to get you coffee. I have thought about it a million times. There must have been poison in the coffee already, or in the cream. I just don't know." She felt his stare as she continued to speak, "I don't know who would do this. The only other people at home were staff, staff you have employed for years. But, it should be on surveillance. You have cameras in the kitchen—"

He interrupted. "All evidence points to you. Then, there is the way you ran to the car and drove away."

She lowered her eyes, she had disobeyed him. She knew not to drive. "I'm sorry." The tears teetered on her lower lids. "It was impulsive. I knew not to take one of the cars. But, I saw the keys, I hadn't had the opportunity in so long, the sky was so blue, and you had been . . . well, life had been unpredictable, and I felt like I was suffocating. I just needed a reprieve, a small break. But honestly, Tony, I was about to turn around to come home. I want to be home. I want to be with you."

He lifted her chin. "Claire, how are your accommodations?" The tears slipped off the lids and onto her cheeks. She didn't reply. Her thoughts were again spinning. His voice was low, no one else could hear. "Consequences, appearances, I thought you learned your lessons better."

"Tony, please take me home. I promise I will never disappoint you again. Please tell them you know I wouldn't, couldn't do this." His black eyes penetrated, but she pushed on, "I know there will be consequences and punishment. I don't care, as long as you are all right. I just want to go home. Please." Begging wasn't planned, but she wanted to be home. "Please, they will listen to you."

Expecting his expression to contain compassion, she was disappointed.

"The entire thing seems to be a colossal *accident*. However, I have done some research. It seems you can plead insanity and receive treatment instead of incarceration."

She sprung from her chair and started to pace. "What are you saying? I'm not pleading insanity. That means guilty and crazy. I'm neither!" She turned to look at him. "And this wasn't an *accident*. I didn't try to kill you!"

He stood and moved very close, looking down at her. "I have found a mental hospital which is willing to accept you. I will pay the expenses so the taxpayers are not responsible for your lack of judgment."

"I have been here for over a week. I've been questioned over and over. I haven't divulged any private information. I have followed all the rules. The only thing I did against your rules is drive a car. That is it!"

"This plea will avoid a trial. It is understandable. You came from a modest background. The life we shared had pressures and responsibilities, with entertaining, charities, and reporters; it is understandable. You just couldn't handle it." Claire sat down, feeling increasingly ill. Tony walked over to her. He bent down to maintain eye contact, "I should have recognized the signs. Perhaps, I was too busy with work. When you canceled your charity obligations recently, I should have realized how overwhelmed you felt." Claire listened as he spoke. It was his expression, a grin, one she recalled from a masquerade dinner almost two years ago, which spoke louder than his words. "You wanted out, and in a moment of weakness—no, in a moment of *insanity,* you decided the only way out was to try to kill me." She watched him. This was a prepared speech. *Oh my god!* "I am only thankful you underestimated the amount of poison needed or you may have succeeded."

The confusion in Claire's mind began to dissipate, the fog cleared, and she saw Tony, his expression and meaning as he spoke. "And if you had succeeded, I wouldn't be here to help you now." She suddenly realized he was done with her. It was like the workers in Pennsylvania, she no longer mattered. He didn't need her anymore! Tony pulled a chair to face Claire. "Aren't you glad I am able to help you?"

The bewilderment turned to realization. He wasn't going to help her. The reality hit her hard, not a physical slap, but it might as well have been. Instead of overwhelming sadness, two years of obedience and submission caused an overpowering rush of hostility. "And, Claire, I hear the rooms at the mental facility are larger than the cells at the federal penitentiary." His grin broadened.

She straightened her neck and met his eyes. No longer did tears flow, instead her eyes sparked with anger. "Yes, Tony, I am so thankful. Would you like me to show you how thankful I am?" Her insincerity and sudden animosity came through loud and clear.

Tony stood, straightened his jacket. "Utilize the time you have to think this over. Don't make another poor impulsive decision. This is your best offer." He knocked on the door. "Goodbye, Claire."

She didn't respond. The attorneys reentered the room. Claire had new resolve. If he was planning to leave her, she was going to start talking.

Mr. Evergreen spoke. "Mr. Task, if your client plans to plead insanity the prosecution will need psychological evaluations."

"Mr. Evergreen, I do not plan to plead insanity." Everyone turned to Claire, the last five days she'd hardly spoken. She continued in a determined tone, one none of them had heard before. "I can assure you, I am not the person that is insane, although I have cause. I am innocent. Now if you will excuse me again, I need to speak to my counsel."

She had entered this preexamination willing to sit passively and wait for Tony to rescue her. Turning to Jane, the only counsel willing to confront her husband, she said, "Ms. Allyson, if we could postpone this preexamination, I believe I have some evidence to share with you and Mr. Task."

Never be bullied into silence. Never allow yourself to be made a
victim. Accept no one's definition of your life. Define yourself
—Harvey Fierstein

Chapter 49

Three days was all the time they had to prepare for the new preexamination. Claire spent hours with her attorneys uncompartmentalizing everything. She recounted everything she could remember from the last twenty-two months. Tony wouldn't approve. Nonetheless, she was brutally honest, recounting details she'd tried to suppress. She explained the initial contact and contract. She said she suspected the *date rape drug* Rohypnol was used to get her to Iowa, because she couldn't remember traveling from Atlanta. This recount could have been demoralizing, but somehow it proved therapeutic -- a catharsis.

She described the respected, adored businessman Anthony Rawlings, as a cruel, vindictive, masochistic, controlling human being. She did leave their home in a hurry. Justifiably, she did it to get a break from *him*, his rules, restrictions, and consequences. If he knew she left the property without his permission, she would've been punished. She explained his punishments could range from verbal, mental, to physical abuse. On one occasion, approximately six months after she arrived on his estate, he nearly killed her. She told about the isolation he used. She also told about the sexual exploits, video recording, controlling nature, domineering manipulation, and constant mental, and on again, off again physical abuse.

At times, her attorneys would stop taking notes and just listen. This was much bigger than anything they expected. Together, Paul and Jane worked to build a case, not of a woman trying to gain financially from the death of her wealthy husband, but of an abused woman, wanting only to flee the situation.

Paul believed she'd been living in hell, but there were points and events she would need to explain. She stated she was kidnapped, yet did she ever try to call for help? Didn't she live in a multimillion dollar mansion? Did she expect people to believe she had no access to telephone, Internet, or anything? Didn't she marry this man she described as a monster? Didn't she accept gifts: clothing, money, jewelry, etc.? Didn't she accompany him on multiple extravagant trips? Didn't she sit with a reporter from *Vanity Fair* and give an interview about her wonderful husband and their amazing life together?

Claire understood how things looked. She knew about appearances. But she knew what she endured. She explained that even after things got better with Tony, there was always the underlying threat of abuse. Things did get better, after the near-death accident. He got better and she believed she loved him. But, *always* there were rules and reminders of consequences for her actions. Any failure to be perfect could result in punishment. The truth would set her free, and she was ready to tell the entire world the truth.

Her legal team prepared a preliminary brief. It informed the prosecution of their defense strategy. By no means all inclusive, it did emphasize the hostile relationship between Mr. and Mrs. Rawlings. It highlighted Mr. Rawlings's aggressive, intimidating, and controlling tendencies. Mrs. Rawlings' only intention on the day in question was to escape the harsh reality of her life. She didn't plan, nor did she execute a plan, to cause Mr. Rawlings harm.

The time for the rescheduled preexamination meeting arrived. Mr. Evergreen and his team, as well as Paul, Jane, and Claire were once again seated around a large table. The only noticeable difference at this meeting was Claire's brown hair. Indulging Claire's request, Jane brought her a box of Chestnut hair dye. She looked younger. The blonde was striking, stunning, and beautiful. Claire didn't feel any of those.

Mr. Evergreen addressed Paul, "How does your client plan to plea?"

"My client is not guilty and plans to plea as such."

"I would like to ask your client some questions to let her know what she will be facing at trial. Mr. Task, Ms. Allyson, do you have any objections to this plan?"

Paul began, "Claire, this isn't a bad idea. This allows us to understand where the prosecution is coming from with their charges. It also lets you experience the questioning portion of the trial. The questions here are not asked under oath. You can refuse to answer, and your answers cannot be used against you in the actual trial."

"All right, please ask away." Claire's mind was made up. She was innocent, and planned to tell the world the truth of what she had endured. Having Marcus Evergreen, a contemporary of Tony's, sitting across the table was unnerving. After all, Marcus attended their wedding, Tony wouldn't approve of her telling him certain things. But she was innocent, and if Tony wasn't going to help her, the truth would.

Mr. Evergreen opened his laptop and began his questioning. "First, Mrs. Rawlings, as your attorney informed you this is not under oath and your answers cannot be used against you at trial. You should also be aware my team and I have read Mr. Task's preliminary brief which discusses the relationship between you and your husband, as well as your allegations to his behavior. I realize Mr. Task and Ms. Allyson plan to use your allegations in your defense. This procedure is a snapshot of how I, and my team, plan to cross examine you. Do you understand?" Claire nodded. "Mrs. Rawlings, please answer all questions verbally." Claire said that she would.

"Please state your name."

"Claire Rawlings."

"How long has that been your name?"

"Anthony Rawlings and I were married December 18, 2010."

"Mrs. Rawlings, I didn't ask when you were married, but rather how long Claire Rawlings has been your name." Mr. Evergreen continued with mundane questions regarding dates and times. Then his questions turned to her life before Mr. Rawlings. What did she do for a living? Where did she live? How did she and Anthony Rawlings meet?

"Why did you move into Mr. Rawlings's house?"

"I didn't move into his house, I was taken to his house," Claire corrected.

"Why were you taken to his house?"

"Mr. Rawlings and I had a business agreement."

"What kind of agreement did you have?"

Claire hesitated. "He hired me to be his personal assistant."

"And how much did he pay you to be his personal assistant?"

"He didn't actually pay me." Claire wasn't sure how to explain this so Mr. Evergreen or a jury would understand.

"You worked for free? Yes or no?"

"No, actually he paid off my debts."

Mr. Evergreen looked curious. "Your debts? He paid off your debts? Did he pay off your car and maybe a credit card?"

"Yes."

"And do you have any idea the total amount of your debts?"

Did Claire know? Of course, she knew. Tony mentioned the amount hundreds of times during the beginning of their relationship.

"Yes."

"Well, Mrs. Rawlings, please share. What was the amount of debt Mr. Rawlings paid off for you?"

"He told me it was $215,000."

"My, $215,000 to be his personal assistant, was that all? Or were there other benefits?"

Benefits? Claire didn't know what he meant.

He continued, "Did Mr. Rawlings provide you housing, clothing, or food?"

"Yes, I lived in his house. The staff prepared my food and he had clothes for me."

"Now, Mrs. Rawlings, were these old clothes or did he buy you new clothes?"

"They were new. But I never asked—"

"Please just answer the question. So the clothes were new. You lived in his mansion, and he paid off $215,000 worth of debt. Tell me what you did as Mr. Rawlings's personal assistant. Did you answer his phone?"

"No." He continued. "Did you answer his e-mails?" No. "Did you coordinate his schedule?" No. "Did you make him food?" No. "Did you make him drinks?" No.

"Mrs. Rawlings, what did you do?"

Claire felt her face flush. "I was supposed to be available whenever he wanted me."

"Can you please explain yourself? What do you mean, available whenever he wanted you?" Mr. Evergreen leaned into the table.

"I was supposed to satisfy his sexual wants and needs." Claire was looking down.

"Did you do your job?"

"I didn't have a choice." Claire was still looking at the table.

"Mrs. Rawlings, I asked if you did your job, yes or no?"

Claire looked the prosecuting attorney in his eyes. "Yes, I did what I was told."

"And, if my notes are correct, you and Anthony Rawlings married nine months after you began your job, is that correct?"

"Yes, we discussed that."

"Yes, we did. I am just trying to understand. At $215,000, housing, food, and clothing for a period of nine months, I figure that Mr. Rawlings paid you nearly *$1,000* a day for sexual pleasure. You must be a great lay!"

Claire glared at the prosecutor. Jane and Paul exploded, "That is unnecessary!"

Mr. Evergreen apologized and continued with his questioning. He asked questions about Claire's claim of imprisonment. Then he showed pictures of her with Anthony at various activities: dinners, fund-raisers, and outings. Claire thought he had a picture of almost every time she was out of the house during the first six months of her imprisonment. "You don't understand. I was only allowed out—"

"Mrs. Rawlings, you'll have the opportunity to discuss your reasons for exaggerating the truth when your attorney is examining you. This is my opportunity. I will ask the questions." He went on in his condescending tone, asking about supposed physical abuse. Did she have any doctor's statements? Had she reported the abuse? Had she even told Mr. Rawlings she didn't like it?

This again got Jane and Paul out of their seats. Claire felt ill. Her head pounded and her blood sugar felt low. She leaned toward Jane. "Could we break for lunch?"

While Paul went to get sandwiches, Jane and Claire spoke, privately. Claire had told them all the information before. She had explained how Tony controlled her, she hadn't been allowed to complain, she couldn't leave her suite for the longest time, and she was never allowed to leave the property without his permission, even after they were married. But the way Mr. Evergreen twisted it, it seemed like she was some kind of prostitute. He made it seem like she was after Anthony's money from the beginning.

Jane reassured Claire the defense had an opportunity to ask more questions following the prosecution. That would be their time to explain things to the jury. Even Jane was concerned about the pictures showing Claire and Anthony out in public. Claire didn't look like a woman being held against her will. Jane had photos on her laptop sent by Mr. Evergreen during the preexamination. She pulled up a picture of Anthony and Claire at an upscale Manhattan restaurant. Claire remembered that night. Tony had completed a big business deal and *celebrated* before dinner. She remembered hating him that night; however, the person in the picture didn't look like she hated him. The Claire in the picture was the perfect companion, exquisitely dressed, beautiful, contented, and attentive. The realization that she'd learned her lessons *too* well began to add to her pounding head.

Feeling more nourished, they resumed the questioning. "Mrs. Rawlings, you stated Anthony Rawlings was physically and mentally abusive, yet you decided to marry him. Isn't that true?"

"Yes."

"Now can you please tell us who took care of the wedding? And if it was nice?"

"Tony paid for the wedding, he hired wedding planners, they did everything, and it was beautiful. You should know -- you were there."

"Do you have any idea of the cost of your wedding?"

"No."

"Well, for your information it came to over $350,000. Your dress alone was over $70,000." Claire really had no idea. "And those figures do not include your rings or your honeymoon. Mrs. Rawlings, can you tell us where you went on your honeymoon?"

"We went to Fiji, to a private island."

"The cost of this honeymoon, Mrs. Rawlings, do you know the cost?"

"No. It was never discussed with me. I didn't care about the money!" Claire suddenly felt tired.

"When you were apprehended you were driving a very expensive car registered to you, wearing multiple pieces of fine jewelry, and expensive clothes. Do you still claim you don't care about money?"

"I drove *that* car because I found the keys. The clothes and jewelry were all because Tony made me wear them. I didn't even choose my own clothes that morning."

Mr. Evergreen went back to his laptop. "Now back to your wedding. Do you know that you and Mr. Rawlings don't have a prenuptial agreement?"

"Yes. He told me we didn't need one. If I ever tried to leave him there would be unpleasant consequences."

"Mrs. Rawlings, I am asking the questions. Did you know that his legal consul wanted him to have a prenuptial agreement?"

"Yes, he told me that the decision was solely his."

"Did or do you understand that without a prenuptial agreement if you and Mr. Rawlings were to divorce you would have claim to half of his fortune?"

"I hadn't given it any thought."

"And, I suppose you hadn't given any thought to the fact that if Mr. Rawlings died you would have sole claim to his entire fortune."

"Honestly, no."

He then showed Claire a picture of an apartment house in Atlanta. "Do you recognize this building?"

"Yes."

"I would assume you would. It is the apartment in which you lived prior to moving into Mr. Rawlings' mansion. How big was your apartment?"

Claire hadn't thought about that apartment in almost two years. "It was a one-bedroom with an eat-in kitchen."

"Now, Mrs. Rawlings, do you recognize this residence?" It was an aerial photograph of the mansion. It showed the sprawling wings of the home, the pool, the long drive, the various patios, and the massive expenditure of land surrounding it all.

"Yes."

"Yes, it is the home you and Mr. Rawlings shared. Is that correct?"

Claire wanted to be done with this. "Yes, it is"

"Mrs. Rawlings, how big is this house?"

"I don't know. Do you mean in square feet?" She was becoming irritated.

"All right then. How many bedrooms?" Mr. Evergreen was smiling. Claire thought about it for a minute. "Honestly, I don't know. Do you want the staffs' rooms counted too? I don't know."

"So let me get this straight. You have been held captive in this home for nearly two years and you don't know how many bedrooms are there? Or perhaps you were enjoying the life of luxury too much to worry about such things?" Mr. Evergreen tapped his computer screen. "Well, let's shift gears. Do you recognize yourself in this photo?"

Claire nodded. "Can you please tell me where you are and what you are doing?"

"I'm in Davenport, shopping."

"You are shopping. But I thought you didn't have any money?"

"Tony gave me a credit card."

"Was this before or after you were married?"

"I believe that picture was before. But seriously, you don't—"

Mr. Evergreen interrupted her. "Mrs. Rawlings, allow me to ask the questions." He paused. "So, Mr. Rawlings gave you a credit card before you were married. Who paid the bill?"

"He did."

"Who is with you on this shopping trip?"

"Eric, Mr. Rawlings's driver was there, in the car."

"So *if* you were a prisoner, wouldn't this have been an excellent opportunity to escape? After all, you were all by yourself in Davenport. Mrs. Rawlings, did you try to escape?"

"No. I was afraid."

"Stick to the *yes* and *no* answers." Mr. Evergreen looked at his notes on the screen. "Did you only use your credit card in Davenport?"

"No."

Mr. Evergreen showed some more pictures: Claire on Fifth Avenue in Manhattan, shopping at Saks Fifth Avenue in Chicago. "Mrs. Rawlings, did you use your credit card on these occasions?"

"Yes."

"Where are you?" he asked, pointing at a photo.

"I was in Manhattan."

350

"So you were shopping in Manhattan. The inhumanity of this prison! How much did you *have* to spend, or let me ask, do you know how much you spent on this particular shopping trip?"

Claire did. "Yes, I spent $ 5,000. But I was told to—"

"Mrs. Rawlings, let's continue. Did you have a credit card once you were married?"

"Yes."

"Did you ever have the opportunity to use it?"

"Yes."

He was looking right at her. "This money thing wasn't so bad now, was it?"

"I didn't want the money. I don't want the money. I told Tony I didn't care about his money—"

Marcus' associate showed Claire an e-mail address and telephone number, as Mr. Evergreen continued the questioning. "Mrs. Rawlings do you recognize this e-mail address?"

"Yes."

"It is yours. Is that correct?"

"Yes, it is, but—"

"Mrs. Rawlings, whose cell phone number is this?"

"Mine."

"Mrs. Rawlings, I thought that you said you were isolated, no way to communicate. Let me see, I believe I have photos of you and your husband in Hawaii, Lake Tahoe, San Francisco, and yes, in Europe. Mrs. Rawlings, did you enjoy the south of France?"

Claire's head pounded with increasing intensity.

Mr. Evergreen went into a long tirade about how an unemployed *weather girl* deep in debt latched on to a lonely wealthy businessman with no heirs. This was an entrepreneur that not only made his fortune through hard work, but was highly regarded due to his benevolent endeavors. She then seduced him into *employing* her as a live-in prostitute and lured him into marrying her without a prenuptial agreement. Given the perfect opportunity, this tawdry woman put poison into her poor unsuspecting husband's coffee. If that wasn't enough, she sent his driver away on a wild-goose chase, and drove away. It would have worked, except with technology as it was, fifteen people witnessed the collapse, and help arrived in time. The prosecution had many character witnesses willing to testify to the generous spirit and good-heartedness of Mr. Rawlings. No one would back her slanderous accusations of this respectable man.

Hadn't Claire been told over and over again, appearances were everything? The small room became smaller. Claire's head hurt, her heart hurt. She saw the pictures and the expressions of her attorneys. She heard Marcus Evergreen's accusations and tasted the sour bile as her stomach twisted and turned.

*We cannot change our memories, but we can change
their meaning and the power they have over us.*
—David Seamands

Chapter 50

He stared at the paint on the cinder block wall. Why did they always use the same pale green? If it was supposed to look cheery, it failed. Anton continued to watch the wall even though he heard the door and knew the guard and prisoner had entered. He couldn't bear to see his grandfather being led around. Anton waited, hands in pockets, until he heard the door close again. Turning around, he met the eyes, the dark defiant eyes. *If* his grandfather were wearing a suit and *if* the metal table were a mahogany desk, Nathaniel would look like he did in Anton's memory. His expression hadn't changed. They may've put him in this damn prison, but they sure as hell weren't keeping his mind here.

"So, boy, did you learn his identity?"

Cole Mathews had worked side by side with Nathaniel Rawls for almost two years. The day before Nathaniel's arrest, he didn't show for work. He didn't call. He disappeared. Almost a year later, information only known by insiders, helped lead to Nathaniel Rawls' conviction. During the trial it was revealed that an FBI agent had been embedded into the inner workings of Rawls Corporation to investigate federal allegations.

Of course, to protect his identity, the name of the agent was never released. But this was the eighties, and Anton Rawls knew his way around a computer better than most. *Hacking* was such a negative term for research.

Anton placed the manila folder in front of his grandfather. "Yes, sir, I found his name and enough personal information to track him down."

"I knew you wouldn't let me down." Nathaniel opened the folder and scanned the contents. "He has a wife and family." He spent a few more minutes reading the pages. Then abruptly, Nathaniel shut the folder and slammed his hand against the table. "This son-of-a-bitch will pay!" His chair hit the wall as he forcefully stood. "Do you hear me, boy?"

"Yes, sir, I hear you." Anton watched his grandfather pacing in his prison garb. "Not just him. Hell, no. He took away my world. He took my family. His damn kids, their kids, their kids . . . they will *all* face the consequences of his actions! He took everything." Nathaniel's eyes darkened as he moved closer to his grandson. "You know what?"

"No, sir."

"You can't lose everything until you have everything to lose." More pacing, "I had everything, and now look at me! That man and his goddamn family will pay!" He moved very close to his grandson. "The day I get out of this hellhole, they will pay. Every one of them will regret the day he decided to bring me down.

Anton noticed the difference in the sound of their footsteps. His hard soled shoes made a distinctively different noise from his grandfather's rubber soled shoes which squeaked. "There is more, sir."

Nathaniel turned toward his grandson's words. "What? What more did you learn?"

"He had help. He worked hand in hand with a securities officer named Burke. Burke fed Mathews the information. If this securities officer hadn't directed Mathews, Mathews wouldn't have been as thorough in collecting evidence." Anton watched the shade of his grandfather's face grow in crimson intensity as he spoke.

"And, your father?" The blackness of Nathaniel's eyes pulled Anton's gaze to him.

Anton felt compelled to maintain eye contact and surrender the rest of his information. "He testified for the state." Nathaniel's pacing resumed. "It was done behind closed doors, but it isn't secret. The media calls him the hero in our family."

Nathaniel collapsed red faced and defeated into his chair. The realization that his son turned state's witness was obviously affecting him. His tone mellowed. "Boy, you will survive."

"Yes, sir, I will."

"Being here today, discovering this information, and most importantly, having the balls to bring it to me are all evidence of your future. Your father has always been a disappointment, but I believe he was better at one thing than me." Anton sat in the metal chair facing his grandfather. He could hear the sincerity in Nathaniel's tone and words, and asked his grandfather to continue. "Public opinion, I never gave a damn what anyone thought. I worked hard and deserved all the money, possessions, and everything I earned, and wanted more. That was never a secret. Remember this, you can want the whole goddamn world, but *never* show it." Nathaniel stared up at the camera in the corner of the room. "If they know what you want, they'll watch you and take it away. Keep up appearances, boy. If you do that, you can take everything you want. The whole damn world is yours."

Happiness doesn't depend on any external conditions
it is governed by our mental attitude.
—Dale Carnegie

Chapter 51

Claire had been incarcerated for over three months and had come to terms with the realization it would not end soon. The claustrophobic cell and virtual isolation were her new norm. Surprisingly, like in traumas before, she was adapting. It was difficult at first, but with time, she developed strength and resolve.

On April 18, 2012, the courtroom sat empty, except for the judge, defendant, and legal teams. Each word resonated throughout the cavernous room. Claire Nichols stood in front of the federal court judge and with the help of her legal team pleaded *no contest* to the charge of *attempted murder*. As the judge explained the consequences of Claire's plea, she listened, felt the smooth finish of the chair she used for support, watched the judge's lips, and wept silently.

This plea saved her the indignity of a jury trial. She didn't admit guilt, but would not, could not challenge the charges. Therefore, she would take a lesser sentence but couldn't later decide to appeal. She would avoid Mr. Evergreen and his questions. She would escape the dark, penetrating eyes of Anthony Rawlings as she testified. She wouldn't need to explain to the entire world how she was forced to do things and how things were so different from how they appeared. She could just go away quietly.

The court of public opinion had not gone well, either. The people of Iowa City, of Iowa, and of the United States all found her guilty. They tried her as a gold digger. Of course, most of the information hadn't come out. Even that shared with the members of both legal teams remained private. Anthony Rawlings made sure of it.

The federal judge sentenced her to seven years in prison, minus time served, to be served in a moderate security federal penitentiary. The severity of her crime required a moderate security facility. Apparently, even her ex-husband testified to the judge, asking for a minimum-security facility, more evidence of his forgiving, kind character.

Counsel on behalf of Anthony Rawlings filed the necessary paperwork to dissolve the marriage between him and Claire Nichols. Of course, there was no contest. With a few connections, the court papers were expedited. The divorce was finalized on March 20, 2012. Since they didn't have a prenuptial agreement, Claire received no financial compensation for her fifteen-month marriage. After all, she was charged with his attempted murder. Why would she get any financial compensation?

According to the smut television shows which played in the common area of the prison, Mr. Rawlings was having no problem finding women to take her place. The world rallied around him and his unfortunate situation. Even Rawlings Industries stock soared.

The small window in the door of Claire's cell allowed a minimal amount of florescent light to penetrate, making the walls drab and colorless. Turning on her desk lamp filled the room with illuminated warmth. Her small cell at the Iowa Correctional Institution for Women would be her home for at least another four years. Although she was sentenced to seven, she would be eligible for parole in four. Claire was good at following rules.

She had a twin-sized bed, dresser, an open hanging area, a few shelves, and a desk with a chair. It wasn't much, but she felt content. She'd experienced more but that hadn't worked well. Existing in a comforting sameness day to day helped Claire survive. There were no surprises, everything was predictable. Day after day, the same routine: wake, dress, and breakfast, then back to her cell, alone, until lunch. Lunch was followed by a one-hour block of free time, either in a large gymnasium, the prison library, or an outside court. Claire loved the outside. She went there whenever the weather permitted. Then back to her cell until dinner. After dinner there was optional common time, if you earned that privilege, for another hour. Claire earned it, but opted for her cell. Companionship required trust in the other person. Claire's trust no longer extended beyond herself. She stayed in her cell until her buzzer rang. The buzzer indicated it was time to shower; following the shower, back to her cell, lights out at 11:00. Simple and predicable, Claire had suffered enough unpredictability.

She spent her free time reading. Emily tried to send her books as often as possible. Having a sister and husband in jail was hard on Emily. She was asked to leave her teaching job in Troy. The private school system needed to maintain its reputation, and apparently some donors were concerned about her influence on young children. She went back to Indiana to familiar surroundings and taught for a public school system near Indianapolis. The money wasn't good, but at least she could survive.

*****

It was a two-hour drive from Iowa City to Mitchellville. Brent Simmons should have utilized a driver. It was four hours he could have worked, but he chose to drive. He wanted to be alone and come to terms with the assignment ahead of him. Claire Nichols needed to be informed of a possible pending civil lawsuit. Brent knew as the head legal counsel for Rawlings Industries he could have sent someone else. He wanted to send someone else. However, Mr. Rawlings made it clear, that wasn't an option.

The July sun shone bright on the pavement ahead of him. Momentarily, he was distracted by the illusion of shimmering liquid in the distance. He didn't want to face Claire, to see her in the correctional institution. He knew she didn't belong there, and he hadn't helped her. She probably, justifiably, felt abandoned. She was. Brent's mind went back to January, to that terrible phone call telling him and Courtney someone tried to kill Tony. They were planning to return from Fiji in three days, of course they flew home immediately.

When they found Tony, still hospitalized, he looked and sounded healthy. His disposition wasn't, as he informed them all evidence pointed to Claire. Devastated, Courtney argued with Tony. After she left the room, Tony informed Brent, they were not *allowed* to visit or help Claire after what *she* did.

That didn't go well with Courtney, who went anyway. Somehow Tony found out, and Brent had hell to pay. Brent wasn't directly involved in the criminal suit. Actually, the State Of Iowa accused Claire Rawlings of attempted murder, not Tony. But Brent was involved in an expedited divorce. Marcus Evergreen, chief prosecutor for Johnson County, had information Brent needed for his petition. Mid-February, Marcus' secretary utilized a courier to deliver a flash drive to Brent. It contained the documents he needed. He planned to leave it at the office, but at the last minute decided to take it home, to *take a look at it.*

Courtney was out to dinner with friends when Brent pulled up the drive on his home computer. There was only one folder: "Rawlings, Claire." He opened it. It contained multiple files. The one he needed was "Rawlings vs. Rawlings." It should have been the only one on the drive. It wasn't. The one titled "State of Iowa vs. Rawlings: Preliminary Brief-Task" sat right in front of him. It was unethical and probably illegal, but he opened it. Young attorneys get wordy. Paul Task's preliminary brief was 147 pages! Brent grimaced and shook his head at the inexperience of Claire's attorney. He started to close the file when he focused on the words, suddenly transfixed.

Two hours and three Blue Label's, straight up later, the entire brief was read. The descriptions and details of Claire's life while with Tony were nauseating. It was stated more than once, this was only a sample of the treatment she endured, there was more. How could this be going on and they not know? Brent panicked, thinking he shouldn't have read it and should delete it.

However, instead of deleting, he made an electronic copy on a personal flash drive and printed a copy. Then he deleted it from the original drive. If questioned, he would deny it had ever been present. He wanted to punch Tony, but Brent knew he could never let Tony know he had read the brief.

Planning to keep it to himself, he decided to hide the paper copy in his safe and put the pin drive in a special box in the drawer of his desk. Before he had the chance to follow through on those plans, Courtney came home. She knew immediately something was amiss and assumed Tony was responsible.

Maybe it was the whiskey combined with helplessness for Claire, but Brent handed Courtney the paper copy. In hindsight, it was a mistake which almost cost him his twenty-eight-year marriage. When she finished reading he asked two simple questions, "Do you believe it? Do you think she's telling the truth?"

Courtney erupted! She believed every word and wanted Tony's head on a platter. She also wanted Brent to quit his job, move far away from Iowa City, and most importantly, help Claire.

Downtrodden, Brent explained none of that was possible. "We can't."

"Why not? She told me at the jail she didn't do it! I knew something was wrong. I kept asking. Why didn't I push more? God! It said he hurt her in California. We were with them! Brent, think about Claire, her age. What if those things you read happened to our daughter?"

"I would kill the bastard! But they didn't. And not only is he my boss, he is now Caleb's boss. Don't you think in light of this new information it is coincidental that he recently offered Caleb such a great job? Now, not only does he own us, but also our son and future daughter-in-law."

"This is America, just quit!"

"Courtney, I can't. You don't walk away from Tony. Ask John Vandersol." Brent hadn't meant to divulge that information, it just slipped out. Courtney sat dazed. She poured herself another glass of cabernet and reread the brief. The next day, while Brent was at work, Courtney left. He came home to a note: "If *anyone* asks, I'm taking care of my sick mother. Do not attempt to call or communicate, I will *not* be available."

Brent tried numerous times. Over a week later she returned. Brent remembered worrying what she would say. He fully expected, "You are weak and I'm done, I want a divorce."

Instead, Courtney apologized. "I wasn't there for Claire and apparently can't be there for her now. I can be here for you. You shouldn't have to face that bastard every day without support. I love you and will support you. But know this: I want out of here and away from him. From this point forward we slowly, inconspicuously move our assets away from Rawlings stock and work to liberate our family. That will start with Caleb before he gets in too deep. Do you agree?"

Brent did. He wanted out, too. The first time Courtney needed to see Tony face to face, Brent worried. She did fine. Courtney said if he could muster a false smile and Claire could do it, she could too. They were already laying the ground work for Caleb's move to another place of employment.

As Brent got out of the car and walked into the institution, he worried about Claire, what would she look like? Had she been able to survive? How? He hated Tony and damned him with each echoing step down the long, tiled halls.

A guard took him to a small dingy room, illuminated with a florescent glow, containing a steel table and four chairs. Brent set his briefcase on the table and waited. Looking around, he noticed the conspicuous camera in the corner. It reminded him of the videotaping mentioned in the preliminary brief and of his conversation with Tony:

"You want me to go tell Ms. Nichols (Tony didn't like to hear her first name) you are considering a civil lawsuit against her, for what?"

"Slander and deformation of character."

"Why, what did she say?"

"It doesn't matter. You don't need to know. You just need to do your job." Tony's voice was flat and authoritative.

In actuality Brent was fishing--would Tony share the information Brent already knew? He also wondered if Tony knew he knew--apparently not. "Tony, there are many members of the legal team who weren't as involved with Ms. Nichols as I. Perhaps one of them could inform her of the impending suit?"

"No. It will be you." His tone was firm and his eyes intense. "Have you ever noticed the nice cameras in those visitor rooms? Those tapes are available for a price. I assume you will not relay information to her that is not related to the suit. As a reminder, this will *not* be a friendly visit." Brent said he understood.

*****

Claire was reading in her cell on that July afternoon when her buzzer sounded. The sound meant she needed to go to her door. She would be receiving something, usually a package. This time a guard informed her she had a visitor; her presence was immediately required in the visitor area.

Claire had only received two visitors since her arrest. The first was in Iowa City, before she gave her plea and was transferred to the correctional institution. That day, following a guard, she found her best friend. Courtney was in Fiji during Claire's arrest and came to the jail as soon as they returned to Iowa. Visibly distraught as Claire was escorted by a guard, Courtney apologized to Claire for not being a better friend. If she had pursued her concerns more, perhaps Claire wouldn't have felt the need to resort to such drastic measures to get away from Tony. Claire assured her, "I did not try to kill Tony. Please don't believe everything you hear or see. Remember Tony's regard for appearances. Many times, things were not as they seemed." Courtney said she understood and would try to help her, but . . . Brent, his job . . . Claire hadn't heard from her since. Honestly, she understood.

The only other visitor since her incarceration was Emily. Claire knew the trip to Mitchellville, Iowa, was difficult for her. When Emily had time to travel she wanted to visit John in New York.

Now, Claire curiously followed the guard down the halls and through multiple gates, each one locking, unlocking, and making the electronic beep sound. Wearing her prison clothes she entered a room to find Brent Simmons. It had been so long, she momentarily thought she was seeing a friend visit a friend. Brent's expression instantaneously changed her mind. Claire sat where the guard indicated. The guard then stepped from the room, leaving Brent and Claire alone.

She knew this was *business,* but he *was* her friend. She couldn't stop herself. "Brent, how are you? How is Courtney? When is Caleb's wedding?"

358

Stone faced and sober, Brent replied, "Ms. Nichols, I have been instructed to inform you of an impending civil suit in which you will be named the defendant."

Creating an equally professional persona Claire responded, "Okay. Thank you for informing me. May I ask the grounds for this suit?"

"My client has reason to believe you have spoken slander against him. This defamation of his character is considered a ploy to damage his personal and professional reputation." Brent said what was needed, with the demeanor necessary, but his thoughts were elsewhere. Claire looked different from what he expected. It wasn't just her hair and the clothes, she had confidence and strength. These qualities had never been evident before. He recalled seeing her for the first time on Tony's plane to New York. She looked nervous and insecure, yet tried to appear otherwise. Now after almost six months, three in a federal penitentiary, Claire seemed independent and strong. He knew it wasn't where she'd been, but where she hadn't. She hadn't been under the gaze of the black eyes. Just like actual black holes, they sucked strength, confidence, and assurance out of anyone close enough to be pulled into their orbit.

Carefully considering Brent's words, Claire laughed and replied, "Thank you, Mr. Simmons. I'm very concerned that your client will want my allegations made public as would happen in such a suit."

"Ms. Nichols, damage to my client's professional reputation could result in a loss of income. A civil suit is meant to subsidize any loss of income."

Smiling, she said, "And of course I have the necessary capital to subsidize your client's income."

"It is my responsibility to inform you such a suit is under consideration, and if filed, you could be found liable." Brent stood to leave.

"Brent, can you please talk with me for a minute?" The defeated look of his eyes said *no*. Brent was just north of fifty but his face looked much older. There were lines and definite circles under his sad eyes. He continued to gather his belongings.

"Mr. Simmons?" They made eye contact. "Your wife told me one time that life was not a daily test. She said perfection was not always necessary. I want you to know that I know. I know better than anyone else, today you just passed a test." She saw the change in his eyes. They glistened with a minuscule amount of moisture, and he ever so slightly nodded his head in agreement. He started toward the door. "Mr. Simmons, two more things." He stopped, she sounded so confident. "Should the subject come up for discussion, I welcome the suit. It will give me the opportunity to make my allegations again, perhaps to a larger forum." He nodded with a knowing smile. She was right. Tony would never risk that exposure. "And the other thing, I truly love and miss your wife. If she cares, please tell her I really am fine. More fine than I used to be."

"Thank you, Ms. Nichols. You have been notified."

"Yes, Mr. Simmons, I have. Thank you." He knocked and the guard opened the door. He left.

The guard took Claire back to her cell. Walking through the halls, through the various locked gates, Claire couldn't help feeling sorry for Brent. His prison was more of a hell than hers.

About three weeks later she received a short note in the mail. The return address was a PO Box in Chicago. She didn't recognize the name, but the note filled Claire with love and support. It wasn't much, but it was something. To Claire, that was a lot!

I care. I'm glad.
I'm sorry. I miss you too,
and I hope to be able to do more.
love you! Cort

Claire kept the note and read it daily. Over time more notes arrived. Sue and Tim had a healthy baby boy. Caleb and Julia's wedding was to be in June of 2013, little bits of information always signed with love.

You have to accept whatever comes and the
only important thing is that you meet it with
courage and with the best that you have to give.
—Eleanor Roosevelt

Chapter 52

When the package arrived in October of 2012, Claire assumed it was from Emily. After all, the label had her return address. However, when she opened the box, she knew otherwise. It contained old magazines, newspaper clippings or photocopied clippings, and some photographs. Everything in the box was meticulously organized and in chronological order. The first item was a note, not signed but it didn't need to be:

Consider this information perhaps the only act of complete honesty I have ever shown you. I didn't need to do this, but I chose to educate you some more. Hopefully, you will understand that you were but a piece of the puzzle. All behaviors, good or bad, have consequences, and even the truth can't fight appearances. As I assume you have plenty of time available to you, read it all. You will find it enlightening. In another life, under different circumstances, it may have been different. You taught me much. I believe you learned lessons, too.

PS. I told you once, your appropriate responses benefited you. The consequence could not be improved, but you did have a positive effect on the actions, for that we should both be thankful. I am.

Sitting the box in the corner of her cell, she began with the first item. Dated 1975, it was a copy of an old newspaper article which talked at length about Rawls Corporation, a privately owned company specializing in textiles. The owner, Nathaniel Rawls, was interviewed because Rawls Corporation went public. It opened on the NYSE at fifty cents a share. In the first day, it raised to eighty-nine cents a share. Claire didn't understand the significance of this information. But Tony told her to read it *all*, so she did.

As she viewed the next item, she realized the significance. It was a magazine article from *Newsweek*, 1979. What caught her attention was the picture of a house, looking very similar to Tony's. Standing in front of the house was a family. The caption read, "Nathaniel Rawls, wife Sharron, son Samuel, daughter-in-law Amanda, and grandson Anton." The boy looked twelve to fourteen. Even at that young age, she could see his dark eyes. The article expounded on the success of Rawls Corporation. A recent stock split confirmed what everyone was saying, *this was an up-and-coming company.* Nathaniel's family enjoyed a lavish lifestyle brought on by his success. The Rawls family lived the American dream—they had it all.

The 1982 *Time* magazine article only had a picture of Nathaniel and was entitled, "Continued Success." It quoted a lot of important investors stating the attributes of Rawls Corporation, which was now expanding its ventures with continued success, run mainly by Nathaniel, but also by his son Samuel. There was a quote from Nathaniel about grooming his grandson to take over one day.

The next was *Newsweek* 1986. It wasn't just a story; it was the cover. In large letters, with a picture of a house of cards, it read "The House of Rawls Falls." The story was short, considering it had been a cover story. The gist of it explained Rawls Corporation stock plummet due to allegations of wrongdoing. The magazine couldn't say too much, due to an ongoing federal investigation. As investors pulled their money, the corporation was folding before their eyes.

There was much more information in the following article from *Newsweek,* dated 1987. There was a picture of Nathaniel Rawls wearing prison garb entitled "Nathaniel Rawls Convicted." Based on evidence from a two-year undercover FBI investigation and testimony, Mr. Rawls was found guilty of multiple counts of insider trading, misappropriation of funds, price fixing, and securities fraud. The family's assets were being sold at auction to help recoup investor loss. Distraught investors were quoted, "We lost everything, and it is good to see the entire family lose everything." The Rawls were living the high life, homes, vacations, and belongings. Now they had nothing.

A short newspaper clip dated 1989 indicated Nathanial Rawls dead at sixty-eight. Mr. Rawls died after only twenty-two months in a minimum-security facility. The cause of death was a massive heart attack.

The buzzer rang. Claire didn't want to stop reading. She thought she should grasp some revelation. But other than that Tony's name had been Anton Rawls before Anthony Rawlings, she didn't see it. She had to follow the rules, so she put the articles away and turned off her lights.

Her journey resumed the following morning after breakfast. Copies of court documents from *New York State vs. Nathaniel Rawls* were the next items in the box. Though lengthy, after time, Claire realized a few key testimonies aided in the conviction of Mr. Rawls: first, from his son Samuel who had turned state's witness, second, from an undercover FBI agent

362

embedded in the corporation for two years, and lastly, a securities investigator. Accompanying these documents was a report stamped "Top Secret." It gave the unreleased names of the strategic individuals: securities investigator Jonathon Burke and FBI Agent Sherman Nichols, Claire's grandfather.

Though warm in her temperature controlled cell, Claire felt a sudden shiver. The next discovery was a newspaper article also dated 1989: Samuel and Amanda Rawls found dead in their rented Santa Monica bungalow, bodies discovered by their twenty-three-year-old son. Based on the evidence from the scene, it appeared to be a case of murder/suicide. Claire thought back, *Tony mentioned his parents' death was an accident. That seems to be an all-encompassing word.*

NYU News, 1990: Anthony Rawlings with Jonas Smithers started a corporation. While completing their master's degrees, they filed the necessary paperwork to start Company Smithers Rawlings, CSR. The article said CSR wanted part of the Internet pie.

New York Times article, 1994: Anthony Rawlings buys out his friend and partner Jonas Smithers for 4 million dollars. CSR was now Rawlings Industries. The *New York Times* predicted it was on its way to being an Internet giant.

Newsweek, 1996: Rawlings Industries begins to diversify. Anthony Rawlings, determined to not have *all his eggs in one basket*, entered the realm of entertainment and transportation.

Time magazine, 2003: One of the men mentioned as a runner-up for Man of the Year, Anthony Rawlings. This designation came mainly because of his dedication to people evidenced by Rawlings Industries' recognition as one of the top ten philanthropic companies in the USA. Mr. Rawlings was quoted, "I plan to spend my life and fortune looking for opportunities to amend my grandfather's life. Every person is important."

Indianapolis Star and News, 2004: Obituary of Jordan and Shirley Nichols. Claire felt ill as she read the accompanying article with a different mind-set from when she was a grieving child. It talked about the unfortunate *accident* which claimed their lives, about her father's police service and full police honors as tribute, and her mother's devotion to her family and teaching. The accident was believed to be caused by wet roads and newly fallen leaves. Photographs taken at the gravesite were clipped to the obituary. One of John embracing Emily, *John and Emily* written on the back; and another of Claire sitting alone, with *Claire* written on the back in handwriting she recognized. Words came back to her, "Because I wasn't able to support you when your parents died . . . you had to go through your parents' death alone. Emily had John but you didn't have anyone." With a sudden sickness Claire realized Tony was there. He saw her grief first hand.

Valparaiso University Newsletter, 2005: During the time Claire was a student. The picture showed Anthony holding a giant check for 5 million dollars. His donation to the university made more scholarships possible.

Again, the buzzer rang. Claire had to wait to continue this journey. She slowly understood her encounter with Anthony Rawlings in March of 2010 was predestined.

The next items were more actual snapshots, pictures from John and Emily's wedding. A few even zoomed in on Claire, wearing the ugly sea foam green, maid-of-honor dress. Emily and John looked so young and happy, *2005* and *Claire* written in the familiar handwriting. She wondered, *was he there, too?*

Albany Post, 2006: Appointments to a local law firm. The second name listed was John Vandersol. The article discussed John both professionally and personally.

Another 2006 article, "Rawlings Industries Continues to Diversify". It discussed the continued success of any venture Anthony Rawlings put his mind to. Rawlings Industries broadened into television with the recent purchase of TTT-TV.

Atlanta Daily Journal, 2009: TTT-TV acquires WKPZ. The acquisition resulted in multiple layoffs. Anthony Rawlings promised that as the economy improved so would job opportunities. He was dedicated to employment and worried about each individual who was out of work.

Claire now saw, all of those people who were so nice to her, who helped her with her dream, all lost their jobs - because of her.

People Magazine, August 2010: the article which almost killed her. She didn't need to read it, but she did: "Questions Answered, the Mystery Woman in Anthony Rawlings's Life Agrees to a One-on-One Interview." These articles were no longer revelations, mere confirmations.

December 19, 2010: Her wedding picture, a smiling her next to a smiling him. She recognized the picture but the unfavorable article was new to her. It talked about how fantastic Anthony was and asked how such a smart businessman could be as gullible as to marry this woman with no prenuptial agreement?

Vanity Fair, April 2011: Anthony's and her smiling face on the cover. It hit Claire at that moment. The woman in that picture didn't even look like her. She was beautiful, blonde, sophisticated, elegant, and way too thin. Not until now had she realized the magnitude of the transformation. She placed a picture of her from Emily's wedding next to the magazine cover. She didn't change, she was changed. Why hadn't she seen it before?

November 2011: Copy of the printed newsreel Tony brought home. "Tragic Accident Claims the Life of Young Gaming Phenomenon Simon Johnson."

Albany Post, January 2012: column listing arrests: John Vandersol, 32, charged with embezzlement and fraudulent client billing charges, arraignment pending.

Iowa City News, January 2012: Headline, "Anthony Rawlings Alive after Attempted Murder by New Wife". No wonder so many reporters were on the courthouse steps!

Iowa City News, April 2012: "Claire Nichols (formally Rawlings) avoids trial, pleading *no contest* to the attempted-murder charge," accompanied by more unfavorable articles.

Iowa City News, July 2012: "Anthony Rawlings's Efforts to Save the Iowa Taxpayers Their Money". The picture, black and white, showed a

364

warehouse full of tables lined with merchandise: jewelry, shoes, handbags, clothes, etc. The article explained how Anthony Rawlings, uncomfortable that the taxpayers of Iowa were held responsible for his ex-wife's pretrial expenses, held an auction of her belongings. It raised enough money to reimburse the state for her counsel and court costs. There was even an additional $176,000, which was donated to the Red Cross of Iowa. Mr. Rawlings explained that this charity remained dear to him because it was Claire's pet charity. A strip of newspaper stapled behind the first, had another picture, a close-up of some of the jewelry. The picture was not large, but center frame was a black velvet box containing a white gold necklace with a large pearl centered on a white gold cross.

As Claire was about to close up the box, something caught her eye. Folded in the bottom was a napkin. She pulled it out and unfolded it. On the napkin in scrolling red letters: Red Wing. Under the words on each side were signatures, Claire Nichols and Anthony Rawlings. Above the red letters: "Job Contract", and the date, "March 15, 2010". She turned the napkin over, no other writing. There was no agreement, no definition of duties, and no life-changing event -- just a napkin with signatures.

Claire's mind swirled with possibilities: she could take this information and ask for a new trial. No. She had entered a plea of *no contest* and by definition couldn't appeal. Tony knew that. Besides, the legal system and the court of public opinion didn't believe her before, they wouldn't believe her now.

She questioned why he would share the information. Obviously, he didn't view her as a threat. As Claire repacked the box, she contemplated and found a better reason. Tony spent years—no, decades—planning his vendetta. He liked recognition for his accomplishments. He required gratitude for his deeds. There was no one else with whom he could share his hard work. She wondered what sort of recognition he expected, perhaps a "*well done*" note?

She kept some of the photos and papers, put everything else in the box, and rang her buzzer. Claire requested permission to incinerate the box. The guard consented and accompanied her to the basement. As they walked the passages, thoughts and ideas began to flow through Claire's mind. She believed her actions kept her alive. She also knew that obedience took more strength than retaliation. With each echoing step, her new knowledge empowered that strength.

She lived her life governed by her grandmother's and mother's words which encouraged truth and forgiveness. The truth did *not* set her free. The thoughts of revenge weren't fueled only by *her* consequences, but the consequences of her parents, John, Emily, Simon, her friends at WKPZ, and even her grandmother's necklace.

Opening the incinerator, she felt the warmth. It reminded her of the fires in her suite, Tony's suite, and Lake Tahoe. Throwing the box into the flames, she watched the contents ignite. The flickering of the flames brought back the flames of her past: love, fear, contempt, desire, passion, pain, and sadness. As the fire consumed the memories, it fueled a new determination. Two and a half years ago, she had one goal—survival.

Now she had a new one – revenge. Mr. Anthony Rawlings would learn that *his* actions have consequences. Claire contemplated her decision. According to Catherine, Claire had received the *rare* opportunity to truly know Anthony Rawlings. With that knowledge, she had four to seven years to plan his demise.

Turning back to the guard, her mind spun with possibilities.

Immediately, the uniformed man noticed something different about the prisoner. It was her smile. How could he not notice? It extended into her emerald eyes.

In three words I can sum up everything
I've learned about life: it goes on.
—Robert Frost

Afterward

The Massachusetts autumn remained cooler than normal. Shivering, Sophia entered her art studio thinking about the events of the last few weeks. First, she presented a hugely successful gallery exhibit. Guests and investors from all over the East Coast were in attendance. Her dream was becoming reality as word spread about her art. Then, in the course of a day, her whole world fell apart.

The call came just as she left for her studio two weeks earlier. She almost didn't answer but decided to pick up after the fourth ring. The New Jersey police called to inform her, a blue Toyota Camry was found by passing drivers. The accident must have occurred during the night. It was believed that perhaps her father lost control on the wet leaves, or it may have been an acceleration issue. She could request tests. The policeman offered his sincere condolences. Could she possibly travel to New Jersey and identify the bodies? Both her mother and her father were killed instantly.

Sophia had so many responsibilities, so many activities; the next week passed in a blur. There was the funeral planning and settling of their estate. That would take months or years. Sadly, she hadn't realized the debt her parents incurred helping her with her studio.

Now, with a minute to herself, she couldn't stay home. She feared she would do nothing but cry. That was why, even on this cloudy Saturday afternoon, Sophia decided to come into the studio. Putting her purse in the office, she heard the bell on the front door. Damn, she had meant to lock that. It wasn't that she was afraid. This was a great town. She just wanted some quiet time alone.

As she stepped into the studio, the man at the counter looked familiar. Maybe he had been at the gallery event, or she had seen him on TV? She couldn't be sure, but his eyes were so dark and mesmerizing. "I'm sorry, I'm not open today. I just forgot to lock the door," Sophia said as she approached the handsome stranger.

"That is all right. I can come back," the dark-eyed man said with an agreeable smile. "It is just that I travel a lot and happened to be in town. A friend of mine told me about your gallery. He was here a week or so ago and bought three pieces. I'm very interested in nature, and he said you have a wonderful selection."

Sophia exhaled and smiled. "Are you a friend of Jackson Wilson?" The man's smile widened as he nodded his head. She continued, "He is one of my biggest fans."

"I don't get this way often. Are you sure you couldn't give me a speed tour? By the way, my name is Anthony, Anthony Rawlings."

Sophia stuck out her hand. "Where are my manners? I'm so sorry. My name is Sophia, Sophia Burke. I would be glad to give you a tour." She couldn't stop looking at those eyes.

"With one condition," Anthony said, his eyes shining, "you let me buy you some dinner and a drink after the tour."

Sophia gently took the man's elbow to lead him around the studio. After a few minutes of enjoying his charm, she decided why not? She'd just experienced a very difficult few weeks—what harm could one dinner and drink do?

TRUTH
(Book 2 of the CONSEQUENCES Series)

All truths are easy to understand once they are discovered;
the point is to discover them.
-Galileo Galilei

You know the CONSEQUENCES...
Learn the TRUTH!

Don't miss the continuing saga of Claire, Tony, and Sophia. Discover the secrets, ambitions, deceptions, and emotions that fuel their tangled web. Can Claire follow through on her plan? Is Tony's façade impenetrable? Did love ever truly exist? Will revenge prevail? What will happen to Sophia? Whose vengeance will triumph?

Be among the first to learn the TRUTH, the much anticipated sequel by Aleatha Romig. November 2012

Then stay tuned for CONVICTED... the final installment.

CONVICTED
(Book 3 of the CONSEQUENCES Series)

You must stick to your conviction,
but be ready to abandon your assumptions.
-Denis Waitley

Contact Aleatha:

Please share your thoughts about Consequences on:
    *Amazon, *Consequences by Romig*, Customer Reviews
    *Barnes & Noble, *Consequences by Romig*, Customer Reviews
    *Goodreads.com/Aleatha Romig

Stay Connected...
"Like" Aleatha Romig @Facebook.com/Aleatha Romig, to learn the latest information regarding Truth, Convicted, and other writing endeavors.
And, "Follow" Aleatha Romig on Twitter!

Made in the USA
Lexington, KY
07 August 2013